© 2024 by Rebecca Quinn.

This is a work of fiction. Characters, names, dialogues, and incidents are the product of the author's imagination or are used fictitiously. Any resemblance to actual persons, whether living or dead, businesses, locales, or events other than those specifically cited are unintentional and purely coincidental or are used for the purpose of illustration only.

The publisher and author assume no responsibility for errors, omissions, or contrary interpretation of the subject matter herein. The author and publisher assume no responsibility or liability whatsoever on the behalf of any purchaser or reader of these materials. The publisher and author do not have any control over and do not assume any responsibility for third-party websites or their content.

Cover, dust jacket and interior art design by Justine Bergman.

Editing by Kate James.

ISBN: 978-1-9231960-0-1

Ensnared

Brutes of Bristlebrook
Book One

Rebecca Quinn

CONTENT NOTE

Hello lovely readers, naughty and nice alike.

First of all, thank you! Thank you so, so much for picking up my book. It's a crazy world as an indie author, and it's gorgeous, wonderful people like you who make it all possible.

Secondly, and quite importantly, I would like to gently direct everyone to my website, https://rebeccaquinnauthor.com, where there is a list of all tropes and content warnings for this book. While it may not be the darkest many of you have read, it's also not light. This book contains several scenes and situations that readers may find triggering, so I would encourage everyone to look those over before proceeding.

I've tried to be as comprehensive as I could with that list, but please, if you have any questions or concerns, or believe anything should be added, contact me at admin@rebeccaquinnauthor.com

Finally, this book contains depictions of BDSM scenes and dynamics. While I hope you have fun reading it, please remember that this is a work of fiction, and should not be taken as instructional reading. Events are dramatized, timelines are shorter than advised for real life, everyone has acceptable breath, we're not stopping for enemas, and there are conflicts included for the sake of the story.

It's fun! But if you're inspired to try any new kink (heck yes!), please look to non-fiction, *reputable* sources for information, or seek advice from experienced, reputable members of the community, and keep things safe, sane, and consensual.

Okay! Serious stuff done. Now go and get Quinnky!

Lots of love,

Becky Quinn

Dear Satisfyer Pro2 Rechargeable Clitoral Stimulator,
Our time together has been a glorious, passionate affair.
Here's to many more years together, gorgeous.

(And no, I promise I wasn't eyeing off a newer model . . . yet.)

CHAPTER 1

EDEN

SURVIVAL TIP #51
Carrots aren't worth your life.

Branches whip my cheeks as I run, slicing through dirt-caked tears. My lungs burn with each labored breath.

Can't stop. Don't stop.

My bare feet slap the earth—I abandoned my flimsy shoes hours ago when the strap gave out. I've barely stopped to eat, and I certainly haven't slept. I push my glasses back up the bridge of my nose and risk a glance over my shoulder as I dart through the trees, but I can't see them. The shrub is too thick, and they're far more used to hunting than I am to running.

"Almost got you, slut!"

The shout echoes through the forest, and I can't tell how close they are. I'd thought I had a good fifteen minutes on them, maybe more.

But it sounds like it's a lot less.

Panic claws at me, and I push faster through the undergrowth.

For four years, I avoided attention. With my lonely cave and my little vegetable garden, I was getting by.

But then I heard voices.

How heady, how purely intoxicating to hear people after so long. I couldn't stop myself from creeping out for a look. Just a *look*, I'm not an idiot. I thought I was subtle. Sneaky. But, clearly, I did something to draw their attention.

Maybe I'm wrong. Maybe I am an idiot.

When I came back after checking my traps, I found my garden uprooted, my meager belongings raided and scattered . . . and two men waited by the mouth of my cave, tearing into my carefully grown carrots. It shouldn't have hurt, not so much. It was just a place, after all. They never mean anything. But I was so startled— so *furious*—that I just stood there, staring.

And they saw me.

One glance at the hunger in their rough faces, the predatory glints in their eyes, was enough to convince me that these were not men I wanted to be better acquainted with.

So I ran, and they chased.

More men quickly joined the first two. They're part of a large group, the kind I always avoid because they're drone bait. For the first time since the Final War began, I've actually prayed to see one of those deadly machines carving the sky, to watch it drop another devastating explosion on the mass of heat signatures behind me.

But I haven't seen a drone for years, and I can't expect a miracle.

So I keep running.

"Come on, baby, this is getting boooring!"

That one sounds closer. Is he closer?

I scramble over a fallen tree, grazing my palms and knees on the bark. *Have to keep moving.*

Two nights ago, I thought I'd escaped them. I laid two false trails and hid up a tree, trembling as the twenty or so heavily armed men stalked beneath me. It took all my courage to climb down after they left and find a new hiding place. I cried in relief that night. I started making plans for a new cave and fretted over the veggie seeds I'd left behind in my flight.

But they found me, curled under my silly bush that suddenly seemed like no protection at all when their leader—Sam—dragged me from it. He stank like filthy thoughts and sour sweat, but he was so distracted calling for the others that his grip slipped, and I bolted. I *escaped*.

You haven't escaped yet, I remind myself, fighting down the sick fear that claws at my belly. My arm is bloody and hot and sore where a bullet grazed me; I've seen worse, but it needs attention.

Howls and catcalls chase me. My glasses bounce off my nose, and the attached chain around my neck threatens to strangle me as I duck under a branch. It's another miracle altogether that I haven't lost them in my flight.

Running water sloshes and babbles somewhere close. Making a quick decision, I round a tree and dart off the path I've been following. I need water. Desperately. I've been sweating and bleeding and running, and I've only had what I could quickly scoop in my palms from the tiny brooks that crossed my path.

My body is flagging.

I glance back again, and the motion costs me. A sharp rock pierces the sole of my foot, and I cry out, stumbling.

Darn it all!

I stop, clutching at my foot. I shove my glasses back on only to see the offending stone topple innocently beside me, its dagger point dropping to the side. Blood wells, and an aching bruise starts swelling the sensitive flesh.

A twig cracks.

My head whips around, and I study the green depths around me. A bird? A hunter?

No no no.

They can't be *that* close.

Biting my lip, I rip a strip of cloth from the bottom of my filthy blouse and wrap it hastily around my foot. Panting through clenched teeth, I hobble as fast as I can toward the sound of water and try to stop panicked thoughts from taking me over. No matter how I push them down, though, my stabbing steps reveal a basic truth: this is *bad*. I need to run. It's the only thing keeping me free.

The sight of the sparkling river makes my pain ebb for a moment, and I stumble between the trees.

Only to stop.

My stomach drops to my feet.

Three tall, muscular—and very heavily armed—men watch me from the riverbed. One of them, with half his dark-blond hair tied in a topknot, slings back his rifle. The colorful carnival scenes tattooed down his defined arms catch the dappled light, and he grins under his short beard.

"Well hello, sweetheart."

CHAPTER 2

DOMINIC

SURVIVAL TIP #220
Don't risk your men.
No matter how pretty she is.

I watch the play of emotions on the woman's face at Lucky's teasing. Her large gray-blue eyes, made even larger by her black-rimmed glasses, widen. The flush drains from her pale, muddy cheeks. Those big eyes dart between the three of us and, before I can move, she spins to bolt away.

At least, she tries.

As she turns, her bandaged foot collapses beneath her and she lets out a muffled cry. Beau jumps into action, lowering himself as he strides forward as though that might make his size less intimidating.

Lucky moves to help, but I shake my head and nod at the river. When he hesitates, I bite back a curse. I know it's bad if *Lucky* is testing my authority. But damn it, we're here for a reason—we need to replenish our water supply and keep moving or we'll never make it back before dark. The years since the Final War have been harsh and there are too few of us left; I'm not risking my men by spending another night in the open. Whatever this woman is about, we don't have time for it.

Lucky pouts but, with a regretful glance at the girl, he does as he's told.

I walk over to the woman. She scrambles until she's sitting with her back against the tree, watching the now-crouching Beau as though he eats babies for breakfast.

" . . . not gonna hurt you. Just want to take a look at that arm of yours, 'kay, darlin'? That's a nasty scrape you've got there."

I just barely stop myself from rolling my eyes. Bastard's laying on the apple-pie accent thick. He always does it when he has a crush; it might have been a while, but I'd recognize the tone anywhere. God *damn* it. I just have to be out with the two bleeding hearts of our fucked-up little group. Why isn't Jasper with me instead? Hell, even Jaykob? He would scare her off for the fun of it.

Beau edges forward. The woman flattens herself against the tree.

He stops and lifts his hands like she's a frightened mare. "That foot needs some attention too, huh? My name's Beau, sweetheart. I'm a doctor. You don't need to be afraid of me."

Dark suspicion fills her haughty features. Her chin lifts and her thin cheeks make her cheekbones seem higher than is natural. I'd bet she hasn't had a decent meal in a while. Not many people have, lately. Though women aren't often found these days either, and certainly not alone, and yet here she is.

Trouble in a shapeless sack of an outfit.

As I move closer, her attention fastens on me, evaluating the new threat. Those gray-blue eyes hit me like a punch to the gut. Piercing, intelligent—in seconds that gaze has me stripped bare and measured from the toes up. Her eyes would be almost too light for her face, if not for the striking darker blue ring around her irises and the thick, sooty lashes that frame them. They're so long they brush her glasses as she blinks.

I set my feet and quirk a brow, meeting her stare and giving her the same once-over, strangely unsettled. My skin feels hot and tight in the face of her frightened pride.

Her thick, dark hair is secured in a tight bun, though sweaty, curly strands fly about her jaw, pulled from their confines. She has a regal face, but full, sensuous lips belie her stern expression. Those lips are trembling now, though she's trying to press them together.

And that's a problem.

Her nervousness excites me—it pricks my instincts hard—and a raw, unexpected picture of those lips wrapped slickly around my cock slides into my mind.

Fuck. We don't have time for this. Damn her for being nervous.

Damn me for wanting to taste her fear.

I drag my eyes to the man next to her. "Beau, forget it. Let's go."

My friend snorts, not even looking back at me. This time I can't suppress a scowl. The others follow me pretty much without question—even Jasper, no matter what he pretends—but it's hard to order someone around who's pulled shrapnel out of your ass.

The girl's attention goes back to Beau as he gently grasps her ankle. Her bulky pants have been torn and mended so many times the length is uneven around her calves.

"Don't," she whispers.

My jaw clenches. Her voice is deeper than I was expecting, rich and husky as hell. A voice made for sex.

Beau tenses as well.

No. We *definitely* do not have time for this.

"Beaumont," I warn.

He glances back at me with a dry look.

"Dominic," he mimics.

"It's not happening."

"Just gonna get her fixed up is all." Beau doesn't shift from his easy crouch, though his thumb starts stroking gentle circles on the girl's tense calf.

I'm going to kick my friend's Southern ass from here to home if he doesn't move.

Slowly, Beau's other hand moves to the heavy pack at his side and rummages about, and he pulls out a small brown bottle, then turns it so she can see the label. She tracks every move.

"Iodine, darlin'. Nothing to hurt you." He pauses. "Well, she might sting like a bitch, but I'm guessing you've faced worse." His voice is low and soothing as he unwraps the filthy cloth around her foot. She flinches, but he doesn't slow. "Come on, now. Infection is worse than I'll ever be, I promise you that."

She doesn't relax but doesn't stop him either. After wetting the area, he wipes away the grime around the wound with a clean cloth and then soaks a fresh one.

Beau has always been good with women.

And horses.

And children.

His steady manner puts people at ease. Unlike me, who puts people on edge. Heather was the only one who never backed down from me—she threw back every bit of temper I had with an impressive one of her own.

Unexpected pain slices into me and I scowl. The fuck? I haven't thought about Heather in months.

My expression frightens our little field mouse again, and she pulls back like she's planning on melting into the tree. This one is no wildcat, that's for damn sure.

Beau shoots me a dirty look. "Stop scaring my patient."

The words are light, but they carry an edge that tells me Beau is liking the idea of this *patient* far too much. Also, funny how his accent just smooths out to a barely perceptible drawl when he's sniping at me. The petty part of me wants to point it out to the mouse.

I flip him off, then pause as my gaze catches on the girl again.

Oh, great. Real nice.

"How did you hurt your arm?" I snap. The wound is fresh, still leaking blood.

The woman flinches, then instinctively looks to Beau for help. Beau frowns at me, then hesitates and studies her bloody arm himself. Worry and anger darken my friend's smooth, tanned face.

"Who shot at you, darlin'?" he asks gently.

She hesitates, wound tight. Then she takes a deep, shuddering breath and closes her eyes.

"I need to go. I have to go." Her voice is tentative, like she doesn't use it often. She looks at Beau, studiously avoiding my livid gaze. "You should go too. It's . . . not safe here."

"Oh, sweetheart, it's not safe anywhere. Didn't you get the memo?" Lucky saunters over from the river, giving me a wide-eyed 'don't get mad, I'm done' look.

His cheek dimples as he smiles at her, clear even under his short beard. Women always love Lucky's dimples.

Dick.

"Don't you worry your pretty head, though. We'll take care of you now. I'm Lucky—and I guess you are too, since you found us."

Lucky seems oblivious to her unimpressed grimace as he eyes her approvingly.

No, *enough*.

"Shut up, Lucien." His nose crinkles at the use of his full name, and he tosses me a wounded look that I ignore. "We're not taking her anywhere. We're sticking to the plan. Beau, finish up; we're out."

Beau opens his mouth to protest when a punishing crack of gunfire thunders through the forest. And suddenly her fear clicks.

Shit. They're tracking her.

The woman's gaze swings to mine, those unusual eyes filled with dread, and I'm caught. Accused. Her naked fear tugs at all my protective instincts—but this isn't the old world, and I'm not putting my men at risk for a stranger. We don't do that anymore.

Beau stands up. I'm only an inch taller, but I use it to glare down on him.

He shakes his head, not biting. "Cool it. How far away?"

It only takes me a moment of thought. "Five minutes, maybe less." I set my jaw and meet my friend's eyes. "Dump her and let's go."

"Fucking Jesus, Dom," Lucky mutters, but my gaze doesn't leave Beau.

Beau wavers. A muscle in his jaw ticks. Then he scrubs a hand over his short brown hair and looks back at me. His eyes are gentle with understanding. "Can't do it, my friend. Won't do it. We need her."

Not. Fucking. This. Again.

Before I can speak, my friend of over fifteen years says, "Get on if you have to. I get it, I do. But the rest of us just don't see it the same. We've been waiting for this."

Another shot sounds.

It's close.

CHAPTER 3

EDEN

SURVIVAL TIP #12
Laugh lines can be deceptive.
Sure, maybe this person is good humored and trustworthy.
But maybe they laugh while they dismember corpses.
Exercise caution.

The second shot has me back on my feet, iodine and pretty doctors be darned. The ground is especially harsh against my now-bare wound. The three men tower beside me, still arguing among themselves. The large man's dark eyebrows are slanted in anger over his caramel eyes. *Dom.* His short military cut is longer on top, and his broad shoulders flex as he gestures.

While I'm not sure what I've done to warrant the frustration in his eyes, I do agree with him on one point: it's time to go.

I gingerly put weight on my leg, scanning the clearing for the best exit or a place to hide. At this point, I'm wondering if jumping in the river and praying would be my best option. I grit my teeth and turn south, not *quite* willing to risk the rapid, icy water—not yet—but I'll need to be quick to make up the time I've lost.

I have to force my trembling legs to action; they beg me to stay seated.

"Woah, darlin', slow down." Beau clasps my uninjured arm. His hand wraps around my whole bicep.

The hard planes of his face are cleanly attractive, his jaw squared. Light laugh lines branch from the corners of his hazel eyes, somehow relaxing me, just a little. How long has it been since I laughed? How often does this man do it for it to mark his face?

"I have to go," I repeat, more insistent this time.

I can hear them clearly now; the cracks of branches and their shouts are way too close. But . . . he's been kind to me. Darn it, why aren't they running too? Guilt and indecision make me pause again, even as I curse myself. This isn't how I keep myself alive. Dump them and go—cold as it is, I can't help thinking Dom is right about the sentiment.

"There are too many of them." I'm dangerously close to begging. "Just run. *Go.*"

Beau considers me. "How many?"

I tug, trying to pull my arm away, but he holds fast.

"Tell me how many, darlin'."

The quiet command in his voice has me impatiently answering before I can think. "Fifteen? Twenty? I don't know."

The long-haired one with the wicked smile—Lucky? Lucien? —groans. "Twenty? Sweetheart, there are a lot of words I want to hear come out of that mouth, but that's not one of them."

I shoot him a level look, not enjoying his flippancy. He winks at me.

Another shot echoes through the forest.

"Too late to run now," Beau says, sounding unfazed. "Dom?"

"There was a ledge on our way down the mountain, two klicks northwest." Dom casts a quick, irritated look at me. "Take her, then. But only until this is sorted. Then we'll talk."

Before I've puzzled that out, I'm being swung bridal style into

Beau's arms. I let out an embarrassing yelp. "What are you doing? Put me down!"

"Hush." His slight smile gentles the word. "You can't run; let us help."

Alarm shoots through me, and I *do* struggle then. "You can't *fight* them."

All of my efforts barely seem to register. He simply tightens his arms, holding me against his hard chest.

"They'll track us. You *can't*."

Lucky laughs. "Just wait and see, beautiful. Didn't anyone ever tell you to have some faith in people?"

My mouth tightens. I've always been a lot of things—smart, polite, kind—but never beautiful. And faith? If people were as good as he says, then I wouldn't have needed to run until my feet bled.

The men set a quick pace, their long legs easily covering more ground than I could. The catcalls behind us make my stomach turn, but . . . I'm so tired. It's good to stop running. Maybe this will be the end. These men around me are well armed and seem almost casual, if annoyed, at the prospect of a fight. But I've seen my hunters. They're dangerous, they're patient, and they aren't going to give up.

I shift to touch the small knife at my waist. Would I have the courage to end it myself? Better that than to let them have me. My fingers tremble on the worn hilt.

Beau gives my thigh a reassuring squeeze. After a moment, I rest my head against his chest; he smells clean, like soap and fresh, male sweat. I can afford to wait a bit longer. If it looks like they'll take me, then I'll use the knife.

Within a few minutes, we're fronting a steep cliff face beside the water. There's a small clearing between the trees and the rocks, but I can't see anywhere to hide.

"Lucky, trees."

Lucky gives Dom an exaggerated salute, tosses me a smile, and kicks off his shoes. He tucks them behind a bush at the base of a large tree and begins climbing with easy confidence. Though he's leaner than the other two, his colorful, tattooed arms ripple with muscle, and he whistles cheerfully as he moves. A long rifle swings from the strap around his neck.

Beau moves toward the cliff. I crane my head up.

Dom is climbing along a nearly invisible path up the cliff face, aiming for a ledge I didn't notice from front-on. I have a great view of his tight ass as he pulls himself up.

No, bad Eden. He is *an ass. You shouldn't be noticing his.*

Wait! *Pulls* himself up?

I've changed my mind. To call it a "path" is laughable.

It's a rock-climbing route.

"I'm going to need my arms for this one, darlin'," Beau murmurs.

My heart sinks. There's no way I'll be able to get up there, not with my arm numb and useless as it currently is—not to mention my injured foot. Beau sets me down, then calloused fingers tilt my chin up to look at him.

I pull back from the intimate touch. He may have been kind to me, but that doesn't entitle him to touch me any way he wants.

"Climb on."

I blink and raise an eyebrow at him.

Amusement dances in his pretty eyes. "Arms around my neck, legs around my waist. Give me the monkey hold."

My mouth drops open. "You can't carry me while you climb, Beau."

Something flashes in his eyes that makes me take a step back.

After a tense moment, he mutters, "I like the way you say my name, darlin'." I don't know how to reply to that, but he saves me the trouble. "Now, you should stop telling me what I can't do, or I might just get offended. Climb on, you're no weight at all."

Still, I hesitate.

"You didn't think I'd leave you behind, did you?"

I shake my head. Not in disagreement, but . . . he doesn't know me at all. Why should I assume anything of him?

A loud bang echoes through the trees too close to us, and I decide now isn't the best time for modesty. I slide my hands up around his neck, hissing at the hot stab of pain in my injured bicep, and shift so my other arm holds most of my weight. He bends and lifts me, hands hot under my ass. I wrap my legs around his toned waist, avoiding his eyes as my cheeks heat. We're close—closer than I've been to a man for years. Years before the strikes decimated our world, even.

"Hold on tight, darlin'." His Southern accent is thick and sweet as honey. "Don't want you falling off halfway up."

I nod against his neck and squeeze closer.

Beau scales the path surprisingly fast, despite my awkward weight. When we reach the ledge, he stands long enough for me to drop my legs, but his hands linger on my hips, holding me close to him for a moment too long. I'm unable to miss his interest—it presses insistently against me.

I stagger backwards, startled, and he gives me a rueful smile.

"Girl." There's even more snap to Dom's rough voice than before. He kneels behind a large boulder and peers down at the clearing. His heavy gun is nestled in his arms. "Get down. Sit behind this rock and don't move."

It takes me a moment to realize he's talking to me.

"It's Eden," I mutter, but I quickly do as he says. Girl? I'm twenty-seven. I haven't been a *girl* for years. It's even worse than 'sweetheart.'

Beau settles behind a smaller rock, swinging his gun around and into position. I peek around to scan the trees. Nothing. I search the upper branches but can't see Lucky. I hope that means they won't be able to either. He's stopped whistling, and I miss the jaunty tune. As ridiculous as it was to hear amid the gunshots and bellowed insults, it made me feel oddly safe. All I can hear now is the nearing crash of my hunters, their shouts growing louder and louder.

My anxiety kicks up a notch. I crane my neck around the rock as if a new angle might give me x-ray vision. Everything in me tells me to run.

"What part of 'don't move' don't you understand?"

I pull back with a scowl, then wish I hadn't obeyed quite so fast. Amber eyes, molten with ire, glare at me. Dom's skin is dusky brown and stubble lines his strong jaw. He really is a beautiful man. Or he would be if he weren't so cranky.

The crashing sounds stop.

"Come on, bitch. Enough games," a loud, nasal voice shouts from below.

Another joins it. "Come out, come out, wherever you are!"

I swallow hard, hand seeking my knife. More hoots and jeers follow. I know what will happen if they catch me. I've seen the leftovers of others caught by men like this, and the images still haunt my nightmares. Unfortunately, most people who survived the lawless years after the strikes aren't the sort I want to be caught by —which is why I hid myself away in my cave for four years. A woman alone is far too vulnerable.

From my crouch, I look at Dom. His focus is entirely on the clearing in front of him. Why isn't he doing anything?

"I know you cunts like to play hard to get, but this is getting ridiculous!" the first voice calls again. Scattered laughter sounds from below. "You'll pay for our trouble, slut. You'll get it in every fucking hole."

Dom's lip tenses, almost a curl, his brows lowering with unholy rage.

I tremble. I *will* use my knife. Anything is better than being taken by them. I rub the hilt between my fingers in a silent, fervent promise.

"Cover your ears," Dom mutters.

I ignore him. I've heard worse from these men before. It isn't their *words* that puts the queasy churn in my insides. This is hopeless. Ridiculous. There are too many of them, they will—

Crack!

The sound of the gunshot beside me is deafening. Then a flurry of them follows. My ears ring. I swing my head around, then push my slipping glasses back into position. Dom's broad body shifts rhythmically as he fires, but I can't hear anything. Releasing my knife, I finally slap my hands over my ears.

Too late.

The ringing reverberates in my skull until even the gunshots are drowned out.

My eyes travel to Beau, who looks grim but calm as he fires. Biting my lip, I close my eyes and try to focus on my breathing.

In.

Out.

Everything will be fine.

In.

Out.

I *will* use my knife if it comes to it.

In.

Out.

One quick, deep slice across my throat will do it.

In.

Out.

A rough hand shakes my shoulder, and I fumble to find the knife. It only takes me a moment to realize there's no need.

It's . . . over.

Dom pulls back when my eyes open and he stands up. He waits for a minute, watching the clearing, then nods and looks down at me. He says something, but I shake my head, my ears still ringing. He scowls.

I'm floating with shock. It can't have been that easy. There were so many of them.

Dom gives me a vexed look and walks toward the "path" back

down the cliff. Then Beau is in front of me, forehead crinkled in concern.

I squeeze my eyes shut again. This is too much. Relief and fear and confusion clog my throat with hot tears. They leak between my lids. How can it be over so quickly? I've been running for *days*. *At least* days. A sob escapes, quickly followed by more I can't hold in.

Strong arms lift me, and I wrap myself around Beau again without thinking. I cry into his dusty T-shirt on the way down the cliff. When we reach the bottom, I realize I can hear my own soft weeping, and the deafening ringing in my ears finally settles into a soft, background twang.

CHAPTER 4

EDEN

SURVIVAL TIP #38
Cheese = safety.

My three rescuers are waiting for me, I know, but I need a minute before I face the destruction in the clearing. My freedom. The 'what's next' problem. There are too many things to think about and I just . . . don't want to think anymore. I don't want to *worry*. Right now, I just want to be held.

As though sensing my thoughts, Beau doesn't set me down.

"Is she hurt?" Lucky sounds alarmed.

Dom stalks toward the viscera in the clearing. "She's fine. Don't know why she's crying; we just solved all her problems for her."

His displeasure cuts through my moment of self-pity. I raise my head, but Beau's arms just tighten.

"Fuck off, Dom," Beau says mildly. "She's been through a lot."

The larger man crosses his arms. I try not to notice the way it pulls his V-neck tight over his broad chest.

"We can't bring her back," he says, voice tight. "She's a deadweight."

"Doesn't seem like she weighs much to me. Hey, Beau, let me try!" Lucky tugs at my blouse.

I shake my head, like that might clear it. What am I *doing*? The frantic panic is fading, but a new uneasiness is settling in. What do these men want with me? Bring me back? Back where?

When I shift back from Beau, he reluctantly sets me down. Tender on my foot, I turn to face the two other men and immediately wish I hadn't. Dead bodies are strewn around the clearing, fallen in awkward, final positions. Blood and chunky body matter coat the grass and the smell of charred flesh wafts to me. I've seen some terrible things over the last four years, but this is among the worst.

Dom bends down to examine the partially dismembered hand of one of the hunters; it's branded with a tattoo of a coiled snake. He moves and looks at another with the same symbol.

For a moment, I'm worried I'll lose my stomach—not that there's much to lose—and, as he straightens to look back at me, Dom's bored expression tells me he's expecting it. That alone is enough to make me swallow hard and look away.

"I . . . " I take a deep breath, trying to summon some of my old poise. Once upon a time, I was known for my manners. "Thank you. I appreciate your help but there's no need to go to any further trouble on my behalf. I'll just . . . I'll leave you to it."

Beau's face grows darker by the word, making me falter as I turn to leave.

Lucky shakes his head, his brow puckering in concern. "We didn't get them all, sweetheart. The rest ran off when they realized they'd lost half their number. It's not safe. You should come with us."

Lucky seems younger than the other two, closer to me in age than Dom and Beau, who I'd guess to be in their early thirties. But despite the lightness in his demeanor, that teasing voice still has a bossiness to it I'm not sure I appreciate.

A muscle ticks in Dom's jaw. "Goddamn it, Lucky. This won't

work. We all pull our weight, that's the rule. She can't even take care of herself."

For the first time, I see discomfort in him. In another man, I'd call it panic.

Beau snorts. "'Course she can. She'll do her part."

The confident implication in his voice has my stomach flipping and dropping all at once. Are they arguing over whether to *keep* me?

One look at Beau's expression tells me that my suspicions are correct. And Dom . . . well, it's clear Dom doesn't want me. He couldn't look more disgusted by me if he tried.

Not that it matters, I don't want to go with them anyway. Of course I don't. I really, truly don't. This was a fluke. One slip in four years. I'll just be more careful next time. I don't need them at all. I don't need anyone.

So why does it sting so much? a voice taunts, one I thought I'd banished years ago. *The only woman within who knows how many miles and you're still not good enough.*

I cringe.

No. I need to leave. These men might not have thrown me on the ground and ravished me, but to have survived this long, they're surely not so different from the men I've been running from. Right? None of them, not even jaunty-whistling Lucky, have spared more than a glance at the body pieces that splatter the clearing like a Jackson Pollock painting.

But . . .

Beau's gentle touch as he tended my foot flashes into my mind. The way he cradled me against his chest as I cried.

My emotions are smattered and smeared, my thoughts a jumble.

"She'll do her part," Beau repeats.

"This isn't necessary," I interject, banishing my internal chaos and forcing librarian sternness into my tone. "I can take it from here. Truly."

Can I, though? I've been running for so long, I don't even know where I am anymore, let alone how to reach the nearest town to resupply. I keep my face composed, but the thought of starting again, by myself, from scratch, with nothing but the knife at my belt and the clothes on my back, is not a pleasant one.

Lucky seems to sense my doubt and moves closer, slinging an arm around my shoulders conspiratorially and ticking off his fingers one by one. "We have showers and spare beds. Proper cooking equipment. The place is completely hidden, very high-tech, so it's secure against assho—" He coughs. "Uh, charm-challenged folks like your friends here. There's also no chance of a drone spotting us, on the off chance one happens to pop up again. We have clothes, food. I could go on."

He's so close, and sizzling warm, and all firm and confusing, and even the thought of food is enough to make my whole body clench hungrily. I shrug him off, feeling overwhelmed. By him, by *all* of it.

As soon as I pull back, Lucky gives me an apologetic wince. "Sorry, sweetheart. Not pushing, I promise." He hesitates, looking me over, then frowns. "I bet you haven't eaten much, huh?"

He opens his pack, pulls out a wrapped cloth and hands it to me. After a moment of wavering, I peel back the corner of the fabric . . . to find a large chunk of hard cheese. *Cheese*! My mouth waters.

"It's not much, but it should be edible. I made it. Kind of. The goat helped." He gives me a nervous smile, but I'm still staring at the gorgeous hunk in my hands. Actual *cheese*. He must mistake my awe for hesitation because he adds, "I mean, I have jerky too, but . . ."

We both avoid looking at the vile clearing.

Despite my resolve to walk away, it's his kindness—as much as the cheese—that makes me pause.

"Thank you," I murmur, my voice husky and thick. "This is wonderful."

It would be more polite to wait until I was alone to eat, but my stomach has been gnawing on my nerves for days. I break off a piece and pop it in my mouth . . . and only just manage to muffle a soft groan of pleasure. Quickly, I devour two more pieces. It's incredible. Almost orgasmic.

And the cheese, more than anything, makes me wonder what this home of theirs must be like. It takes resources to make cheese. Time. Security. Patience.

Forcing myself to pause, I give Lucky a small, grateful smile, and his face relaxes in relief.

"Come with us, sweetheart. We'll keep you safe," he says, so softly. "You won't have to worry about this sort of thing"—his head tilts to indicate the corpses decorating the area—"ever again."

It sounds like a promise.

Swallowing, I take a calming breath. How am I meant to keep my resolve while he's looking at me like that? I *can't* be considering this.

There's always a catch.

I lift my chin and raise a cool eyebrow. "In exchange for . . . ?"

Lucky awards me a cheeky, dimpled grin. "The best orgasms of your life?"

My breath catches despite myself, and my skin tingles like he's just kissed his way down my spine.

That smile is deadly.

I know I should stop staring at him, but I can't seem to work up a suitable response.

Dom snorts, and his voice turns exasperated. "She can't even do that, Beau. She's intimidated by *Lucky*. How do you think she'd go with Jasper?" Beau grimaces, but Dom keeps going. "Jesus. Or Jaykob? There's. No. Point."

He looks down at me, and I finally manage to tear my eyes away from Lucky's dimples.

"Can you hunt? Skin a deer? Can you fix the plumbing?" Dom asks. "Are you a scientist? A doctor? An engineer?"

I purse my lips. "I was a librarian. I have a masters in information science and librarianship."

The tip of Lucky's tongue wets his bottom lip. He bites down and lets out a pained groan.

"A librarian? You're joking, right?" Something hotter, more intent, joins the twinkle in his eye. "That's . . . Damn it, Dom. I want her. Gimme."

Beau nods his agreement.

Dom swings his glare between them, then he fixes it on me, seeming to sense an opportunity. "And you, little librarian? You want to come with us?"

Do I? In the last hour, with these men, I've felt safer than I have for years. They killed people, yes, but they did so in my defense. If I'm honest, I'm far from feeling judgmental about that.

And a bed? How long has it been since I slept in a real bed?

"Is there hot water in the shower?" I ask hesitantly.

Lucky's eyes dance at the measly joke, but Dom's not letting up.

"If they both want you to come, then I won't say no, but there are rules, Eden. Rules I don't think you'll be so quick to agree to."

I give Dom a sharp look, unsure if I'm more unsettled by this idea of "rules" or that he actually caught my name earlier.

Beau shifts. "Is this really necessary?"

One of Dom's midnight brows arches. "You going to keep your hands off her?"

My eyes widen. Beau's Adam's apple works as he swallows. He says nothing. When he looks at me, his gaze is considering. Wait. Hold on. He actually wants to . . .

I look at him, properly now. The man is huge, well over six feet, and better looking than any man has a right to be. Where Lucky is impishly beautiful, with those long lashes, devilish smile and glorious hair, Beau is golden tanned and clean shaven, all hard planes and angles. And Dom . . . Dom is dark and dangerous. Stubbled and broad and deadly.

Keep their *hands off* me? Sweet raspberry popsicles. I feel faint.

"There are five of us at Bristlebrook, darlin'. We've had women there before and it . . . Well, it doesn't work too well. Not when there's the chance she's the last woman we'll ever see, you understand? Too much jealousy. Whole heap of drama. Whether you can pull your weight or not, well, that isn't really the problem." Beau's voice has taken on that slow, coaxing tone again, like he's worried I'm going to bolt. I'm not altogether sure I won't. "We decided after the last time that if we had a woman under our roof again, she'd belong to all of us. Equally. Or she couldn't stay."

My mouth forms a small *o*, mind racing.

Belong? What an unattractive word. And unfortunately, not an unfamiliar concept for me.

Except . . . they want me to belong to *all* of them?

That part is new.

Dom cuts in, a grim, knowing expression on his face. "You ever even been under a man? Well, how about five? Not that we'd all take you at once—" He tilts his head as if considering that, then shrugs. "Probably not, anyway. But none of us have been with a woman for nearly three years now. You think you're ready to keep up with that kind of demand?"

Dom leans in close enough that I can smell his warm, earthy scent. His voice is full of delicious threat. "You think you're ready to keep up *with me*?"

An image pops into my mind, of Dom shoving between my thighs, that same dangerous look in his eyes. Of him punishing my mouth with his tongue and teeth. Of our bodies slick with sweat, fighting, aching, until I whimper and writhe beneath him.

Heat pools low in my stomach with a vicious suddenness I've never felt before.

Dom pulls back, a frown flickering across his face as he studies me.

I avert my eyes and take a shuddering breath. He's right. There's no way I can do that. I've only ever slept with one man—

my husband, Henry—and he was always less than impressed with his frigid wife. Quite simply, I don't enjoy sex. To even think of sleeping with five different men is . . . well, it's . . .

My heart is racing again.

"It has to be your choice, darlin'," Beau drawls. "We won't take anyone who isn't willing."

I stare at him. For some odd reason, my feet won't move.

The silence stretches a little too long, then Dom shrugs. "All settled then. We'll walk you back to the river and see you off."

His relief is insulting, but he also reminds me of my burning thirst. I nod once, mind racing, and hear Beau let out a hard, disappointed breath. Cheeks hot, I don't look at him.

It's just because they haven't had a woman in months, I remind myself as we make our slow way around the clearing and back into the woods toward the river. *Nearly three years, they said.* It's a supply and demand issue, that's all. It's rude, really. My only value isn't in my body. I kept myself alive all this time, didn't I? So many others haven't.

Again, I avoid looking at the putrid corpses. They won't take long to sour in this heat and birds are already starting to flock to the fresh meat. I tuck the remaining cheese into my pocket for now. I don't think they'd ask for it back, but I'm not taking any chances.

Beau is close behind me, raising the hairs on my skin like static electricity. Lucky walks to my left, shooting me glances clearly designed to catch my eye. I study our feet instead. He has a musical walk, as though he's just a step away from dancing.

My foot throbs against each brush of grass, and I wonder if I'm in any position to ask for that strip of iodine-soaked cloth Beau had earlier. Sweat dampens my back and arms, stinging my bullet wound. Should I be worried by how little I can feel in that arm now? Beau said he was a doctor, didn't he? I can't possibly ask for more help, though. Not now.

I think of the remaining hunters, out in the woods somewhere.

Are they still around? Have they scattered? I'm in no state to keep running, and my little knife seems more pathetic than ever.

By the time we reach the clearing, I'm trembling from head to toe. The days of fear and running and scrounging crash in on me, and I have to lean on Lucky's muscled arm for support. He helps me to the riverbank, and I sit with a grateful sigh, moving my toes through the cool, silky liquid.

Edging forward, I wash the dirt from my hands, then cup them to catch some water. It trickles from the creases in my palms too quickly, but I lick every drop I can. If I didn't have company, I'd be tempted to stick my head in.

A hand touches my shoulder. Lucky offers me an empty tin bottle with a small, sad smile. He looks like a Viking with that long, tied-back blond hair, albeit a very clean one. I take the bottle with a grateful nod and fill it to the brim.

When I finish drinking, Beau sits beside me and opens his bag.

"You don't have to—" I protest, but I'm cut off as he grasps my elbow, gently pulling the injured arm closer.

"I didn't finish," he says gruffly, "and this arm needs to be looked at."

I close my mouth as he tends to me and decide to let him work. Truthfully, I'm glad for the help.

I made a few sneaky trips to the library in the last few years—for some reason, no one ever thinks to raid a library—and I picked up some books on herbology to try to cover the medicinal basics I need. I know better than to attempt to find drugs these days; the places they might have been found are either long since hollowed out, or they're war zones. The books were sufficient, and I learned enough to get by, but nothing replaced modern medicine.

Or, at least, what used to be known as modern medicine.

I grit my teeth as he cleans and disinfects the wound.

"This needs stitches." He sighs and rubs a hand over his face. "I don't have anything to numb the pain."

I grimace. "Just do it. I'd rather have them."

Beau's eyes flick to mine, gauging my reaction. Then he pulls out what looks like a small sewing kit, though the needle is wickedly curved and unlike any I use on my clothes. He tugs me closer, and his other arm holds me steady. Small flecks of golden brown warm his green eyes. His hair is tousled and small beads of sweat cling to his hairline from the soupy heat of the day.

The first suture drives all thoughts of his face from my head, and I cry out in pain despite myself. His lips compress and eyebrows lower, but he keeps going.

"Beau, you can't torture her for not coming with us," Lucky calls. "You know that, right?"

My gaze catches on Dom. I could have sworn he was watching me, but he's so absorbed on re-loading his gun, I must have been mistaken.

I try to breathe through my nose until Beau pulls back to examine the tight, even stitches. When he's finished, I let my pent-up breath out in a rush, and he quickly wraps a clean bandage around the area. He doesn't leave, seeming to fight with something in himself.

"Beau—" I begin.

"Is the thought of it really so awful for you?" he asks, voice low and demanding. His eyes flick up and there's a fire lit behind them, the gentleness gone. "Would it be so hard for you to give yourself to me?"

My breath catches when I realize his face is only inches from mine. I want to look away, but his gaze won't release me.

"I— I just . . . it's not that simp . . . " Heat floods my cheeks. "I've never . . . "

A different look crosses his face then; a calculating light enters his woodland eyes.

I shiver. "Beau—"

His hand slides from my shoulder up my neck and into my bound hair. The pressure yanks my head back, and before I can react, his mouth covers mine.

I freeze, then soften against him. Hot. His lips are scorching as they caress mine, and my breath hitches. My lips part on the sound, and he slides his tongue into my mouth, slick heat stroking mine. He tastes amazing—light and tangy and delicious—and his plundering kiss demands a response. Tentatively, I stroke my tongue back against him, and he groans against my mouth.

The steely strength of his arm locks around my waist, and he pulls me onto his lap. I can't protest, don't want to, can't string together a thought complete enough to know where I'd begin if I did. I'm needy, out of control. He's hot and hard between my thighs.

My blouse lifts with his grip, tangling precariously under my breasts as he grinds me against him, a parody of the close grip we shared earlier. I shift over his hardness, shuddering in shock at the feel of him pressing against my core. There's almost nothing between us, just a few shifts of fabric and we'd be—

Liquid heat floods me. I cling to his hard shoulders as the pressure on my hair makes my back arch. I press my chest against him, my hips down over him, shivering at the friction as he rubs his tongue across mine. His teeth catch my lower lip, and I gasp, arching more completely against him.

I burn. Ache. I have to do *something* to ease this terrible, incredible tension inside me. Mindless, I shift again so I can rub against him, panting against his punishing mouth.

"Fucking hell. Cool it, idiot. I'm not watching you fuck her on the bank."

The snapped words don't completely register; my fingers dig into his shoulders. He's so much bigger than me. How can his lips be so soft and so hard at the same time?

Thoughts that aren't really full thoughts swim blurrily in my head. Our mouths part for just a moment, and I run my tongue across his lower lip with a whimper.

"Beau!" the voice barks.

"Fuck," Beau swears, breaking the kiss. His hand eases from my hair in a soothing stroke down my back.

My breath comes in hitching pants. My head is spinning. It takes so much effort to lift my heavy lids. Absently, I push my glasses back up. Sweet sunshine, what on earth just happened?

I want to squeeze my legs closed against the throbbing, wet ache between them, but it only serves to push my core against him again.

Beau's gaze crashes against mine, dangerous desire turning them a darker shade of emerald, drowning out the golden flecks. I stare back at him in shock, too stunned to blush, part of me wondering whether it would be impolite to tear open his pants and beg him to finish what he just started. I've never felt like this my entire life, and it frightens me as much as it thrills me.

He rests his forehead against mine as we both try to catch air.

"Come with me, darlin'. You don't belong out here," he murmurs, voice deep and cajoling. His grip around my waist hasn't eased and he deliberately strokes himself up against my center, making me shudder. "You can leave any time. What would it hurt to try, hmm?"

"Beau." The stern voice is warning this time.

I try to regain control of my thoughts. I've always been so good at thinking. How did he short-circuit my brain with his tongue?

"But it's . . . it's not just you."

It's too much. Isn't it? How could I possibly do *this* with *all* of them? I'm no virgin, I've had sex before, but this kind of chemistry doesn't just happen. Sex usually just sucks.

Beau presses his lips to my forehead. "What would it hurt to try?" he repeats against my skin.

I'm trembling. What *would* it be like to be with a man like Beau? Can I really walk away without finding out?

That thought makes up my mind.

As my stomach dips in nervousness, I nod.

A slow smile creeps across his face, and he drops a light kiss on my nose. "You won't regret it, darlin'." Pulling us both up, he calls to the other two, "She's coming."

"I knew it!" Lucky grins, a godless glint in his eyes. "Eden could never resist temptation."

Beau snorts at Lucky. "That's Eve, idiot. Didn't your mama ever send you to Sunday school?"

He helps me up and leads me over to the others.

"My mama had an upside-down cross hanging in her studio. Does that count?" Lucky waves off Beau's rolled eyes. "Fine, I guess we're going to plunder her secret gard—"

Beau smacks him lightly on the back of the head, and Lucky snickers. Then, eyeing Dom, he takes a cautious step behind Beau.

Dom's expression is a thundercloud, dark and ready to spit lightning.

"I hope you know what you're in for." He stalks toward the south. "If she can't keep up, she gets left behind."

Beau ignores him and holds out his arm, his smile full of promises. I take it hesitantly. My head spins, and I can still feel the impression of his lips against me like a brand.

What on earth did I just agree to?

CHAPTER 5

EDEN

SURVIVAL TIP #2
Don't wait for the next bad thing to happen.
Move on before it does.

After traveling for several hard hours at a grueling pace, I'm worried. At this rate, I *will* need to be left behind. Darkness has bled through the forest, turning everything to cool shadows. Lucky hasn't stopped whistling, and the lighthearted sound is beginning to grate.

I'm running on empty. Even the prospect of a bed isn't enough to keep my shaking legs moving anymore. Or maybe they're still shaking because of that kiss. I haven't been able to look at Beau since we left the clearing. I've never behaved like that in my life. No kiss has ever made me feel like that. No, forget a kiss, full-blown *sex* has never made me feel like that.

It has to be my exhaustion. At breaking point, some people get furious, some cry—and I apparently become wildly aroused. It definitely makes sense. It's science. Added to the fact that I haven't so much as spoken to another person for four years, and it's no wonder I reacted that way.

My legs wobble, and I pause, resting against a tree. I need to stop, just for a moment. My eyelids droop.

"Ohhh, no you don't."

The whistling stops. Relieved, I drag my eyes back open.

Laughing baby blues meet mine. "You're not getting away from us that easily. Come on, it's really not much farther. Barely an hour."

My shoulders slump. "I truly don't think we have the same understanding of 'not much farther,' Lucky."

He snorts softly. "All right, hop on up then."

My mind flashes to the way my legs were wrapped around Beau. "Oh, that's okay," I say hastily. "I can walk."

Did I say that too quickly?

Lucky laughs, then turns around. "Unlike Doctor Desirable over there, I'll have you know that I have a little class. Only pure, Catholic, functional piggybacks for me, no matter what salacious siren spell you try to cast." He looks over his shoulder, and my hanging mouth clicks shut. "I'm a respectable gentleman, you know. I need to be wined and dined."

I huff a laugh, and he indicates for me to jump on. I wish I were strong enough to say no—I haven't been carried since I was a child, and now twice in one day—but my damaged body won't let me pass up the offer.

Resting my head against Lucky's back, I let the easy rhythm of his steps lull me, ignoring the way the position jostles my glasses. He's wonderfully warm, and I nestle in closer, hoping he won't notice.

When he begins to whistle, I moan. "Please, no more, anything but that."

"And here I was, composing a masterpiece just for you." His voice is scandalized.

"I'm sure you'll survive."

Lucky tuts. "Fine, then we're going to play a game."

"Like . . . I spy?" Trees, trees, and more trees!

"More like twenty questions. Here's how we play: I ask you twenty questions and you answer them."

He's caught up to the others quickly now I'm not dragging us back. At the last comment, Dom grimaces, pushing forward so he's out of earshot. Beau drops back to stroll beside us. It's not fair that they don't even look tired. The fact that, between them, they just killed upwards of ten men doesn't seem to faze them either.

I sigh. "How about five questions?"

He doesn't hesitate. "Why did you choose to become a librarian?"

"I like things to be organized," I answer after a moment. "I like things neat and logical. I love to learn and helping others to learn. Knowledge is how our world grows, how people do, as well. You can never experience as much in your lifetime, or see through so many eyes, as you will by reading what others have to say. Books will glue our world back together, if anything can."

"Hmm." It's a thoughtful sound. Then he adds, "See, I was never so good with books. To me, they just take so long to get to the point. It's all information this, information that. Music fills your soul. Movies make you laugh. Books just seem so . . . I don't know. Drab."

"What!" I cry in disbelief. I shift so fast he has to readjust to stop me from slipping off his back.

I'm not sure I've ever heard anything so offensive in my life, so much that I can't articulate a response. After the Final War, at first my days, like everyone's, were about survival. The initial strikes came out of nowhere. Intercontinental ballistic missiles obliterated a dozen key strategic locations across the US, from major cities to military bases to the Pentagon.

Day Death, they called it.

It was shocking how fast it happened. How quickly everything went dead. International tensions had been growing worse each year, relationships between the major nations disintegrating into masses of sanctions and warnings and weapons manufacturing . . . but no one truly thought anyone would take it *this* far.

Everyone was desperate for details, for confirmation of who and why and what was being done. It never came. People certainly weren't turning up for their day jobs to produce the seven-o'clock news, and only a bare handful of emergency radio broadcasts ever reached the public.

We heard a toneless recitation of the cities and military bases that now lay in ruins. An assurance that a national response scenario would soon be implemented. A declaration that martial law was now in place. An instruction to follow local authorities' guidance.

I know people were desperate for more information. I saw them freeze in place, waiting for it. But from the start, I didn't care who started it or why they wanted to end it this way. Knowing wouldn't change the facts.

And knowing wouldn't keep me safe.

In the wake of all the carnage that was left, it wasn't enemies across the sea that were the true risk. It was the people around me. As soon as I heard about the initial strikes, I got myself out of town and secluded deep in the woods. It was the only place I could think of that wouldn't be subject to rioters, or people out of their minds from fear. The only place that might be secluded enough for me to remain undetected.

And so, by the time Day Death drew to a close, I was tucked away. I was safe as hospitals were torn apart for supplies and supermarkets were gutted. When people were attacked for the weapons they had or the food they hid.

And I was secreted away when, just days after the first attack, the second wave hit. Devastating drones prowled our country—as best as I could tell, they were programmed to target masses of heat signatures. Our remaining major cities and military bases were eviscerated. Telecommunications infrastructure went down. The power went out. Smaller cities began falling like dominos.

After six days, there were no more emergency broadcasts.

There wasn't much of anything, anymore.

I had no idea when the next strike would happen, or which places, if anywhere, were safe. I didn't know whether aid was coming, or if a land war was imminent. There was no presidential announcement to confirm what had happened in the world beyond.

There was no president left to make an announcement.

In the end, it didn't matter. Our reckoning was over, and it wasn't pestilence, or death, or famine that killed us.

It was war.

After the first year, I stopped seeing drones scouting the skies. Some of the panic eased. I survived, and my daily challenge, insidious in its own way, became boredom. Boredom and loneliness. Books were my one true pleasure. The *one thing* that kept me sane.

And Lucky calls them *drab*!

Beau laughs. "Don't get too worked up, darlin'. He's teasing you. I've seen circus boy with his share of books. Not as many as Jasper, of course, but still."

With a small huff, I resettle myself. He must be part imp. Joking about books, of all things.

I want to ask about the other two, the ones I haven't met yet but . . . "Circus boy?"

"These are *our* questions, no hijacking," Lucky complains.

"Did you really work for a circus?" I press, curious.

"You don't understand how to play games at all. We'll have to work on that. But yes, of course. Where do you think I learned to juggle and eat fire and do trapeze?"

I frown at the back of his head. Luscious strands of long dark-blond hair are escaping the tie. I notice there are a few braids scattered through the length and wonder if he did them himself.

"Is he joking again?" I ask Beau. "I can't tell if he's joking or not."

Beau shoots me an amused look.

"Joking! Me? No, no, beautiful, I am never anything but deadly serious. How else could I have tamed the lions?" Lucky protests. "They respect strength, you see. Discipline."

I can't help but laugh.

As he adjusts me against his muscular back, he continues, "I'll have you know that I was the best acrobat in our troupe. It was one of the best and most beautiful shows in the US. I'm also an excellent dancer and am quite good at making balloon animals."

Beau snorts. "Don't take it personally. He gave us all so much grief on tour we just about agreed on friendly fire."

"You were . . . *all* in the circus?"

Dom is stalking ahead; I try and fail to imagine him performing in front of a crowd. Maybe twirling some batons or something.

Lucky starts laughing so hard he has to set me down. Bewildered, I look at Beau, who rolls his eyes.

"Rapid deployment, darlin'. We were Rangers."

Oh. I study them both.

"That makes more sense," I mutter.

Lucky wipes his eyes from where he'd bent over. "Oh, Beau, can you picture Jayk in a leotard? Maybe I should get him one on the next run."

"He'll kick your ass."

An eager glint appears in his eyes. "Worth it."

When he's recovered, he helps me back up. After a few moments, I relax against him, soothed by the rocking motion and his easy, constant chatter. It doesn't take long at all for my weariness to drag me into sleep.

CHAPTER 6

EDEN

SURVIVAL TIP #230
Beautiful men make your brain fuzzy.
Thinking is important.
Abort!

When I wake, it's slow and reluctant. I'm surrounded by clouds, white and fluffy and warm. I blink and let myself adjust. A bed. I'm in a real, actual bed. As I shift to look for my glasses, the sheets slip silkily over my skin.

My bare skin.

I freeze, then throw back the covers. I'm still in my long button-down blouse, but my filthy pants are missing. My cheeks heat.

Crap. Which of them undressed me?

Feeling around, I find my glasses on the bedside table and put them back on. The room is large, surprisingly so. It makes me nervous. A big room means a big house, and a big house—one that looks like it's in active use, anyway—is always a target.

In my sleep-muddled mind, though, I remember them telling

me that their home is hidden from drones. How did they manage that? Some of my anxiety eases with the memory.

The room is all dark wood and deep, luxurious colors. There's a bookcase and desk in the far corner of the room, and a small sitting area has been splendidly arranged on a lower section by a crackling fireplace.

God. This is stunning. The luxury feels almost profane after years of cave living.

Midnight blue blackout curtains run from the ceiling to the floor and sit half-open across the large windows. The bright light tells me it's past midday. I must have slept for nearly twenty-four hours.

There's a door to my left and, closing my eyes in a brief, hopeful prayer, I slide out of bed toward it. I moan in delight at the extravagant bathroom I find, complete with heated tiles, a shower big enough for a small elephant, and a standalone porcelain tub that begs me to soak.

After relieving myself—the toilet *works*—I wash my hands, though I keep my head down out of habit. The mirror is large and demands my attention, but I don't even want to know what I look like. Not yet. It's been a long time since I've seen myself as more than a blurry reflection in the lake, and I want to be clean before I reacquaint myself. I've been living rough, with very little food, for too long. I've never been a beauty, but I still dread seeing the damage this life has wreaked.

I notice a man's large button-down shirt is draped on a hanger beside the sink and grimace. Wearing their clothes feels odd, but it's better than my own filthy, blood-stained outfit. With a longing glance at the tub, I leave my glasses on the sink and limp to the shower. I don't know how long I slept, but I want to be out of the bathroom and dressed before they come looking for me.

I strip off quickly and turn the shower on, grinning at the heavy burst of water. Not having anything to replace my bandages with, I leave them on. Hopefully Beau will help me replace them later.

Stepping into the slick steam, I gasp as sizzling hot water splashes my skin, then laugh, the sound rusty and unfamiliar. It takes several minutes to calm my excitement enough to investigate the amenities. Perfumed shampoo and conditioner, luxurious body soaps, a brand-new razor, exfoliants . . . I sigh in pleasure.

The familiar hunger gnawing at my insides finally drives me from the steamy bliss. I wonder if they have more cheese. Maybe even other food. *Real* food. None of the men had exactly looked peaky. All three were hard and strong and clearly healthy. It takes a lot to maintain that kind of muscle mass. I've been living off the fruit and vegetables I'd been able to grow in my garden, and the occasional fish or rabbit I managed to trap. My attempts were getting better, but meat had nevertheless been scarce.

After towel drying my hair, I pull on the white silk shirt. It's long on me but still barely brushes mid-thigh. There's no fresh bra or underwear to be found, but I'm not about to put my soiled undergarments back on after finally getting clean. It would probably be better to burn them. I worry my lip between my teeth, feeling exposed.

Wonderful.

It's hardly their fault, though, I reason nervously. They hadn't been expecting company.

I pick my glasses up from the sink and, after a moment's hesitation, rub the cloudy mist from the mirror.

Long dark-brown hair wetly snarls around a face so pale it's almost translucent. The damp ends are doing obscene things to my white shirt, so I quickly twine the length up into a messy bun and secure it with my last hair tie, ruing the lack of a brush or comb to tame the mass.

The angles of my cheekbones and jaw stick out sharply, and I wince. I've lost a lot of weight over the last few years—too much to be healthy. My too-wide mouth now seems ridiculous to me. I sigh. I've always prided myself on being neat and tidy, at least, but between my hair and clothes, I can't even manage that.

Not that it matters, though, right? An internal voice taunts me. *You're here and you have the right parts, checklist done.*

The thought twists my stomach.

On the bright side, I'm no longer lumpy and unfit. I can see the ad campaign now. *Starve yourself skinny: the Apocalypse Diet.*

Tossing a last, irritated look at my reflection, I stalk back to the bedroom—and right into a tall, warm wall of man. Strong arms steady me, and though I don't recognize him, his scent—books, ink, and parchment—settles me instantly.

"Easy."

His voice is soft and controlled. I try to step back, but his grip, though gentle, is uncompromising.

After a moment, he murmurs, "Look at me. I want to see your face."

With a shiver, I look. In the flickering light of the fireplace, I make out a sulky, almost femininely curved mouth. The second thing I realize is that this man is starkly, utterly beautiful. His angular face has an underlying masculine strength to it that belies the thick eyelashes and sweet softness of his lips.

His eyes are darkly shadowed and fiercely intelligent as they study me. Small lines fan from the corners. Older than the other three, in his early forties perhaps, his steady maturity is both unnerving and comforting.

This is not a man to be trifled with—but his quiet authority is all the more vital and interesting to me because he *doesn't* radiate raw strength. It's in his obvious self-assurance. In how he radiates this inexplicable dual sense of threat and safety.

What I can't explain is why that sends slow, heavy tendrils of heat licking through me.

His eyes gleam in the firelight as he takes in the damp, clinging shirt, lingering on my breasts. He's clad in an elegant pair of trousers and a similar silk button-down, and I wonder if the one

I'm now wearing belongs to him. Suddenly, the fact that I'm wearing someone else's clothes doesn't feel odd. I *like* it.

I like it a lot.

After a long moment, he nods, seeming to decide something. A hand trails from my upper arm to my chin, and he brushes a thumb over my lips, tracing the sharp indent at the top. The movement shivers through me, and I jerk my head back, feeling abruptly vulnerable and overwarm. He lets me retreat, though something predatory moves in his gaze as I do. A faint smile curves his lips, as though I did something interesting. It isn't like Lucky's delighted grin, or Beau's slow warmth. It's restrained. Bitingly amused.

Uncomfortably flushed and unsure of what that gaze means, I look away.

"I am Jasper Douglas. A pleasure to meet you, Eden," he says, soft and cultured. "Please come with me. We have drinks ready in the gaming room, and I understand you are yet to meet Jaykob. I'd be pleased to introduce you."

My stomach jolts. Just what I need, more men.

Jasper escorts me through the house, built entirely in rich dark wood and stone, with warm golden lighting. I would have called it a log cabin had it not been so massive. It drips luxury, decorated with artifacts and carpets and paintings so clearly expensive that the owner might as well have glued money up on the walls and have done with it. I wonder if the Asian influences are Jasper's doing. Something about it calls to me. There's a care and a warmth infused into the design that softens the obscene wealth.

Jasper leads me to an interior balcony at the end of the hall, which overlooks the sprawling lower level. Glowing lights dangle through the middle of the house from the high ceiling. An imperial staircase curls its grand, matching flights down to the first floor.

As we descend the left flight of stairs, I pause by an exquisite artwork. It features three silhouettes under a vibrant cherry blossom tree, with some artful calligraphic characters in the corner that I think might be hangul. I'm caught by the way the female silhouette is reaching for the young boy playing just out of her grasp. The way the man has his hand tangled in the strands of her hair as he watches them both. There's something deeply warm and cozy in the silhouettes that makes my chest ache.

Jasper steps in behind me, and his breath stirs the small hairs on the back of my neck. "It says 'family is always in reach.' Or near enough."

A tiny chill accompanies the ache in my chest, and I turn away from the artwork.

"A pretty thought," I say with forced levity.

"My mother was a sentimental woman."

There's a fondness in his tone that makes me glance up—and that may have been a mistake. Jasper is drinking me in, absorbing me with his gaze until I'm dizzy and floating inside it. I'm not sure there's air, here in the ether of his eyes. If there is, I can't find it right this moment.

His expression grows soft. "Family is who you choose to make it, Eden."

My lips part, and there's a small lump in my throat. He's trapped me inside of him, unraveling me in moments. I don't know how he managed to figure me out so fast, but I'm sure he did. I'm sure he just drank down all my secrets. All my fears. I'm almost afraid of the implication in his words.

Family. It *is* a pretty thought.

I take a delicate step out from under him and down the stairs, sucking in a needed breath and rubbing my hand over the raised hairs on my arms. He lets me escape, but his clever, curious interest follows me.

Casting about for a distraction, I eye the wide, clear windows that line the entire front wall of the sitting room, inviting me out into the sunshine. A large, solitary apple tree stretches its laden limbs toward the house.

"How could this possibly be hidden from the drones?" I ask as we pass the windows, changing the topic.

Jasper allows the shift, directing me with a firm hand on the back of my shirt, just lower than is proper. I shiver under the proprietary touch, so warm through the thin fabric.

"The lodge is built into the side of a cliff, which overhangs our valley. It's protected on three sides by the mountain and the fourth is concealed by the forest. It's impossible to see from above from any angle, and you would have to know where you were going—or be incredibly lucky—to find it from the ground."

I frown, letting the new puzzle take the place of my discomfort. "What about heat signatures?"

He shakes his head once. "We're too deep into the rock. Even if we weren't, we've seen no evidence of drones since the first year after the initial attack. Whoever was sending them is either now unable to or has given up their efforts."

"You don't know who sent them?" I ask. "I thought, perhaps, since you were Army . . ."

"The men were on leave when it happened; I had recently retired. They were summoned back to base when the first strikes hit, but by the time we arrived, it was too late. Our base was gone, as well as a dozen others." He lifts one shoulder, his soft lips forming a hard, grim line. "Our team eventually tracked down one of their satellite phones, but by the time we were able to contact our international embassies, no one answered. As there has been no land invasion here that we know of, nor any aid delivered from our allies, we can only speculate regarding the state of other nations. Mass devastation, surely. Whether they were entrenched in the Final War, or wiped out as surely as we were, the silence speaks for itself. I don't expect they're any better off than we are."

My stomach drops at the confirmation. It was everything I assumed, everything I feared. It doesn't change anything, not really, but it still hurts to hear how irrevocably our world has been torn apart. I suck in a deep breath.

He pauses. Taking my arm in a gentle grip, he draws me to a halt. "I apologize, Eden. That is not news I should have delivered so casually."

I can't help but sink into him. Just a little. He lets me, but the decadent silk on silk press of my body against his isn't as relaxing as I thought it would be. He's too warm. Too firm. He smells too much like the books that kept my imagination vivid and awake through these last four lonely years.

"Oh, that's quite all right," I say, my voice on the wrong side of breathy. "It's, well, it's surprisingly hard to hear, but it's not like I expected help to arrive after all this time. I'm not quite that naive." I shake my head. "I'm okay. I'm sorry."

"Hm." He cups my chin in those long, elegant fingers, but I can't be snared in those eyes again. I try to turn my face but end up rubbing my cheek into his palm instead.

He releases a long breath, then murmurs, "Did help not arrive, though?"

He brushes his thumb over the seam of my mouth. My eyes flutter closed as a shiver traces its way over my scalp and down my spine, and I need to force them back open. I blush at how intensely he regards me. I don't think I've ever met someone with such single-minded focus. Like the whole world has just faded away and we stand together, alone in some kind of hazy, dreamy abyss.

"I—" I clear my throat as his thumb dips briefly into the warm, slick heat of my mouth before he withdraws. I only just stop myself from panting. "I suppose it did."

Those pretty lips take a sweet, lunate curve, and then he draws me back into motion down the hall. I'm reminded that there is, in fact, a world around us. And there are four other men awaiting me. Four men who are expecting to form a ridiculous sex pact that is slowly sounding less and less ridiculous with every moment I spend in Jasper's company.

He leads me around a corner, deeper into the lodge. Rosy lights brighten the spacious hall. Jasper matches my slow steps patiently, in silence, until the air between us swells, growing heavy and electric.

I have to fight to stop my hands from fidgeting, my body tingling and pulsing with . . . nerves? Surely it's nerves.

"You have a lovely home," I blurt.

The curve to his lips deepens, but he says nothing.

I'm not usually a person who needs to fill silence, but my pulse is jittery. Carbonated. It's making things bubble out of me.

"So have you lived here long?" Just stop talking, Eden. Please, for the love of God.

Jasper quirks a brow and lets me stew in my embarrassment for a moment, damn him.

"Yes, I have," he finally says, then adds, "This was my family home, and later my personal retreat, before the world disappeared. My mother was from Gangnam-gu, in Seoul. She fell in love with an American businessman, my father, though she insisted that she fell in love with the scenery first. They built Bristlebrook, and it was their sanctuary for many years before they retired in Seoul."

We pause in front of a heavy door. "They left this home to me, and I was in the process of moving here after my retirement when everything fell apart. I suggested the Rangers join me when it became clear we could do no good where we were."

I press my lips together. There's a bitter undercurrent in his tone. I want to touch him, to offer him some small comfort, but I'm scared that if I do, I'll end up floating away again.

I need to stay grounded right now.

"You're too young to be retired," I say instead of pressing.

"It was foolish of me, but there was something I thought I could outrun. In the end, it only ended up chasing me here." The smile on his lips turns cold, self-deprecating, but he grimaces. "Enough of that."

The crease deepens between my brows, and I open my mouth, confused, but he cuts me off and pushes open the door.

"Welcome to Bristlebrook, Eden."

The low murmuring in the room tapers off as the door swings open and it takes a moment for me to gather my courage and step inside. Dark floorboards span the room, covered in the center by a plush rug. The natural gray rock of the cliff forms the walls and ceiling of the large, cave-like room, reminding me of my last home.

Golden light bathes long leather couches, which frame the room on three sides. A floor-to-ceiling television takes up the fourth, complete with gaming consoles and controllers. On the opposite side of the room, a raised platform behind one of the couches houses a well-stocked drink bar. It's a complete man cave, albeit a classy one.

Lucky is sprawled far too close to the massive television, an open bottle of whiskey beside him and a game controller in his hand. He gives me a wink when I enter, then his eyes run over my silk shirt and color creeps into his cheeks. He glances up at Jasper, but the game draws his attention back quickly.

Dom and Beau are leaning forward on the couches, heads bent together as though in mid-conversation. A half-read book rests open and forgotten on Dom's lap. They both look up as I enter. Something flares in Dom's eyes as he takes in my skimpy, damp shirt.

I don't recognize the fourth man by the bar but this has to be the mysterious Jaykob. As I watch, he cracks a bottle open on the belt of his jeans, letting the bottle top fall to the floor as he takes a drag.

I purse my lips. He had better be planning on picking that up.

The man is tall, about Beau's height, but stockier with it. His face is rough-hewn—rawly attractive rather than classically handsome. He has elaborate, full-sleeve tattoos on both thickly muscled arms and his once-white T-shirt strains across his chest; it's dirtied with some sort of black paint. Not that he seems the artistic type. Despite his stillness, his eyes hold a kind of dangerous turbulence that makes me uneasy . . . even as I wonder what kissing him might be like.

What maybe more than kissing him might be like.

The thought pulls me up short. What on earth has come over me? Since when do I think about, well, about *more than kissing?*

It's as though Beau sparked something by the river, then Jasper fanned the flames, and now Jaykob and Lucky and Dom are just sitting around like sexy man kindling.

This needs to stop—*now*—or I'm going to end up embarrassing myself.

I shiver and look back at Lucky's game, which seems the safest option at the moment. A mocking snort comes from the scary artist's direction.

"The mouse?" he scoffs. His voice is gravel and windburn. "Whatever. I'll make do."

I flinch, and Jasper curses softly behind me. My gaze swings back around to find Jaykob stalking up to me. I barely see the dark intent in his midnight blue eyes before his hand grasps my chin and his mouth fits flush against mine. My lips part on a sound of surprise, and he takes the opportunity to plunder my mouth. His grip moves to the back of my head, almost painfully, and his other hand grasps my backside, pulling me hard against him.

I shudder, shocked, lost in his demanding mouth. With a whimper that gets lost in our tangled tongues, I raise my hands to his chest, not sure if I want to push him away or pull him closer. No one has ever been this rough with me. My breasts rub against him, shockingly sensitive through the thin silk.

Then he's yanked away, and a hand grasps my elbow, keeping me upright.

I suck in air, panting jaggedly, heat rising in my cheeks as I take in the scene in front of me. Jasper, who had been closest, was the one who dragged Jaykob off me, and Beau is helping him hold back the now-swearing man. Lucky has abandoned his game and stands between them and me, and Dom . . . Dom has my elbow. I look up at him, wide eyed and damp lipped, and he gives me a stern, searching look.

"The fuck was that?" Beau snaps.

Jaykob smirks at him, chest heaving as he half-heartedly tries to shake the two men off. "It is what she's here for, ain't it?"

My cheeks burn. Was I confused before? I *definitely* would have pushed him away.

Eventually.

Before I think about what I'm doing, I stalk up to the three men and slap Jaykob hard across the face. It barely moves his cheek and my hand stings from the impact. I curl my fingers into my palm to soothe the sudden shock of pain.

Everyone stills. The burly man gives me a look of darkening disbelief.

Immediately, guilt pricks me. Stabs me, really. It's as unacceptable for a woman to strike a man as the other way around, but memories of the men in the woods are still too fresh for cold fear not to prick me at his roughness—even if that fear is only filtering through now. And he *did* grab me first.

"Whatever I agreed, you do *not* have the right to manhandle me like that unless I give you permission!"

My voice is only half as stern as I'd have liked it to be, my body still roiling with . . . I purse my lips. Even if I am attracted to him, it's not okay for him to just paw at me like that. I don't know this man.

"You will— You will treat me like a lady!" I add, trying to keep the indignation in my tone and wishing I didn't sound so much like Scarlett O'Hara on the verge of a swoon.

My stomach dips again when I see the angry red mark growing on his cheek. I've never hit anyone before. Even frightened, I'm better than this. I'm certainly smarter than this. Guilt makes maintaining my anger difficult.

I'm about to apologize when his eyes trail over me obnoxiously, lingering on my breasts. I don't have to look down to know my nipples are tight and hard against the thin silk.

Traitors.

The urge to apologize dies, and I lift my chin.

Jaykob meets my eyes and sneers. "Lady, is it?"

The scorn in his face makes me cringe, though there's a flash of something small and bitter in his downturned mouth that makes me wonder. Why should *he* be upset?

Then he rubs a hand over his reddened, stubbled cheek and the look is gone.

He looks at Dom. "Got a type, don't you? Just so it's on the record, hypocritical bitch ain't mine."

Beau's brows lower in a menacing look that would make Dom proud, but Jaykob pulls his arm free of Beau's grip and moves toward the door. Just before he leaves, he turns. "If she's staying, she'll do her part for all of us. Or she's out."

The door slams behind him.

CHAPTER 7

EDEN

SURVIVAL TIP #238
You won't actually pass out from embarrassment.
It's not a good defense mechanism.

I tremble, looking at my feet. Their gazes sear me, and I swallow, trying not to let my panic grow. I cannot, *will* not, have sex with that man. A dark stain on my new shirt catches my eye, and I examine it. Not paint, I realize. Grease. His shirt had engine grease on it.

A hand grasps mine, gently twining our fingers. Lucky tugs me toward him into a loose hug. My head barely tops his shoulders. He rests his chin on the top of my head, and his chest rumbles with a nervous laugh. "You know, that went better than I thought it would."

Just like that, the wary tension in the room eases.

Jasper gives a wry laugh. "Would you like a drink, Eden?"

Dom sits back down across the room, flipping open his book —somehow managing to do all that without once looking my way, as though he hadn't just been holding me up.

Beau slumps on the couch, right by where Lucky and I are standing.

"Better than you thought it would? What did you think was going to happen?" he asks incredulously. "Another whiskey, Jaz? Make it a double."

"I want a double monkey master mix! Get us two!" Lucky calls to Jasper.

The light catches on Jasper as he looks down on us from the raised bar, making a halo of his dark hair and turning the angles of his elegant face wicked.

To my surprise, Lucky stills entirely under the stare—it's the first time he's stopped moving since I met him, I'm sure of it. I twist to take in his expression, but he blinks and then shoots me a grin, as though he hadn't just drawn taut as a bowstring.

With an easier smile, Lucky waves off Beau's question and addresses me, "Aw, Jayky's okay, he just gets nervous around pretty girls. Trust me, he's more scared of you than you are of him. Deep down he's a real sweetie."

"He pawed at her," Jasper cuts in smoothly. "It's inexcusable."

Lucky sucks in his lower lip, considering that. "Deep, deep down."

Jasper gives him a disparaging look, but I think I detect a hint of humor in the too-determined press of his lips. He pours the whiskey and his own glass of red wine with exacting precision. "I don't know how to make your ridiculous drink, Lucien. You need to make it yourself."

Lucky huffs and releases me.

"You'll see that I do *all* the important jobs around here." That earns a reluctant smile from me, and Lucky joins Jasper up at the bar. "And he was always going to paw at her; he's an animal. It's all those primal instincts—pheromones, you know."

I shift. "Would he have . . . ?"

"No," Dominic says, finally looking up from his book. "Jaykob might be rough, but he wouldn't hurt a woman without a damn good reason. We wouldn't keep him around otherwise. He wouldn't have touched you if we hadn't already told him you'd agreed to this. But he *is* rough. He likes it that way. He is that way." He grimaces. "If I had to guess, that was a test."

I cross my arms, realizing with relief that the movement covers my breasts. The silk shirt truly hides almost nothing. "A test I failed, I take it?"

He gives me a blank look. "Did he hurt you?" When I stay silent, he shrugs, turning back to his book. "Not really that different to what Beau did at the lake then, is it?"

Beau scowls at his friend, and my back stiffens.

"That was not even close to the same thing," I mutter.

When Dominic looks up again, I try not to squirm. He reminds me of a medieval king. There is something so forbidding, so rough with power about him, that I feel the urge to kneel and ask for mercy whenever he directs the full weight of his attention to me. His presence is a physical thing.

He studies my face. I know Beau is looking at me too, but I can't bring myself to meet his eyes. I've been in the wild long enough to know to keep my eyes on the biggest predator in the room, especially when he seems about to pounce.

Dominic's lips purse in a considering way and he shuts the book with unnerving finality. "You liked the way Beau touched you?"

His golden gaze traps mine and won't let go. Mortification spreads through me.

"Answer me, little librarian. This is just the beginning of the inquisition."

An inquisition. Oh, yes. I could just imagine him now, giving direction from his throne. Demanding cuffs and chains and exquisitely painful torture devices. Watching with those heavy-lidded eyes as his inquisitor spreads me open, bare and naked for the king. The two of them working me over until I scream and expose my every secret. Expose every part of myself and . . . and . . .

My breaths start coming in shallow pants I try to hide but know he doesn't miss.

Lucky gives a low laugh from the bar. Jasper makes his way back down and hands off a whiskey each to Beau and Dominic, then takes a seat beside the king.

Jasper would make a good inquisitor, I think before I can control my ridiculous fantasy.

Dominic is still waiting on a response, but embarrassment makes me snarky. "I'm here, aren't I?"

A golden-tanned hand catches the bottom of my silk shirt and tugs. After a moment of hesitation, I let Beau pull me down. At the last moment, he directs me to his lap, rather than the seat beside him, and I shoot him an indignant look. He smiles lazily and picks his drink back up from the side table. His other hand remains wrapped around the hem of the shirt, his fingers stroking absently over my inner thigh. I become very, very conscious that I'm wearing nothing under the dress shirt.

Lucky comes down from the bar, two large, bright orange cocktails in his hands.

"C'mon, Dom, you saw it. She practically mounted him on the bank." He offers me one of the frothy concoctions. When I hesitate, eyeing the obnoxious color dubiously, he says, "You should take it, sweetheart. The boss man will want to cover the bases, and I'm thinking you might need some good ol'-fashioned liquid courage. Double monkey master mix'll sort you out."

I dart a look at Dom and take the drink. Lucky settles himself back in front of his game, only partially turned our way. His own drink is precariously balanced on a raised coaster beside him. With his long dark-blond hair escaping down his back, I can't decide if he looks ludicrous or completely right.

After a moment of strained silence, Lucky laughs and adds more quietly, "He'll cover *all* the bases with you. First, second . . ."

Beau throws a pillow at him.

Looking for any distraction, I take a sip of my drink and immediately wrinkle my nose. It's cloyingly sweet, almost a syrup, and obviously devastatingly alcoholic. I'm running on an empty stomach too, but I don't want to seem as though I'm complaining. I'll just go easy on the booze.

"How many men have you slept with?" Dominic asks bluntly, drawing my attention from the frosty glass.

"Is this really necessary?" I reply, a prim press to my lips.

To my surprise, Jasper answers from where he's perched beside Dom. Not a hair is out of place around that breathtaking face. "We need to understand who we're dealing with, what kind of experience you have. We're not going to treat a virgin the same way we would someone who has been in the lifestyle for years."

"The lifestyle?" I tilt my head, confused.

Beau reaches up and plucks at the tie in my still-damp hair. "Kink, darlin'. Someone experienced with BDSM."

I move to pull my hair out of his grip, but it only tightens. His lips tilt in an entertained smile, and I sigh, deciding it isn't worth the struggle. As soon as I relax, he resumes pulling the tie out of my hair until the locks tumble down my back. Looking at Beau seems like the safest option at the moment, now I'm cradled on his lap—at least while Lucky is only half paying attention. Or pretending like he is, anyway.

I lick my lips. "So are you . . . ah, all into that kind of . . . ?"

His hand trails down my back, then down my hip until he goes back to making those slow, shivery strokes along my inner thigh. "Mm-hmm. To different extents, and in different ways. We were all in a private kink club off base when the first strikes went down—a couple of us used to go there to blow off steam whenever we had leave. We hauled ass to get back to base, but it was blown to shreds by the time we got there. We stuck around for a bit to see if there was anything we could do, but it was chaos. We couldn't find the rest of our platoon. Not . . . not much of them, anyway."

His face grows grimmer as he speaks. I can almost see the memories scarred in his eyes. Without thinking, I lift my hand to brush my fingers over his cheek, wishing I could brush away the hurt as easily.

Beau leans into my touch for a moment, and continues roughly, "Jasper guessed his retreat might be safe—he was our shrink, and our friend, before he retired. Dom and I'd been out here a few times and agreed it was our best option."

"You know I don't like that term, Beaumont," Jasper says, disapproval sharp in his tone. The way his chin lowers makes the angles of his face seem sharper, pooling darkness in the hollows.

Lucky mock gasps. "Yeah, we're not *friends*."

"Don't test me, Lucien." Jasper isn't warm and bookish now. "I do not find derogatory remarks amusing."

Lucky glances up from his game at Jasper and color floods his cheeks when he takes in his expression.

"Our psychologist," Beau corrects, inclining his head apologetically.

"Sorry, Jasper," Lucky mumbles.

I'm grateful for the brief reprieve, because my mind is still caught back at "kink club" and "BDSM." Burying my face in my drink, I take a long sip to try and collect myself. Okay. Not only am I agreeing to a crazy sex pact with five strangers, but they're five strangers into the kind of kink I don't even have the experience to *imagine*.

Right.

No problem at all.

I mean, sure, I've delved into the racier sections of the romance shelves before, but my memories of the brief pages I was able to bring myself to read in no way make me more comfortable right now. Darn it!

Dominic clears his throat, his annoyance far less measured than Jasper's. "If you're done getting off topic, she still hasn't answered the question."

I scowl.

"Are you a virgin?" he demands.

"One," I mutter, realizing I'm not going to be able to escape his questioning. No torture devices needed, apparently. I have the backbone of a kitchen sponge. "I've slept with one person."

There's a momentary silence. Jasper leans forward, concern creasing his brow. "Please tell me I misheard that."

I sigh, cheeks pink, and my gaze drops back to my drink. How can I possibly *still* be considered a dud in these circumstances? The quiet rejection stings worse, in its own way, than Jaykob's harsh judgment. "My husband is the only man I ever slept with. We met when we were teenagers."

When I was so desperate for a friend. When he was so desperate to be someone's hero. Back before he lost everything and realized I wasn't worth the cost.

"Sorry you lost him, beautiful," Lucky says, turning from his game to look at me seriously.

I give him a stiff smile and shrug awkwardly. "It's fine. I mean, it's not, not really, but it's . . . well, it's been a long time now."

In the end, while his passing during the strikes was certainly sad, I hadn't been heartbroken. But I'm hardly going to get into that now.

"Anal."

My head snaps toward Dominic.

"I beg your pardon?" Ice chills my voice.

He rolls his eyes upward, for all the world like he's praying for strength.

"Have you had anal sex before?" He runs a hand over his jaw. "Never mind, I can see that's a no. Something easier, then. Has anyone ever gone down on you? Can you give a blow job?"

My mouth drops open, and his sinful lips curve, though amusement is scarce in his eyes. "Yes, that's the general idea, but I would prefer a verbal response."

My jaw clicks shut, and my eyes narrow. My one experience attempting a grand oral seduction had ended after all of five seconds, with Henry pulling my mouth off him and telling me I was prettier when I acted like a lady.

I hadn't exactly protested, though. The clinging odor of urine had turned my stomach and left me wondering if I would embarrass myself further by vomiting all over his crotch.

That probably wouldn't have been ladylike either.

"No," I mumble, deciding *not* to share that detail with the class. I take another deep draw of my sugary drink and the syrupy flavor of Skittles slides over my tongue. Oddly, it's growing on me.

"Maybe it would be quicker to cover what you *have* done. How many times did you have sex, ballpark? Did you do *anything* other than missionary?"

He sounds frustrated. Bah. Kings don't usually need to sleep with silly, inexperienced women. He's used to having his pick. How disappointed must he be?

Jasper has settled back into the chair, but the crease in his brow deepens with my every response.

I clear my throat.

"He . . . I mean, we did it from behind. Once." At the silence, I moisten my lips and huff. "He was deployed a year after we were married, and I left him about two years after that. But, well, we weren't . . . together . . . all that many times. He was out of the country so much . . . Things were so intense overseas. And I think, I mean I know, he didn't really— I wasn't what he—"

I can't get the words out.

Dominic tensed during my speech. Now contempt touches his regal features. "You left your man while he was deployed?"

I stiffen, my nervousness of him temporarily leaving me at the disgust in his tone. Expression turning to stone, I say, "I am not answering any questions about why my relationship ended with Henry. That has nothing to do with this, and I do not need to explain or justify myself to you."

Dominic regards me with a shadow of surprise, and only the background noise of Lucky's game breaks the silence. His lips tighten, then he asks in exasperation, "Did you even enjoy having sex?"

Jasper gives a single shake of his head, not even waiting for my response. "She's too inexperienced. This isn't a good fit."

Lucky snorts, eyes still caught on the game as he shoots his way across an abandoned airport. "She had shitty sex a half a dozen times as a teenager. Probably in one position, no foreplay, with the lights off. Making out with Beau was probably the highlight of her sexual career. She'll be fine. She just needs to get *Lucky*."

I squeak in utter humiliation. Though I have to admit . . . he pretty much summed it up.

Beau's chuckle shoots right through me. There's a clink as he sets his glass down on the side table. He leans forward until his lips brush against the shell of my ear, the warmth of his chest flush against my back.

"That right, darlin'?"

His warm breath in my ear makes me shiver. My nerves skitter in a way I'm not used to at all.

"I—" My voice is lower, huskier than it should be.

A hand reaches around and gently extricates my drink from my grip, then sets it beside his. Then his arm reaches back around my waist, holding me to him. I twist slightly in protest, but he corrects my position with firm movements until only my face is turned to look up at him. His other hand, still on my thigh, hitches higher, raising the silk shirt into precarious territory.

"Do you want me to fuck you?"

The dirty words make my breath catch in shock, but my eyes drop to his lips.

"I want . . . " The words stall in my throat. I'm breathing embarrassingly hard.

"Say yes, pet."

Pet? I feel like I should have a problem with that word.

Beau rests his forehead against mine, and his closeness is decadent. Inebriating.

Maybe later I'll have a problem with it.

"I—" His mouth tasted like a promise. Like sin. But surely that was just sleep deprivation. Surely it wasn't that good.

I should probably double check.

"*Yes.*"

The word escapes me like a sigh, like a plea, and Beau's lips curve as his hand flattens on my thigh, gliding up and inwards. Tensing, I try to clench my legs to trap his hand, but his knees are inside mine and, with a quick, brutal motion, he uses them to push my legs apart. Too far apart. His other arm holds firm around my waist.

I'm trapped. Exposed. Dominic watches me with heavy-lidded eyes, unfazed and confident on his throne. His expression is detached, almost careless, as I'm manhandled and stripped in front of him.

Why does that turn me on even more?

"Fuck." The hoarse curse from Lucky makes me turn. He has abandoned the TV completely and all humor has drained from his face. Strain lines his tight jaw as he stares between my now-open thighs. With no underwear, I'm completely bare to him.

My cheeks flame, but before I can squirm away, Beau's hand moves to cup my slick, silky flesh, and despite myself, I let out a low, hitching sigh. His head dips and his lips skim the side of my neck, over the soft skin beneath my ear. My eyes slide closed. The hand around my waist shifts upwards, palming my heavy breast through my shirt.

Stop, stop, stop, one voice chants. *They're all watching!*

Another voice—a better voice, I decide—gasps a husky, *I know. Hot, right?*

Beau's fingers curl in to pinch my nipple, tweaking the stiff peak, rolling it between them, and my weak inner protests die on a throaty moan. The motion stings; light pain and heavy pleasure zing through me. He gives the other the same treatment and electric sparks charge and heat my blood until I'm tingling everywhere.

I twist, not to escape this time, but to push against the hand that is just resting against my scorching sex. It's not enough. I need so much *more*. Even just cupping me as he is, I know I must be coating his palm—I'm embarrassingly wet. Dripping. But I want his fingers sliding through my drenched folds, need them stroking my clit.

At my squirming, the gentle lips on my skin part and his teeth bite down on the sensitive flesh between my neck and shoulder. Hard. Heat spears me. I arch my back with a gasp as he licks over the bite.

"Stay still for me, darlin'," he murmurs, voice deeper than usual, his accent thick. "You tell me to stop if you need to."

I still. Everything in me wants to shiver and grind against his hand until I come but, God, I want to do this right for him. I want to be good. And I really, really don't want him to stop.

So I obey, but I can't help my tremble.

He squeezes the hand at my core, and I whimper, but don't move. Don't move even though I desperately need him to touch me *properly*. My body throbs, begging to be filled. I'm not the type of person who often makes demands, but I want to demand now. Or beg. I'll crawl naked across the floor to him if he only promises to *touch me*.

Feverish, I look back over at Dom, needing to see if he's still unfazed. If I'm being good enough. If he likes me like this, wet and squirming on his friend's lap. But when I look at him, he's not looking at me at all. He's looking down at his book, jaw tight.

"*Dom,*" Beau says in a strained, rough voice.

His knees inside mine nudge me open further until my thighs strain and I'm all but dripping onto the floor. He tilts me toward Dom like a virgin sacrifice. An offering to our king.

But the golden eyes don't lift. He turns another page.

Shame tangles around my lust, spicy and barbed, as Beau's chest vibrates. The sound he lets out is suspiciously like a growl.

Before the hurt can set in, I become aware of footsteps, and someone standing in front of me. My eyes fly open, and Jasper's savagely beautiful face is intent as he looks down on me.

The arm around me tightens in warning, but I've stilled completely. The steely thighs that spread me flex, taking me to my limit, making room for the other man to step between them.

"A pretty sacrifice," Jasper murmurs approvingly, echoing my thoughts. His fingers brush over my hair, and he adds coldly, "One only a fool would pass up."

There's a rough thump in the background, but in my haze of arousal, I'm lost to wondering what Jasper's mouth tastes like . . . and how it would feel if his tongue replaced Beau's hand between my slippery thighs.

I catch my lip with my teeth to avoid another whimper at the visual. *Bad. Bad librarian.* My lids wilt, heavy with lust; it's an effort to keep my eyes open.

"Interesting." Jasper's thoughtful tone is far too liquid and cool against the raging heat inside me. Steam. That's what we'll make together. Hot, wet, cloudy steam. He bends on one knee, between my and Beau's thighs, and his graceful fingers stroke over my chin.

"It was until you ruined the damn view." Lucky's voice holds more than a hint of bite.

When I work up the courage to glance at him, though, he doesn't look irritated. There's an ache in his eyes as he looks at me and Jasper that makes my breath gush out all over again.

My head falls back limply against Beau's shoulder, and his lips resume their wet, delicious movements along my neck. Jasper's fingers trace the column of my vulnerable throat, down to the front of my shirt.

Before I can work out what's happening, he's freeing one button after the other. I jerk in protest, but then a determined finger —Beau's?—slides between my folds, brushing my clit, and I cry out, all thought and uncertainty chased from my mind by pure want.

"Beau."

"Fuck," he swears, hips jerking upwards, pushing his hard length against my ass.

"If you don't mind," Jasper says wryly as the motion jostles his movements on my shirt, which is now mostly unbuttoned.

How did he do that so fast?

Beau licks the shell of my ear, all hot, heavy breath, and whispers, "I told you I love it when you say my name, darlin'. Such a good girl."

The finger between my legs strokes firmly, up and down first, then in circles, discovering what makes me shudder. Beau's approval makes me weak. My breathing becomes more urgent, panting. My eyes squeeze shut, trying to close off at least one element of overwhelming, riotous sensation, and I hardly notice as the silk shirt is pulled to the side, revealing my naked body to the room.

There's a sharp intake of breath, and I vaguely hear someone ask, "Uh, should Jayk be here for this?"

And someone on the other side of the room replies with a growl, "He left. His own damn fault."

Cool fingers run over my chest. Tension coils low in my stomach as someone else rubs and strokes my clit. My own arousal slicks my thighs obscenely. I can hear every wet motion, but I'm too far gone to care. I want them to know how much I want this. How good they're making me feel.

Lips replace the hands at my chest, and my own hands lift, tangling in thick hair. There's a scorching, wet drag of a mouth to my ear, making me arch into another pair of lips as they close around my left nipple and suck.

My hands tighten in that thick hair, and I let out a sobbing cry, lost to sensation, my eyes fastened shut. The mouth moves to my other nipple as the maddening finger flicks over my clit again, making me jerk. The finger drags down, teasing my entrance, circling it, before plunging in. Then another finger works inside, joining the first, filling me.

I try to grind against the pressure, but sudden hands at my hips hold me firm.

Those fingers continue to move in and out of my tight hole, stretching me, punishing me. Teeth join the damp, determined lips at my breast and the sharp sting sizzles over my skin, like a live wire to my core.

Tears leak from the corners of my eyes. I can't track who is doing what—it's all just pleasure. At another sharp, wet tug on my nipple, I clench around the thick fingers inside me. The sensation is foreign, invasive, delicious. I've never been handled like this in my life. Beau groans into my neck.

"Do you have any idea how good your pussy feels, darlin'?" he whispers roughly. "So tight. You're dripping over my fingers, dirty girl. You're going to come all over my lap, aren't you? Jasper and I will take care of you."

I want his filthy mouth on mine. I want to swallow the sounds. My hands are frantic, but I can't reach skin.

Just when I think the pressure inside me can't build any further, the fingers inside me crook, rubbing a magical spot that makes lights dance behind my eyes. Everything in me tenses. I think I stop breathing. A thumb circles wetly over my clit, faster and faster. I teeter on the brink, breathless and gasping. The build inside me is strange and desperate and tears are in my eyes, and I don't know exactly what it *is* but I know I'm so *close*.

"Be a good girl, darlin'. Come for me," Beau orders.

Then those scraping teeth bite down hard on my breast as a hand roughly tweaks the nipple on the other. The sting of pain, the excruciating fullness of the fingers in my pussy and Beau's hungry command work like raw dynamite and I explode. I shatter. I hurtle over the edge, drowning in full-body ecstasy. A scorching mouth meets mine, swallowing my wild cry, and the fingers inside me are unrelenting, eking out every last wave of pleasure. Every squirming shiver.

My toes actually curl. I always thought that was just a myth.

The cruel mouth on my breasts turns gentle, soothing. The hurt has settled into something luscious. My head is turned and a new pair of lips licks and nibbles against mine, encouraging my soft moans. I relax into the lazy kisses, until finally I give a last shudder, limp and spent.

The mouth on mine moves to pull away but I suck weakly on the delicious lips, not ready to relinquish them. The amused laugh muffled against me isn't familiar and my eyelids, heavy with pleasure, flutter open.

Jasper studies me, and there's a smoldering satisfaction behind his eyes that makes me swallow. *God, he really is lovely.*

Beau's hand lifts from between my legs, drawing my gaze. He licks his glistening fingers and smirks when my mouth drops open at the slide of his pink tongue cleaning off my juices, though my breathing is still too ragged to protest. I bite down on my lip. Hard.

"I've changed my mind; she's a perfect fit. I'd be pleased to have her," Jasper says in a low, silky voice.

I blush and my gaze catches on the very noticeable bulge between his legs. Guilt washes through me.

"I—" I begin, and then clear my throat. My voice is so husky it's unrecognizable. "I can . . . "

Can . . . what, exactly? I don't even know where to begin. The tempered heat in Jasper's face gentles somewhat, and he bends to give me another brief kiss on my lips.

"Very kind, but not necessary. I think that's enough for one afternoon."

He turns and gives Dominic a cool look. Catching sight of him makes me distinctly aware that I'm completely exposed.

My breasts glisten damply in the warm, low light, my nipples are obscenely puffy and red, and there's a distinct bite mark on my right breast. My legs are still split over Beau's thighs and my slit is wet and swollen and bare and in full view. My long, still-damp brown hair tangles over my arms and Beau's shoulders. I can even feel the dark blush in my cheeks.

With Jasper out of the way, I note with relief that Dom has finally abandoned his book. His golden gaze rakes over me, and Lucky blatantly watches, his eyes sliding between me and Jasper. Jasper raises one brow at him before leaving the room.

I clutch the sides of my shirt and pull them closed over my chest. The movement makes me shift in Beau's lap, and he groans, his arm tightening around my waist. The hardness of him is insistent against the seam of my rear, covered only by the straining denim of his jeans. I fight the urge to turn around and press against him. Delicious little aftershocks still tingle under my skin but there's a hollow, empty ache between my thighs. As wonderful as his fingers were, what I really want is that thick length buried inside me.

I jump off Beau's lap, pulse erratic. What in holy hell is wrong with me? I *never* think like this.

Dominic stands up slowly and walks over to me. "You have one week to get comfortable here, then we're drawing straws to work out the roster. Two days on, one day rest, continuous— unless you and those involved agree to swap days, or take more than one per day, but you sort that out between yourselves."

He leaves with me still gaping after him.

CHAPTER 8

EDEN

SURVIVAL TIP #124
Everyone has a past.
Make sure theirs won't come back to bite you.

More than one of them in a day? How in the world does he imagine *that* working? Though, I mean, I guess it just had.

I shift, looking down. My etiquette lessons didn't cover this kind of thing, and embarrassment is fast swallowing my brief moment of abandon.

Beau stands behind me. My cheeks feel hot. He just . . . His hands were just . . .

He bends and presses a firm kiss against my lips. Shockingly chaste, considering what he was just doing to me. I can taste myself on his mouth. He pulls back and makes to leave, and I clutch his arm, feeling like I should say something—thank him, maybe? Demand an explanation?—but my tongue feels clumsy in my mouth.

Beau misinterprets. "I need to cool off, darlin'. Lucky'll get you sorted."

Letting out a slow breath, I nod. With a final squeeze of my arm, he leaves as well.

Not able to look at Lucky directly, I stare at his shoulder as I squeak a request for the bathroom. With a far-too-cheerful bounce to his step, he shows me the way and tells me to meet him in the kitchen when I'm done, giving me brief directions I pray I'll remember.

Closeting myself in the bathroom, I quickly relieve myself and clean up, feeling swollen and tender from my encounter. My head is spinning slightly, whether because of the ridiculous drink Lucky gave me or my combustive orgasm, I'm not sure.

Washing my hands, I study my face in the mirror. The cheeks that were ghostly pale less than an hour ago are full of color, my blue-gray eyes luminous and glassy, my lips pouty and roughed red.

I run a finger over the pink mark on my neck, examine the one on my breast—while trying *not* to examine why I feel a sneaky sense of pride when I look at them. My hair is a mess around my face, kinked at the back where it rubbed against Beau's shoulder as he—

The tap is still running.

I turn it off with a curse and take a deep breath, bracing myself on the sink. I can't remember the last time I looked so . . . *pleasured*. Have I ever looked like this before? Why does it make me feel just a little bit . . . pretty?

A frown crinkles my forehead. What is *wrong* with me? Years of propriety and reserve melted in moments under Beau's touch. Jasper's lips. Dominic's kingly, heavy gaze. Lucky's intense, playful heat. My thighs clench.

If I'm brutally honest with myself, I even responded to Jaykob's rough handling—though that had to be some sort of post-traumatic reaction, I'm sure of it.

I meet my own lust-drunk gaze in the mirror.

"You're behaving like a slut," I admonish myself.

Yeah, well, apparently being slutty is really fun, my heavy-lidded reflection purrs. *Let's be slutty again. Right now.*

Despite the glee of my vixen twin in the mirror, my long history of disillusionment warns me not to get too excited. My situation isn't so simple, after all. The things they want to do to me, what they expect . . . it's overwhelming.

My reservations cast shadows across my features, dimming some of the rosy glow.

How can I possibly juggle the needs and desires of five men when I haven't ever been able to hold even one man's attention?

I swallow, thinking that over. I can't. That's the simple fact. I won't be able to, even if I can bring myself to do all the things they're asking. Who could? That has to be a superpower reserved for gorgeous sex sirens with mystical ambrosia vaginas and charisma on par with Santa Claus.

But how can I leave?

I slept in an actual bed last night. They have real drinks, and I'm about to eat a proper meal. Made in a *kitchen*. Comforts I forced myself to forget about for years are now a very real possibility.

My mind flashes to the ease with which they handled the men who'd hunted me.

I wouldn't have to watch over my shoulder constantly, could stop flinching at every broken twig, stop wondering if the animals are just a touch too quiet for safety.

I wouldn't have to be lonely anymore.

A thick lump lodges in my throat. It's so damn *nice* to have someone to talk to. Day after day, that was what threatened to pull me under. For someone who lived most of her life as a loner, it had stunned me how much I craved casual conversation. A passing touch. All those little things I always took for granted. Those things I left behind without a second thought.

Over the years, as the quiet grew deeper and colder, there were times I considered seeking out one of the packs of armed, careful men that occasionally prowled by. I was almost willing to take the chance that *these* ones were good and honest, just so I wouldn't have to deal with that biting, wintery loneliness. If I'd seen any women among them, I probably would have taken the risk.

I was sorely tempted by a group of about fifty I saw in the city about a year after everything went down—children and men and women all banded together. They were casual. Barely armed. I followed them for a while, soaking in their affection for each other. They laughed. The kids played in the street as they walked. Men and women flirted.

But deep in my heart, I didn't believe they would make it. They stood out too much. They were too slow. Too noisy.

They were prey.

Worse, they were stupid prey. And they were going to die.

So, in the end, alone and grief weary, I crawled back to my cave. For months afterward, stinging with loneliness, I cursed myself. Maybe I was wrong. Maybe they were fine. Maybe I could have reasoned with them, showed them how to be careful. Maybe I could still have tracked them down. I was sick and ashamed of myself.

But I never went after them.

The thought of returning to that quiet, hungry existence hollows my stomach. I can't start over, not alone. Not again. Even having a home for a little while—until they tire of me—has to be better than going back to that, right? My body seems such a small price to pay for company. For safety. Especially if *that* is what they plan on doing to it.

I can always leave if it's too much. If the loneliness ever seems like the better option, then I'll take it.

But I have to give this a shot.

Straightening my shoulders, I finger-comb my hair again as best as possible and go in search of the kitchen.

Three wrong turns later, I finally find it. It's on the ground floor—and it's massive. Spacious and kitted out with every modern convenience, it's a chef's dream. I've always been more of a utility cooker, but even I start plotting what I might be able to make on that stove.

Lucky is sizzling baked beans in a pan and the fragrant smell of garlic and onion almost has me swooning. There's a kettle heating on another burner beside it, and two mugs sit like little temptresses on the counter. He shoots me a dimpled grin and the sight of it tightens my throat.

Those dimples could do more damage to me than any one of their fancy rifles.

"A Lucky specialty," he declares, and I could kiss him for not bringing up the porn show from earlier.

Wandering into the room, I admire the way the floor-to-ceiling windows showcase the apple tree and the dark, towering forest just beyond. But just to myself, I admit that the better view is behind me. I take a seat at the breakfast bar in front of Lucky, watching his forearms flex as he stirs the contents in the pan. With a wink, he goes to the fridge and pulls out a wedge of cheese, and he grates it over the steaming meal.

Sinful, decadent, it melts through the sauce like liquid gold.

My stomach growls a demand. Loudly.

"Ah, damn," he curses, giving me a guilty look. It pulls the firm swells of his lips into an almost-pout that I have the insane urge to nibble on. "Should have done this first."

He spins to the flick the burner off and pours steaming liquid from the kettle into the mugs. The scent of coffee floats through the room, and I close my eyes for a moment against a sinful rush of pleasure almost on par with my earlier orgasm. Coffee. For real, actual coffee. I mean, it must be instant, but *still*.

I can't help the smile that blooms across my face and, as Lucky catches sight of it, the worry that made little lines in his forehead eases.

A few minutes later, he sets the meal down in front of me.

Coffee and cheese. Maybe I'm wrong about all of it. Maybe I

wasted away from sadness and exposure out in those woods, and I've somehow found my way to heaven.

"Don't eat too fast," he cautions firmly. "Your body won't be used to it."

I raise an eyebrow. "Oh, sure, *now* that's a consideration."

Lucky's eyes lighten to sunny skies. "Always a consideration. We're very considerate people." The dimple flirts with his cheek again. "'Specially me."

Shaking my head, I huff a laugh. I've never been a playful person, but it's impossible not to warm to Lucky. He's pure sunshine.

Unable to resist any longer, I drive my spoon into the fragrant, savory mixture and bring it to my lips, only just remembering to blow on it before shoveling it in. Garlic, melted cheese, and tomato explode on my tongue. I moan, eyes rolling back slightly. It has been *so long* since I tasted anything this good.

My embarrassment vanishes under my appetite and, despite Lucky's warnings, I make quick work of the bowl. Grasping for the coffee mug, I drink deeply. The rich, once-familiar flavor makes me grin.

God. *Yes.*

Draining the last delicious drops, I remember myself and glance up at Lucky. He's watching me intently, an amused smile peeking through his short beard.

"Sorry," I mutter.

Damn it. What am I doing? We might have lived in a dingy, beaten trailer, but my grandmother brought me up with impeccable table manners; she would be appalled. I can imagine her now —*low cash doesn't mean low class, Eden!*

"Been a while, huh?" he deadpans.

I narrow my eyes at him but decide against commenting on *that*. Getting up, I take my bowl to the sink and flick the tap on.

"Just stick it in the dishwasher," he calls casually.

After a pause, I open the wooden panel under the sink and

find the dishwasher. Unbelievable. They have a working *dish-washer*? How on earth did they manage that?

Lucky grins. "Whole-house generator. Jasper's parents had it built so it's completely self-sufficient."

I stare for a moment, then put it in, shaking my head. When I straighten, I bite my lip, at a loss.

"What's up?" he asks.

I spread my hands over the cool marble countertop. "What now?"

His head cants to one side questioningly. Strands of hair have escaped from his messy bun and slip along his neck in long, traceable lines.

"Is there something I can do to help? What do you all do all day? Do we need to go hunting or something?"

Understanding dawns on his features, then he laughs. "You don't need to do anything. You have your daily chore ticked off."

His tone is teasing but the way his eyes light with blue fire leaves no doubt in my mind he's replaying the scene from earlier.

My cheeks heat, but only partially from embarrassment. I'm worth more than just sex.

Irritation makes my voice crisp when I say, "Well I'm hardly going to spend all of my day walking around and parceling out orgasms. I need something to do."

"Shame." Lucky smirks, then stands and wanders over. "What did you do before, when you were alone?"

What *did* I do? The days and months are blurred together, a hazy mix of hunger and fear and boredom. I shrug.

"I usually checked and re-set my traps. If I was lucky, I might have caught something. I wasn't usually lucky. I'd collect my herbs and vegetables for the day. I'd wash my clothes. Very rarely, I had to go into a town for supplies." I grimace, remembering the throat-closing fear that all but paralyzed me with every trip. "Mostly, I read. I'd bring books back from the library. I'd take some non-fiction—on topics that would help me stay alive, of course—and some fiction, so I wouldn't go stir crazy. Whatever I could get my hands on, really."

Horror tightens Lucky's features. "I'd put a bullet in myself before living like that."

"Not all of us had these luxuries," I tell him quietly.

His eyes widen and he shakes his head. "I didn't mean it like that; it's amazing you stayed alive. I just can't deal with being alone. I'm a people person. Even these idiots are better than nothing. You're tougher than I am, is all I meant."

His voice is so earnest, I relent. I give him a rueful look, very aware of what a hot mess I look like right now. "I don't feel very tough."

Lucky tugs me into his arms before I can protest, like he did after Jaykob kissed me. I should have known he'd be a hugger. My instinct is to tense, but there's nothing loaded or suggestive in the way he holds me. It's more like he's drinking in the sensation, and I can't help but want to take a sip as well.

I rest my head in the nook of his neck and, after a moment, tentatively wind my arms around his waist. His short beard tickles my forehead, and I find myself enjoying the unfamiliar sensation.

After a moment, he says, "Jasper has a lot of books. I'm sure he'll share if you ask nicely. As for jobs around Bristlebrook, we kind of split tasks. Dom and Beau do most of the recon and raids for parts and essentials; sometimes I sub in, but there's always at least two of us out together at a time. We try to keep Beau there in case anything goes south. He's handy with a rifle as well as the med kit. If I'm not with the others, I'm usually out hunting. The three of us are gone on and off about half the week."

"Hm. And Jasper and Jaykob?"

His hands trail over my hair, twining through the strands and stroking them between his fingers. "Jayk is extra muscle, if needed, but he's pretty handy, so he mostly works on getting shi— Uh, *stuff*, up to scratch. Handles most of the mechanics, wiring, weapons, that kind of thing. And Jasper is our housemaid. He cleans the place, monitors security for Bristlebrook and surrounds, takes care of the farm, fixes our heads, and does most of the cooking. He's not as good as me, obviously, but even he can't have everything."

I don't crack a smile; my mind is caught on something he said. "Did you say 'farm?'"

He releases me with obvious reluctance. "Oh. Jasper didn't give you the full tour, huh? He's usually perfect." His cheeks color, and he clears his throat, avoiding my eyes. "I mean, perfect at that kind of . . . You know what, never mind. Follow me."

Grabbing my hand, he tugs me out of the kitchen and into the sitting room, walking slowly to allow for my injured foot. A huge stone fireplace is unlit, but sunshine dances outside, warming the room. He tugs open the sliding doors, letting me see the code to lock and unlock the house. A cozy swing chair stuffed with soft cushions is perched on the wrap-around deck.

The large front yard brackets the house, extending to the line of the woods. There's a barn far to our left and a small shed about thirty yards back from that. The two towering barn doors are closed tight.

I take a step toward it, but Lucky drops his hands on my shoulders, spins me, and nudges me in the other direction.

"Unless you feel like another run-in with Jaykob, we should go this way." He bites down on the corner of his bottom lip, but his smirk is irrepressible. "The barn is where he works. And sleeps. Where he spends most of his time—since he's a damn recluse. The shed is for dressing, drying, and stocking our meat, and we keep a locker for our heavy-duty weapons in there. Not that *I* have a key." He pouts. "Dom has a 'thing' about keeping explosives in the house."

I don't particularly care about the weapons, beyond being glad that I'm not sleeping on top of a powder keg, but the memory of Jaykob's scathing scowl makes me step a little faster.

I fastidiously ignore Lucky's snicker.

He slows as we pass the apple tree and plucks a ripe orb from between the leaves. He rubs his thumb over its crisp, ruby red flesh, and I'm so caught up in watching the provocative slide that I'm a beat too slow when he tosses it to me and fumble it awkwardly.

"Want a bite, Eden?" he asks, his smile making a reappearance when I finally catch it.

I lift a brow. "Kind of low-hanging fruit, don't you think?"

Lucky laughs, then leads me to the right side of the house until we reach a hidden tunnel leading into the cliff. The sneaky entrance is tucked between folds of rock and can only be seen from a certain angle. The stone is rough under my palm as I gingerly pick my way inside. It smells cool and wet. We're only swallowed by the dark for a few moments before it opens out into a grassy cavern.

There are openings in the rock above where sun shines in from several angles, and an underground stream bubbles along one rock wall, trailing in from deep within the cave network. Wire fences enclose the space neatly, blocking off several dark, snaking trails.

What truly catches my attention, though, is the multitude of animals bustling around the enormous space. Chickens, goats, and pigs share the clearing, perhaps two dozen of each trotting comfortably alongside one another. Realizing my mouth is hanging open—quite improperly—I shut it with a click.

"How . . . ?" I ask weakly.

Lucky rubs his hands together, delighted. "It wasn't easy. It took ages before we could get this many. The cocks were especially bad—they kept going after each other until we started keeping them penned. Fighting over the hens, you know?" He indicates a few small pens toward the back. The dimples are back, and I notice the one on his left cheek is particularly pronounced.

He opens the feed bin beside us and draws out a scoop of mixed vegetables and scraps. "You should have seen Dom and Jayk trying to get the pigs from the farms. They had to take the Jeep, and by the time they got back here with the first load there was shit all over the seats and Dom was just about ready to start the slaughter early—starting with Jayk." He grins. "Jasper refused to clean it."

He starts laughing, and my lips twitch at the image. It's hard to imagine stern, domineering Dom wrestling dung-covered pigs.

Lucky opens the latch on the wire fence and steps into the clearing, indicating with his head for me to follow. I take a cautious step in, and immediately the animals seem to perk up, shuffling our way.

"It took months to get all the basics here. I wanted cows, but Dom said unless I could ride one in here, it wasn't going to happen. Always been a spoilsport." He sighs and starts scattering the food around. "They only get sunlight during certain hours, but it doesn't seem to bother them too much. They keep breeding anyway."

"So, you eat them?" I ask, watching a baby goat nuzzle its mother.

Lucky studies me. "Are you a vegetarian? You said you caught rabbit and fish, right?"

"No, I'm not, but they're just so . . . " *Cute*. Damn it. I trail off, realizing how stupid I sound. It's been a while since I've seen anything so soft and sweet—innocent things don't last long these days. It's never been a sentimental world, and it's only gotten worse since the strikes.

A twinge of guilt twists my guts. Memories of the small, hungry faces in that group haunt me, as they do every few days. What would they have given for a home like this?

A small pig presses its wet little nose to the back of my bare legs, snuffling, and I reach down to scratch its pink ears, hiding my face.

Lucky grins at me, oblivious to the dark turn of my thoughts. "We don't usually kill these guys. Mostly, we use the eggs from the chickens and the milk from the goats—you can thank Billie and her sister Baa-bara over there for the cheese. When I go hunting, I usually pull us enough meat that we don't need to worry. Rabbit and fish are pretty much a given, sometimes turkey or pheasant, but I'm after the deer, mostly. A good-sized buck will feed us for weeks—months if we really ration it. We only crack out the pork and bacon if we're running low, or for special occasions."

My forehead knits, and I straighten again as the pig gets distracted by the produce. "But feeding them alone would take so much work. How do you even get all of this food?"

Lucky plucks up a particularly fluffy black hen, nuzzling into her.

"This is Henrietta. She's needy," he explains. Then he lifts one shoulder, refocusing on me. "They do okay. We had a couple shi— sorry, crap—years when we couldn't get anything to grow properly. We have the veggie patch over by Jaykob's workshop. Berries, cabbage, pumpkin, tomatoes, corn. Lots of corn. We also let it pretty much run wild in here, so they get insects and worms and shi—ah, stuff—too. Thought Jasper was going to shoot one of us and use the corpse to feed to the pigs before he finally got the hang of it."

God. How can they have *so* much? I stay quiet, just watching the animals and thinking, until Lucky starts shifting beside me, his smile slipping.

"Eden—"

"It's just— Don't you ever feel guilty?" I can't stop the words; they bubble from some dark, envious vault inside me. I starved and scraped through for *years* while they had all of this? "People would kill for what you have. Literally kill for it. People starved, good people, who needed homes and safety and food—and you had all of this! How is that fair? Why couldn't you share? There's room. There's so much room. With these caves . . . How many people could you have saved? You were Army, right? Doesn't that mean you have to protect and serve?"

My hands clench around my shirt, twisting it. The events of

the last few days, weeks—heck, *years*—are bubbling over into my emotions. I want desperately to understand. I need to.

At my words, Lucky's face turns grim, its playfulness stilled. Henrietta lets out an anxious squawk, and he sets her down with an absent, soothing rub of her feathers.

"That's the police, I think. We're 'Rangers Lead the Way,'" he mutters as he shoves his hands in his pockets. His gaze skirts mine. "Maybe you should chat to Dom about this one, I—"

I lift my chin and force my hands to unclench, and he breaks off with a grimace. I like Lucky. He's easy to be around and has made me feel welcome and included, without the underlying pressure I feel from the others. But it just isn't fair, and I can't pretend it doesn't matter to me.

If I'm being honest, I wouldn't have just killed to have what they *have*—the things or objects. In the early days especially, I was so desperate to feel *safe*. I'm not a fighter. I don't have any crazy, special survival skills. Even when everything went dark so suddenly, even though the broadcasts stopped, I was so confident the Army, the cops, *someone* would get organized eventually. That sooner or later they would sweep through, take control, and protect us. That we would recover some semblance of government and order.

But it never happened.

I learned to protect myself, and I'm better for it. Not with guns and fist fights, but with learning and patience. But how many others died who really needed the help that these men—trained and so much more capable—could have given?

Sure, the Army was scattered, destroyed. But surely even the five of them could have done something on a small scale. Couldn't they have helped innocents on the ground, rather than holing up together and only caring about themselves?

I *can't* let this go.

So instead of backing away from the confrontation, my usual instinct, I take a deep breath. "No. You brought me out here.

Explain it to me. Make me understand why you all felt it was okay to hide out in paradise while innocent people were butchered."

Lucky blinks at me in shock.

"Well, damn, sweetheart. And here I thought you were sweet and shy." He runs a hand into his hair, seeming to forget it's in a bun. He scowls when it loosens, and his arm drops. "We did try, okay? We tried a couple times early on."

He hesitates a moment, like he's trying to find the right words. He looks as though he'd rather be anywhere else. "When we first came out here, we collected nearly twenty people before we even had resources to support them. A few families, some couples, a handful of loners. We lost four on the way—attacked by asshole marauders like your friends from the other day. They were attracted by a big group of soft targets, I guess. We fought them off, but there were too few of us to protect that many in the open. A woman died, two men . . . and a kid. Wouldn't have been eight years old."

My stomach drops, and I bite my lip.

A brown feathered chicken plucks at Lucky's shoes and he scowls down at it, but I'm not sure what he's seeing. There's a vulnerability in the downturn of his mouth. The memory clearly hurts him.

My self-righteous anger melts into concern. Gently, I take his hand again and tug until he lets me lead him out of the clearing. Lucky drops the scoop, but when I move to release his hand, he squeezes it. Avoiding my eyes, he stares at our cupped palms. We're standing too close, but I don't move away again. Absently, I run my thumb over his wrist.

When he continues, his voice has steadied. It's matter of fact, like he's reading a report. "It got tense after that. A few people started thinking that they could have done better, wanted us to share around the weapons."

He snorts, and the sound is colder than I thought him capable of. "Like we'd hand our weapons over to civilians who don't know their asses from the right end of a rifle. 'Specially ones muttering about how they'd be better in charge. By the time we got to Bristle-brook, it was a pot ready to boil over. The rest of the group was picking sides, who they thought would win out. We got the most, but Sam—the loudest of the assholes—got the ones willing to cause trouble." He grimaces. "Everyone was distracted the first week or two, but it didn't take long before they tried a coup."

The final residues of my anger wither like fire-caught parchment. I'm such an idiot. Clearly I'm too emotional right now. What was I thinking, accusing him of not caring? Beau's first reaction on seeing me was to calm me down and tend my wounds—and Lucky instantly wanted to bundle me up and cart me back with them. Of course they would have tried. Imagining them asleep and helpless while the people they'd protected came after them . . .

I'm beginning to get a bad feeling about why they're alone.

"Dom had figured them out, though," Lucky continues, almost motionless. It's unnerving. Like he's been powered down, all that joy and animation sucked into some dark, yawning black hole. "He was watching Sam's group closely, so they didn't catch us unawares and take us out in our sleep like they hoped. We caught them in the act. Subduing them was easy, at least—they weren't so keen on fighting us while we were awake and armed, funnily enough—and soon we had 'em tied up all nice and pretty. But then we had to figure out what to do with them."

Lucky looks back at the clearing, his neck corded with tension. Henrietta is nestled up against the wire fence, as close as she can get to him. A beady black eye rakes me head to toe. If I were a more fanciful person, I might think the ruffle in her black feathers is aimed at me for upsetting her friend.

Shifting my hand, I twine our fingers together until our naked palms are pressed against one another.

"We told the rest of the civilians the next day, asked them what they thought we should do." The grim cast to his face is so unlike the Lucky I've seen so far, I feel the urge to cuddle up to him. "There was only one *smart* thing to do. They knew where we lived, they were full of hate, and they wanted what we had. We didn't have the resources to keep them as prisoners, so . . . the group wanted us to . . . to take them out." He swallows, then looks at his feet. "I mean, it made sense. Would've been safer, you know? To kill them."

A chill seeps into my skin, and I barely hear the last part. Did he say 'take them *out*'?

I take a breath. Would *I* have been able to let those men go if I had them at my mercy? Knowing that they knew where I was and when I'd be vulnerable? Knowing they could, and most likely would, come back for me at some point?

He catches my expression, and his face softens. "We couldn't do it. It's one thing to kill someone in combat, it's a whole different thing to execute civs in cold blood, even ones who attacked us first. We're not murderers." Rubbing the back of his neck, he sighs. "We exiled them. Don't know if you know this about Rangers, but we get pretty extensive surveillance training. We made it clear they weren't allowed within fifty miles of Bristle-brook, and we spent weeks setting up motion sensor cameras, remote controlled cameras, the works, just in case they came back."

"And did they?" I ask.

Lucky shook his head. "We've seen others, and we stopped them before they got too close. But no, they never came back."

I nod, thinking that over, and we watch the animals in silence for a moment.

"What happened to the others? The families who were here," I ask softly.

Lucky shrugs one shoulder, but the movement is slow, like he's become too heavy to shift.

"It all fell apart after that. About half of the remaining civs decided to leave—the two families, actually. Said that we couldn't protect them, that we wouldn't do what needed to be done. They wanted to try to set up somewhere themselves." His voice is a little bitter at that. "Dom took it pretty hard. But most of the women stayed, and a couple men. It worked for a while, but we had problems. People didn't want to pull their weight. Jealousy. People hoarding supplies. Then there was everything with Heather, and the drama with Thomas, of course."

Thomas? And was this the woman they mentioned earlier? The last woman they had here? As casually as I can, I ask, "Heather?"

Finally, a smile touches Lucky's mouth again. "Nah-uh. That's a *whole* other story. And not mine to tell. You'll need to earn that one."

I pout, humor lightening my mood again, and he chuckles.

"Whose story is it then?" I venture.

"Dom's, mostly. Kind of Beau's." He sobers again. "Look, I will say that there was a lot of drama. The fallout of that relationship hit our whole group pretty hard, burned away a lot of trust. So just go easy on us for a while, okay? They'll see you're different soon enough."

Well, that isn't confusing at all.

I look at him sideways. "How could you know that already? That I'm different to Heather."

Lucky laughs then. "Oh, sweetheart, you couldn't be more different."

"Jaykob said—"

"Ah, don't listen to him. Jayk can't see past his own prejudice. The only thing you have in common with Heather is that you both talk kind of fancy."

I shake my head, disbelieving. *Fancy*? If he only knew. Maybe they aren't seeing through me as easily as I thought they were.

"Hey." Lucky nudges me with his shoulder, drawing my attention. "I want you to know, we have helped people over the years. We keep an eye out for anyone who needs help, but it really isn't that simple. Most groups want nothing to do with us. Anyone who's survived this long is careful—they don't exactly run our way." He lifts a brow. "And if they do, they're not usually the type we want to bring home for supper, if you get my meaning. If there are women like you around, they must avoid us like the plague."

Didn't I do exactly that? I saw several groups of men over the years and not once did I work up the courage to go up to any of them.

Or perhaps I just had the sense not to.

There were signs that other women survived—tampons raided from supermarket aisles, diapers depleted—but my actual sightings of them were few and far between. Those large packs of families and soft, smiling people disappeared years ago.

Lucky grimaces, taking in my expression, as if the confirmation hurts him. "Beau's stitched people up while we've been out, we've traded news or supplies, but most of them have their own plans now. They trust their own, that's it. And it's not like we're going to point signs to where we are for just anyone to find, either." He looks me in the eye. "It's not as easy as wanting to help. People have to accept it."

It reminds me of Jasper telling me family is who I choose to make it.

We both fall silent, lost to our own thoughts.

"Have I scared you off already?" I can feel Lucky's gaze asking me to understand. He's clearly trying to keep his tone light but failing spectacularly.

And in that moment, I see it in him. There's a melancholy under his brightness that I feel in my bones.

I wonder what causes someone as warm as Lucky to burn so quietly cold.

I wonder if any of the others notice.

Hesitating, I look up at him. "It's a lot. It's all been a lot. But I'm not leaving until I have time to take it all in."

I don't want to leave at all. The forest is a frightening place to live alone, and it's hard to draw boundaries for myself when all I want to do is hide under my new silk sheets and read and eat delicious cheese and claim cuddles and let them erase the last four years from my mind.

But I need to be tougher than that. Experience has taught me that gift horses should not only be looked in the mouth, but examined for fleas and attitude problems and secret, nasty packages strapped to their saddles.

Just because I want it, it doesn't mean I get to have it.

And it certainly doesn't mean I'll get to keep it.

Relief touches his features. He blows out a breath then holds out his hand. "Come on, then. Let's head back inside and you can get some rest."

He walks me back and lets me go when we reach the house. I walk up to my room, my mind tripping over a dozen stumbling thoughts. I'm readying myself to sink into another deep, pillow-soft sleep when I spot a book by my door.

Bending, I pick it up. It's a glorious hardcover of *Little Women*. I let myself into my room as I examine it and curl up on one of the soft armchairs by the dying orange coals of the fire. I crack open the front cover and a note slips out.

This family of ours is messy.
Complicated. But try to be brave
Eden. Our pieces may fit together
better than one might think.

—Jasper

I stare at the note for a long time before I finally set it down and turn the first page of my present. It's smooth and comfortable in my hands, just like the hundreds of books that have been my only friends for too many years now. It has a familiar weight, and a familiar smell, and it's enough to make me emotional after such a flood of unfamiliar things today.

Did Jasper see this in me today, while we were alone in that abyss together? How quickly he worked out just what I needed.

The next page slides between my fingers in a soft caress, and I read until day fades into shadows, and long into the night.

CHAPTER 9

BEAU

SURVIVAL TIP #85
Deal with your messes when you make them.
The longer you leave them, the harder they are to clean up.

Another yawn cracks my jaw as I step through the thick
forest, armed and ready. But I have to fight to keep from
glaring a hole clear through the back of Dom's head. Now, I generally consider myself a man slow to anger, but I have been known,
on a handful of not-so-proud occasions, to boil over to bursting.
And this morning? I'm struggling to keep myself to a simmer.

Between trying to scare Eden away from coming home with us,
shunning her in the games room, and then dragging me out of the
house at the crack of dawn this morning before I could even steal a
good-morning cuddle, Dom is getting on my last nerve.

He's lucky I'm so even tempered. Not one to hold a grudge. In
fact, it's only because I'm *such* a professional that I haven't given
him the old what for. Nope, you'd best believe that I've kept my
mind on the mission and eyes on the trees—and not on the Judas
to my right.

Though I am counting every one of my lucky stars he isn't at my back.

Since I'm running out of places he can stab me in it.

"So," Dom begins, breaking the four-hour silence between us. He nods at the river of wildflowers running between the trees. "Should I be picking you a nice bouquet to get my ass out of this doghouse?" He looks over at me and lifts a brow. "Or is this a fancy tennis bracelet kind of deal?"

I blink, spluttering a laugh—then can't help but roll my eyes. "You know damn well I won't wear a tennis bracelet." Checking my MK 16, I add with a prim sniff, "Not without the matching earrings."

His mouth snags up in a half-smile, and I scowl . . . because it makes me want to smile too. Damn it. I hate that he can do that—get me laughing when he hasn't even apologized yet. But no, that would require Captain Slade to actually admit fault, and I've never met anyone so sure they're right. Or harder on themselves when it turns out they're not.

But it takes a good dose of hard reality to smack him round his thick head before he ever comes to *that* realization.

I lower my rifle even as I raise a scolding finger, just the way my ma used to.

"Don't you just brush over these last few days, I'm—" I break off, grinding my teeth.

Nope. There's no point in getting all worked up. I'm calm. A breeze through a cornfield.

I'll be back at Bristlebrook and helping Eden get settled in tonight. It does *not* matter that Dom seems to be doing his level best to keep us apart. It doesn't matter that he's been rude and mean and petty about her and not at all willing to consider what she could mean for us.

It. Does. Not. Matter.

At all.

I turn abruptly, stalking ahead through the undergrowth.

Dom sighs. Sighs like *I* am the problem here. "The word is 'mad,' Beau. Say it with me, 'I. Am. Mad.' The world won't break."

Ducking under a low branch, I squint into the greenery. "How about we just focus on cleaning up our tracks? I'm good with silence. Real good with it."

Dom follows after me, watching my back.

"No? Let's try something easier. How about 'Why, Dom, I am just *fixin'* to rearrange your features,'" he mocks in the most atrocious accent I've heard in my life. "Heavens to Betsy, I have never been so riled up in all my born days."

I stop and gape. "I don't sound like that. I've never sounded like that."

Dom rolls his eyes, then continues in the same exaggerated drawl, "Well, howdy, Miss Eden. Ain't you just plump as a peach. Let's get you back to the farm now, and I'll have you barefoot and pregnant before this here night is out."

At the mention of Eden, my teeth grit again. "It's 'plump as a dumplin'' and you're not even a bit funny." Dom doesn't respond but gives me a dry, sideways look, and I add, "*I'm not mad.*"

"Right," he mutters under his breath, then pauses. He crouches to study the ground. As he smooths over the boot print in the dirt with his palm, his lips compress.

Concern replaces my frustration. "They didn't track us, Dom. We would have seen them by now, or some sign of them anyhow."

He stands and keeps walking, careful to leave no trace, but his fingers curl into a fist. I follow, moving up until I'm by his side, like I have been for the past four hours. Like I have been for half my life. We find our rhythm again, falling into step like an old married couple—just without the man-on-man action.

Or the communication skills.

Finally, the grim line of his mouth cracks. "It was careless. We should have realized there were survivors—Eden *told* us how many there were—and I led us straight back to Bristlebrook. Didn't even attempt to cover our tracks." He lets out a hard breath. "We got lucky that they didn't follow us."

Dom shakes his head once, a sharp, angry gesture, and I can just about see the silent self-flagellation he's delivering. He's been this way ever since military school. He liked to get a head start on beating himself up over his so-called failures before his pa, Colonel Slade—the piss-your-pants terrifying, legendary head of the 75th Ranger Regiment himself—could voice his disapproval. I'm half sure Dom wasn't born so much as carved out of the *Ranger Handbook* and made flesh by sheer force of the Colonel's will.

And there are no mistakes in the handbook.

"You don't think any stragglers might have been put off by the giant pile of their dead buddies?" I ask.

Dom's dark brows lower. "Maybe."

"There were three of us out there. Not just you. We all messed up," I offer, knowing it's useless. To Dom, it's all his responsibility.

He makes a noncommittal sound, his shoulders still tense boulders beside me. We pick our way through the forest carefully, making our way back to the clearing-of-death. It's slow going—we need to stop and erase every sign of our passage from two days ago. Dom is right about that, at least; we don't want any surviving hunters tracking us to Bristlebrook.

After thirty minutes, he's still kicking his own ass, and it helps me push down my prickly feelings. I've always been better at soothing tempers than stoking them.

"We're making good time," I try again. "At this rate, we should be able to make it back home by dinner."

Dom's head swings toward me. "We're going to town, then home through the caves." He snorts, shaking his head as he keeps moving. "I'm not about to undo half a day's work so that you can bat your eyelashes at the new girl."

I grab his shoulder and yank him to face me before I even clock the impulse. Dom studies my hand on his shoulder, then looks at me with a curious tilt to his head. He looks *amused*.

"That will take *days*," I grind out.

"Three, probably. Maybe four." Dom picks my hand off him, then shrugs. "But that's no problem, right? After all, *you're not mad*."

He smirks, and I press my tongue against my teeth so hard I reckon I might pop one out. Days. Eden is skittish. In days, she could be gone.

A breeze swirls around us like it's trying to cool us down before we get too hot.

"I'm fine," I reply automatically, but the words come out stiff . . . and tasting slightly of sour bubbles. My mama would have rinsed my mouth with soap for telling such a bald-faced lie.

Dom rubs a hand over his face. "*Fine*?"

"And dandy," I assure him tightly.

"Oh, sure. Sounds like it."

We stare at one another for a moment, and I work to stifle the words pushing at my lips. Dom sighs again, then turns like he's about to keep on, and it all just comes bursting out.

"Look, I just think it's real funny how—"

Dom's head drops back. "Here we go."

"*How*," I repeat, ignoring him, "you managed to find a reason to drag both of us out of Bristlebrook the second she got there. Because me myself? *I* was planning on seeing what our pretty new houseguest looked like all tangled up in her sheets. Help her get settled in. Make her some breakfast. You know, actually make her feel welcome instead of dumping her on the others and bailing."

"You planning to wipe her ass for her too?"

I grind my teeth. I didn't even get a chance to see her last night before she ducked off to bed—and I'd wanted nothing more than to crawl in beside her. Instead, *he* had me out here at the ass crack of dawn like he can't bear to be in the same house with her.

I sling my weapon over my shoulder before I'm tempted to use it on him. "You had no right to drag me out here on some useless exercise because you can't bear that she makes you tingle in your happy places."

Dom shoots me a warning look. "Don't start on that shit with me, Beau. I need your head in this—so pull it out of your ass. We have bigger things to worry about than some girl. Move west; the clearing was that way."

He turns to stalk off, and I pick up the pace so I'm stalking beside him. We're not going to avoid this conversation like we do all the others. It's past time we talked through our shit.

"You're keeping me away from Eden, so I'm gonna go ahead and say you started this one," I bite back. "She's most comfortable with me; it was a dick move to drag me off before she's even settled."

Dom doesn't even look my way, every inch the stern CO, utterly unfazed by my irritation. He steps over a log, checks the compass on his kit and keeps moving. "We need to do recon. There are others still out here, I'm sure of it, and there could be trouble. I'm not compromising our security because you want to get your dick wet."

Dick wet?

"You trying to piss me off?" I ask between gritted teeth. "Kiss my ass, Dom. You need someone out here, fine, maybe you're even right about that, but there's no reason that had to be me. I brought her in. I convinced her to stay. She's—"

"Yours?" The calm breaks, and Dom snaps his own golden glare my way. "She's not yours, Beau. She's everyone's. She's no one. She's just some girl we picked up. *Two days ago.* What is with this insta-love shit?"

"She's ours, Dom," I bite out. "Maybe you don't remember what that's like, but I sure do. And for the record, you don't have to be in love with someone to show them a little good old-fashioned hospitality."

"*For the record*, I don't think your mama would agree with your idea of 'old-fashioned hospitality.'" Dom rolls his eyes.

Rolls. His. Eyes.

Is he really trying to pretend this doesn't even faze him?

"If she's just some girl, then how come you can't bear to be in the same room with her?" We pass the stream where I tended to Eden. Where she kissed me like she wanted to drown in my arms. I drag him to a stop at the lip of the forest. "If she's just some girl, it should've been real easy for you to work her over with me yesterday, burn off some of that tension from the last three years."

Dom snorts. "You're not going to bait me into fucking her, idiot."

"Like I need to. You might take your own sweet time about it, but you'll snap sooner or later—you always do."

He glowers at me, and I glare back, trying to figure out how to get through to him. I want to ask if this is about Heather, but if I do, this conversation will be over. I'd just about need to pull out the cuffs and catch him by surprise to get him to go *there*. And anyway, I don't want to be making this about her when it should be all about Eden.

"You got no interest whatsoever in pinning that girl between us and seeing how many times we can make her come? You don't want to watch those pretty eyes beg for more? You really saying that you don't miss waking up with a warm, pretty girl snuggled between us?" A muscle ticks in his jaw, and I press on. "You know how alone she's been. You telling me you don't want to give her a friend she can count on? You really want me to do this without you?"

"I don't want a mouse for a pet!" he bursts out, eyes flashing with temper. "God damn it, I want—"

Dom's mouth snaps shut, and my lips twist bitterly, choosing to ignore that he's insulted Eden twice now.

I won't let it slide a third.

"She's gone, Dom."

He shakes his head sharply, like that wasn't where he was going, even though we both know it was.

"You just want her because she's here," he says softly. "It's not a good enough reason. Not for this, not for us."

Us. Yeah, right. *Us* has been on the rocks for a long time.

For a way longer damn time than that, though, Dom was my brother. In greens and out. We met in military school and got tight *fast*. We fumbled through learning how to top with some seriously patient subs together. We got our first girlfriend together. Got dumped by that same girlfriend, also together. We graduated together, did our Ranger training together. Even when I did my surgical training and he started working his way up the ranks, we stayed partners. And as soon as I graduated, we pulled every string we had to make sure we were in the same squad.

I always thought it'd be him and me, preferably with some pretty subbie between us, right up until we got dusted. That had always been The Plan.

Then Heather happened, and suddenly Dom was telling me good and clear that I didn't feature in his new idea of Happy Ever After. That it wasn't going to be me and him and *our* girl—it was just him and *his* girl, and maybe Beau as a little side piece whenever Heather was feeling *adventurous*. Like I was an extra man-shaped dildo they could pull out when I served a purpose. He loved her more than me, and so fifteen years of friendship and The Plan got nuked with one brutal conversation.

When Heather blindsided all of us and ran off with Thomas instead, I was there with him, despite it all. But this resentment won't let me alone; I can't push it far enough down this time. At the same time, I haven't been able to bring it up, not when our friendship is this weak. It's like it's lacking its old foundation—a mis-healed bone that's still too tender to take our full weight. Since Heather left, we've been gentle with it, not pushing it too hard.

But it has to end.

Eden could be our last chance at happiness together. This time, I know I've got to tell it to him straight—he's right on the brink of fucking this up for the both of us.

"That ain't it, Dom. It's not just because she's here. She's more than just convenient; I want to know her better. And you don't get to make the decision that I don't, just because you're scared I'll choose her over you, the way you chose Heather over me."

He stiffens. "I didn't—"

"Don't. Don't lie to me," I warn, chest tight.

Jasper's been trying to get me to talk to Dom about this for years, but I haven't been able to find the words.

"Dom—"

"For fuck's sake, would you just—"

A bullet explodes into the tree beside my head. Chips of bark spray us both as Dom yanks me down under him, pulling us both behind a tree. He scans my face as bullets pepper the trees around us with brutal, bursting thuds, and I pull back to look him over, breathing easier when I don't spot any blood.

"I'm okay," I assure him quickly.

Damn it, my gun is under me. Why the hell did I sling it?

He squeezes my arm, then releases me to peer around the trunk. "Firing from seven and ten. Semi-auto. You good to split?"

Assaults through heavy thickets are tough. Being surprised by a firefight even tougher. We'll have to be quick and use the terrain for camouflage to regain an edge. Misdirect if possible. My heartrate kicks up, and I nod. All thoughts of Heather, Eden, and our fucked-up issues vanish.

This is where we shine.

"Good. Move out." He pulls back behind the trunk with a curse as more bullets fly our way. "And be careful—don't want you going Swiss on me."

I breathe a laugh as I nod, adrenaline purring through my veins. "No new holes today. Promise."

Dom grins back, color high in his dark cheeks. I push off the tree and brace myself for an ugly fight.

Dom dumps another body on the pile, then rubs his jaw. There's a nasty bruise blooming where one of them clocked him, and he's salty they got one in. Still, he came out better than I did. I caught a knife across my chest and left arm. Nothing too serious, but it stings like a pissed-off jellyfish.

We're back in the clearing where we took out Eden's hunters two days ago, discarding the remains of the assholes who fired on us. Five more hunters had been lurking in the woods around the area, and it took us hours of cat and mouse before we got them all.

And the five of them must have been hard at work for the last two days because there's now a deep pit in the clearing, and it's filled to the brim with more than half of the old bug-ridden bodies. Just one big rancid puppy pile.

We've been tossing today's fresh ones over the top, but this time, as the last body thumps over the others, it groans.

Dom frowns. He crouches and grabs the corpse's hair as its eyes crack open.

"You're meant to stay dead, you know," Dom scolds mildly.

I set my rifle across my shoulders and rest my head back against it. "Must have been a sloppy shot."

Without looking up, Dom flips me off.

Blood bubbles from the dead man's lips. "H . . . help."

Poor lamb.

"Hmm. Seems like you're in dire need of medical assistance," Dom muses, a hard glint in his eyes. But this breathing carcass is part of the group who chased Eden—the same coiled serpent brands his hand. Whether he likes her or not, Dom has no patience for predators. "What do you think, Beau? You know anyone who might be able to help with that?"

I cluck in disappointment. "It's the darndest thing—in all this commotion, my training has just flown right out of my brain."

"That *is* a shame."

"A damned shame," I agree.

Turns out, I don't have all that much patience with predators either.

The man's gaze falls to the side, and he seems to realize he's in the grave, sprawled over the leaking, reeking bodies of his comrades. He squeezes his eyes shut, shaking.

"They'll f-f-find . . . you." His breaths start rattling. "Th-they're . . . com . . . coming."

Dom's attention sharpens. "There are more of you?"

"More than you . . . can stop," he whispers, then he coughs, coating his lips in blood.

The man goes limp, and Dom and I exchange a look.

"Fuck!" He stands and shakes his head. "We should have taken a hostage."

"Oh yeah? Did you have an opportunity for that? Because I sure as hell didn't. You know as well as I do not to fuck around in this terrain. You get the shot, you take it."

Dom rubs a hand over his mouth, glaring down at the corpse pit like he could revive one of them with the force of his ire.

I grimace. "Look, the others need to know about this—we should go back to Bristlebrook."

"We have a camera set up about a klick from here. I told Jasper to keep an eye on it—I'll put up a sign so they know to look out for another group."

Irritation spikes again, fueled by my buzzing adrenaline. "Unnecessary. We can cover our tracks, Dom. We'll be careful this time. There's no reason to take the long way."

Damn it, I want to go home and kiss our girl again, not be stuck out here with his sulky ass.

Dom just raises his dark brow in the condescending way he knows I hate. "They could be coming right to this clearing—we don't know how the groups were communicating, or what their rally points are. It's safer to leave a decoy trail. If we go through town and the caves, they have no lead on Bristlebrook. Not to mention, your pet might appreciate some clothes of her own. We can use the trip to stock up."

That . . . Damn it. She probably would like that.

The smugness comes now, hiding in the tuck of his smile. Dick. He knows he has me now.

But the real joke's on him, because this only proves my point. Even if he's using it to manipulate me, he's still thinking about her. He pretends to be the aloof, in-control CO, but he's more considerate than he gives himself credit for. He's still thinking about what she needs.

He's acting like her dominant.

So, fine, Dom can pretend he doesn't care till the cows come, but I know him through and through. The man was hooked the second she turned those big eyes on him for help, and he was lost the minute she submitted to me and Jasper right in front of him.

I'm sure it pissed Dom off that I shared her with the sadist instead of him.

It was *meant* to.

The proud asshole could choke on that one for being a dick to our girl.

I let out a long sigh. "Fine. We go through town. But in five—I need a break."

After walking upwind of the fetid clearing, I sit, stretching back against a mossy tree. To my surprise, Dom sits next to me, pressed against my shoulder. I pull out my canteen to take a sip, then spot the hole going right through it. I toss it down.

Wordlessly, Dom hands me his, and after a moment, I take it and drink deep.

"Thanks," I mutter, handing it back.

As he screws the top, his jaw flexes tight. "Our friendship can't take another hit, Beau." He looks up at me, golden eyes solemn. "We're full of holes as it is."

"I didn't break us, Dom." I smile at him, a little bitterly. "You did."

His eyes flinch shut, and his head drops back against the tree. "I know."

The words float between us, like a musty old secret freed to fresh air. Just hearing him acknowledge it, finally, soothes some of the sullen ache in my gut. But it also births a new pain. Because he thinks it too. We're broken, riddled with wounds, and we have been for three years.

"Maybe," I start, then stop, trying to find the right words. "Maybe we shouldn't have left those holes to fester. Maybe we should find someone to help us heal them. We've always been better with a third."

"Or maybe we should fix ourselves first before we try to involve anyone else." Dom's voice is full of rebuke. "I won't do it, Beau. Even if we were ready for that, the girl isn't right for us—she's too timid. She'll be gone in a week."

Eden melts through my memories—her chin lift, her clever, quiet regard—and I give Dom a grave look. "You're wrong about her. And if you wait too long, she'll move on before you realize exactly how wrong you are."

His mouth curls up in a half smile, his eyes full of phantoms. "They always move on, Beau. That's why I need you."

My eyes travel over his face, hurting for his pain. "You always have me, Dom. Always."

He swallows hard, and ducks his head to examine his compass for a beat too long.

My own throat feels a little thick, and I stand. I offer him my hand, and he stares at it before he takes it. I pull him to his feet, and then into a tight hug. He squeezes me back, pressing his face into my shoulder, and it's like he's squeezing my heart through my chest.

I miss my friend. I don't want to abandon The Plan.

When he has himself together, he steps back and nods in the direction of town.

I follow him . . . and start my plotting.

I need to figure out how to make the asshole fall for Eden. Whatever he thinks, we *need* a third. Someone smart, someone kind—someone who can soothe over the scar tissue that's forming between us.

We need Eden.

But I have to get Dom on board, because no matter what he's afraid of, I could never choose *anyone* over our friendship.

CHAPTER 10

EDEN

SURVIVAL TIP #166
Don't upset large predators.
Watch, listen, and learn . . . and maybe they won't eat you alive.

The next week passes quickly, and I have the days more or less to myself. Dom and Beau headed out the day after I arrived to collect some essentials, and Lucky seems to spend most of his time hunting. One day, he even came back grinning as he dragged a 120-pound deer carcass behind him and into the stinky meat shed I try to avoid. Jaykob has been hiding out in his workshop in the large barn, with only the occasional clang and loud grunt alerting me to his presence.

Jasper was neatly helpful after the others took off, showing me where to find fresh bandages for my arm and taking me on a brief tour around the garden, which I offered to take over maintaining. After that, he mostly kept his distance . . . except that, every other day, I receive a new book with neat, handwritten annotations in the margin. The librarian in me wanted to cry when I first saw them, but for some reason, I haven't said anything.

Maybe it's because, tucked in the neat swirls of his pen, a

sharp, mischievous humor soaks through the pages. Seeing my old friends—*Frankenstein, The Hobbit, Pride and Prejudice*—through Jasper's eyes is a seductively intimate experience.

I discovered he empathizes with Victor Frankenstein's flaws, and that his heart shatters over the creature's unending rejection, hating it with a level of addictive loathing I don't quite understand but am endlessly fascinated by. I know that he doesn't share Bilbo's reckless inclination toward adventure, sympathizing instead with the steady rhythms and quiet life of the Shire hobbits. And I learned he loves the word "ardently," and that he thinks Elizabeth Bennett is a "saucy minx"—a scribble that startled peals of laughter from me.

Some nights, I even find myself curling up in the downstairs sitting room before the crackling fire, and he joins me, elegantly draped in the large armchair opposite my own. We quietly turn our pages and sip our steaming tea, and I work hard not to stare at him in the flickering firelight. And work *very* hard not to notice the coiled intent in his dark eyes as he stares back. The male need under his cool demeanor.

Despite my curiosity, I'm grateful for his silence—for the breathing room they've all given me. I've needed the space to catch my breath. Despite their distance, I still feel overwhelmed. Overwhelmed by this new world, by their story, by the sudden, abrupt rush of grief-relief over losing my safe haven of the past four years.

Most of all, I'm overwhelmed by *them*.

Masculine energy pulses in every nook and line of this place, from the tools, weaponry, and rigorous security to the overabundance of meat and the size of all their clothes in the washing basket, all the way down to the clean, pleasantly male scents that permeate the house.

It may be elegantly presented. Tidy. Oh-so expensive. But it's unmistakable.

It makes me feel strange. Overtly female. Every example of their hard discipline makes me hyperaware of my softness. The height at which they keep the showerhead reminds me how small I am. Even the size and weight of the heavy doors makes me feel fragile. This is a man's house, and it is aggressively obvious that men own this space.

I was raised by my grandmother, and lived barely more than a full year in total over my marriage with a man who didn't have an ounce of this virile presence. I've never felt anything like it. And after years of fending for myself, of the unending responsibility, and dirt, and *toil*, it's so lovely to allow myself to *be* soft. Just a little. Just for a while.

As the days pass and I'm able to think, to relax, I reach the uncomfortable realization that, despite the tremendous onslaught of *new*, I don't feel threatened here. Or if I do, it's in a secret, delicious way that I struggle to admit even to myself. I feel protected. Pliant. I want to yield to the strength around me. It makes me want to temper some of the harshness, to balance it somehow, though I'm not sure where to begin.

Or if I'm allowed to make that kind of impression here under the strict, subservient terms of our deal.

Being constrained by their rules bothers me, but I can't put my finger on why. Between my strict grandmother and my perfectionist husband, I should be used to living by the whims of others. Why does it feel so strange to me now? Perhaps I'm just out of practice. I've spent a long time making decisions for myself, after all.

It's like I've grown a new skin over these last few years—one thicker and steelier than I had before. Perhaps that old skin of mine is just too thin, too soft, to contain me now.

Can I force myself back into the person I was before?

Do I *want* to?

The thoughts are uncomfortable, but ultimately useless to me. I know what I signed up for, and my feelings don't matter. Survival does. And maybe, if I'm very lucky, I will have the chance to not be alone. I can give up my independence for that, I think.

I have to.

I can't take another year by myself.

Eventually, I find a gentle rhythm to my days. I throw myself into the huge vegetable garden, enjoying the familiar task amid the upheaval of the last few weeks. I tend my now almost-healed wounds and play in the ridiculous kitchen. The decadence of my room hasn't worn off, and I soak myself in scalding water each night, luxuriating in the soft soaps and scented oils.

And I suffer through my least favorite self-allocated task—washing and mending clothes. Today I decided to move a large tub near the apple tree so I could work outside. It's a messy job, and I'm tired of cleaning suds from the laundry floor.

Instead, I'm outside and up to my elbows in soapy water as dusk descends into magenta and moonlight. Hazy stars tease twinkle-bright over the towering trees, and the temperature has dropped enough to lend a nip to the apple-scented breeze.

I'm hopeful Jaykob might be able to fix the broken washing machine Lucky mentioned soon—though the way Jaykob scowled when he saw me scrubbing clothes the other day didn't exactly inspire hope that he'll help me out. The memory of my awkward little wave and the abrupt way he stalked past me still makes me cringe.

With a stifled sigh, I pull the final item from the hamper—and blush when I realize it's a pair of black boxer briefs.

I really need to stop doing that.

But though I try to lose myself in the task before me, unfamiliar tension is coiling tighter and tighter.

Today, my reprieve is over.

Dom and Beau arrived back about an hour ago. Lucky is cooking up a big venison dinner. No one has said so explicitly, but I know it's time to work out the schedule.

I'll have to sleep with one of them tonight.

God. Have I ever been so nervous? I can't tell if I'm excited or terrified. Or both. Or if maybe, somehow, I'm excited *because* I'm terrified. That thought I bury quickly because it's too scandalous for me to contemplate.

And if the more I dwell on my nervousness and shame about what I'm about to do, the wetter and needier I become, well, I can ignore that too.

Pressing my hand to my stomach, I decide I need to put on my big girl panties—and while that might be easier if I currently owned any panties, I can't procrastinate any longer.

I've already spent a frankly creepy amount of time on these boxer briefs.

Piling up the washing, I make my way inside quietly and try to convince myself that I'm not sneaking. But when I round the corner, I collide with Dom.

He catches my basket quickly, steadying me. I silently curse myself as my eyes fly to his, and I'm surprised that he looks as caught off guard as I am. He's freshly showered, still damp and rosy from the heat. Then his gaze flickers over my wet shirt and muddy knees and whatever momentary boost of confidence I felt shrivels.

Then I notice the bruise shadowing his jaw, angry and a touch swollen.

"Are you okay? How did that—?"

"Dinner's ready in ten minutes," he says, cutting me off. "Get dressed."

I swallow hard and nod once. I step around him and into the laundry room, not looking at him again. Jerk. God forbid I show a hint of concern.

Oddly, though, his tone knocks me back onto familiar ground. My grandmother would have given me the exact same distasteful look if she had seen me looking like this.

Some of my nervous-excited flutters have stilled, and when I'm safely closeted inside, I dump the basket and shove the wet clothes into the dryer. I don't even sort them.

Dom can deal with lint balls for all I care.

Tears prick my eyes as I make my way to my room. Damn it. This is going to be a disaster. I'm not even naked yet and his disappointment is still enough to chill me to the core.

Then I see the clothes.

Spread across my bed are jeans, blouses, sweaters, activewear, loungewear, boots, and pretty dresses that I itch to slip into. I wonder if I could get away with wearing dresses like those while I'm here. It's been years since I've been able to wear anything but the most practical clothing.

Sitting beside my new clothes, piles and piles of lacy, sinful lingerie beg for my attention.

I finger the edge of a satin lavender bra that has clasps around the throat with a touch of wonder. I've never worn lingerie like this in my life. Eyeing the tag, I realize that they even managed to get my sizes right. Not that I should be surprised. They certainly had an eyeful that first night.

Conscious of time, I speed through my shower routine, glad I washed my hair earlier. Confronted again by the multitude of underwear, I pluck the least outrageous set from the pile. They're a shimmery, metallic cream, silky soft and cut low. See-through lace peekaboos my bare skin on either hip.

The bra has a simple hooked front clasp that looks like a shining *s*, and it isn't until I fasten the clasp that I realize exactly how dizzyingly high it pushes up my breasts.

After a moment of indecision, I brush past the activewear. I slip into a short, flirty blue dress and leave my room before I can let my dread convince me to do something stupid.

Like lock myself in the bathroom and refuse to come out.

God. What if it's Dom first? If he looks at me with that kind of disgust while I'm with him, how will I ever be able to respect myself again? What if I cry? What if I'm so bad that they immediately demand I leave? Is there a notice period for my eviction? Am I going to be graded on this?

I stop outside the kitchen, breathing fast. Why can't I choose who is first? Beau wouldn't be so bad. The memories of his fingers and indecent mouth are fresh. He's thoughtful and sexy. I think I could bear it if it was him. Or maybe Lucky. I'm sure he'd be gentle with me—though he's so carefully friendly, I'm not sure if he'll inspire that same kind of thrill.

And, so far, I have been thrilled. Somehow. Despite everything.

Jasper. He had his mouth all over me, his teeth pushed me over the edge, and his kindness with the books warmed me to him . . . but something in that dark, dangerous control of his makes me certain I'm deeply out of my depth. Then there's—

The kitchen door swings open.

"Come on in, darlin'. We're waiting." Beau's voice is kind, inviting.

I am so screwed.

CHAPTER 11

EDEN

SURVIVAL TIP #200
A safe place is worth any price.
Even your pride.

D amn it, Beau!" Lucky complains from behind the beautiful
doctor. "I bet a week of chores that she'd come in by
herself!"

Pushing my glasses up my nose, I go inside. All five of them
stand about the room. Lucky and Jasper are working over the
dishes on the countertop. Lucky's wearing a *Kiss the Cock* apron
that makes my cheeks color primly.

"She wasn't coming in, idiot. She was standing outside hyper-
ventilating." Jaykob is sprawled by the small table, flipping his
pocketknife. He doesn't look at me.

Ignoring him, I meet Dom's gaze. He towers by the door to the
dining room, and I can't read anything in the regal lines of his face.
Impassive and assessing, he takes me in. Sourly, I decide he must be
great at poker.

"You're late," he says. "Grab the plates, Lucky."

As he turns and pushes into the dining room, Lucky rolls his eyes at me. He picks up two plates, muttering, "Yes, oh lord and master. Shall I shine your shoes too, your highness? Perhaps you'd like a neck rub?"

My lips twitch, some of the heavy lead in my stomach lightening. Jasper is watching Lucky closely from behind his back, an almost-smile playing around his mouth.

Lucky winks at me and raises his voice as he makes his way to the dining room. "Goodman, shall I cut your venison into tiny bite-sized pieces?" He hip-bumps the door open and he croons, "Oh no, mustn't strain yourself, sire. Allow me to feed you!"

There's a loud thud followed by a muffled curse. Beau squeezes my arm and collects two plates, and Jaykob brushes past me to grab the last two.

Jasper shifts his attention to me from behind the counter, and I'm struck again by how beautiful he is. The others are dressed nicely enough, though casually, but Jasper doesn't seem to wear anything but his elegant silk button-downs. This one is black, open at the collar, and the sleeves are rolled up to his elbows. The muscles in his toned forearms flex as he leans forward on the counter.

"You look beautiful, Eden," he murmurs, and a few strands of sable hair fall over his forehead.

His dark eyes devour me. They lay me bare. But the simple, approving words are surprisingly calming, and my shoulders unknot just slightly.

"Thank you," I whisper back.

"Would you like wine with dinner?"

I huff a laugh. "Yes. I would love some wine."

He doesn't smile, but his face softens. "You had better go inside. I'll bring it. I wouldn't put it past Dom to have Jaykob fetch you, and I don't imagine you'd enjoy that."

I nod and head into the dining room, taking a seat at the monstrous table beside Lucky and across from Beau and Jaykob. Dom sits to my other side at the head of the table.

The meal sprawling between us looks incredible.

"Venison backstrap with blackberry sauce, roast potatoes, pumpkin, and asparagus," Lucky announces proudly.

Half his long hair is in Viking braids today, not in its usual messy bun. It makes the angles of his face more pronounced. He even tidied his close-cut beard.

I smile at him. "You look very nice tonight, Lucky. Thank you for cooking."

He blinks at me, seeming taken aback by the compliment. Then a smile blooms across his face. "I didn't want to show you up, but my natural beauty is hard to hide. Should have known you'd outdo me again. We'll have to swap grooming rituals later."

Beau snorts as I laugh, my nerves making it a husky sound. I realize Dom is staring at me, a frown marring his forehead, and I push my glasses back up the bridge of my nose. As soon as I risk a peek at him, he refocuses on his plate.

Jaykob is the only one already eating, not bothering to wait. His dramatic tattoos are particularly dark on his thick arms. This close, I can see heavy skulls nestled among black leaves and flowers, with vines snaking through the empty eyes and mouth. The designs are beautiful . . . but unsettling.

Jasper walks in with two bottles of wine and pours us each a glass. I try not to seem too eager as I take a sip. At Dom's curt nod, everyone starts eating and I dig in, sighing over the incredible flavors.

I notice Beau is favoring his left arm, and under the collar of his shirt, I spot a bandage.

Patting the corners of my mouth with my napkin, I ask worriedly, "Did you run into trouble on the trip?"

After a moment, Beau replies in a guarded tone, "Trouble?"

I look between his shoulder and Dom's bruise, not failing to notice the heavy silence that has fallen across the table.

"Nothing serious," Dom cuts in, though he's looking at Beau, not me. "Just the usual scuffle over supplies."

Scuffle. Did he classify the shoot-out in the clearing as a *scuffle* as well? I take another sip of wine.

I can't let myself forget that theirs is a bloody, rough system. There's little doubt in my mind that, sooner or later, they'll have other run-ins, fights. Deaths. They have too much to be desired. Too much to defend. Violence doesn't come naturally to me, but if it means my safety, I'm pragmatic enough that I won't quibble about their methods. It is why I'm here, in part.

I want to ask the details, to absorb myself in their problems, the way friends should. The way *family* does. It's the kind of beginning for us I might like, the kind where I help ease their burdens. It might make this whole sordid deal feel less . . . transactional.

Except that Dom's tone doesn't invite further questions, and the way the others avoid my eyes tells me well enough that they plan on keeping plenty between themselves.

The realization, right in the middle of the friendly meal, is sudden and painfully sharp. I am not one of them, and they have no intention of letting me try to be. Jasper misled me, and Beau did too.

I'm not their equal . . . I'm just their *pet*.

And a silly, stupid girl.

Hurt unfurls in my chest, but also something else. Something *new*. Something hot, and stubborn, and singed at the edges. Something that pushes against my soft feelings with angry little claws.

Thankfully, my indoctrinated manners save me, and I swallow around the lump in my throat and mindlessly change the topic only a heartbeat too late. "Well, thank you for the clothes; it's nice to wear things that fit again."

Irritation flickers over Beau's face before his features smooth, and I only have a moment to wonder if I said something wrong before he smiles at me. "My pleasure. Had more fun than I thought I would, actually, picking out those . . . bits and pieces."

There's a naughty edge to that smile that makes my stomach

flip and helps the hurt work its way into a little box. I have dozens of them crammed tight and packed shut inside me.

"Which ones are you wearing?" he prompts.

I clear my throat as I realize they're all looking at me. I focus on the food in front of me, cutting into the meat.

"Well, I suppose one of you will find out," I mutter, more tartly than I'd intended.

Jasper leans back with a soft, "Hmm."

Thankfully, Lucky changes the subject, chattering about the deer he hunted and about showing me the farm. Talk turns to what I've been doing, and how I like the garden and animals—easy conversation led by Beau and Lucky, with Jasper chiming in now and again when we reach a lull. Dom mostly watches from the head of the table but trades surprisingly warm jokes with the three, though he doesn't say a word to me. Jaykob stays quiet, finishing his meal first and then playing with his pocketknife again, flipping it dexterously between his fingers.

Between my glass of wine, the delicious food, and the innocuous conversation, by the end of the dinner, most of my dread has eased and the sting of rejection—and that odd burst of anger—has faded. But when the last fork drops and the words peter out, I know my payment is due.

I take a deep breath.

"Little librarian, are you still sure you want to stay?" Dom asks, deep voice carefully neutral. His eyes are as piercing and predatory as a wolf at bay.

Wetting my dry lips, I nod once.

Beau sits forward, favoring his injured arm just slightly, and he awards me a relieved smile. He looks gorgeous today, in a simple navy shirt and jeans.

"Well in that case, we should cover off a couple of things before we get started," he says, his drawl is slow and careful as he measures my response. "Before the strikes, we all had sexual health tests done regularly for the club, but it's been a while and we've had other partners since."

"Not all of us," Jasper breaks in coolly before taking a sip of wine.

Lucky is stiff and uncomfortable beside him. Catching my stare, he shifts in his seat and offers me a smile that's really more of a grimace.

"Now, darlin', I've done regular checkups for all of us and as far as I can tell, we're clean—but we don't have modern testing available, so there's no way to be sure. Some diseases are asymptomatic, so there's always a risk. And then there's pregnancy to think about."

I'm grateful he's bringing this up, even if the whole conversation makes me want to run in the opposite direction. "I have an IUD—the copper one. I don't think it's meant to expire for another five years. And I was clean. I was tested after . . . well, after Henry. There hasn't been anyone since, like I said. I haven't had any checkups or anything though, obviously."

I stammer to a halt and take a deep drink of my wine, so I don't have to look at anyone. They all seem content to let Beau take the lead on this one.

"If you've been tested, you shouldn't have anything to worry about, but a general health check is worthwhile. We'll take care of that soon," Beau promises. "We have condoms, of course, and we've kept them in the best conditions we could, but they're at the end of their shelf life. We have a few boxes left with a few more months on them, but the rest are recently expired. Better than nothing, but knowing these assholes, those few boxes aren't going to last us real long. I'll do a checkup for you soon, darlin', but we might have to revisit this conversation when we run out of the good stuff."

Revisit. As in, potentially decide not to use protection?

"Ah," I squeak.

The thought of them going bare, of them filling me up and

leaving me dripping and slippery with their cum, sends a flush of wild, unexpected heat through me. I duck my head into my wine again, hoping I hid my shiver in time. I've never done that before . . . but the idea is filthy. Erotic.

Shockingly appealing.

"That work for everyone?" he asks, and sounds of assent ripple around the table.

I nod as well.

"If that's done"—Dom stands and picks up a small bag from the side of the room. He pulls out five playing cards—"it's time to organize the roster, starting tonight. Ace to five, ace being first. You shuffle."

The five thin cards are heavy in my hand when he passes them over. I shuffle them uncomfortably; I've never been one to play card games. Or games at all.

I only hesitate a moment before dealing them out, face down. My heart pounds, and my nerves roar back to life. "I— Okay. You can, um, turn them over."

They look at their cards, but not one of them has the grace to flip it where I can see it.

"Five," Dom says carelessly.

"Two," says Lucky, and Jasper gives him a look I can't decipher.

Beau gives me a rueful look and says, "Four."

My stomach clenches. The smirk on Jaykob's face tells me all I need to know. He flicks the card on the table, and the ace of spades winks at me.

"Looks like we've got a date, sugar. Time to strip down."

My breath hitches. I remember the way Jaykob grabbed me as he kissed me. Hypocritical bitch, he called me.

Of all of them, why does it have to be him?

As though he can read my thoughts, his mouth twists. "Or leave. Don't bother me either way."

"Perhaps you could give her a moment, Jaykob, rather than

behaving like a beast. You might do well to recall some of our discussions about the benefits of civility." Jasper's tone is chilly.

Under my lashes, I can't stop staring at Jaykob. He's too big, far too big. Huge. And I hoped for gentle Lucky? Jaykob will snap me like a twig.

"Maybe this wasn't a good idea. Can't we let her choose? Just for the first night? Ease her in, you know?" Lucky asks Dom, frowning at Jaykob, whose face darkens with every word.

"Oh sure, all's fair till it's not you. Carnie cheat."

Lucky stands up quickly, knocking his chair back.

"No favoritism. That's the rule," Dom says sharply, but he's watching me.

It's hard to breathe.

"Whatcha thinking, darlin'?" Beau asks me gently, ignoring the others.

My eyes latch on his, then dart back to Jaykob, who's still glaring at Lucky. Jaykob flips his knife again, deliberately, all tattoos and scars and sneering anger.

"I—"

Tearing his eyes away from Lucky, Jaykob looks to me, taking in the white press of my fingertips on the table. Then he scowls and turns, stalking toward the door.

"Wait!" I call, my voice strangled, but he doesn't stop.

Trembling, I push out of my seat and stumble after him.

"Eden, it's okay—" Beau starts.

"No, it's not," I snap, then I follow Jaykob out, catching his arm just outside the kitchen.

It isn't okay. I agreed to this. I spent the last week thinking over what Lucky said. I promised equality; I can't just play it safe with Lucky and Beau. It won't work for the others, and then I'll be out.

And also, it *really* isn't okay. Because just before he turned to leave, I could swear I saw a hint of self-conscious bitterness shadowing Jaykob's eyes—and *that* is a feeling I know well. And maybe

I'm projecting, but I can't let him walk away from me like that, even if he has been a complete jerk to me.

As I catch his arm, he whirls around so fast I flinch back. He looms over me, pushing me into the wall. If I did see any vulnerability in his eyes, it's gone now.

"Wait," I repeat at barely a whisper.

"Takes a minute to get over the disappointment, huh?" His voice is gravel, rough and rude.

It sparks something defiant in me, something like that hot feeling when they all dismissed me.

"You really do have a chip on your shoulder, don't you?" I ask, trying to match his tone.

He doesn't say anything, but his scowl deepens.

"I—" I start, then clear my throat and try again. "I don't know what I'm doing."

He snorts. "That's pretty damn clear, princess."

Swallowing hard, I lift my hand to his chest—not to push him away, but just letting myself, and him, get used to my touch. I went horse riding once and they told me to keep my hand on the horse as I moved around it, so it wouldn't startle. Maybe that will work here too.

After a moment, I slowly lift onto my toes and brush my lips across his, fully conscious that this is a man who can throw me over his shoulder without breaking a sweat. His full lips are hard and unyielding, and I press a second, gentle kiss to their firm crease, my pulse throbbing fearfully.

Before my heels have even dropped back to the ground, he's spun again and is halfway toward the sliding doors that lead outside. Embarrassment is just starting to crash in on me when he looks over his shoulder.

"If you're coming, move your ass."

The mannered girl in me frowns at his language, but it doesn't stop me from darting over and following him out into the darkness.

CHAPTER 12

EDEN

SURVIVAL TIP #278
*When manners fail,
go primal.*

Jaykob's workshop is huge. A large jeep is parked in the far corner and machines of all shapes and sizes sit haphazardly throughout the room. Beams of wood and piles of metal crowd the space, and the walls are lined with every kind of tool imaginable. A small kitchen is just visible from where I stand. The room is only dimly lit, even with the light on.

I glance around, looking for a bed. He doesn't wait for me, ducking under a hanging beam and making his way to the back of the workshop. I trail after him. There's a door at the back of the workshop, only visible after I round the half-repaired washing machine. I eye it longingly, wishing I could press some kind of priority sticker to its front.

He opens the door, flicks on the light, and jerks his head for me to go inside.

The room is fairly small, almost entirely taken up by the large bed and a small bedside table. As soon as I step inside, he shuts the door behind us.

Turning, I open my mouth to ask him if he has any refreshments, but he presses me into the closed door. Thrusting his hand into my hair, he tugs my head back and claims my mouth in a rough, punishing kiss. His tongue tangles with mine, invading, demanding. My knees fall out from under me, but he shoves a thick thigh between my legs, pinning me to the door. His weight presses against my core.

I whimper my shock into his mouth, and his tongue coaxes the sound into his own. Despite myself, I shiver in pleasure. He tastes like blackberries and the wine he had with dinner. My hands flutter to his shoulders and clench in his shirt, holding on for dear life.

My head is spinning from his kiss and the wine, but my nerves are fading. The spark of irritation I've been nursing for him, though, that's stoking higher with each demanding stroke of his tongue, with each throb of arousal that pulses inside of me.

"Wait," I try to say into his mouth, but he licks the sensitive inner rim of my lips, throwing my mind to carnal places, sending me shuddering.

I press back into the door away from him, needing air, needing to think, even as my hips tilt into his.

Traitors.

He crowds me closer, not letting me escape, his other hand cupping my waist, then moving up to my breast.

Breath catching in shock, I bite his lip.

Jaykob jerks his head back, and if I wasn't reeling, I would laugh at the shock on his face. Then he smirks, something close to surprised pleasure creeping into his expression. He touches his lip where a bead of blood has welled. Desire whips his eyes into stormy seas.

"If you want it rough, princess," he drawls, "all you gotta do is ask."

My eyes widen, and I squirm, instinctively trying to get out of his grip. All it does is rub me against the hard, insistent length of him until his jaw tenses.

"Just . . . slow down! There's no need t-to throw me around like this."

"You want me to stop?"

He's everywhere. Big and broad and—God, does he have to feel so good? "I— N-no."

He snorts, and my cheeks burn. I glare at him.

"Did no one ever teach you basic manners? And . . . and can we turn off the light? Please?" The throaty sound of my voice spoils my indignance.

The smirk deepens. "Manners, hmm?"

He steps back, and I'm about to reward him with an approving smile when he grasps the straps of my dress and yanks them down to my waist, completely exposing the top half of my body. My breasts swell wantonly over the cups of my bra.

I choke on a gasp, eyes widening in anger. "You—"

The words die in my throat as he yanks his own shirt off. He towers over me, and I greedily take in the miles of corded, thick muscles now naked in front of me. Tattoos cover his chest, and the intricate skulls and vines on his arms stand out in sharp relief.

His skin is taut and smooth over his powerful muscles, except for a smattering of circular scars that pattern his upper left shoulder and a thick white scar that wraps horizontally across his stomach. My eyes dip as his rough, calloused hands grasp his belt and pop it open. It's impossible to miss the tight, *substantial* strain below the buckle.

I grab hold of the door handle, worried I'll lose my legs again. I try to work moisture into my dry mouth, but it won't come. While I know the men I'm living with are in good shape, I've never seen an actual eight-pack before. Some deep, buried part of me wants to lick my tongue over the ridges.

"There," he mocks. "Very fair. Reciprocal. See? I'm a fucking gentleman."

His hand leaves his belt and wraps around my throat possessively, then strokes down my front, over my breasts.

"You got some real nice *manners* right here too, princess."

My chest lifts too quickly under his wide, warm hand. His hard-earned calluses scrape over my silky soft skin as he traces the edge of my bra.

"I— I don't. . . Maybe we could just talk first?" I stammer.

Jaykob's stormy eyes narrow. "Sugar, I'm not your boyfriend. You wanna have a heart-to-heart? Go run to Beau."

My breath hitches and when I look up at him, there's more than a hint of challenge in his gaze. A kind of knowing, self-deprecating resentment. He's pushing me on purpose.

He thinks I'm going to run.

And I realize, for all his rudeness, he's giving me enough space to get away from him.

I push my glasses back up, trying to think as his fingers track closer and closer to the clasp of my bra. I lift my hand and press it against him, but instead of pushing him away as I intended, my hand flexes on his tight abs. He smells good, I realize. Like cars and wind and raw man.

"Let's try a different game," he says with none of the humor Lucky might have teased me with, "'cause I don't feel like playing 'will I or won't I' all night."

My cheeks burn. He steps closer again, and using one of his boots, knocks my feet wide, unbalancing me. His hand dips to the hem on my dress, then slides up my inner thigh.

"Three options, sugar." His eyes glint. "One. Turn around and leave right now, then tomorrow you pack up your things and get out."

I glare at him. I've already made up my mind, the jerk. There's no way I'm running off now.

He continues, and his breath fans my lips. "Second option.

You can walk out that door and I'll even be a gentleman and tell the others we fucked. No questions asked." He smirks. "*If* you can prove you don't actually want me to bury my cock deep inside that princess fucking pussy of yours."

His hand hitches higher, and I squirm. I'm slick and wet and wondering if he can feel the heat of me already. My cheeks redden at the thought. Something about his rough, mocking smile is starting to get to me. His fingers are coarse on the sensitive skin of my inner thigh. So male to my female.

Jaykob's voice lowers as he presses his face close, his lips an inch from mine. "Or, if you're as soaking wet as I reckon you are, you shut up with your good-girl protests and let me fuck you. Not with the lights off, not with a please and thank you and seven hours of foreplay. My way." His lips brush mine as his fingers catch on the edge of my panties. "Fast, rough, and messy."

Oh, God. Time to turn your eyes away, Jesus.

I'm panting against his mouth, and I can't do a thing to stop it.

I know what he'll find if his fingers dip any further.

When I don't move, he pulls my panties to the side and then plunges two fingers into my slick, wet heat. I clench around the tight, sudden pressure with a gasp, and roll my hips forward urgently, pressing him deeper.

When I meet his eyes, he gives me his first real smile. It's small and slow and full of male satisfaction. Unable to stop myself, I widen my stance further, allowing him better access. His coarse fingers fill me, stretch me. I'm dripping around him.

He presses his forehead to mine. "Filthy bitch."

I hate that he sounds approving. I hate that I care. I hate that him using me this way, talking to me this way, makes me hot and liquid and dangerously desperate.

Embarrassed and annoyed and more turned on than I can believe, I close the short distance and press my mouth to his, wanting to wipe the amusement from his face.

He grunts, lips parting. His thumb moves so it rubs my clit as his fingers pump in and out of my soaking core. Head spinning, I let out a sobbing moan and scrape my nails down his chest to the top of his jeans, shuddering at the feel of his firm skin under my fingertips. He draws my tongue into his mouth and sucks on it hard.

I rock myself instinctively against his fingers, sending pleasure crashing over me. It's not the deliberate build I felt with Beau and Jasper; it's wild, raw passion. I'm so close. My traitorous body feels out of my control, chasing pleasure with a desperation I've never felt before.

My nipples ache, rubbing against my bra. It pisses me off. It leaves me breathless. Our mouths break apart and mine presses to his throat, nipping and licking the salty, delicious skin there.

The button on his pants is stubborn as I try to work it open, caught tight against the pressure of his straining cock. I sob in frustration against his neck, and his fingers leave me. He bats my hands away and pops the button in moments, then drops his pants and kicks off his boots.

He . . . isn't wearing underwear.

My breath hisses between my teeth. He's thick and huge—bigger by far than anything I've ever had inside me before. My core throbs needily, missing his fingers and protesting the loss of the quick brink he'd brought me to. His eyes gleam as he takes in my expression, and he roughly shoves my dress the rest of the way down. My hair's escaping from my bun, the tendrils teasing my breasts and shoulders.

"Get down," he says, and his gravelly voice grazes over me deliciously.

Down?

At my confusion, Jaykob snorts, grabs a pillow off the bed and drops it to the floor in front of him, tugging me down.

Oh.

The thick, bold length of him is thrust in front of me. A wet drop glistens from the tip, and I can't look away, unwillingly fascinated. My breasts feel trapped and sensitive, and my body still aches, shivering with need. But trepidation trips over me. The one time I tried this, I nearly lost my lunch.

"My way," he reminds me, his voice barely more than a growl. I look up and he's watching me with that mean, knowing smirk again. "The others might be sucked into the big save-me eyes, ladies-first bullshit. But I'm the real feminist, princess. Equal opportunities."

He grasps himself at the root and tangles his other hand in my bun. He rubs the tip over my lips, smearing the dewy drop across my mouth. He doesn't try to thrust past my defenses though—for all his talk, he gives me a moment. Inhaling through my nose, I realize he doesn't smell bad at all, not like Henry did. Slightly musky, his natural scent is stronger here, but it's far from unpleasant. Clean and very Jaykob.

Tentatively, my tongue darts out, tasting the essence he's marking me with. It's slippery, a little tangy, but surprisingly free of flavor. Startled, my eyes fly up and the pure, unadulterated lust in his face brings the banking heat in me back to a full storm.

Hesitantly, I open my mouth to him as he rocks his hips forward. He gives me just a moment to adjust to his size, my jaw straining, before filling my mouth more fully. My glasses slip down my nose, and, with a sound of derision, he plucks them off my face and tosses them on the bedside table. I yelp my disapproval, my teeth scraping him just slightly in warning. His hand tightens in my hair.

"Now that ain't very nice, Miss Manners. Put those away."

I make a helpless sound against him, and he groans.

"Move your tongue, princess. Lick me. Neat and tidy ain't gonna work; get it nice and wet." Very small rocking motions accompany his growled instructions, and I find myself obeying.

He's hot and hard and full in my mouth and, far from hating the taste, I'm shocked to realize I love it. The friction of his movements against my sensitive, soft lips has me writhing and my lids fluttering closed. My lips still don't come close to his pumping hand at the base of his dick.

"Open your eyes. Look at me."

I do, and the angry pleasure on his face fills me with a strange confidence. I made him look like this. He presses a little deeper, but not quite far enough to set off my gag reflex.

"Spit on your hand."

He pulls out abruptly, leaving a trail of my saliva along his cock. A part of me wants to get a washcloth. A bigger part wants to rub myself against him and beg him to fill me with that hard, glossy length until I forget how to talk. He grabs my arm and brings my hand to my face.

"Spit."

Scowling at him, I spit a small drop into my palm and cringe. Rolling his eyes, he spits over the top of my droplet, coating my palm. I squeak in horror, but he pulls my hand to his cock, wrapping it around the base. Placing his hand over mine as he leans back to watch me, he tightens my grip and pumps. The muscles on his chest ripple, making his tattoos come alive.

I stare at him, dazed. I don't think I've ever seen anything so erotic. My slickness drips down my thighs.

"Move your hand while you suck me," he orders.

With far less hesitation this time, I bring my mouth back to him, taking him as deep as I can and running my tongue along the underside. He hits the back of my throat and lets out a muffled snarl, the sound going right to my clit. I move my hand, keeping it tight like he showed me, meeting my sliding mouth with my fingers. Tears prick my eyes, and I remember to breathe through my nose, drinking in the musky scent of him and getting off on the blatant enjoyment he's getting from me. I test my rhythm, finding what makes him shudder.

I am doing that to him.

And it's making me so, so wet.

After a few minutes, I begin shifting, rubbing my thighs

together. Bringing my other hand down, I part my swollen folds and touch myself. I don't do it often—my strait-laced upbringing muffling the pleasure I might have found in it—but under Jaykob's hungry gaze, my usual rules fly out the window.

My unpracticed rhythm on my hot, wet clit doesn't bring the same pleasure that Beau or Jasper commanded from my body, but the small ripples are enough to throw off the rhythm of my mouth. Seeing my distraction, Jaykob yanks my hand away from his cock and wraps both his hands in my hair. My bun is almost entirely loose now.

"Slap my legs if you need me to stop."

My eyes widen as his speed picks up, and he starts thrusting into my mouth, controlling the angle with his hands. He doesn't take it too deep, mostly easing back from the back of my throat, but rubs himself into the scorching softness of my cheeks, the roof of my mouth. In and out until my lips are coated in saliva and he makes a wet slap with every thrust.

I don't want to stop him. Hands free, I touch my breasts, freeing the clasp at the front and pinching my aching nipples, rolling them until the prick of pain make my core clench. My other hand works faster around my slick clit, and I moan around his cock.

He pulls back and picks me up as though I weigh nothing. To him, I probably don't. Flipping me, he pushes me face down into the bed, using the pillow that had been under my knees to prop up my waist. My feet are planted on the floor, and his hand on my back keeps my face pressed into the mattress, ass in the air and completely exposed to him. Then I realize my hand is trapped— with the pillow where it is, I can't touch myself.

"Asshole!" I swear at him, and I don't even flinch at the curse word. I'm too hot and damp and hungry and so, so close. My hips shift restlessly, but there's nowhere for me to go.

A hand comes down hard on my right ass cheek. "Shut it, sugar."

The bright sting of pain is almost enough to send me over the edge.

Before I can squirm into a more accessible position, he grasps my panties and rips them through on one side. They flutter to the floor. His hands part my legs further and then his mouth is on me.

Scorching hot, his lips part over my aching center, his tongue tunneling obscenely through my drenched folds. The old me, the me before this mindless sex-crazed version, wants to protest, conscious of the view he must have, of my scent, my taste, but all that comes out is a ragged, keening cry. His tongue flicks over my clit, then thrusts in and out of the most intimate part of me. His fingers thrust into my hole and, with his other hand, he parts my ass cheeks obscenely. I jerk but he holds me in place.

"Asshole, was it? Your wish, sugar."

His wet fingers move from my pussy to tease my tight rosebud, right as he angles his head, draws my clit into his mouth, and sucks.

"N— Jayk!" I cry, shocked.

I can't shift away from him; his other arm is banded like steel around my waist, holding me to him.

His finger slowly pushes past the tight ring and eases in and out, and he flicks his tongue rapidly, firmly over my clit. I feel the strange intrusion in every part of me, unable to escape it. Not sure I want to. My body tries to adjust to the sensations, overworked, overstimulated.

The pressure inside me heightens until my vision blurs and his mouth, his fingers, are all there is, pushing and taking and claiming me. Then, with a blinding wave of wild, overwhelming pleasure, I come apart, sobbing into the mattress, not sure if I'm cursing or thanking him.

I shiver as the aftershocks of pleasure ripple through me, making me tingle. Blinking on my way back to sanity—my vision not the best without my glasses—I realize I'm now on my back and Jaykob is between my thighs. There's a raw violence in his motions as he covers himself in a condom that probably should make me nervous, but somehow doesn't. Not with pleasure drugging my veins and excitement again re-starting my heart.

He grips my hair and pulls me so I'm sitting up. With a savage snarl, he captures my mouth, making me taste my own orgasm, thrusting his tongue between my lips the same way he thrust his cock there minutes before. My eyes grow heavy lidded. I can't remember enjoying a kiss so much in my life. Right now, it's only Jayk, Jayk, Jayk.

On a muffled sob, I rake my hands over his now-damp shoulders and chest. When he releases my mouth, hand still twisted in my hair, I bend forward and bite his pec hard beside the snarl of a vine, then lick over the mark before he yanks me back. I'm not sure if I want to punish him for pushing me so far past my comfort zone or make him feel as wonderful as I just felt. Violence and desire rock me in a completely unfamiliar way.

He tsks. "That ain't very fucking polite, Miss Manners."

He shoves me back down on the bed, not bothering to be gentle.

Stepping forward, he lines himself up, pushing the flared head of his cock against my entrance. But rather than thrusting forward, his hands grasp behind my knees, and he yanks me toward him, impaling me along his length in one quick motion. I gasp, then shift around him with a whimper, my tight body racing to accustom itself to his size. His eyes slide closed for a moment, jaw clenching as he rocks slightly inside me. I clench against the intrusion, and his eyes fly open again, dark and stormy and intent.

"Don't do that again until I tell you to. Wrap your legs around me. Now."

My heels bite into his lower back, pressing him more deeply inside me. I shudder. *Fuck, fuck, fuck.* I'm over-full. Taken. Overwhelmed.

He cups my breasts, squeezes them, making me groan, then grasps my hips hard with both hands, as though he can't wait. He meets my heavy-lidded gaze. The sneer is gone, leaving only hot, hungry man.

"Hold on."

Withdrawing sharply, he thrusts back in, deeper than before, angling so he hits every delicious spot inside me. Again and again, faster and faster, he finds a rhythm that brings me back to a breathtakingly sudden peak. He pounds inside me so hard it hurts, but I sob at him not to stop. I can feel every inch of him, feel every slide of flesh, feel him filling me with dark, delicious need.

My hands, bunched in the sheets, move to grasp for skin. My long nails dig into his shoulders, and he leans over me, changing the angle, pounding roughly. I scrape my nails down his back until it arches. He hisses and then laughs coarsely. I kiss him again, wanting his tongue in my mouth as he claims my body. We press together, hot and slick and coated in each other.

He speeds up just as I cry out again into his mouth, shattering into a thousand pieces around his demanding, invading body. With a low groan and a final, shuddering thrust, he finishes deep inside me.

It's a long, long time before I can recall how to breathe.

CHAPTER 13

EDEN

When I wake the next morning, I can't help but be relieved at finding myself alone. Jaykob had me twice more during the night, but, despite my delicious soreness, the memories of all the things I let him do to me—the things that *I* did to *him*—have me burying my face into a pillow.

What came over me last night? I was so nervous, then so mad at him. I wanted to push at him, throw him for a loop, like he did to me. Instead, I turned into some kind of wanton, furious, sex-hungry . . . *harlot*!

And with *Jaykob*, of all people. How did I let him bring that out in me? How can I possibly face him again? Just the thought of his harsh, sneering smirk makes me want to bury myself in my room and never come out. I've had bullies mock me before. I should have been collected and calm, the bigger person. I should have talked to him rationally.

I should not have come on his dick a half-dozen times and begged him for more.

The way he spoke to me . . . And I not only let him, I urged him on. I shiver at the memory. He more than obliged.

I'm going to have to do some Hail Marys or something. My grandmother would be so disappointed—she had grand hopes for my purity and godliness. She was the one who'd insisted on my name.

But Eden was never pure.

I was made to be corrupted.

Sitting up and putting on my discarded glasses, I look around the room. It's destroyed. Pillows are flung around the room, clothes litter the floor, and the bed covers are rumpled. It smells like sex and sin. *I* smell like sex and sin.

How strange.

And why on earth do my lips want to twitch in satisfaction at that?

There's an unfamiliar ache between my legs—not the pulsing need from last night, but a well-used soreness that, with every motion, sends vivid memories of how I obtained each spot of discomfort to my mind. Surprisingly, my stomach, arms and legs also quiver with weakness, as though I've put in hours at the gym.

The next room is quiet. He must have gone to the main house. My stomach falls. Is he filling the others in? Giving his review?

I pale. I clawed at him. Did I *bite* him? I wasn't myself at all last night. I was just *awful*.

Though echoes of pleasure still ripple through my body, what if he doesn't feel the same? Someone like Jaykob has probably been with dozens of experienced, sexy women who knew exactly how to blow his mind. I'm barely more than a virgin. What if he left so early because he doesn't want to look at me? He was only "making do" with me, after all.

All the familiar doubts and self-consciousness that somehow abandoned me under his mouth and cock now come roaring back to life.

Though after we . . . did what we did . . . at least he didn't sneer at me again. He'd fetched me water and something to eat, and gruffly rubbed arnica cream over my back and arms and legs, and when he stopped, we'd stared at each other so awkwardly that I was about to crawl under the bed to hide in embarrassment before he kissed me again.

Before he more than kissed me again.

I pick my clothes off the floor, then dubiously discard the torn panties. I'm about to put on the dress when I notice the top half of it is ripped down one side as well. With a sigh, I drop it. Unwilling to go back to the main house in my bare butt—there's been enough of *that* on show, thank you very much—I go to the bedside table and look for a shirt.

A faded picture sits on top of remarkably neatly folded clothes. I pick it up, unable to curb my curiosity. Two young brown-haired boys sit on the fold-out steps of an old trailer, a woman in a long dress standing behind them. The boys have their arms around each other, and the smaller one on the left is missing a tooth as he grins at the camera. The larger boy wears a familiar smirk, though it holds none of the bitterness age would bring. They look happy.

The trailer is worn but well kept, the way my grandmother always kept hers. There's a quiet pride in having nothing, sometimes. Everything you have becomes precious. Something to be protected.

Jayk and I are more alike than he knows.

I brush a finger over the photo. They must be his family. Did they pass away on Day Death? Or after, during the second wave? My chest cramps. By the time everything went south, I didn't really have anyone left to mourn.

I bite my lip. He shouldn't keep something this precious wrapped up in his clothes—it's a good way to lose things. I spot a large metal toolbox on his dresser and slip the photo inside one of the empty compartments, resolving to let him know where I've put it later.

I pull out a blue T-shirt and it falls nearly to my knees. Quickly,

I let myself out of the room and head back to the house, carrying my shoes. I've never done a walk of shame before and want more than anything not to have to face anyone before I've showered and pulled myself together.

Of course, I'm not that lucky.

Dom and Jasper stand by the large stone fireplace in the towering sitting room, arguing in low voices. Though I can't make out his face from my place by the sliding door, Dom speaks with his hands—crisp, clipped motions—and his powerful shoulders are pushed back. I start to assume that he's getting the best of Jasper, but a second glance makes me hesitate, then shiver.

Jasper's motions are precise, careful, and only occasional. There's a sharp expectation, a sense of stillness in his stance that reminds me of the mesmerizing threat of a coiled whip. His beauty is cold, carved with a delicate savagery.

Suddenly, I'm not quite certain which of the two men is the more dangerous.

In spite of my curiosity, my self-preservation is stronger. I can find out what they're arguing about later—if anyone is feeling more willing to share today, that is.

That thought ignites that odd spark of anger all over again, but I shake my head at myself before the feeling grows. I need to get over it. I know what I signed up for. I can take being belittled and condescended to. For comfort and company? I *will* take a good many things.

Last night flashes into my mind, and my hot temper shifts into a different kind of burn. Yes, okay. Perhaps I *already* took a good many things.

There's a lot to be said for this deal, really.

As gently as I can, I ease open the door—though I might as well have flung it open for all my deviousness wins me. Both men fall silent, instantly shifting so they stand shoulder to shoulder. They may have been arguing mere seconds before, but now they look like a team. A team that is one hundred percent focused on me.

I attempt a bland smile and step toward the stairs farthest from the two men.

"Stop, pet," Dom orders, eyes narrowing on me. "Why the rush?"

My lips purse, and I give him a disapproving look, trying not to quail. "You know, it's quite impolite to call me that."

Dom just stares at me, molten-eyed and expectant. Jasper studies me too closely for my liking. I know what I must look like. My hair is a wild mess around me—my hair tie was lost to Jaykob's floor—and I'm in his overlarge shirt, and if I smell even a fifth as strong as the room I woke up in, then I reek of sex. Not to mention, I'm aching everywhere, and covered in sweat—not all of it my own—and other fluids that I do not particularly want to think about in the judgy light of day.

It's no secret what we were up to, but I still find myself wincing at their knowing looks.

"I, ah, need a shower," I mutter, backing up before they can stop me again.

I turn right into Beau's chest.

Why are all these men so tall and constantly in the way?

"Mornin', darlin'. Want some breakfast?" He holds a mug of coffee with one hand and, with the other, he catches me round the waist and pulls me close to his body in a quick hug.

I can't stop my slight gasp of discomfort.

Beau steps back sharply, his smile fading as he studies my face. Before I can flee with whatever dignity I have left, Dom is behind me, lifting one sleeve of the T-shirt. His face stills. Stiffens.

"It's not a big deal," I start, wishing, not for the first time, that I was hidden deep in my old cave.

"How bad is it?" Beau snaps, and I jump at the harshness of his tone.

It's only a few bruises. I've always bruised easily.

But Dom doesn't wait for me to answer. His hand bunches in the back of my shirt and he yanks it up, exposing my bare body to the waist. I screech and try to pull it down with no success.

Beau is quivering. I look up at him, bewildered, as I fight against Dom's grip on the shirt.

"I'm going to kill him, Dom." Fury makes his hazel eyes flash. "And fuck you for forcing this. I might expect her to look like this after Jasper, but at least he knows when to stop."

Jasper? My gaze flies to the beautiful man, my heart pounding in embarrassment and frustration and a renewed hint of fear. The same man who turns each page with mesmerizing, reverent care? *That* Jasper?

Jasper takes in my reaction in one assessing glance and directs a small, chilly smile at Beau. "This is far too crude for my taste. But I do so appreciate you frightening her; that will certainly make this easier on everyone."

His tart words could cause frostbite, and the taste of violence in the air thickens. It curdles on my tongue. Then Dom runs his hand firmly over my bare, bruised hips like I'm an injured animal, and I flinch back.

"Let *go*!" I demand, hating that my voice quakes. "I— I am not some toy to be thrown around!"

The sliding door rolls open behind me, but Dom's grip won't let me turn.

"Got thrown around plenty last night, sugar. Didn't reckon you'd be ready for round two already," Jaykob drawls. "Or that'd make it round four now, yeah?"

His gaze is hot on my ass, and I wince, remembering altogether *too much* from last night.

Given how angry Beau looks, I would have put money on him going after Jaykob, but to my surprise, it's Dom who drops my shirt and storms over to the other man. I spin just as he slams Jaykob against the wall.

"Oh, sure, fucking typical." Jaykob's face darkens as he lifts his heavy arms to push the other man off him. Even while I'm reeling from the sudden attack, I notice he's shirtless.

Dom's grip doesn't budge. "I knew you were rough, but I thought even you had enough goddamn restraint to hold back with someone like her. Did you even bother to hear her limits? Her *safeword*?" He slams Jaykob back again and hisses, "She's not from the club, asshole, she doesn't know how to stop you."

Wait, *what?*

My mouth drops open, but before I can say anything, Beau crowds me protectively. I push against him, my horrified attention still absorbed on the scene in front of me, but it's like trying to push past a stone wall.

"Looks like she gave it her best shot, though," Jasper notes from the side, taking in Jaykob's scratched-up chest.

Dark approval lights his angelic face as Dom's forearm presses against Jaykob's throat. Jaykob grunts, his airway cut off. They're of a size, but Dom caught him by surprise.

Then Jayk jabs a hard punch into Dom's ribs, making him loosen his grip slightly. He follows up with a swing to his jaw, but Dom ducks it, smashing him back again against the wall for a third time.

Evidence of my nails mark Jaykob's shoulders in red streaks, and my bite mark on his chest has bruised.

"Fuck." The whisper is from Beau above me, sounding tortured. I try to wriggle away from him again and he looks down at me as though he's just remembered I'm here. His hazel eyes are haunted. "It's okay, darlin'. It'll be okay. Fuck, I—"

"Whoa, the hell?" Lucky comes in from the kitchen, taking in the scene.

Jaykob jerks hard under Dom's arm, and when Dom pulls a hunting knife from his belt, I finally find my voice.

"No!" It comes out unnaturally shrill. "*No*. Let me go, Beau!"

He does, reluctantly, and I rush past him and over to Dom.

"Stay back. He won't touch you again, Eden." Dom's dark skin is flushed with rage; he presses the knife against Jaykob's throat.

Resignation and anger war across Jaykob's features, and my stomach twists.

"Let him go! He didn't—" The words stick. "He didn't *force* himself on me. I let him do it."

"You don't need to make excuses for him. He shouldn't have been so rough. You didn't sign up for this. We wouldn't ask you to — We wouldn't do *this*." Beau's voice is hard. "Stay back, Eden. Just stay out of it. Dom's handlin' this."

"Or, I don't know, maybe you could listen to her," Lucky breaks in with such an even lightness to his tone that I know he worked hard for it. "She can speak for herself."

Bolstered by Lucky's words, I touch Dom's tense shoulder.

"I'm not making excuses. He didn't do anything I didn't *want* him to do," I insist, trying to make my voice firm, even as humiliation washes over me. "Please, sir, let him go."

The "sir" seems to catch him. Dom looks over his shoulder at me, studying my face. I meet his eyes, holding them steady despite my hot cheeks. Surprise touches his features, and I see the moment he realizes he made a mistake. He eases the knife away from Jaykob's throat.

I yelp and step back as Jaykob takes the opportunity to punch Dom hard across the jaw, sending him staggering back.

"Fuck!"

Before I let myself think how stupid it is, I step between them. "Enough!" I say sharply. I look at Jaykob. "Enough."

He rubs his throat, scowling.

"Eden," Jasper says carefully after a tense moment, a gentle crease between his brows, "an explanation might help . . . ease tempers."

I cross my arms, eyes narrowing. Lucky shoots me a sympathetic half-smile and shrugs, and Beau looks conflicted, watching me worriedly.

Dom straightens and rubs a hand over his jaw, staring at Jayk from under his brows like he's lost for words. I can't tell if he wants to return the punch, or if that's Dom's way of looking horrified.

At least he's put his knife away.

I splutter. "Explain *what*? He drew the card for the first night. We did . . . stuff. The stuff I'm here for. *Consensual* stuff. All very consensual. All *types* of consensual." Then I add in a mutter, "And nobody else's business, thank you."

Why is it so hard to sound prim and proper when talking about . . . stuff?

Dom's eyes press closed at my words, his jaw clenching. He shakes his head just once. At himself?

"Then why in holy flaming hell, darlin'," Beau grinds out, looking between me and Jayk, "does it look like he's come off a war zone?"

As I glance at Jaykob's chest, the heat in my cheeks deepens, then spreads to my ears, then my chest. Despite the bitter resentment behind his eyes, a self-satisfied smirk starts working its way across his face. He raises his eyebrows at me, as if to say, "Go ahead."

Asshole.

"Well, I—um—may have gotten . . . I might have . . . *gottenalittlecarriedaway*." The words leave me in a rush of squirming embarrassment. I worry my bottom lip between my teeth. "I should maybe cut my nails, and—um—you've had your tetanus shot, right?"

Jaykob glances down at his chest. "Might need to get you a muzzle too."

My sympathy eases back, and I scowl. "I wouldn't have done it if I hadn't been so mad that you—"

My teeth clamp down on my tongue, cutting myself off before I blurt to everyone *exactly* what he did to set me off. Despite my indignance, my butt clenches, and I vividly recall the shocked, naughty feeling of over-fullness.

He strolls around Dom and into my personal space.

"Mad, huh?" His lips curve mockingly. "That why you came so hard you ruined my sheets?"

"Y-you—" I spit, unable to get the words out around my anger.

And I just *defended* him!

He leans in close to me, until I can see the ring of midnight around his mocking blue eyes. "But sure, if you wanna test it, I'll go again. Only next time, I ain't going easy on you."

My eyes widen. "*Easy?*" Every inch of me aches, and he's shocked me more in the last twelve hours than I was shocked in the entirety of my marriage. Of my *life*. My voice lifts into a strident screech. "That was *easy?*"

Jaykob's lips curl, inches from mine. True amusement sparks in his eyes. "Yeah, sugar, *easy*. Next time you'll be takin' a whole lot more than my fingers up your—"

My hands fly up and clamp over his mouth in pure panic, stopping him from finishing that *awful* sentence in front of everyone. Lucky starts howling with laughter anyway, and Beau mutters, "Jesus fucking Christ."

Mortification rockets through me. My heart pounds as my wide eyes stare into Jaykob's smug ones. Then he grasps my wrist, thumb lingering over my racing pulse as he tugs my hands from his mouth.

Before he can taunt me any further, I glare at him. "Why did you come barging in here without a shirt on anyway? This all could have been avoided."

And now that Jayk isn't in danger of having them sliced open with Dom's hunting knife, my traitorous eyes can't help but slide over the delicious muscles that I was oh-so-intimately acquainted with last night. A shiver chases up my spine.

Bad librarian. He is not a piece of meat. His eyes are up—

He looks down at my chest. "You stole my last clean shirt."

Oh.

"Well," I mutter, "you ripped my underwear. And my dress."

"Damn. I liked the blue one," Lucky complains. Drama over, he turns back to the kitchen, calling, "Breakfast is here when you're showered, beautiful."

With his exit, the last violent edge of tension eases from the room.

There's a heavy sigh from Beau. "Ah, shit. Sorry, Jayk, I—"

"Save it," he sneers. "Least she's honest, or I guess I'd be over the walls."

Dom curses. "Jayk, I'm sorry. But what the fuck were we meant to think? She doesn't exactly scream claw-your-back sex."

I flinch and look at my feet, his words like tiny cuts of shattered glass.

"Trust me, she screams plenty," Jaykob taunts.

Jasper lets out a low laugh behind me. "Interesting. She may enjoy me yet."

"Ooohhhkay. I think Eden's had enough," Beau interrupts, coming to my rescue as I try my best to become liquid and melt through the floor. A wide hand brushes against the middle of my back, and when I glance up, apologetic woodland eyes peer down at me.

"Whatever. Gimme my shirt back when you're done."

Dom sighs and his voice softens. "Jayk, I'm—"

Jaykob storms out, clearly still pissed.

Honestly, I can't really blame him. They're meant to be his friends. Or co-inhabitants, anyway. War-man partners? While I can't fault their protective instincts, how could they think he's capable of that? He's an ass, sure. Humiliating and rough and rude as heck. But he never made me worry about my safety at any point

—and he might not have been polite about it, but he made sure I wanted him before he touched me.

I somehow don't think he'll be open to a sympathetic hug, though.

After one searching last assessment from those molten eyes of his, Dom leaves for the kitchen, muttering under his breath—I only catch the words "trouble" and "pain in the ass."

After a moment, I nod at Beau to let him lead me upstairs, and his tension finally eases as I allow him to take charge.

"Eden," Jasper says, and I turn, wishing he'd just let me hide in peace. He continues carefully, "If you want to talk—about anything—you can talk to me. It's not entirely possible, clearly, but I will try to remain impartial."

I remember that he's a psychologist. He surely means well, but the veiled hints and threats about the nature of his *preferences* unnerve me. And then there's this coiled, threatening stillness in him. I glimpsed it my first day here, but seeing him now, so malevolent and impenetrable, I can't believe I managed to fool myself into thinking he was a kind, bookish safe haven.

"What were you and Dom arguing about when I came in?" I ask.

Jasper gives me a long, measured look. Finally, and oh-so-politely, he replies, "With respect, it's not your concern."

A chill runs up my spine, and I'm conscious of the line he's drawing.

No, not drawing—a line he's *reinforcing*. Dom and Beau were the first to dismiss me last night at dinner. I suck in a painful breath. It hurts coming from Jasper, who just a week ago was so sweetly reassuring, talking about family and our pieces fitting together. But they aren't keeping me here to start a relationship. If I fit at all, it will be between their sheets, or under their feet.

If I'm to keep any pride at all, I need to keep my emotions contained.

You're here for yourself, *Eden, not for them*, I remind myself. *For as long as it works for* you.

"Then no, I believe I'll decline your offer," I reply, forcing my tone to remain even. I glance at Beau. "I can see myself to my room, thank you."

The concerned warmth on his face dims, but I brush past him, up the stairs, and into my room before he can speak.

CHAPTER 14

LUCKY

I flip the pancake into the air, trying to get it to do three spins before it hits the pan again.

"Can you just cook the damn things instead of playing with them?" Dom barks, pacing the kitchen behind me with the charged energy of a panther lashing its tail.

"Art. This is *art*, boss man. Don't mess with it. And don't get pissy with me just 'cause you didn't think before you swung this time." Before oh-leader-supreme can bite my head off, I slide the pancake off the pan and onto a plate, and then plant it on the edge of the counter for him. "Just swallow it and apologize. Plenty of sugar in these babies to help it go down right. Jayk'll bitch, but he'll get over it. We'll need him on side soon enough."

Dom scowls . . . but stalks closer to the pancakes. He'll settle once he's eaten.

"Not the point. I shouldn't have gone after him like that." He stabs a fluffy pancake with his fork, sounding almost sullen. "She's just got those big, prissy fucking eyes. She isn't the *type*. What was I meant to think?"

He stabs the pancake harder and it splits in a fluffy spray.

A laugh snorts out of me that I can't keep in, despite the glare I receive in return.

I hold up my hands in surrender. "She got naked in front of *four* of us on her first night here and came all over Beau's lap." Lucky bastard. It should have been a *Lucky* bastard. "She might not know what the hell she's doing—and she might shock herself into a nunnery—but she's definitely *the type*. Whatever that is."

And she's cute. And smart. And I have a mother-flipping date with her tonight.

Beau eyes me sideways, and I realize I'm grinning like a five-year-old with pockets full of candy. Ah, whatever. Why not? It's been ages since I've felt this excited about something, and I'll be good for her, anyway. I'll make sure she has a bit of fun—the girl needs to lighten up.

Well, all of them need to lighten up, really, but I'm pretty sure it's a lost cause with the guys. I've been working on 'em for years and I can still only get them to crack a smile once a month.

"She won't want anything from us if we keep lying to her," Beau says quietly.

I shoot Beau a sympathetic wince over Dom's shoulder as the full weight of the bigger man's displeasure lands on him. "Since when do we explain our decisions to civs?"

The doc—brave guy—rolls his eyes. "I think that ship has kind of sailed, don't you? She has a right to know if another group of hunters is hanging around these woods. I want her around as much as anyone but it could influence her decision on whether she wants to stay or not."

Choosing self-preservation on this one, I pop a hunk of chocolate chip pancake in my mouth.

Beau and Dom's recon mission had mixed success. The guys covered their asses by heading to town, but after they flagged that there could be another group out there, Jasper started running through our camera footage. Sure enough, there's a huge group of hunters slowly making their way in our direction. Right now, they're about five days south of us.

So in the understatement of the year, it's not great. These guys are getting closer and closer to Bristlebrook, they're seriously kitted out, and if they don't already know their friends were taken out, they will soon. I'm guessing they aren't going to be too happy about that.

And worst of all, it's making Dom cranky.

The captain's prickling anger is tangible as he narrows his eyes on Beau. "This wouldn't even be our problem if we didn't bundle her up and play knights in shining khaki for her. She's been here a week and she's already started infighting and brought a goddamn militia down on our heads."

Beau meets Dom's gaze, and I'd give my left nut to have that level of calm under our CO's rage.

"Eden didn't pull that knife on Jaykob, Dom." He runs a hand over his head. "We shouldn't have assumed anything, that's on us. We should have known better. Jayk is a good dom. He's a good man. *We're* the ones who fucked up, not Eden."

Dom grunts sourly, and I go back to flipping pancakes, shamelessly eavesdropping.

The doc leans back casually and shakes his head. "And I find it hard to believe that forty-plus men would take this many risks for one woman, no matter how hard up they are. They were already in our woods, close to our home. Did you stop to think about why they're all here in the first place? It has to be territorial, right? A push out from Cyanide, maybe?"

I grimace at that thought. Cyanide City is the closest city to us, about a week south—called Cyanide because it's damn suicide to go there. After the strikes settled down, it became a war zone, with every gang around trying to claim their corner, and every stupid asshole who managed to get his hands on a gun trying to loot supplies.

We decided early on not to risk trips out there unless it was absolutely necessary. There are other towns around that, while less abundant in supplies, are a heck of a lot less dangerous. None of us wants to get a bullet in the ass because some trigger-happy civilian wants to throw his dick around.

Dom ducks his head like he's thinking it through, a grim cast to his mouth.

"Eden was just a surprise bonus for them, and you know it, Dom," Beau presses. "This is not her fault. Best I can tell, our librarian's cave was more or less on the fringes, and she just happened to run our way. And a party that size? Pushing through our woods? They were going to get close to Bristlebrook sooner or later anyway. It's better we found out about them now and not when we have our pants down—we haven't been monitoring our cameras half as much as we should."

Dom shakes his head like he's about to argue, but Beau cuts him off. "Just shitty luck, Dom. Don't blame the girl for it."

The door swings open and I look up hopefully, but it's too soon for Eden to have showered and come down already. If she's even able to work up the courage to face us after this morning.

Seeing Jasper gives me a familiar jolt, though, and I slide the fresh fruit salad I prepared into a bowl and place it in front of him. From under my lashes, I take in the familiar icy irritation in the set of his angular jaw and silently add a piping chocolate pancake to a plate and slide that over too. He'd never admit it—he's always rigorously in control of what he eats—but I know he loves the sweet stuff.

The muscles in my back clench as I turn back to the stove. Memories of Jasper's cruel care, the torturously perfect pain he can inflict, are too vivid, even after all this time, for me to ever relax properly around him. Now, normally I would say that letting your psychologist whip you until you come somewhat stretches the bounds of friendship—but lying to myself isn't my kink.

Jasper *is* torturously perfect. Perfectly painful. And if he'd wanted to work me over every night since our very own D-day to satisfy his frustrated sadistic needs, I'd have buckled the handcuffs myself.

But I'm not that lucky.

In the long years in our new base camp here, our relationship has changed. No matter how he tries to insist otherwise, I'm more than his patient now. More than his friend. Even if he's still never accepted pleasure from me. Even if he only doles it out so sparingly I could starve between the nights he really looks my way.

And if my stomach still twists every time he talks about his ex-wife, or I still stare too long when his eyelashes cast secretive shadows over his face, and if I still think he's the most beautiful man I've ever seen, well, we've both gotten pretty good at ignoring that too.

An image flashes into my mind of Eden kitted out in leather and whips, and I can't help but snort at my own fantasy. Dirty she may secretly be, but somehow I seriously doubt she has it in her to take control like *that*.

The image is chased away by another, of her kneeling next to me, our trembles and tears mixing as we wait to serve a different master.

I choke on my chocolate chips.

"Is there some part of this I'm missing that is funny to you, Lucien?" Dom glares at me.

I turn the stove off, angling my body behind the counter so they don't catch sight of the erection suddenly tenting my apron, and give him a wounded look. From anyone but Jasper, "Lucien" means I'm in trouble.

Well, fine. If I'm in trouble, then I'm keeping the rest of the chocolate pancakes for myself. And for Eden, I guess. If she's nice to me.

I really hope she's nice to me.

"Nah, boss. Your call, one hundred percent."

Over Dom's shoulder, Beau's look turns dry, and I can practically see him calling me a coward. But whatever. Ole Doctor Decent knows I agree with him—I just have better self-preservation skills than he does. I give him a one-shouldered shrug when Dom turns back around, and he rolls his eyes.

"And you?" Dom snaps at Jasper, who's perched elegantly on the breakfast bar stool, for all the world as though it's a throne. "You think we should tell her about the hunters?"

Jasper sips from his coffee before answering, the measured delay after Dom's demanding tone clearly deliberate. As the military psychologist, Jasper is the only one of us who hasn't been directly under Dom's command. He was responsible for our debriefings, supervised our reintegration, and because of the nature of our specialist deployment, we'd all had regular—and mandatory—sessions with him to work through our shit. Before he retired and left us, that is. Between that and the fact that this is still Jasper's home, he made it clear early on that his obedience to Dom is just a courtesy.

"I don't think we should tell her, no."

Jasper neatly cubes his pancake and quiet pleasure unfurls in my chest, even though he doesn't so much as glance my way.

Still, I really wish he wasn't taking Dom's side on this one. I hate this authoritarian crap.

Well . . . for this kind of thing I hate it.

Jasper continues, "She's frightened and skittish, only just now recovering from days of running from these men. We don't yet know to what extent—or if—we're even facing a threat. They might not even be aware their comrades are dead. Telling her about them now would be premature and perhaps send her into a flight that would only put her in more danger. We need to assess the danger, prepare accordingly, and inform her calmly when we have the facts and can be sure she won't put herself, and us, at risk."

Dom nods once and Beau shakes his head with a frustrated hiss.

"Ridiculous," he says under his breath.

Jasper ignores him.

"It's final; no one says a word to her," Dom says firmly. "Clear?"

"Clear, Cap," I say with a pang of regret, and Jasper murmurs his agreement.

After a beat of silence, Dom's golden gaze swings back to Beau. Their eyes lock.

Even after all these years, I'm not sure I completely understand their relationship. For a while I thought maybe they were like me. But I figure I've got secret desire pretty much locked down by now, and I just don't see it curling between them.

The team is tight enough, but we all know these guys are partners. They balance each other, watch each other's six, and they'd leave the rest of us in the dirt before they'd leave each other.

But things have been off with them since the Heather drama, and I do *not* love the weird tension. It makes me itchy.

That push and pull is there between them now, the kind of questioning that never existed before Heather—or BH, as I call it —when Dom repeats, "Clear?"

Finally, Beau drops his gaze. He scrubs a hand over the scruff on his chin that he usually keeps shaved. "Clear. But for the record, she's smart enough to know something's going on. It's not going to make her any more trusting of us if we keep lying."

"I'm more worried about keeping the hunters off our backs than coddling her feelings. She'll need to toughen up if she wants to stick around." Dom's voice is hard. "Now if we're done, can we move to the study and figure out how to stop these assholes from killing us in our sleep?"

"Should I get Jaykob?" Beau asks, and everyone tenses. "He should be a part of this."

Dom rubs his forehead. "Not . . . now. I'll talk to him later."

"Barring Lucien, we all miscalculated there," Jasper says in a grim voice. "Unfortunately, I anticipate this incident will exacerbate some of his more problematic behaviors. I will make my apologies shortly, and I strongly suggest you both do the same. In the interim, Lucien, it would be good if you could visit with him. He's not half so antagonistic with you and we need to keep him from feeling too isolated."

"Yeah. I mean, yes. Sure. I can do that."

I shut my mouth and internally kick myself. No one acknowledges my clumsy reply, but I know Jasper, at least, noticed. Damn it. Through the years, I've become real good at keeping this shit locked down, but ever since Eden arrived, it's like I've taken a dozen fresh cuts and my emotions are bleeding out everywhere. Hearing my name on his lips tangles my tongue, seeing him eating the food I've prepared makes me weak. I'm pretty sure I'm broken.

And I know why.

Seeing them together the other day wrecked me. I'm still not sure how it can be the hottest thing I've ever seen and yet still make me want to yank my heart out through my mouth just to make it stop hurting. I've gotten myself off six times since, just picturing him pleasuring her, remembering the short, gaspy pants she made and the look on her face when she came—and it only made me cry once.

Okay, twice.

Fuck. I'm a mess. And he's going to see it.

"Study in five," Dom orders.

I salute my assent and quickly gather the plates as Dom and Beau leave the room, not wanting to leave a mess for Eden to find. When I move to take Jasper's plate, his hand grasps my belt under the counter, and I still. I think I forget to breathe.

His dark eyes pierce me, but I don't lift mine to meet them. I don't want him to see everything writhing around in there right now.

Screw the mess, I should have left while I still had the chance.

"Look at me, Lucien," he murmurs.

Reluctantly, I do.

The icy irritation has melted from his features and he's looking at me with his Sir eyes. He's looking at me like. . . Fuck, the curve of his mouth is so pretty. *He* is so pretty. I've never seen softer-looking lips—except maybe Eden's.

Eden.

Shit.

I swallow hard and wrap my hand around his wrist, tugging gently so he'll remove it. "Jasper, I can't—"

His brow kicks up in surprise. His hand doesn't budge.

Damn it. One more minute and he'll have more than my buckle to hold on to.

Jasper ignores my protest. "It's your night with Eden," he muses.

Oh. Ohhh no. Yeah, I am *not* having this conversation.

"Dom said five, right? We should get moving. I—"

Those beautiful lips purse into a severe line. "Captain Slade can wait."

There's a threat in his words, a warning, and that tone from him is like the bell for Pavlov's dogs. I'm so hard I hurt. I ache.

But I'm used to aching for Jasper.

I nod in response, not trusting my voice, and the line of his mouth softens in approval. He likes it when I disobey Dom for him. I know he does. I just wish Dom didn't hand me my ass every time I did it.

Right now, it seems like a good deal though. It's still early, but Jasper is groomed and pristine. His shirt is immaculate, and the combination of silky soft fabric and hot, hard man always unravels me. During one of our scenes, after he'd whipped me until I was wrung raw and crying at his feet, he rewarded me by wrapping one of those used silk shirts around my swollen cock and stroking me until I spilled everything I had into the fabric. Even the thought of it makes me want to pass out all over again.

Sometimes I wonder if he ever wears that shirt. If it could be the one he's wearing right now.

Or if I ruined it that day as much as he's ruined me.

Jasper stands up, so very close. He's taller than me and it makes me want to straighten—some small, heteronormative part of me I thought I rationalized away years ago wanting to prove that I'm just as tough. That just because I'm submissive to him, it doesn't make me less of a soldier, or less of a man.

Ridiculous.

He knows that as well as I do. Hell, he's the one who helped me work through a lot of my conflicted feelings about my sexuality. But still. I stand straight, shoulders back, and it brings our lips within inches. We haven't been this close in almost a year and a half. Just for a moment, I wonder if he's finally going to kiss me.

Instead, he lifts his hand from my belt and cups the side of my face. A few strands of inky, satin hair fall over his forehead. He's not teasing now. He's not severe. Dark, grave eyes caress my face.

Tension coils inside me, and I tremble under his grip. I've never seen him look at me this way, not even in the depths of a scene.

"You seem very taken with her," he says softly, and I can feel his breath on my mouth.

My erection strains for attention, but there is an inch of space between every part of our bodies, except where his hand holds me in place. Where he stops me from floating away. I feel magnetized against him, like that space can't be closed. Like it won't ever be, not with us.

"So do you." My words are just as soft as his, but they're glass in my throat. It hurts, it hurts, it *hurts*. He looked at her like he was *captivated*. Owned. Alive.

But not at me.

Not like that.

I'm not usually a jealous person, but I'm jealous of him. I'm jealous of her too. I'm jealous that it's so uncomplicated for them to be together but for some reason it's the hardest thing in the world for us.

It must be because I'm a man, but the conversation has never been on the table, and I've been too chicken shit to ask. I never wanted the confirmation that there's no hope for us.

"She could be the solution to a problem of mine." Jasper rests his forehead on mine, and my breath falters at the contact. His thumb moves along my jaw. He hesitates, and the moment is so unlike Jasper, I wonder if I've been transported to some other reality. Finally, he murmurs, "If I asked something selfish of you, would you do it?"

A shiver courses down my spine, raising gooseflesh on my arms. My mouth dries up. God, I want him to be selfish with me. I want him to take and take until I'm wrung out and spent. Part of me wants to make a joke, to lighten the mood, because he can't be saying what I think he's saying—and if I'm wrong, it really will destroy me.

Because there's this other part of me that doesn't have a sense of humor at all. That part of me is desperate, and lonely, and has ached for him to touch me like this for too many years to count.

"Anything. I'll do anything for you," I whisper, finally meeting his eyes.

I'm shaking, my body fighting against this rising tide of hope. He wouldn't look at me like this if he didn't care, right?

His grip tightens painfully. Then his forehead rolls against mine, just slightly. "You don't even know what I'm asking yet," he mutters, letting out a sound suspiciously close to a groan.

It goes right to my dick. He's confusing me now. For the first time since I've known him, he seems *undone*.

"Jasper? Sir?" His eyes come back to mine, full of a banked heat that thrills me. "Are you okay?"

He doesn't answer, but the pad of his thumb brushes over my lips. I shudder, caught. My every atom zeroes in on that single point of contact.

His thumb drags over my lip harder, smearing it. Owning it.

"Don't sleep with her."

The words are halfway between a plea and an order. They hang in the air for too long.

"Why would you . . . *ask* that?" My stomach is in knots. I can't tell if I'm thrilled or horrified. I think I'm both. I try to move my head back so I can think—so I can *breathe*—but he holds me tight. "You of all people shouldn't be asking me that."

"I know."

"Years, Jasper. It's been *years*. And she likes me. I won't have to be— Damn it! You're doing this *now*?"

No. Okay. I think I've got a handle on this. I'm definitely pissed.

I push him off me and get some distance even though my heart tries to carve its way through my chest and leap back into his arms. Stupid thing is a masochist.

Okay, all of me is a masochist. It's no excuse!

"Lucky, I *know*," he repeats.

The use of my nickname pulls me up short. I've never heard him use it. Not once.

"Are you going to promise the same thing?" I demand.

I look back at him and the delicate line of his throat works. He sighs, looking at the floor, which, really, is answer enough. But . . .

But.

He's achingly beautiful in this moment. Rumpled and vulnerable and raw. I wonder how many people have ever seen him like this.

Jasper has unspooled me before, and I've curled up at his feet and thanked him, but I never thought I'd see him unravel.

"I know it's cruel. I know it's unfair. But . . . I'm asking anyway." Jasper swallows, and his voice is unsteady as he adds, "Please."

Please.

Fuck.

Drawing in a tremulous breath, I have to ask, "Why?"

My voice is too hoarse. My erection has long since deflated—but this isn't about that.

He shakes his head once, and I laugh, a little surprised at how strangled it sounds. "No. You can't ask something like that and not even give me an answer. Even I'm not that much of a pushover."

"You're not a pushover," he snaps, dark eyes flashing like lightning in the night. "Being submissive with me is not the same thing."

And my stupid masochistic heart knocks out a few ribs at his instant defense.

His pale jaw clenches, and his black hair is discomposed. Haltingly, he says, "I need to work through a few things. I fear . . . I fear that I need to make some decisions."

As though that explains anything.

"Decisions," I echo, heart sinking. He *fears*. That doesn't sound like a man ready to make a wild declaration of love. "About me?"

Jasper falters, but there's a hint of shame in his slight grimace.

"Right," I breathe. Everything inside me is shredding to pieces. I've been shot and it hurt less than this conversation. Hot tears prick the back of my eyes, and I rub the back of my neck, hoping it might somehow knock the hot lump out of my throat as well. "So I should blow my chance with Eden and just . . . wait until you decide whether I'm worth it?"

Jasper steps forward again. I retreat but find myself up against a cabinet. Did I think this kitchen was big? It's a matchbox, and he's the lit match, sucking down all my oxygen.

"Lucien—"

"Y'all might want to move your asses, Dom's pitching a fi—" The swinging door crashes back against Beau's outstretched hand as he cuts off, taking in the scene.

Jasper turns, angling his body so I'm not in full view. Instantly, all vulnerability flees from his face, leaving only cold, forbidding marble in its place.

That's what he is, I realize. Unfeeling, untouchable, beautiful art. And I can stare at him all day but, really, he's never going to look back.

Beau looks up at the ceiling like he suddenly finds cornices fascinating. "I'll— Ah. I'll tell him you'll be a few more minutes."

Fucking. Fantastic.

While neither of them are looking, I swipe a hand over my eyes.

Somehow, Beau beats a retreat even faster than he arrived. And right now? That looks like a damn fine idea.

I sidestep around Jasper before he turns back to me and walk toward the door as quickly as I can without being accused of running.

"We're not done here, Lucien," Jasper says, but the hint of panic takes the usual weight from his implied order.

I stop. "I think we are, actually," I tell him as I crack in a thousand places. "We are *done*, Jasper."

Now I just need to get through one whole meeting without shattering completely.

CHAPTER 15

EDEN

SURVIVAL TIP #183
*"The lonely one offers his hand too quickly
to whomever he encounters."*

L ooking around, I finally, reluctantly, have to admit there's
nothing more I can do to tidy my room. I never made it
down to breakfast, though someone—Lucky?—left a plate of delicious pancakes that dripped with melted chocolate by my door,
which staved off my hunger at least.

Before the strikes, I only rarely had heavy carbs or sugar,
though I have a terrible sweet tooth. My grandmother never
allowed it, making it clear she couldn't spare the expense. And
Henry, well, he controlled everything so tightly. At first, he'd
delighted in having me sample every sweet and delicacy I'd never
been able to afford as a child. But over time they became a treat, a
reward only given when I especially pleased him—and that became
a very rare thing.

Lucky's pancakes were delivered free of judgment or condi-
tion, and I savored every morsel with carnal delight.

I'm now glowing clean, the night's sticky sin scrubbed off my skin. My tight bun is back in its place, and I've donned the most conservative clothes that Beau and Dom brought me. Looking down at the tight pencil skirt and silk blouse, I'm reminded more of a caricature of a secretary than anything else, but at least it has the illusion of professionalism.

My very own version of body armor.

Though . . . the way the skirt presses my sore thighs together makes me uncomfortably aware of my body and what it's been through in the last twenty-four hours. Memories of Jaykob's tight grip biting into my hips makes heat snarl low in my stomach.

Shaking off the scandalous urge to dip my fingers between my thighs and relieve the pressure, I leave my room to explore the rest of the house. Crossing the inner balcony, I duck into the left side corridor. One room, a mirror to my own, is open, and a grand piano rests on the raised platform. Cozy sofas and beautiful artwork decorate the room, and the large window opens on a gorgeous view of the woods and mountains.

Deeper into the corridor, creeping into the stone of the mountain, three doors are closed. Those, I ignore. Very possibly they're bedrooms, and I don't want to happen upon anyone if I can help it. At the end of the corridor, there's another open door, and with a moment's hesitation, I step inside.

My breath leaves me in a pleased sigh.

Towering bookshelves of rich, dark wood line the hexagonal room, and shorter bookcases divide the center. Books of all colors, shapes, and sizes fill the space, and comfortably lived-in reading chairs are placed at clever intervals. I'm flooded by scents of dusty pages and leather covers and the uniquely nostalgic scent of the special glue that holds them all together. Warm light slips under lampshades and soaks the room in a romantic golden haze.

I've been wandering for twenty minutes and am fingering a leather-bound copy of *On the Genealogy of Morality* by Friedrich Nietzsche—placed beside Roald Dahl's *The Witches*, of all things

—when a hissing, mechanical sound behind me makes me shriek and spin around.

Jasper steps out from a metal door, then a bookcase slowly swings back into place behind him.

My jaw drops.

Just in that moment before he spots me, something about him seems *off*. There's a cruel set to his mouth, an unhappy cast to his eyes, an unsteadiness in his slow steps. His usual poise is unbalanced, like he's teetering on some unfathomable precipice.

"You— You actually have a secret passageway. Behind a bookcase." I pinch my nose under my glasses, trying to control my rapid, startled breathing. "Did I really just see that?"

Jasper's head snaps up, and his eyes run over me with cool precision. His face barely shifts, but amusement warms his eyes ever so slightly and that *off* feeling recedes. He walks toward me with the casual grace of a dancer, as though that instability I spotted was a dream.

"A little on the nose, perhaps, but I couldn't resist. My study," he explains, "and where I operate our surveillance."

I nod weakly. Searching for something to say, I glance around the room. "I can't believe you didn't show me this library." I smile at him. "It's lovely."

"I've been enjoying sharing my favorites with you." His lips curl up on one side. "And I was worried I'd lose you in here."

I let out a little laugh. "You still might."

He plucks the book from my hands; I didn't even realize I was gripping it.

"Ah, Nietzsche. I find his thoughts on master–slave morality fascinating," he murmurs.

Pausing, I scan his forbidding features from under the rim of my glasses. His sweet, comforting silence is apparently over, and there's something behind his words that puts me on guard. I can't help but remember Beau's words—*I might expect her to look like this after Jasper.*

Nervousness thrills up my spine, and I bite my lip. "I find it hard to relate to anyone who thinks that 'To see others suffer does one good, to make others suffer even more.' It's a rather permissive opinion, don't you think?"

The first full smile I've seen from him creases his cheek, and I can't help but stare at the pleat, my heart stuttering. He catches my stare, absorbing me for the first time since the first time we spoke. That *off* feeling has entirely vanished, and I feel myself floating into his orbit again. Alone in a beautiful abyss with a perilous man.

Something predatory glints in his eyes. "I wonder if you'll feel that way at the end of the week."

My eyes narrow, and my romantic imaginings skid to a halt. Did he mean that as the threat it sounded like?

Before I can respond, Jasper continues smoothly, "But a somewhat simplistic interpretation; he also said, 'Mistrust all in whom the impulse to punish is powerful.'"

I blink. Did he just—? It isn't often I've been called *simplistic*. My lips curve in a wry smile. "So, should I mistrust you, Jasper?"

I meant it as a joke, but I don't win another smile.

He replaces the book carefully, then studies me. A moment of silence, then another, and I become very aware of his hard body right before me and the considering weight of his gaze. I remember the dangerous confidence with which he spoke to Dom this morning and shiver.

"Only if you have done something that warrants punishment," he says finally.

Unbidden, thoughts of Henry come to mind, and I only just stop myself from flinching. He liked his little punishments too. Nothing physical, never that, but he had a perfect knack for petty cruelty.

Before emotion can swamp me, I turn back to the bookshelf and reply, "Show me someone who hasn't in this world." Determined to change the subject, I shake my head and study the books.

"No offense, but this library looks like it was put together by a monkey."

Jasper steps in close behind me. "More insults. You're rather free with them."

He's warm and close enough that I can sense his every movement, but far enough that we aren't touching. Giving me the choice to lean back or not.

I hesitate, torn between shyness and slow, slippery desire. Instinctively, I tilt my head until the breeze of his breath stirs the tiny hairs on the nape of my neck. I shudder.

Darn it, is no topic safe with this blasted man?

Desperate to escape his confusing nearness, I drop into a crouch and pull *The Witches* free.

Compared to the bookish coziness of his presence from the last few days, the sudden onslaught of Jasper's attention feels like a lethal advance. It makes my adrenaline pump and flight instincts flare, warning me to *run*, run *now*, because I'm suddenly sure he's done it on purpose, that he laid his trap and lured me in with books and quiet company, and soon he'll have me pinned, at his mercy, and that's just . . .

I swallow hard. Bad? That's bad, right?

My fingers quiver on the illustrated cover, and I consider that my new position at his feet may not have been the best choice. His presence over me is delightfully omnipotent and reminds me powerfully of Jaykob's hand tangling in my hair while I knelt for him and—

No! Stop, Eden. What on earth is getting into me these days?

"D-do you have an interest in philosophy, then?" I ask, flustered and embarrassingly breathless. Honestly, it would really help matters if I didn't sound like some scarlet woman out of a low-budget pornographic film.

When I'm certain I have myself under control, I show him the miscategorized Dahl classic with a small smile, and manage—in a much more civilized tone—to tease, "Making a statement on the dichotomy of good and evil in children's books?"

Jasper chuckles, rich and smooth as my morning's melted chocolate chips, and swipes a hand over his angled chin. "I do, actually—have an interest in philosophy, I mean. I find it quite relevant to my work. Though I must admit, I haven't made use of children's books just yet."

"Not such a hit with soldiers, I guess." I smile and pluck free two heavy—and beautifully illustrated—atlases. "Though I can't imagine Lucky objecting, for some reason."

"Lucien—" Jasper stops, and I look up to see he's watching me carefully. After considering me a moment, he sighs. "Lucien is an exception. In many respects."

I wait a beat, but he doesn't elaborate. Feeling like I'm missing something, I turn my attention back to the shelves. I wonder if this is yet another one of those things he's decided I'm not to know, and the thought sinks my stomach. He doesn't need to share anything with me, not under the rules of this *deal*.

This deal that is starting to grate in unexpected ways. Perhaps I've been too focused on the perks they included on their end of the deal . . . and not enough on the things they didn't.

"Well, I don't mind the theories," I continue, rearranging the books in my arms and ignoring my thundering pulse, "but so many philosophers just waffle on in self-importance. It's a common fault in clever men—they so like the sound of their own voice. Oh! Get that Frank Herbert novel? That shouldn't be here either."

When I don't get a response, I turn. He leans against the book-shelf. His crisp white shirt is open at the throat, revealing a glimpse of corded muscle. The sleeves are rolled to just above his elbow. He's a study in elegant disdain, regarding me with a neat, arched brow.

I color as I realize I was ordering him about in his own library and am about to stammer an apology when he slowly plucks the book off the shelf, his gaze never leaving mine.

I'm not too dense to miss the gentle mockery in it.

Or the warning.

Moving closer—closer than he needs to—he places it on the pile in my arms. With one finger, he tilts my chin up toward him. "I have found many things are best demonstrated without words."

My thoughts liquify, and I can't remember exactly what we're talking about.

As his finger strokes along my jaw, my mouth grows dry, and I watch as his darkening gaze fixes on my mouth.

"Hey, hands off. It's my turn!"

The sudden sound of Lucky's voice makes me flinch back, and there's an undertone to it that I can't quite decipher. Jasper doesn't drop his hand, though, nor does he acknowledge Lucky's presence.

Lucky comes up behind me. "Come on, beautiful, I have the whole afternoon planned."

I want to greet him, but as though he senses it, Jasper's grip tightens briefly on my chin, holding me captive. His lips thin, and I shift uncomfortably as that *off* feeling returns. "You are more than welcome in my library, Eden. And you may reorganize it if you wish."

Ah. I should have asked before I started doing that, too.

"Do you enjoy chess?" he asks. His dark gaze finally flicks from my mouth to my eyes, and something distant and calamitous lurks in its shadows.

"I—" I pause, hearing how husky my voice has become. His presence isn't Dom's thunizcloud, or Lucky's warm sunshine; it makes me shiver, like ice sliding down hot skin. "I've never played."

"I think you might be good. Join me tomorrow for a game."

My arms are beginning to ache under the heavy books, but I hold his gaze. A streak of daring darts through me.

"If you say please, I might be persuaded," I tell him, though my voice comes out far more shaky and less tart than I intended.

The lighting catches the hollows of his cheekbones as he straightens, turning him villainous.

"A simple, 'Yes, Jasper' will suffice, Eden." His voice is cultured, casual. Rippling with the warning of a great white beneath the waves. "You might do well to teach her a few lessons before she comes to me, Lucien, since you're fond of her."

Indignation pricks me. Now that *was* a threat.

The warm, easy intimacy of moments ago is nowhere to be found, and his chilly censure seems oddly pointed. Is he mad? My gut starts a slow, queasy roll as I run over our conversation in my head, trying to pinpoint where I might have gone wrong.

As I study his punishing face from beneath my lashes, my brief burst of nerve curls up and dies. I can't seem to summon any of the courage I'd found yesterday with Jaykob. Something about Jayk's challenging stare had encouraged me to meet his fury with my own—I understand the chip on his shoulder, even while it infuriates me—but under the faint disappointment in Jasper's expression, I want to cringe into nothingness.

"Ah . . . you know, I'm not really the lesson-giving type." The uneasiness in Lucky's voice catches me, and I dart a glance between them. Lucky avoids my eyes and color is high in his cheeks.

What in the world . . . ?

"Manners should be taught during childhood," Jasper tells me curtly. Everything about him is strung tight now, and I'm sure I've made some horrible faux pas. "But if that was somehow missed in your education, I'd be happy to assist you. Now, I made you an offer. Answer me, Eden."

I stop my lip from trembling. Barely. He brushes the pad of his thumb over my mouth, as though sensing the movement. Lucky sucks in a breath.

My grandmother had plenty to say about my manners, and so had my husband. No matter how I've tried to leave my past behind me, I know my trailer-trash upbringing still shows. It makes me self-conscious about every reference, every turn of phrase, because despite all the books I've read and the study I've thrown myself into, it's those small, habitual slips that will always betray me. That will tip off my *betters* that I am poor, and lazy, and ill mannered, and whatever other attribute they choose to ascribe to me for the past I can never change.

Jasper is as calculated and wealthy as Henry's family was. He's the man Henry always strived to be. Articulate. Assured. Intimidating.

Of course he sees right through me.

Of course he's disappointed by what he sees.

The years since my husband's death crumble, and all at once I'm the insignificant, lonely girl who so desperately craved his approval.

I tear away from his penetrating gaze, lowering my eyes. "Yes, Jasper."

I know this part. I play it as well as any actress.

I'm sorry. Please forgive me. I won't embarrass you.

I'll be good, I swear.

Jasper stills. His stare is intense. Finally, the grip on my chin gentles. After a long moment, he makes a sound of frustration in the back of his throat and drops his hand.

"It seems I'm on a roll today," he mutters, sounding unhappy. "That will be a problem."

Of course I am.

I keep my mouth pressed shut, but the sudden sting behind my eyes surprises me—as does the waver of my lip that, this time, has nothing to do with arousal.

You don't need them, I remind myself fiercely. *You can leave at any time. You're a survivor now. You're not that same girl anymore.*

God, how is it that in one week among people, all my insecurities have returned so viciously? I hate this. Hate the unsteady ground I'm walking on here. At least with Henry I knew the rules.

Why do I always seem to be living by someone else's?

I work to keep my face smooth as I stare at my feet, but tension knots my shoulders.

"Jesus, Jasper," Lucky mutters, "the lot of you need to back the hell off her so she can get her shit together. Between Jaykob hulking out and throwing her against walls and you going full sadist, she'll be completely warped. Let me show her how to have a bit of fun before you start stripping her raw. Please? Just back off of us for a while?"

Full sadist? Stripping me raw?

Despite myself, my gaze once again lifts and slides between the two men. The little comments over the last few days start to make sense. I turn the label over in my mind. *Sadist.*

Jasper doesn't respond right away. That chilling, deadly stance returns as he faces Lucky; it would look almost lazy, if not for the treacherous tilt to his mouth.

Lucky gives an uncomfortable roll of his shoulders under that stare, grimacing. The flush deepens over his cheeks.

He spares a blue-eyed glance at me, then sighs, setting his feet reluctantly, as though it physically hurts to set himself against his friend.

"You *owe* me," Lucky finally says in a low, serious voice.

Something silently passes between the two men. After a long, tense moment, Jasper inclines his head. "Very well." Then his eyes narrow and his voice becomes granite. "Though don't presume, Lucien, that there is any debt between us. We both know better than that. I have never taken more than was offered."

I am most *certainly* not being told everything.

As Lucky's face turns scarlet, Jasper looks at me, and the bright, proud insolence from moments before dims back to his usual detached elegance.

"I apologize, Eden. That was impolite of me. Would you please join me for chess tomorrow? To be clear, you are under no obligation to do so. I would simply enjoy the pleasure of your company."

Frustration and embarrassment make me want to flee to my room. Maybe even from the house. I don't know why I thought I could do this.

"Eden?" he prompts, and this time his voice is soft, gentle as the brush of a feather.

When I look up, his face is lined with deep remorse. It soothes some of the sting, but none of my confusion.

I manage a nod. "Yes. Of course. Thank you."

"I had better get back to work. Have a good afternoon."

With a nod to each of us, he stalks back to his not-so-secret secret study. Lucky and I both stare after him, red-cheeked, as he leaves.

CHAPTER 16

LUCKY

SURVIVAL TIP #212
Laugh when it hurts.
Tears will only dehydrate you.

I turn to see Eden's bewildered expression just as the books start slipping from her arms. I catch them, helping to steady her, then snicker, trying to put Jasper's last comment to me from my mind.

"Weight of the world, huh?" I tease.

Her brow wrinkles. Then she looks at the atlases atop the towering pile and rolls her eyes. We set them on a table, and she worries her lip over the disorder. She's every inch the librarian today, and damn if it doesn't leave me hard as a rock.

"What—?" she begins and then stops, flustered.

"Ah." I rub a hand over the back of my head, wondering how much she picked up on, how much to explain. My T-shirt lifts with the motion, and I pretend not to notice when her eyes light on my bared skin. Smugness makes me want to grin, settling some of my stomach-aching jealousy, though I wish to hell I didn't have to be the one to try and explain Jasper to her.

It seems kind of like adding insult to injury at this point.

After I finally escaped from the group meeting earlier, I'd needed to shower and change before I started feeling anything like myself again. "Jasper is kinda . . . Well. I mean, he's a—"

"A sadist," Eden whispers. Her blue-gray eyes are adorably wide behind her glasses.

I shrug and quirk a smile. "Yeah, I guess. And a dominant. You remember we were in a kink club when it all got real? Well, that's kinda why you got stuck with the more colorful personalities in the troop."

She blinks at me, then leans against the table, seeming to take that in. "So he wants to hurt me?"

Her voice sounds small, and I just barely stop myself from wrapping her in a hug. Damn it. Jasper should be explaining this. I try to think of a way to put it that won't freak her the hell out.

"Only if you want him to. It's only fun for him if you're into it too. I guess— I mean, part of the appeal for him is pushing you to your limits, and making you want to be pushed there. Pain can heighten the pleasure of sex for some people."

Eden turns the shade of sun-curdled cauliflower.

Oo-kay. Screwed that one up.

"Not for me," she insists. One delicate hand flutters to her throat where her pulse pounds. "I wouldn't like that."

I must have hesitated a moment too long because her chin lifts in defiance. "I wouldn't!"

I give her my best grin, lifting my palms in surrender. Then, once her chin starts to lower to a normal level, I add quickly, "But just hear me out."

She huffs in exasperation, but a hint of amusement eases into her features.

Good. I want her to relax around me. Lord-our-deeply-ashamed-father knows she won't get much chance around the rest of these idiots.

"You said you had fun with Jaykob, right?"

Her cheeks pinken.

"Um . . . *fun* might not be exactly the right word," she says, "but yes, I— I did enjoy myself."

"There's nothing wrong with enjoying pain, beautiful. Or putting yourself in someone else's control, so long as you trust them not to abuse it," I tell her gently, earnestly. "You were covered in bruises, and knowing Jayk, he probably threw you around a bit, huh? I'm guessing he was a little rough?"

I don't need her tentative nod to know I'm right; I saw her this morning, and I saw the way the big bastard fucked often enough back in the day. Of the five of us, only Jasper was ever worried about privacy. I've never been able to decide if it was a blessing or a curse that I never saw Jasper dominating anyone else.

The way Eden's eyes cloud with lust does nothing to help my hard-on.

I clear my throat and continue, "But you still had a good time. For some people, that kind of treatment during sex just makes them feel more desired. Like they can't get enough of you. The pain and the pleasure kind of blend together, right?"

Her embarrassment seems to have faded slightly and her look of thoughtful concentration has me biting back a smile. Fuck she's cute. Her lower lip is caught between her teeth and small frown lines appear between her brows. Apparently considering the theory, rather than how it applies to her, is more acceptable.

"So you know that having both pain and pleasure isn't necessarily a bad thing. Now, Jasper, he just kind of takes that to the next level. He likes delivering pain in a controlled way, doling it out like a treat or a punishment until your body wants the pain. It brings your pleasure to a different level. It's full-on. Exhausting, both physically and mentally. But it can feel fucki— I mean, it can feel good. Really good."

Rapturous. Blissful. Agonizing.

I don't have the words to describe this to her properly. How can I explain the need to venerate his cruelty? The craving for the sweet-sharp lashes of his cane? For the unbearably soft kindnesses between? How good it feels to free-fall into darkness with someone, knowing they'll save you and punish you for the favor all at once?

Do I really want to explain this to her? Maybe it would be better for all of us if she ran far, far away from Jasper.

Or maybe it would just be better for me.

She glances up at me at the last, and I ready for her to scold me on my language, but there's something too assessing in her gaze, and I realize that isn't what caught her attention.

I shift. Damn it. I get enough of those looks around here. I want her smiling again. I'm not good with the serious stuff. After today, I've had enough serious to last a lifetime. I feel raw, like an exposed nerve, but being with her is a sweet kind of balm.

"You sound like you speak from experience," she says tentatively, the unasked question clear in her voice.

"Oh. Yeah, well. Yeah. I . . . do."

Smooth, motherfucker. Smooth as asphalt. What the hell is wrong with me? I'm not sixteen anymore. I know how to talk about sex.

"With Jasper, even," I add thoughtlessly.

Her mouth drops open and her eyes widen. Not in disgust, I note, even as I continue to swear at myself for being a fucking idiot. More like curiosity.

"So you're . . . bisexual?"

Aw hell. It's *way* too early to be having this conversation.

"Well, yeah. But not like that. Not with Jasper, anyway. I mean, he doesn't— We don't—" I stop, then start laughing at myself. This is ridiculous. How am I even having this conversation after today? I have to laugh or this is going to turn into some kind of rom-com where she ends up stroking my hair, and I tearfully confess my soul to her. I scrub a hand over my face and give her a rueful look. "I think your tongue-tied disease is catching, woman."

I take a breath and start again. It's not the right explanation, but it's all I can work up right now. "Yes, I enjoy pain and being dominated. I also enjoy dominating, sometimes. I switch, depending on my mood and who I'm with."

Although, now I think of it, the thought of dominating anyone—even with gorgeous and clearly submissive Eden laid out on a platter—somehow doesn't seem so appealing as it once did. Not that the attraction isn't there, because it is. I haven't been this attracted to anyone since, well, since Jasper. But I would much rather both of us be under him, at his mercy, than have her at mine.

But that might be a bit much to cover on a first date.

"I don't enjoy giving pain. Yes, I'm bi. No, I haven't had sex with any of the guys. As far as I know, the others are at least mostly straight."

I think of the way Jasper pinned me today. The way he looked at my lips.

What he asked of me.

To be fair, he's never exactly *said* that he was straight. . . I just assumed because he was married to Soomin, and because he's never tried to take pleasure with me, even while he had me spread and naked and begging beneath him. I mean, I know he gets worked up—it's impossible to miss his arousal during our scenes—but I always put that down to his kink rather than me. More of a "whipping subbies until their sobs soothe my cranky temper" boner than a "Lucky is my one true love and I'd give anything to brand his soul with mine" hard-on.

Heart-on?

I wish I gave him a heart-on.

I shrug it off for now. Plenty of time to torture myself some more over that later.

"Yes, I have bottomed for Jasper before when he needed a

release. We don't have sex"—I push one of the books open, and the hard cover hits the table with more force than I intended. I think of how Jasper was looking at her when I walked in, and how she stared up at him. His perfect, submissive thing. The two of them heart-twistingly beautiful together—"and we . . . we aren't interested in each other that way."

The lie tastes like ash on my tongue.

I shrug like it means nothing. "But he's a sadist, and he occasionally needs to work out his shit on someone who likes to take it. Which I do. So, you know." I want to knock my face into a wall at how I sound, and yet I can't stop my dumb mouth from adding weakly, "It makes sense."

My emotions were just splattered around the room like a toddler throwing mashed peas, but sure, it makes sense. No one usually lets me talk for this long. Apparently it's because the longer I talk, the more I let the stupid out.

She's staring at me, but I can't for the life of me tell what she's thinking. All in, balls out, though, I guess.

"Anyway, my point is that Jasper knows what he's doing. He won't push you beyond what you can take, and the two of you will set out your boundaries before he even touches you."

The thought makes me sick. And hard.

If only I had a psychologist to help work this shit out . . .

Idiot.

Her eyes narrow. "Then what was that before about teaching me a lesson? It sounded to me as though he was willing to punish me if I don't do as he says. What exactly would have happened if I had turned down his chess game?"

Damn, I like it when she gets all snippy—though I know enough about women not to say so.

"If I had to guess, he wanted to turn you over his knee and spank your ass until you agreed to do what he wanted." I snort. "Though I think he's regretting that hard-ass approach right about now. Jasper won't touch you, not without your permission. He'll set out the rules before he punishes you for breaking them."

I watch her face as I talk about Jasper spanking her. Her color is high and, despite the pursed displeasure of her full lips, the hollow in one cheek makes me think she must be biting it.

So, not quite as against the idea as she's saying.

"As for the obedience thing—and I really hate to say it since you're making that face at me—but it's kind of a given with these guys. Dom, Beau, and Jasper are all gonna be pulling that card, so you probably should prepare for that. I mean, Jayk too, I guess, but he's got more of that caveman clobber-you-over-the-head style."

"Don't speak about him like that," she says absently.

My brows fly up, though she isn't looking.

Right. Okay. Go Jayk, I guess.

Then she sighs, looking exhausted. "I suppose it doesn't matter, huh? I'll just take it as it comes."

I shove my tongue into my cheek to stop myself from making a crack about her word choice, then grab her hand and tug. When she finally looks up at me, a new wariness in her eyes, I wink at her.

"Come on, we have some strength training to do."

Ignoring her spluttering, I drag her out and down to the music room where I set everything up and shut the door behind us.

"Lucky, I don't want to work out. *Why* are you making me work out? What are you— Oh."

A Twister mat in a six by four grid of red, blue, green, and yellow circles is laid out on the floor, and a pitcher of my famous orange monkey master mix is perched on the table. Eden is staring at the mat in horrified bemusement. I snicker, and she blushes.

The more we talk, the more I think maybe we can try this without kink. Maybe we can be together, just the two of us, without thoughts of Jasper and pain and tears. Maybe she and I can be enough for each other, and she'll drown out the way I ache for him.

Maybe we both just need a bit of fun.

"Strength training. Now, we're playing this one with a *twist*," I say, and even though she rolls her eyes, she's starting to smile. Some of the snaking jealousy in my chest softens when she does.

I'm beginning to think she has a thing for puns.

Or maybe it's just for me.

"Sit down, gorgeous, and pour yourself a drink. It's time for Eden to sin."

CHAPTER 17

EDEN

SURVIVAL TIP #69
The world will twist you up.
Be flexible.

I don't move. I am not flexible. I don't play party games. I didn't have the kind of childhood that encouraged parties at all, let alone silly activities like this.

"Lucky . . . this isn't really my kind of thing."

Resolved to back away, maybe find something else we can do together, I look up at him pleadingly—only to see disappointment dim those bright blue eyes. My stomach jolts. It's a feeling I remember vividly. How many times did my grandmother tear away my "frivolous" books, or scold me for watching cartoons?

The thought of making teasing, playful Lucky feel anything like that . . .

How am I managing to upset every person I speak to?

"Will you teach me?" I blurt.

He rubs the back of his head the way he does when he's uncomfortable. It makes his shirt ride up again and, like a magnet, my gaze is drawn to the defined V of golden muscle peeking over the top of his low-slung gray sweatpants.

"We can find something else to—"

"No, I'd like to play. I would." Biting my lip and tearing my gaze upwards, I kick off my low heels and hike up my skirt. It's tight, so I have to edge it up bit by bit to my upper thighs so my legs are free to move. Then I kneel by the absurd drink and pour two glasses, making my own smaller as I remember how potent it is.

Lucky takes the glass from me, his eyes snagging on my exposed legs for a few heartbeats too long. His throat works as he swallows, then, seeming to make up his mind, he shoots me a wicked grin and sits cross-legged on the floor.

"It's occurred to me that you don't know how to smile, laugh, or generally have a good time without correcting yourself within about five seconds."

My own smile fades as I stare at him. "I thought Jasper was supposed to be the psychologist."

He waggles a finger. "Not an attack, sweetheart. Promise. I'm making it my personal mission to make you smile."

Well.

I take a sip of my drink, unsure what to say to that.

"So, here's how we play. Since there's only two of us, and I'm not having any of the other bozos crash the party, rather than spinning the wheel to choose where we place our hands and feet, we're going to ask each other questions. If the other person answers truthfully and completely, then they get to choose where to move one of their limbs. If they don't answer to the questioner's satisfaction, however, the questioner chooses where they place their limb. And they get to demand a dare from the other person."

His face was far too innocent as he said the last.

"A dare?" I ask dryly. "What kind of dare?"

Lucky's wicked grin deepens, flashing that dimple at me. "How good's your imagination?"

Before I can protest, he lifts a hand. "No dare is allowed that would injure or unduly embarrass the other person. And as for other basic rules, you need to place your limbs in order: foot, hand, other foot, other hand. Start with whatever you like, but you have to change each time. No just moving one hand around the mat."

Not trusting him a whit, I look around the room as though I might be able to spot a trap as I consider his offer. I only see a few sofas, the intercom, the piano, a guitar in one far corner, a sound system, large microphones in each corner of the room, and an expansive collection of records. That, and the table with the monkey mix on it, a bottle of icy water, and the box that the Twister mat came in. Finally satisfied, I give a reluctant nod.

Lucky shakes his head with a *tsk*. "So distrustful. It's heart-breaking. Good to play? You can start. Ask me a question."

He sets the drink down, walks to the side of the mat with red circles, and looks at me expectantly.

Hmm. Tapping my lip, I think for a moment, then ask, "Were you really in a circus?"

Lucky laughs and then pouts as though disappointed in me. "Yes," he replies, then puts his right foot on a red circle. "Why did you love your favorite childhood toy?"

I scowl at him. Right. Yes and no answers are a stupid idea. I stand, put down my drink and walk to the opposite side of the mat, the one with green circles.

"I didn't really have many childhood toys. I did have an old shirt that I loved when I was little. It belonged to my mother. But I threw it away when I was ten and realized she wasn't ever going to come back." I put my left foot on a green circle in the corner farthest from him. Sensing Lucky's eyes on me, I quickly ask, "*Why* did you join the circus?"

When I look at him, he smiles again, although it seems a little forced, and I'm grateful. I don't like thinking about my absentee parents.

"My parents were both acrobats. They ran a cirque studio and taught classes with other people in their troupe in the off season. The circus itself was only set up during summer. I picked it up over the years, mostly. I was there after school every day, and everyone was willing to teach me. Eventually I started teaching classes too. Easy money doing something fun."

I study him, all lean, catlike grace and power. Yes, I can see Lucky running around with a group of people who laughed and loved as freely as he seems to. The thought has me smiling too.

"I bet you were popular with the students," I say, and then wish I could swallow the words.

My cheeks flame, but he only winks. Then he pulls his shirt over his head in one smooth movement.

"What are you doing?" I squeak.

Smooth, golden skin covers corded, defined muscles. He isn't bulky, but his clean lines and tight, cut abs send me right into danger of combustion. I clench my hands as my fingers itch to slide over him, and I try to keep my gaze somewhere safe.

Damn it, he's gorgeous. Nowhere's safe.

"Twister is a game of strength and balance. I mustn't be impeded by something so insignificant as a shirt," he tells me in a fair imitation of Jasper's haughty, silken tones.

Despite my distraction, I can't help my unladylike snort. As soon as it escapes me, I clap a hand over my mouth, mortified.

He frowns. "Nuh-uh. No smothering laughs, smiles, snorts, or any other bodily functions. Except coughs—because hygiene. Do it again and I'm going to claim a dare."

After giving me a mock-stern look, he dimples and then bends over backwards, stretching diagonally across the whole mat and placing his right hand on the green circle next to my foot. It places his head under me, and I shift back so he can't see up my skirt. His muscles ripple as his back arches in the unnatural position.

I lick my lips and mutter, "Show-off."

Mirth bright in his voice, he says, "Tell me the most ridiculous fact you know."

"The name for a fear of long words is hippopotomonstros-esquippedaliophobia," I reply instantly, relief lightening my voice. I had worried he'd press me more about my childhood, but it seems Lucky really does want to keep it light.

"I am shocked and impressed that you know how to pronounce that."

I study the mat, deciding where to place my hand. Lucky made it hard for me, stretched across the whole mat as he is. If I place my hand on the easy green circle beside his, I'll be bent directly over him with my breasts in his face—and placing my right foot would be very difficult next round.

But if I choose a more comfortable circle on that side of him, I'd have to straddle his head next round in order to reach a circle with my right foot. He would be able to see directly up my skirt.

He's made this impossible.

Even if I claim a blue or red circle with my left hand on Lucky's other side—the side closest to me—I'd need to stretch along his body.

Which would put my face right by his crotch.

But . . . there *is* more empty space on this side. If I start there, then I might actually be able to place my foot next turn without crawling on top of him.

"You know, it doesn't usually take this long to choose a circle. But if you're trying to cheat by tiring me out, then let me just tell you—I can do this all night." To emphasize his point, he lowers and raises himself twice in an odd kind of upside-down one-handed push-up that makes his stomach, pecs, and arms tighten.

I splutter and glare down at him, ignoring the way my pulse skids. Had I worried about not feeling a thrill with Lucky? What an idiot I am. It might not be the maddening freedom I felt when Jayk, Beau, or Jasper took control, but there's something else here. Something joyful and scorching and giddy. Something that makes me want to melt into him and spend days giggling in sun-soaked meadows.

"I do not *cheat*," I say. "I'm strategizing."

He laughs. "Well, all right then, Sun Tzu, take your time."

The usual instinct to bite back my smile rises, but I stop myself, letting my lips curl as I meet his eyes again. It's strange how exposed I feel for doing something so small. Like he might mock me for being amused by him. Or like I'm letting him know I like him, somehow. Like I need to hide it to keep my advantage.

But, for all his teasing, Lucky hasn't once looked at me mockingly. He's always invited me in on the joke—never made me the butt of it.

His expression softens at my smile, and he murmurs, "Good girl."

My stomach gives a low, hard flip.

"Lucky . . ." The word comes out husky. Embarrassingly, transparently lustful.

Lucky's breath snags. His eyes meet mine, and he slowly, so slowly, sucks his lower lip into his mouth. When it pops back out, it's glossy and ripe with color.

Good *God*.

Blushing, flustered, I make my decision and lean forward. My skirt catches and, with a wince, I hike it another inch. Ignoring the pleased hum from the man beneath me, I stretch forward again and place my left hand on the red circle directly across from me.

I'm a little overextended, balanced entirely on my left side, but I'm able to angle my body along the outer edge of the mat so it falls away from Lucky slightly.

And my face isn't *quite* buried in his sweatpants.

From here, I should be able to maneuver in the next round—hopefully *without* putting myself in some obscene position.

"Your turn," he prompts.

Right. "Why did you decide to join the Army, since you loved your job?"

There's a pause. "When I was seventeen, there was an accident on the ropes. One of the teenage students was doing something she shouldn't have and landed wrong. It was . . . It was really horrible. The damage was pretty bad. We had insurance, but the family sued and it got ugly. Insurance came through for the claim, but they trashed our reputation.

"Anyway, the Army was a good way to make a quick buck, especially since I was pretty physically fit and not qualified or interested in much else. Ended up getting pulled into the Rangers when I was twenty and met Dom and Beau then. They'd been in the squad together a while already. Jayk and Thomas came in about two years later—they'd been in other divisions and transferred. All came good in the end. Mom and Dad moved, got a new place. Worried about me too much. You know."

My heart twists at the sadness in his voice. He's open with it and it's clear how much he misses them.

I wonder what that must feel like.

To my surprise, Lucky stretches impressively to place his other foot on the red circle beside my newly placed hand. It means his firm thigh is right by my face, pushing my already precarious balance uncomfortably, and I have to lean backwards to avoid falling down on top of him.

And yet *he's* annoyingly stable. *And* he's crowding all the space I had to move.

Despite myself, my eyes skim over him and I can't fail to notice the hard length of him, er . . . at attention.

And very, very close to my face.

That seems to be the only strain on him, however, and, when my gaze finally makes its way to his face, he catches my shocked look with a cheeky grin.

Something about the naughty curve to his lips has me wondering what it would feel like to have them buried between my thighs. My core throbs and my balance wavers. I swallow hard, looking away as heat flames in my cheeks.

"What was that thought?" Lucky asks, voice dipping into a low, rough drip that shivers down my spine.

I half-shake my head before I stop myself.

"Nuh-uh." Lucky laughs. "That's my question, beautiful. What thought had you turning that pretty shade of scarlet?"

I glare at him, suddenly liking this game a whole lot less. I shake my head again.

Blue eyes dance. "If you don't answer, I'm going to claim my dare. *And* I get to choose where you place your foot."

Why did I agree to this stupid game again? Nervousness crowds me, and I lick my lips. Is it worse to tell him, or let him claim a dare? He seems creative; I'm not sure I trust him with a dare.

Decided, I open my mouth to tell him that I was fantasizing about him licking me . . . but the words won't come.

He catches my panic, and his smile turns slow and lazy. "All right, beautiful."

His free hand wraps around my free ankle and tugs, nearly sending me off balance. Biting my lip, I let him guide me, and he sets my right foot on the other side of him. My balance shifts until my body is curved over the top of his.

To my surprise, I realize the position stabilizes me—but it means I have a foot placed on either side of his head, and my skirt now barely covers my ass. He must be getting a full view of my now-soaking lacy blue panties. In this spread position, I feel my swollen lips part. My breath strangles.

"Um, what—" I clear my throat to try and rid the thick, raspy tone from my voice. "What is the dare?"

Hot lips brush the sensitive flesh behind my knee, nearly making it buckle. He smiles against my skin.

"Haven't decided yet," he says, all smug amusement. "Maybe after the game."

His tongue rasps up my thigh, and I shudder, flinching away from the sumptuous contact. Goosebumps tighten my skin and wetness pools at my core, slicking me further. I want to clench my thighs together, sure he'll be able to see my growing arousal, but it isn't possible in my position. His spare hand lifts again and his fingertips skim up the back of my thigh.

"Lucky, I— That's . . . cheating . . . " The last word comes out on a sigh.

The hand flattens on my upper thigh, fingers brushing against my panties, just barely. He rubs slightly against the silk, and the wetness makes his hand slippery. I can smell my own musky sweetness.

"Fuck, beautiful. Do you have any idea how good you look?" Lucky groans.

He squeezes my thigh, then pinches my ass. I squeak, and he laughs, though the sound is tortured.

"Touching is not against the rules," he informs me after a moment of shared unsteady breathing. "That would be a stupid rule."

Oh, really? My eyes narrow, though he can no longer see my face. Sneaky blasted man. My gaze returns to all the delicious golden skin under me and competitive giddiness bubbles up.

I blame the monkey mix.

Before I can stop myself, I move my remaining hand to his stomach, lightly tracing the lines of his abs. The soft skin tightens at my touch and Lucky releases his breath. Hard. His thumb strokes the inner curve of my ass, baring me further to his gaze.

Trembling, I roll my lips together and trace my fingers down his V, right to the spot where it disappears into his pants. I love the textural feel of his skin, so different from my own, so different from Jaykob, even. So sensitive, like he can feel every brush of my breath like static electricity. I love his little shivers.

"Now who's playing dirty?"

Despite the delight in his tone, there's a hot edge to it that makes me want to moan. A pleased smile teases my lips at knowing I'm affecting him.

His fingers catch the edge of my panties, and I whimper as he peels them to the side and cool air teases my heated flesh. My fingers tease the tie at the front of his sweatpants, held tight by the strain of his erection.

I shake my head slightly, trying to think. What am I doing? Two men in two days and I've been turned into a puddle of lust by both of them. I can't help but be shocked by the sharp suddenness of my attraction to Lucky. Maybe I should—

Crack.

His palm comes down hard on the curve of my ass, and I gasp against the sting. It's chased by a low, throbbing ache that reminds me I'm still a little bruised from last night.

"Stop thinking, sweetness. It's your turn to ask a question." Then his voice turns sly. "If you can hold up that long."

His fingers return to my panties, only this time he parts my wet folds with his long, clever fingers, sliding up and down but somehow missing my clit on each stroke. My arm wobbles underneath me, and I arch into his hand, but every motion to bring him closer to where I want him has him pulling back teasingly. A frustrated whimper escapes my throat.

My mind is utterly blank of questions, and I know I have to end this soon if I want to win. Why does winning suddenly matter so much to me? I've never won anything before.

His fingers circle tortuously around my clit again, not quite touching.

Biting my lip, I yank at the ties on his pants, loosening them enough that I can pull them down slightly, exposing his hard length. I can't help my pleased gasp. He isn't as thick as Jaykob, but he's big enough that I know I'll have trouble with him. Lucky lets out a smug, happy sound that tugs a return smile back to my own lips.

Wrapping my hand around the base of his cock, I give it a tentative stroke, then another, more confident. In reward, he finally slides that teasing finger against my clit.

"Oh!" I cry out, a shudder racking my body. My legs wobble, and he kisses the back of my knee again, scraping his teeth against my skin as he increases pressure against my clit. Then his fingers part and press inside me, disturbing my clumsy rhythm on the scorching, velvet length in my palm. I'm adrift, whirling. I can hear the obscene, wet smack of his pumping fingers. I clench around him greedily, needing more.

"Fuck," he swears on a groan, "you're soaked."

I suck back a sob and realize I have to up the ante fast before my legs give out. Before I can think about it, I remove my hand from his cock and flatten my hand on his tight stomach for balance. Then I lift onto my tiptoes and angle myself over him.

My lips brush over the glistening, florid tip of him, then part, sending warm breath down his length. He makes a surprised sound, and his fingers hesitate inside of me. I clamp around them again as I slide his swollen, needy cock inside my mouth, swirling my tongue around him.

He only just catches me by the hair to steady me as he collapses. His back hits the mat, and I fall with him, the sudden movement burying him deep in my throat.

I lift my head in shock, licking him as I go, then beam at him. "I won!"

Lucky snorts a laugh, then his fingers tighten in my hair. "Sure did. Congrats. Very proud." His voice is raw and throaty. "Now have mercy on me and put that sexy as fuck mouth back on my dick."

My nipples tighten in my bra at the desperate request, and I obey, ridiculously thrilled. I realize I'm still mostly dressed, but it really doesn't matter right now. As soon as my lips close around him, he moans helplessly, his hips rolling like he can't help himself.

That's it, it's official: I'm a sex goddess.

He wraps his other arm around my waist and tugs me backwards. I pause; I'm kneeling over his face.

"Don't stop on me now, beautiful." It's a plea, not an order, and suddenly I'm powerful—in control of giving or taking away his pleasure. And, with a desperate, warm ache, I realize I want to make him happy. I want to drive him wild.

"God damn. It's been . . . so long," he groans.

I let my mouth slide over him wetly, before tightening my lips for a firmer stroke. I quickly realize I can't suck to his base without the wide head of him hitting my gag reflex so I wrap my hand around him again to make up the extra length.

He lets me work him over for a minute, testing different rhythms until he shudders encouragingly. Then he pulls my panties aside again and yanks me down onto his face, parting his open mouth right over my heat and sliding his tongue around my clit in a firm stroke.

I cry out around his cock, and he chuckles against me, those wicked lips as delicious as I imagined. More delicious, even.

It's different to Jaykob's wild, messy hunger. Lucky savors me like I'm made of candy, with teasing, naughty tastes. We find a rhythm together and as his fingers join his mouth, rubbing and fucking my tight, wet hole, a now-familiar tension begins to crest in my center. I shiver and squirm over him, my mouth growing wetter and sloppier and more frantic.

A part of me is appalled by the mess I'm making, another part is worried I might suffocate him like this, but the needy side of me —fueled by the lost, wild noises Lucky is making—tells them to shut the hell up. My rhythm is fast and frantic and his hand wraps over mine, steadying me, tightening as he pumps my hand along his length to my mouth. The tangy, delicious taste of him coats my tongue, and his smell fills my nose.

I pull back slightly. "Lucky," I beg, breathless.

"Hmm?" His tongue circles me, and I shudder.

Words are hazy, hard to find. "Lucky, please. I need you to fuck me." In this moment, the wicked word fits in my mouth. In this moment, my mouth is filthy, my mind debauched, my body lost to carnal, wanton sin. This moment is for cocks and cunts and tongues and obscene orgasms. "I need— I want you to—"

His tongue falters on me, and my body wants to scream.

Don't stop. I want him inside me desperately.

"Lucky!" I repeat urgently. "God—"

Then the fingers that had been plunging inside me crook and rub against an incredible, magic spot, and he sucks hard on my clit. Unable to help myself, I explode against his fingers, pleasure shooting through my spine and arching my back.

As if my release sets his off, his cock tightens under my fist, and he thrusts up into it desperately until I take him in my mouth again.

"Fuck, fuck. Take it, beautiful, taste me. Drink me down. Every fucking drop."

Caught off guard and shuddering through my climax, I swallow the hot spurts that hit the back of my throat.

When he's done, I tremble against him, my tongue still lapping in tiny licks, until he tugs my head back and off him.

Lucky gives me a few open-mouthed, carnal kisses as I sit up on his face, riding out my last shudders of pleasure. His fingers slide out of me, and I sigh. In moments, he has me spun around and tucked against his side, his hands running over every bit of skin he can reach.

Lucky presses a kiss to my forehead. "Good game, beautiful. You're a natural."

I go to scowl at him, thinking he's teasing again, but the warm, happy light in his eyes melts it before it begins. Giving up, I huff a laugh into his chest. "You're impossible."

Part of me wants to ask why he didn't do what I asked, why he didn't finish inside me, but I'm too shivery with pleasure to care overmuch.

I lift a hand to my mouth and surreptitiously wipe the moisture from around my lips. His hand is lazy in my now sex-fucked hair.

"You, um, wouldn't have a breath mint would you?" I mumble, embarrassed.

Lucky snorts, then starts laughing. He pushes me onto my back and then the hand in my hair fists as he brings his mouth to mine and kisses me deep. His tongue works mine and, despite my very recent orgasm and the fact that I *know* where both of our mouths have just been, my body begins to tingle.

When he finally pulls back slightly, he rubs his nose against mine.

"You're too cute. Don't stress so much." Lucky grins, and his dimple creases his cheek. "Just remember, it's been years since any of us have gotten laid. We're happy for what we can get."

Ouch.

My smile withers.

Lucky's eyes widen. "Whoa, hey, I don't mean it like that! I just meant that something like how your breath smells is so far down the list of priorities right now. Y'know, when I have a fucking half-naked bombshell in my arms after she just blew my mind. Never mind what Jaykob said. He's a complete asshat and even he is clearly into you."

My cheeks burn and I try to twist away to avoid his earnest gaze, but he presses his forehead to mine.

"If you think I'm anything but completely kid-in-a-candy-store-who-also-has-ten-million-puppies level of happy to have you here, you need a brain transplant."

It is *really* hard to argue when a man's slightly sweaty and decadently hard body is pressed up against you, I decide, and I slowly relax back into him. It's amazing how he does that. Just smashes right through every insecurity I have.

A moment later, I'm running my fingers through his short beard, enjoying the soft, springy bristles.

"I like your beard," I whisper.

I'm fairly sure my inner thighs are now thoroughly abraded, to add to the collection of sex badges I'm accumulating, but I'll take it. Turns out, beard burn is hot. When his lips curve, I trace their shape as well. He lets me touch him as much as I want, watching me with warm, hooded eyes, like he's just soaking in the happiness the same way I am.

"You want some more monkey mix?" he eventually asks.

I laugh, sitting up beside him, keeping myself in the curve of his body. Touching him like this is addictive. I never knew I was a cuddler. "Are you sure that's a good idea? I'm a bit of a lightweight. I'll be no good to you if I have much more."

He teases a lock of hair that's hanging loose over my shoulder. "Oh," he says casually, "I just figured you might need some Dutch courage. Y'know. Considering you have that dare to do and all."

My liquid body freezes solid again, and I stare at him with wide eyes. "Um. Right now?"

"Oh yeah, beautiful. Right now."

CHAPTER 18

BEAU

SURVIVAL TIP #301
*When in doubt,
fight it out.*

The first drops of daylight spill through the trees, a lazy, watery shine that steeps into the darkness, brightening it in slow drips. The apple tree stretches its limbs to an easy breeze, and Bristlebrook nestles into the gray cliff face, sleepy and shadowed in the early morning light.

Hooking my foot behind Jasper's leg, I slam my shoulder into his chest and bring him down hard into the grass.

Again.

Today really isn't his day.

Then again, today doesn't seem to be anyone's day, except maybe Lucky's.

The five of us usually meet out on the lawn at oh-five-hundred for our daily workout, but this morning Jayk's barn was silent and sullen, Dom had to drag Jasper out of the surveillance room when he didn't turn up—by God Almighty, I don't know why he was in there at that hour and not sleeping like a normal human—and

Lucky strolled in out of the woods a full half hour late, grinning from ear to ear.

Of course, I may have *also* tried to bail on training this morning. I had grand plans of stealing Eden away for a few hours, taking her for a stroll, picking wildflowers sparkling with morning dew, kissing her frosty fingers warm, and settling in on a thick picnic rug with a thermos of piping hot tea to watch the sun rise . . . except that when I went looking for her, she and Lucky were nowhere to be found.

But Dom was, and he dragged me outside like a wayward puppy right alongside Jasper, once again blowing to hell any chance I had of spending time alone with Eden.

Damn it, where did Lucky and Eden go? I know they were in the house at some point yesterday—it was impossible for *any of us* to miss the Twister extravaganza. Lucky, little asshole that he is, set it up in the music room, and that damn room is *designed* for sound to travel. Their giggles, squeals, and moans floated through every single room of the lodge.

And I can't even be mad about it.

Those sounds are just about the most delightful thing I've heard in years, and I'm stupid happy that Eden had a good day, even if it wasn't with me.

Wouldn't have stopped me from hauling her out of Lucky's arms the second I tracked her down, though.

Under me, Jasper makes a sour sound in the back of his throat, then taps out. I don't let him up this time. His face is red and sweaty—it always is when we spar—but there are rough, tired rings around his eyes that I don't like, and he's been feral as a pissed-off badger all morning.

I frown down at him. "Where's your head today? That's the fourth time I've pinned you."

"This is a waste of my time." His eyes flash dangerously. "I should be on surveillance. Do you know how difficult it will be to make up two hours of missed footage on thirty-seven cameras?"

I grimace. "How close are they now?"

"They stopped last night and set up camp," he says in a clipped voice. "Last I saw, they hadn't yet moved."

Easing my grip, I soothe, "So it's not an immediate concern. We can help you with the cameras later." I hesitate, then add in an undertone, "But are you sure that's what this is about?"

His face takes on such an unholy light that I back up fast and watch him warily as he shoves to his feet. With a chilling curl of his lip, he yanks down his rumpled, grass-stained shirt.

Beside us, Dom breaks Lucky's hold around his neck, then throws him flying over his shoulder and down hard into the dirt.

Lucky wheezes.

Jasper fires a vicious glare at Dom. "Would you be careful? I was under the impression that we're here to train, not to snap one another's necks."

He whips his towel off a low-hanging branch and swipes at his flushed forehead.

Dom catches me looking, then rolls his eyes skyward, and I cough to hide a laugh.

"Pulling punches in training is a fast way to get people killed in action. We don't do that here. You'd know that by now if you didn't keep skipping out on us." Rubbing his neck where Lucky half-strangled him, Dom adds wryly, "And my neck is just fine, thanks for the concern."

Jasper gives him a withering look.

Lucky groans good-naturedly as he sits up. "You know, the rear naked choke always ends differently in my head."

Ignoring that, Dom nods at him. "It was good. You're coming in faster. Much better than last week."

Lucky shrugs one shoulder, but there's a pleased glow to his smile as he grabs his bottle for a drink. Guy would roll over and show his belly for a compliment, I swear.

Dom reaches out a hand to help Lucky up, but instead of taking it, Lucky launches forward into a somersault, somehow ending up on his feet. He bounces on his toes with the same buoyant energy he's had all morning, as if he's burning extra bright today to make up for Jasper's gloom.

"Don't get too cocky." Dom frowns. "Your offense is strong, but you leave yourself too exposed. If you don't fix up your evasive maneuvers, you're going to catch bullets sooner or later."

Lucky re-ties his loosening hair, then waves his hand dismissively. "Don't you know? Tragic hero is my aesthetic." His dimple flashes. "Just like bossy jerk is yours, grumpy Hulk is Jayk's, self-righteous sweetheart is Beau's, and sexy nerd is Eden's."

I choke on my water. "I am *not* self-righteous!" I scoff. "I'm a doctor. I *help* people!"

Lucky inclines his head at Dom. "See?"

"Idiot." I twist up my towel and whip it so it cracks against his ass. He yelps, cackling as he spins to face me, and Dom snorts.

"What does that make mine, then?"

Silky. Indolent. The words slice through the levity in a single, neat cut. Despite his still-pink cheeks, Jasper's glittering eyes warn of poisoned waters and blackened, roiling skies.

Lucky straightens, and I don't know why it strikes me now, but I realize for the first time how much older he is than when I first met him. There's a seriousness and a hardness in him that seems suddenly obvious now he's stopped smiling.

He looks Jasper over. "That makes you the one getting saved, I guess." He shrugs and picks up his bottle again. "Especially if you're letting yourself get pinned four times in one morning."

Oh, shit.

I freeze, glancing between the two of them. Watching Jasper's face is like watching an avalanche descend, wintry and ruinous. Lucky casually sips from his water bottle.

For the four years we've been at Bristlebrook—and years before that, even—the two of them have circled around each other with gravitational force. Now, within just a few days, they're on a collision course.

Maybe Dom is right. Not about all of it, of course, but there's no pretending that Eden isn't stirring up a whole pot of emotions here.

"Did I or did I not see you writhing on the ground yourself just moments ago?" Jasper snipes.

Lucky tilts his head as if puzzled. "Which time? I've been rolling around all night."

Dom and I exchange a loaded married-couple look.

I raise my brows, and glance at them without moving my head. *Should we do something?*

Dom lowers his chin, then tilts it in a negative. *Not our business.*

"Don't test me, Lucien." Jasper takes a sharp step forward, and I ease up onto the balls of my feet anyway in case I need to intervene. "You forget, I've been watching the cameras. What were you and Eden doing out in the woods? I saw the two of you leave together."

Lucky smiles, maliciously innocent. "I didn't forget." He pauses, sliding a sidelong look at Dom that's about three shades too casual. "Hey, did you spend much time in your room this morning?"

That catches the boss's attention, and Dom narrows his eyes. "No." When Lucky's lips roll in like he's trying to hide a grin, Dom demands, "*Why?*"

Lucky's eyes widen, and he shrugs. "No reason."

I groan.

The man can be reckless to the point of stupid for a good adventure. One time he begged me to race him on a climb up the cliffside—only to realize it's a lot fucking harder to climb down fifty feet without gear than it is to go up. We waited on a tiny little ledge, arms aching, for two hours before Dom and Jasper came searching for us, and another hour on top of that while they worked out how to get belay equipment up to us. And the idiot laughed the whole time. Of course, he wasn't smiling overmuch after a livid Jasper got him back to Bristlebrook.

Point is, Lucky is not to be trusted.

"Lucky," I warn, narrowing my eyes on him too. "Why were you in the woods?"

Mischief dances over his lean features. "Sorry, Doc, that's need to know."

I jump to my feet. "Where is Eden?" I demand anxiously . . . and immediately cringe. I sound like my ma after she learned a burlesque club was moving into town.

Dom snorts, and the derisive sound pricks at me like a thousand needles. It's not enough to crap all over my chance at happiness, he has to mock me for it too?

"Eden's inside. She came in through the caves 'cause she was afraid of—" Lucky stops, eyes sparkling with fiendish innocence. "You know what, never mind. She's freshening up."

Thank God she's safe at least.

My eyes drift back to Dom, who seems to have lost interest in the conversation.

"Have you talked to her at all since we got back?" I ask him abruptly, apparently just as unable as Lucky and Jasper to keep my mess contained today.

He tenses but slings his towel around his neck like he's unbothered. "I've been busy."

"So make time."

There's too much testiness in my tone, but my temper is growing shorter and shorter with him. He's not even trying—he barely spoke to her at dinner, and he's still interrupting every potential moment for me to be alone with her. I'm starting to wonder if I'm wishing on a star here. Maybe it was a pipe dream, this idea of us staying close and making a family together with the right girl. Something born of teenage hormones and a friendship that hadn't really been tested yet.

Dom doesn't respond, leaning down to pick up his shirt. He sniffs it, then grimaces and sighs.

"Why don't I have any clean clothes?" he asks the group instead, changing the subject.

I narrow my eyes. "Because Eden took over the washing and Jayk still hasn't fixed the machine. And because there are six of us in the house now and somebody keeps chasing her off, making it so she wants to hide in her room instead of being around us."

"I'll tell Jayk to make the washing machine a priority," he says, ignoring the rest.

"I hope you plan to apologize first, for your assumptions the other day," Jasper cuts in sharply.

Cocking a brow, Dom asks, "Have *you*?"

"I have." Jasper grimaces. "It didn't go well."

"Were you nice, though?" Lucky mutters.

I run a hand over my hair, frustrated by them, by Dom, by Jayk and all of it, when I see the curtains in Eden's room twitch. A small, pale face peeks between them.

And just like that, sweet heat slides like syrup through my veins.

"We should do one more set," I blurt.

Beside me, Lucky frowns, then follows my glance. He sneaks me a grin where the others can't see, then wipes the smile and turns. "I agree. One more to finish."

Dom and Jasper stare at us.

"I'm going to shower," Dom finally says, forehead crinkling. "But knock yourselves out."

Jasper shakes his head, then follows him as he heads inside.

"Bet I can embarrass you in front of our girl," Lucky teases.

Our girl.

After Dom's rejection, the phrase is like cool water on a livid burn. *Our* girl. Not just mine and Dom's. Mine and Lucky's. Jayk's. Jasper's.

I never pictured the three of them when I thought of The Plan . . . but I could be okay with some modifications.

If that's what Eden wants.

If they treat her right.

"Eden's going to be embarrassed *for* you once I show her what I can do." I step back and whip off my shirt. "I've got moves you can only dream of."

"I'll let you know, since your *moves* usually put me to sleep," Lucky quips, tearing his own shirt off.

We're both damp with sweat, and daylight has finally soaked in through the forest enough that it gleams off our skin.

Lucky darts forward quickly, feinting up, then sweeping low in the next instant to try to take my legs out. I'm familiar enough with his fighting style to anticipate the tricky move, and I swerve to the side so he slides past me. I aim a quick kick to his ribs while he's low, but he's already spinning away from me, coming up with a right hook that I block and follow with an uppercut. Back and forth we fight, pushing and pulling, straining and slamming into one another until we're sweat-slick and showing off and snorting with laughter.

Finally, Lucky makes the mistake of glancing over at the distant face still peeking down at us through the curtains, and I manage to kick out the back of his knees and knock him, face first, into the earth.

"Fuck," he groans.

I crouch beside him. "It's just like Dom said," I tell him smugly. "Got to work on those evasive maneuvers."

Brushing my hands on my pants, I step on Lucky's bare back and saunter over to say hello to the pretty girl I've been missing since we met.

CHAPTER 19

BEAU

As soon as I turn toward the house, the face disappears and her curtains are yanked back into place. A slow, stupid smile works its way across my face.

Nice try, little subbie.

I let myself into the sitting room, planning on hunting her down . . . only I don't need to.

"Oh. Good morning, Beau."

Eden looks down on me from the top of the stairs, haloed by the lights behind her. The sight of her slides into me like a needle, and I'm not sure if I'm being infected with the cure or some terminal disease. Eden's in a cute little dress today—a pink one that sets off her mahogany hair and brings out the flustered color in her cheeks. Her hair is out of its usual bun, and I'm surprised to see it flows almost to her waist.

I want to see it spread out beneath her as she comes apart.

"Mornin', darlin'," I finally say, remembering I have a voice.

Her mouth swings up on one side in a sweet smile, even while her eyes dip down and linger over my bare chest. Seeming to remember herself, she snaps them back up.

"Were you working out?" Eden asks, pure and innocent as her namesake.

And a filthy little liar, apparently.

I bite my lower lip, then release it with an amused smack. "You just finish cleaning up?"

She smooths out invisible crinkles in her dress. "Mm-hmm."

Like she wasn't just staring at us like she wants me to pocket her eyes just so she can keep them on my ass.

Crossing my arms, I lean against the wall. "Come on down here, then."

She casts her eyes around the room, lingering on the partly open curtains behind me.

"Is, um, Dom around?" she asks.

Dom.

Jealousy cuts through my amusement in a way that never used to happen before. Before, we always shared. Before, having a subbie ask me about Dom would have filled me with satisfaction. Now I'm just wondering if she's asking because she likes him more.

God *damn* Heather.

"He's gone upstairs for a bit."

Eden darts a startled glance behind her, then starts down the stairs, a definite haste to her steps. When she reaches me, she looks back at the top floor with a frown between her brows, anxiously adjusting her glasses. "Will, um . . . will he be out soon, do you think?"

My annoyance turns to confusion. She's not asking because she wants to see him. She's asking because she *doesn't*.

I sigh. Why doesn't that make me feel any better?

"Not sure, darlin'. I'm not his keeper."

Casually, I stretch my arm up on the wall so I'm leaning over her, then flex my pecs. Just a bit.

Eden blinks and then focuses her attention back on me fully. She looks down, then jolts as she notices how close we're standing. The delicate line of her throat works as she swallows. Her eyes lift until she's peering up at me through her lashes, and her fists tangle in her pink skirt.

"Hi," she says again, softly.

My heart melts in my chest with one tiny splash. It's as natural as breathing to press a light kiss against her rosy lips.

"Hi," I murmur back.

I win that small, shy smile from her again, and I'm about to steal another kiss when Lucky bursts through the door, whistling obnoxiously. Eden jumps a foot in the air, pressing a searing, steadying hand against my chest.

When recognition crosses her face, she scowls.

Huh. Not the warm response Lucky usually evokes. Especially not the one I thought she'd be giving him after what I heard yesterday.

He strolls over and leans against the wall on Eden's other side, effectively pinning her between us, and presses a kiss to her cheek. "Hey, beautiful."

"Lucky?" I prompt. "Do you mind?"

It does sound a lot like "fuck off" when I say it out loud like that.

Lucky looks at me in surprise. "Oh! Of course. Sorry." He leans up and kisses me on the cheek.

"You're beautiful too, Beau," he says seriously.

I snort, but Eden sucks in an audible breath, eyes darting between the two of us from under her glasses, then back at our half-naked bodies pressed around her. Her hand absently rubs against my chest for one cock-stirring moment before she snatches it back, cradling it against her throat as if she felt the blistering heat as fiercely as I did.

"S-sorry," she stammers.

I give her a slow smile. "You don't ever need to apologize for touching me, Eden."

"Yeah. Or for peeking through your curtains and eye fucking us for forty minutes. We're cool with that too," Lucky chimes in cheerfully.

Eden's head whips toward him. "What?" Her voice is pure panic. "I did *not*—"

My lips twitch. "Word to the wise, darlin', it ain't a real good idea to lie to your dom."

Her mouth opens, then snicks shut, and I watch as the rose color in her cheeks deepens, then rolls into the tips of her ears.

"You really saw me?" she asks in a small voice.

"Oh yeah." I grin. "We saw you."

She squeals, burying her face in her hands.

Lucky snickers and ruffles her hair. "I'm going to make breakfast. You watch that sweet butt of yours, Eden."

She bats his hand away and glares after him as he leaves.

At my confused look, she scowls. "Lucky is the devil himself, and if he gets me killed, I would appreciate it if you buried him next to me so I can haunt him in our next life."

I frown. "I thought y'all played a game of Twister. That doesn't sound—"

"Have you ever played one of Lucky's games, Beau?" she asks in her gorgeous, husky voice. The blue-gray of her eyes spears me, not seeming at all shy in that moment.

The sound of my name rolling off her tongue hits me low in my stomach.

"A few times," I tell her, surreptitiously looking her over for burn marks. "I'm usually his best bet for anything close to a game."

"Well, I'm surprised you escaped unscathed," she hisses, darting another nervous glance at the stairs. Then she blinks and bites her lip with a little wince. "I don't want to talk about Lucky."

I don't really want to talk about Lucky either.

Taking her hand, I lace our fingers together and tug gently. "Come sit with me for a minute."

Hesitating, Eden looks up at the top floor, then at me. But when she meets my eyes, her shoulders relax, and she follows me easily.

I walk backwards toward the sitting-room chairs, enjoying the bashful little looks she's giving me. As we sit, I shift the med bag I dumped when I got back the other day.

To my surprise, she looks it over curiously. "Are those your medical supplies?"

"Some of them."

It's not often anyone pays any mind to my gear. Not unless they need me to patch them up, that is. Or when they get carried away on the booze and come begging for painkillers.

"May I?" she asks.

Tickled by her interest, I unzip it for her and lay it out on the coffee table. She leans over the bag, examining the contents with open fascination. She turns a bottle with one slender finger.

"You have diazepam, morphine—oh, and a cricothyrotomy kit! Narcan, antibiotics . . . " She shakes her head, and her hair shivers prettily around her shoulders. "You could have bars of solid gold in here and they'd be worth less."

I nod absently, then nudge her with a questioning look. "How do you know about all this? The guys went through first responder training, and some days I still doubt they'd be able to perform a crike, even with the kit."

Eden sits back. Rueful eyes meet mine. When she twists her mouth like that, I notice how her nose crinkles . . . though I have no idea why that detail should have my heart thundering like a herd of horses.

"I don't know that I could perform one, either. I've only read about them." One shoulder lifts lightly. "I studied what I could, but the herbology books were more helpful, since I didn't have access to medicine like this. But I'll take any tips you have, in case this doesn't work out."

Something in my gut drops. "Why wouldn't this work out?"

Dom. Damn it, I knew he was scaring her off.

"Oh, I just mean, I . . . " Eden pushes her glasses up the bridge of her nose. "I'm not sure this is sustainable. What we're doing. And all these rules . . . I don't know that it . . . That *I'm*—"

"Eden, you don't need to worry. You're perfect—more than enough for any one of us." I take her hand again, rubbing my thumb over her knuckles. "No one's kicking you out. You haven't done anything wrong."

She stares down at our hands, and a strange look crosses over her face. After a moment, she shakes her head, disentangling our fingers. "I know I haven't," she says quietly. "I'm following your rules perfectly."

Something about that hits all wrong, but I can't pinpoint why.

Then she takes a deep breath and smiles up at me nervously, and I'm distracted by the curve of her breasts. The trepidatious quaver of her lips.

By all that's holy, she's the prettiest thing I've ever seen.

"Actually, I did want to ask about something," she blurts. "Ask *you* about something, specifically, I mean. You're a doctor, you see." She winces. "I don't know why I said that like you don't know. Oh, I'm saying this all wrong, but *because* you're a doctor, I was going to ask—"

My lips twitch despite myself, watching her get all flustered. My darker side wants to come out and play, but unlike some of the others, I do actually have some restraint, so I force myself to be patient.

"You want to ask me a medical question?" I prompt, having mercy on her.

Eden blows out a breath. "Yes. Yes, a medical question," she agrees, tugging one of her elegant fingers anxiously. "I wanted to talk about—To ask about—" She clears her throat. "You said the other day you would do a check-up for me. So we could revisit the conversation about protection. We're going to need to do it sooner or later, isn't that right?"

Blinking in surprise, I study her. "Darlin'—"

She rushes on. "I do know that we need to think of diseases, and be careful, but you said you were as sure as you could be that the others were clean, right? It would be good if I could offer the same thing, is what I was thinking. But I don't want to impose on you, because you're so busy, and I really don't want you to feel uncomfortable—"

"Eden—" I try again, amusement bubbling.

She frowns but doesn't seem to hear me. "I'm not even sure how we do this without testing available. Do you still take a swab? No, that would be pointless, I suppose. So I guess you must just ask me questions, and—"

"Eden!" I break in, voice edged hard in stern command. "*Enough.*"

At my tone, she pulls back, her mouth snapping shut, and her hands clutching at her skirt. Her eyes darken with awareness, and spots of ardent color appear on her cheeks.

As much as I like her sweet, trusting looks, I also like this . . . the fearful way she trembles, caught in that nectarous place between arousal and alarm.

Hiding a smirk, I lay my arm along the back of the couch behind her. If she thinks I'm all apple pie and slow talk, she's in for the shock of her life.

"You want me to give you a check-up, is that what you're askin'?" I drawl.

She stares at me wordlessly, her breaths shallow. Her pink tongue darts out to swipe at her lower lip, and the wet trail it leaves is nothing short of profane.

"I— Maybe?" Her voice is gorgeous, husky. Ripe with desire.

"That's very considerate of you," I tell her, and start playing with the loose strands of her hair. Goosebumps lift the small hairs on her arms. "Gettin' yourself prepared so we can all spread you out and fill you up with our cum."

Eden's hand flies to her throat, and her pulse pounds like frantic wings against the delicate skin. "Beau . . ."

My cock thickens, and I part my legs to make room, drawing her eyes. They press shut, then flutter open again, her pupils blown as she takes me in.

"You want me to do it here?" I ask thickly. "Open you up and see where you're all pink and pretty? Right here, where anyone could walk in?"

My finger trails down the line of her throat, then along her collarbone, following the low collar of her dress. My fingertip grazes the tops of her breasts, and she trembles.

"Does it make you wet? Thinking about me spilling inside that sweet pussy of yours? You want me to take you bare?" I run my other hand up the inside of her thigh, and her legs part so eagerly that I need to adjust myself. "Do you want me to fill you up? Or do you want me to paint those pretty breasts?"

Eden's breath is snared by a moan as I taste her lips with the barest brush of my tongue. "I'm askin' as your doctor, pet."

And as if a whirlwind had blown through the room, I feel her arousal snuff out. She stiffens under me, but I'm already pulling back, searching her face.

"What's the matter?" I ask gently. "Talk to me, darlin'."

She closes her legs, eyes averted, and slowly pulls the fallen strap of her dress back over her shoulder, not speaking.

Finally, she asks, "What do you see me as, Beau?"

"See you as? What do you mean?" I reach out to touch her hand, and she pulls back, out of reach.

My stomach drops as I realize I've hit her somewhere soft.

Her eyes meet mine, soft and serious. "What is my role here?"

I hesitate a moment too long, trying to work out what answer she's wanting here. "You're here for us. So we can keep you safe."

I know I got it wrong when her shoulders square.

"Where were you and Dom the other day? What happened during your 'scuffle'?" She purses her lips. "What aren't you telling me?"

I grimace, shifting. "Where's this coming from? You don't need to worry about any of that, pet."

Eden's hands clench around her skirt, her lip trembling . . . but it still takes me a second to recognize it for what it is.

Anger.

She takes a deep breath, then smooths her dress back out deliberately.

"I'm not your *pet*, Beau," she says. "I am your equal, despite what you all seem to think. I'm more than just your plaything. I can choose to leave at any time if this isn't working for me." Her chin lifts with quiet pride. "I'm here for myself—not for you."

"I don't want a mouse for a pet."

Dom really should take five minutes to speak with her. Eden is no mouse.

She's a force to behold.

And his stupid, patronizing plan is going to drive her away from us.

"Eden, if any of us have made you feel . . . if *I've* made you feel—"

A door slams loud enough to echo through the house, cutting me off and shattering the serious moment.

"LUCKY," Dom roars.

All color drains from Eden's face, leaving her white to her lips.

Ah, shoot, now that's a shame. I give her a regretful look.

Maybe Lucky really will get her killed.

CHAPTER 20

EDEN

SURVIVAL TIP #245
Find the biggest predator you can.
Then hide behind them.

O h, *shit*," I swear. All thoughts of their silly rules, and my
place here, and being kept like a stray dog vanish in a crash
of terror.

Lucky peeks his head from the kitchen just as Dom rounds the
top corridor, livid. In seconds, he's rushed down the stairs and is
stalking for the kitchen.

I should be moving. I shouldn't be here. But my head feels
light. Floaty.

Am I going to faint?

I might faint.

The rest of Lucky pops through the door, with a huge, shit-
eating grin on his face.

Dom grabs the front of his shirt, shoves the smaller man
against the wall, and crowds him with every broad-shouldered inch
he has. "Give it back now, Lucky, and I won't take your head off.
We had a deal."

I lift half out of my seat, debating whether I should rush in and stop Dom again or just let Lucky get the ass kicking he probably deserves. My hands twist into a white-knuckled knot in front of me.

Beau looks over at the scene, leaning back in his chair to watch, seemingly entertained. Lucky is still grinning, that *damnable* dimple of his winking like a bad joke. I dart a look at Beau, like he might help, and he glances back, giving me a curious once-over. I can practically see him putting the pieces together.

Lucky clears his throat. "Technically the deal was that *I* couldn't take it from your room."

That catches my attention. A low, sick moan escapes me, and Beau's brows shoot up in surprise. I need to go.

Now.

Dom freezes, then his head turns until he looks at me. Like something out of a horror movie, I wonder if it will keep spinning.

"*You* stole the bazooka from my room?"

I back up a step, releasing a gust of nervous air. "I— *Well*, I—"

Beau rubs a hand over his lips, not quite able to stop his stunned amusement from showing.

My eyes shoot back to Dom as his expression darkens. He releases Lucky and steps toward me, his face set in narrow-eyed disbelief. Dangerous intent lines his muscles.

"You went into my room." *Step.* "Without permission." *Step.* "Rifled through my closet." *Step.* "And *stole* from me?"

Panic. PANIC. Damn it, why can't I *move*? I'm frozen still; someone's dipped me in ice.

"I— It was a bet. I had to. I lost, and I *had* to do a dare, and I didn't have a choice, and I—"

Dom's brows lower. It isn't a pleasant expression. "Interesting that you're more afraid of Lucky." *Step.* "Than me."

He's close now, and I'm quivering. For the first time in years, I start praying under my breath. My legs need to start working. Yesterday.

God, he's huge. Was he always this big?

Dom tenses, and I see the moment he decides to pounce.

Lucky must too, because he yells, "Run, Eden!"

Dom lunges and—*finally*—startled into movement, I twist away with a shriek. As I try to flee, though, I slam into Beau's chest. With blatant enjoyment, he grasps my upper arms, and I give him a terrified, wide-eyed look.

When did he move? How did he get behind me?

"It'll go easier if you submit to your punishment, darlin'," he murmurs, his high school–sweetheart face filled with predatory delight.

I squeak in fear and, before I can think the stupid, stupid idea through, I kick Beau hard in the shin. Utter shock crosses his features, and his grip loosens.

Before he can recover, I spin out of his arms just as Dom pushes forward to grab me. Dom stumbles into Beau, who reaches out to steady him.

I don't waste any more time, already darting out of the glass doors and across the front lawn to Lucky's wild cries of, "Run like the wind, babe!"

I dare a look over my shoulder as I bolt outside. Dom has pushed off Beau and is moving quickly toward the glass doors after me. I can't help but shriek again and glance back as I scatter.

Lucky, I'm going to murder *you for this!* I swear inwardly as his bright, elfin laughter follows me from the building.

I can hear Dom's footsteps too close behind me as I scram. My pulse thunders in my veins. The door to Jaykob's workshop is open, and I adjust my course.

"Stop, Eden!" Dom growls.

No, no, no. No *way* am I stopping. Submit to punishment, my ass!

I put in an extra burst of speed and fly toward the building, taking full advantage of my slight lead. I round the door at speed, the momentum sending me crashing against a bench just inside.

Standing by a half-dismantled washing machine, Jaykob looks up, startled. Grease smears his white tank and the left side of his face, but he runs a bemused look over *my* disheveled appearance.

The nerve.

Hearing Dom's footsteps, I squeak again and run right for Jayk, his muscles and tattoos and irritated scowl seeming a beacon of safety.

"What the fuck—"

I duck around him and bury myself in his back.

"Lucky made me do something," I explain calmly. Or that's what I meant to do. In reality, my voice sounds high and breathless as a rubber duck being strangled by a four-year-old. "Please, please, please just help me and I'll do anything you want."

Jaykob tenses for a moment, then snorts as Dom stalks into his workshop. I clutch at the back of his shirt like it's a lifeline, suddenly unsure why I thought *Jaykob*, of all people, would be willing to save me. He hasn't spoken to me since our night together. Though, since Dom went after him yesterday, maybe he'll be more inclined to take my side.

Oh, good Lord in heaven, I'm an idiot. A *bazooka*? How stupid could I be?

"Hand her over, Jayk," Dom grits out.

Jaykob tosses down an oily rag and leans against the washing machine, turning slightly so he can look down at me. The bemused look is still on his face.

Please, please, please, I silently beg up at him through my lashes, for the first time wishing I knew exactly how "womanly wiles" were meant to work.

After a long moment, he finally looks back at Dom and drawls, "Nah. She's good here."

My bones go weak, and I melt into his side. He shifts so I'm pressed more closely against him. Peeking, I see Dom standing tall and dark and frightening just a few feet away. Uneasily, I wonder if

Jayk would even be *able* to take him. He's huge and deadly-seeming in his own right, but there's something about Dom that commands absolute fear and respect. Lethal violence lives in the hard slash of his jaw and the blunt strength of his wide, rough hands. Hands that could break every bone in my body to use as toothpicks.

Jaykob's voice hardens. "You can get out of my shop now."

Dom crosses his arms as he studies Jayk.

"Seriously?" he asks dryly.

He doesn't sound angry. Bolstered by Jaykob's warm strength, I study Dom. His stance seems relaxed.

Jayk lifts one shoulder in a shrug. "Go beat on Lucky. He put her up to it."

"She stole a bazooka," Dom retorts.

Yep, definitely dry.

Jayk rolls his eyes. "Yeah, she steal it so she can play with it? The circus rat has a thing for explosives. It's why you hid it in the first place."

Dom sighs, then turns his golden gaze on me. Rather than molten, blazing fury which, let's face it, is the main expression I'm used to seeing from him, all I see is firm exasperation.

"Stay out of my room. You try and take anything else that doesn't belong to you, and I'll hold you down and have Beau beat your ass so you can't sit for a week. Running off to Jayk won't save you then either. Understood?"

I flush and duck my head. "Yes, understood. Sorry, sir."

Dom nods once, and gives Jaykob a final, puzzled glance before he shakes his head and leaves.

I heave a sigh of relief.

"Ohhh, thank you, thank you, thank you," I murmur reverently, not sure if I'm praying to God or thanking Jayk.

When he doesn't say anything, I look up. He's staring down at me, almost as puzzled as Dom. I'm still nestled into his side but I can't bring myself to move, enjoying the comfort of his closeness. I become very aware of the delicious, very male scent of him. I color, shifting.

"What?" I ask.

I touch my hair, annoyed with the strands that became tangled in my flight, and my glasses slip down. Jayk nudges them back up my nose, careful not to touch my skin with his oil-greased fingers. My lips part in surprise at the gentle touch.

"Why the hell did you run in here?" he asks, sounding uncomfortable.

My gaze drops from his eyes. It lands on his lips, and I vividly remember how they felt branding my skin. Shivering slightly, I press closer again. There's nowhere to go, of course. We're as close as we can get with our clothes still on. The adrenaline is settling but my body still feels wired, electric.

"I'm not sure, I—"

Jayk shifts again, this time moving so I'm no longer pressed against his side. He nudges me with small, insistent pushes, until I'm pressed back up against the wall and his front is flush against me. His hard length is hot and insistent against my stomach.

"I just thought that . . . you might help me?"

I didn't mean for that to come out as a question.

"Because we fucked?" he presses.

How can he look so good covered in grease?

Without stopping to think about it, I let my hands run up his chest. Ridges of muscle play against my palms. He said he went *easy* on me last time. What would hard be like?

He's waiting for an answer.

"Yes? No. I don't know." I search his face, then give a tiny shrug. "I just feel safe with you, I guess."

Dirty blond brows lower, and I can't help but smile at his consternation.

"Does that really surprise you?" I ask. I'm not sure what it is about him, but he makes me bold. I let my fingertips rub over a spot of engine grease on his thick bicep where it mars one of his tattoos. "I can't imagine why. You're strong." I lick my lips and force myself to continue. "Attractive. You took care of me the other night, even though you pretended you wouldn't."

He glances away, jaw flexing, and mutters, "That wasn't taking care of you."

My chest twists, though I'm not sure why. Running on instinct, I lift on my toes and brush a light kiss across his check.

"Thank you for helping me, Jayk."

His gaze swings back to mine, a deep, beautiful midnight blue. Something glimmers in their depths like stars, so unfathomably inside him, I wouldn't have seen it if I hadn't been soaking them in.

Red rolls into his cheeks, and he pulls back abruptly. He shrugs. "Yeah, whatever. Don't get used to it or anything."

My lips purse, though it's more to hold in a snort of laughter than in disapproval.

"Uh-huh," I hum through closed lips, and he glowers at me. Then I glance around the workshop, realizing I have a day to kill. I could spend it doing the few chores I've assigned myself, but I have zero desire to do anything else that makes me feel like their sexed-up maid.

The pile of laundry can *wait*.

My eyes linger on the washing machine that I would commit all kinds of sins to have fixed. That broken beauty belongs back in the house with the rest of the equipment.

As far as I'm concerned, it's *mine*.

"Need a hand?"

CHAPTER 21

EDEN

SURVIVAL TIP #173
*Settling for less than you need
only guarantees a slower death.*

T *hud.*
Frowning, I ease my door open gingerly, looking down
to see what I bumped. There, on the floor, is a glorious, embossed
copy of *Dracula*. I pick it up with a hungry eagerness. It's been
days since Jasper last left me a book—since we had that entrancing
and awful encounter in the library. Whenever I think of it, my
stomach flips and churns all at once.

It's Jasper's "day," and I'm so nervous I could heave.

Will he expect sex? Of course he will, won't he? Lucky said he
would set boundaries with me before we did anything . . . but he's
a sadist. Can my boundary even be "don't hurt me"? Where does
that leave us? Will he want me to try, at least? Take off my clothes
and let him chain me to a wall so he can whip me until I scream?

That's what sadists do, don't they? They whip?

I haven't forgotten Jasper's dismissiveness when I asked him
for answers, or the cutting cruelty of his words in the library.

Yet . . . he brought me my dearest friends to keep me company when I was confused and alone—the one gift that could have made me feel at home. He listens so carefully, absorbs me so utterly in his attention, that after so many years of walking unseen and unheard through the forest, I'm turned real, turned flesh, just by the weight of it. Flesh that feels. Flesh that craves.

And he does have such lovely, clever hands.

God, I'm such a mess.

Ever since I left Jayk's workshop last night, I've been plagued with worries. I fully expected today to reduce me to a puddle of nerves, except that I woke to Lucky staring at me with puppy-dog eyes, begging to spend the day with me.

Whether he'd forgotten it was Jasper's day or simply didn't care, the distraction suited me just fine. I let him drag me away to spend half the day giggling and cooking with him in the kitchen. I had half a mind to let him suffer for the trouble he got me in with Dom, except that he was moving so gingerly, I didn't have the heart.

Dom apparently thumped him soundly—mostly because Lucky still hasn't returned the bazooka from his hidey stash. I only hope that Dom doesn't work out I know where that stash is. Let's just say Lucky has more than a bazooka in there, and I will sing like a canary if he questions me.

Still, despite Lucky's protests, I begged off cooking an hour ago and came back to my room to think.

Well, and to shower, since I was covered head to toe in about a dozen different ingredients.

I can't procrastinate any longer. I need to make a decision.

Do I go and find Jasper to fulfill my end of this bargain? Or risk a refusal?

I turn the book over in my hands, and it naturally parts at chapter five where he's bookmarked the pages with a simple note.

Chess in my room at 3pm
Please?
—Jasper

On the first page of chapter five, he had—heartrendingly—highlighted several lines: "I am longing to be with you, and by the sea, where we can talk together freely and build our castles in the air."

Please.

Does that mean I'm getting lovely, bookish Jasper today? One who will talk with me freely about all the things they're keeping from me?

Or is his scary, sadistic evil twin playing games with me?

I flick through the pages of the book, searching for his notes, the little insights and witticisms I've come to crave, but they're naked of anyone's thoughts but Stoker's. I frown, tapping the spine with my finger.

Is the book itself the message? A more sensual choice than some of the others . . . but also screaming with misogyny. He chose a quote from Mina, a praised and perfect Victorian woman. Is that how he sees me? Intelligent and beautiful, fine, but a woman whose success, whose value, is assigned by how she props up her male counterparts?

Maybe I'm being too sensitive.

My frustration with the men is growing—their insistence on secrets is infuriating, these unexplained tensions in the house are confusing, and the whole farcical bargain is starting to grate. It pushes me into a position in the house that is becoming more uncomfortable by the day.

If I'm being honest, it's *because* I'm enjoying myself so much that it's beginning to hurt. The last two days have been . . . surprisingly pleasant. No, more than that. They've been delightful.

Yesterday, I worked in Jayk's barn until night fell and he fixed me a bland but deeply appreciated meal of dried jerky and garden vegetables that he fidgeted over for far too long. We fell into a quiet rhythm as we puttered, and for the first time since I arrived, I felt *useful*. Like I was contributing in a meaningful way.

His gruff corrections didn't sting like failure and his rare approving nods had me glowing. When it grew late enough that I decided I should probably get some sleep, I left with the greatest reluctance. I'd even found the courage to ask if I could help him again soon and received a rough, "Suit yourself" in response.

From Jayk, I'm pretty sure that counts as an open invitation.

My sneaky satisfaction with him, the sweet heat I feel with Beau, laughing with Lucky, all of it has me wanting . . . more. Maybe even everything.

A greedy, impossible thought.

But an honest one.

I stifle a sigh. How can I ever even hope for more when there is such an imbalance between us? While they're making the rules, how can I make my own? And I do want new rules, I think. To finally make some for myself.

I want to be able to speak my mind without fear of consequence.

I want to fill my days with whatever or whomever I want.

I want to be able to form real relationships. To know that if we're together, it's because that's what I want, and what they want, and to know it's based on more than convenient sex.

Ducking back into my room, I check the grandfather clock. It's two fifty-five. Decision time.

I look down at the highlighted words. "I am longing to be with you."

Longing seems too soft a word for all the things I want.

I place the book on my bedside table and make my way to Jasper's room.

"Come in, Eden."

My hand pauses where it's raised ready to knock on Jasper's door, then drops to press against my stomach. I glance around the hall for a camera but can't see one. Perhaps Jasper's latest book delivery was a hint, a telling clue that he truly *isn't* human, but rather some kind of ancient, beautiful vampire lying in wait for his unsuspecting prey.

Only, I'm more than a little suspicious of Jasper.

And I only feel about sixty percent like prey.

Steeling myself, I open the door.

Large, elegant, and understated. Jasper's room is decorated thoughtfully, and surprisingly cozily. There's a lovely picture of him with an older couple who I assume must be his parents in front of a beautiful palace, and a hand-knitted blanket is draped over one of the armchairs. The chessboard is set up on an artful table by a toasty-looking heater, and delicate classical music wends through the room. Soft light turns the rich colors misty. Romantic.

There are no whips, or chains, or bloodied nail marks on the walls.

If he's a vampire, he's a very tidy one.

I decide it's safe to step inside.

Jasper stands beside a small kitchenette, pouring from a teapot that seems to be fused by veins of gold. The lines at the corners of his eyes seem more pronounced today, and there's an exhausted drag to his movements, like his limbs are falling asleep before his brain has agreed it's time.

The familiar scent of chamomile soothes me . . . though the

cream sweater he's wearing riles my insides back into instant, passionate riot. It looks gloriously soft, and I have the absurd urge to bury my face in him.

It.

In *it*.

"I think I've read about that," I offer into the lengthening silence, hoping he doesn't notice how flustered I am. When he looks up at me from under sinfully sooty lashes, my mouth goes dry, and it takes me a moment to gesture at the teapot he's holding. "It's broken pottery, isn't it? Mended with gold and lacquer?"

"Kintsugi," he says, setting it down. "It's a Japanese art form."

He hands me a cup and saucer. Our fingers don't brush, but I track the near miss with obsessive focus.

"To show that sometimes the greatest beauty lies in our flaws. The most strength, in the ways we break."

They're pretty words, but they ring hollow, and his expression is so carefully still, I know he's hiding something.

Again.

"Talk together freely," my sweet behind.

I bite the corner of my lip, then bury my face in my cup.

"What was that?" Jasper muses, and I lift my eyes over the rim to see him taking me in with those sharp, sharp eyes.

The hot liquid burns my tongue as I swallow too fast. "P-pardon?"

"If you have a concern, Eden, I would prefer you voiced it." His lips compress unhappily.

"I— I'm sorry. I just . . . "

Why am I always on the wrong foot with him? Will he turn me over his knee if I make him unhappy enough? That was what Lucky said, right? Unlike Lucky, though, I'm not sure my body "wants the pain."

There's no way he brought me into his private room on *his day* just to play a board game. Right?

My eyes stray to the very large, very inviting-looking bed on the far side of the room.

I clear my throat and snap my eyes back to Jasper. "You don't sound like you believe the philosophy."

"No?" He stirs steaming ripples in his cup, and I'm mesmerized by the graceful curve of his wrist. "No, I suppose I don't. At least, not with regard to myself. I have flaws I'm not so proud of, Eden. I've broken in ways that shame me. I haven't yet found a way to turn them into something I can find beautiful."

I stare at him, taken aback by the raw honesty in his tone. Cryptic as ever, yes . . . but it feels like a confession.

"I think you're beautiful," I whisper, before I can think better of it.

With a startled blink, Jasper looks up at me, face softening, and my cheeks begin to burn. "Darling girl," he murmurs.

A shiver skates down my spine, then erupts over my skin.

Those dark eyes move over me like a caress, and he steps in, cupping the back of my neck with his free hand. He's tall, standing above me, but he doesn't crowd me, doesn't loom like some of the others. Subtle pressure eases me forward, and I sigh a breath as he directs me to an armchair.

There's something erotic about the press of his fingertips on the sides of my neck, in the confident lack of force by which he moves me. By the time I'm at the chair, my knees feel weak, and my teacup trembles on its saucer.

"Sit, Eden."

My knees drop out.

I think about taking another sip to ease my parched throat, but then think better of it. I need a bucket of ice, not to raise my temperature any further.

Jasper takes a seat across from me, on the opposite side of the chessboard, and sets his saucer down on the side table. Sitting back in his armchair, he crosses one leg over the other. The tiny teacup seems unbearably delicate in his elegant fingers.

I set my saucer down too and examine the board. Apparently, we really are playing chess. "How do we play?"

Jasper shakes his head neatly. "Chess isn't a game so much as it is a battle of minds."

Comforting.

"Okay." I clasp my hands together on my lap. "Let's spar."

CHAPTER 22

EDEN

Don't enter a battle if you don't know the lay of the land.
You'll lose.

A t the word "spar," Jasper's eyes narrow on me, and I give him a demure smile, remembering the way I watched Beau knock him to the ground again and again yesterday morning.

"Did you—?"

I take a sip of my tea as I grin, and pink rolls into Jasper's cheeks.

With a grimace, Jasper explains the rules to me, and he was right—the orderliness and the strategy concept are appealing. He lets me choose a color, and his slight smile when I choose black tells me instantly that I picked wrong.

Biting my lip, I duck my head again and survey the grid— numbers down one side, letters down the other—and I move my black pawn to E5. Jasper moves his knight to F3, putting my newly moved pawn under threat. Scanning the board again, I move my pawn to D6 to protect it.

When I glance up through my lashes again, Jasper gives me a

slight nod, and a smidge of my anxiety eases. He's overwhelming, sitting back like an indolent prince, and playing a game of wits against him seems like an unwinnable exercise.

Is this really how he wants to spend his day with me? Or is this just the warm-up? Something to lull me into a sense of safety before he pounces?

He's quiet now, but I can't tell if that's because he's not one who needs to fill silences, or if it's because he's waiting. Maybe it's part of his psychologist training, to let others speak first.

"Do you play often?" I ask as he moves another pawn, taking it to D4.

I frown, studying the move. I could take that pawn, but it would open up the board for him. I think. Biting my lip, I try to play out the next few possible moves in my head.

"Dominic is the only one with the patience for it. We play occasionally," he replies.

I have to suppress a flinch at the name, remembering my wild flight from him yesterday.

"Oh, that's interesting," I say absently.

Looking back at the board, I hesitate. There are so many options. I'm afraid of mis-stepping.

"Interesting?" There's a curious cant to Jasper's head; it makes his silky black hair fall forward slightly.

"I just . . . didn't think the two of you got along very well."

"Oh?" Jasper rests his chin on his fingers. Settled back in his chair, he's relaxed and watchful. "And why do you think that?"

My fingers hesitate over the pieces as I eye him. This feels like a trap.

Flustered, I move my bishop to G4. "You were arguing. When I saw you together— Oh, I don't know. Just a feeling, I suppose. I'm sorry. I didn't mean to offend you."

"Eden, would you do me a favor?"

His dark eyes snare me, fathomless and shadowed. I nod, swallowing.

"Please stop apologizing," he tells me gently.

I release a breath. I've only technically apologized to him twice today, but I know he's asking more than that.

"You intimidate me," I confess quietly.

Jasper's chin dips. "I'm aware."

"Of course you are."

He actually smiles at that, and small and neat as it is, it changes his whole face. I stare at him, lips parting, my eyes tracing over the tragic delicacy of his cheekbones, the way I've been doing each night before I slip into a sweet, feverish sleep.

"I would be lying if I said I don't enjoy a sub being nervous around me. You being afraid, however, does not appeal in the slightest."

Thinking that over, I nod slowly. I can appreciate the distinction.

Jasper adds, "There has been some talk of punishment that I fear has misled you. To be clear, I don't intend on causing you any harm, or crossing any lines you aren't comfortable with me crossing. You can always refuse, Eden. Always. And with no consequence to your position in this house."

His need to make me understand is tangible, and although my fears and frustrations and desires go far deeper than that, I'm comforted by his reassurance. He's giving me an out, despite the group's earlier agreement, and it's a huge weight off my shoulders.

No whipping necessary today.

I tilt my head. "Dom said—"

"Ah," he breaks in gently. "Dom may lead the men, Eden, but this is my home. If he has a concern about my guests, he can discuss it with me."

When he sees his words have sunk in, he picks up his pawn at D4. Some of the tension around his mouth and shoulders has eased.

"Occasionally there will be consequences for your actions, however," Jasper tells me with a dangerous glint in his eye. He indicates the board with his head. "Such as for that move. That one was a mistake."

With precise motions, he takes my pawn at E5. I'm now left unprotected and retaliation in that spot would be futile. I scowl, and he chuckles softly.

"In answer to your earlier question, I like the captain just fine. We both have competitive natures and occasionally that leads to conflict, but I respect him. He's a good leader."

I move my bishop to F3 to take his threatening knight. As soon as I do, I crinkle my nose. I'm going to lose that piece. It's utterly unprotected.

Damn. I need to prepare better against his attacks.

"May I ask something of you, Eden?"

"Mm-hmm," I mumble, still puzzling over the board.

"Will you tell me about your husband?" The words are careful, calculated—like he timed their delivery to the second.

My hands clench hard, and I realize he's knocked down my defenses. Smooth and deadly, Jasper takes my bishop with his queen.

A clean kill.

I force a smile, though it feels more like a grimace. "Trying to shrink my head?"

"Trying to get to know you, actually," he replies with gentle reproach.

I lift my eyes to his, feeling shame sting my cheeks. He's right. That wasn't fair of me. Thinking about Henry upsets me, puts me on edge, but that's not his fault, and it's a fair question. I'm curious about his past too—about all of their pasts. I've shared my body with both Lucky and Jaykob, but I've only gleaned the tiniest teases of information about who they are and where they've come from.

And unlike my body, their pasts are not on offer.

Taking a moment to collect myself, I use my pawn to take his at E5.

"My husband—" I start, then cut off, not sure where to begin. Frustrated, I blow out a breath. How can I even begin explaining all these complicated things I'm feeling? "I don't know how to—"

Jasper nods once, and his expression grows thoughtful.

Moving his bishop on white to C4, he says, "I was married for ten years. We divorced a year before the strikes. One of the last conversations I had with my mother was about the divorce, actually. Despite her years here in America, it was still not something she felt comfortable with. Nor did I, for that matter." Jasper picks up his tea and sits back in his chair. His fingers stroke the rim absently. "I loved Soomin . . . very much."

Jasper was *married*? I don't know why that surprises me so much. Maybe because he seems so lonely to me, so distant and hard to reach. The lines of his throat are taut, like he's holding in some strong emotion. It's almost incredible to me, how the rest of him seems so calm and relaxed. Unless you were watching closely, you could think he hardly cared at all, despite his words.

Wanting him to keep talking, I stay silent and focus on the board. Jasper's pieces seem more involved—and far more exposed. I want to get more pieces out to play; I'm feeling timid and trapped behind my line of pawns.

I move my knight to F6.

"I grew up in a trailer park," I offer. Sucking in a deep breath, I continue, "My mother was an addict—I don't know who my father was—and after I was born, she left me with my grandmother."

"What was your grandmother like?" Jasper slides his queen to B3, placing several of my pieces in direct danger again.

Nerves slide like oil through my intestines. Needing to defend myself, I move my queen out to E7 to protect my pawn from his bishop.

"She was fine, as long as I followed her rules. But I minded my manners and went to church when she told me to, so we didn't have any problems."

His eyelashes shade his eyes, and when they fly open again, there's a crease between his brows. "What I said to you, in the library, about your manners . . . that wasn't based on anything you said or did, Eden. I'm sorry if I hit a nerve. I was upset about something else, and I have an unfortunate habit of cruelty when I'm caught off guard."

I study him. "Is that one of the flaws you mentioned earlier? That you're not so proud of?"

He looks away, unseeing, toward the teapot where it cools on the benchtop.

"It's one of them," he murmurs.

"I met my husband, Henry, when I was eighteen," I quietly offer in return. "He was handsome, and wealthy, and I thought he was so kind when he did me the high honor of lifting me out of poverty. He worked so hard to help me slide easily into his world. To . . . correct . . . all my embarrassing behaviors." My throat feels sore, no matter how I swallow. "And in exchange, I adored him."

I falter again. What a humiliating thing to admit.

Rather than taking another piece with his queen, Jasper moves his remaining knight to C3. Distracted, I try to figure out what he's doing. I'm exposed, and I don't understand why he's not attacking.

"When did you realize?" I ask, wanting desperately to even the playing field. "That you liked . . . That you were a—"

"A sadist?" Faint amusement lightens his features. "A frightening word, isn't it?"

Of course he's amused—he's the one on the safe end of the whip.

Jasper appears to think it over. "It was from a fairly young age—certainly from the time I was old enough to start thinking about sex. I can't remember a time where it was separate from pain in my mind."

He grows silent for a moment, and it's like he gathers the shadows, becoming something still and slightly frightening.

Something unholy, but divinely in need of worship.

"As I grew older, I learned. My body called for control, for *pain*. Craved it like air, or water. It wasn't a desire . . . it was a vocation." His eyes gleam in the soft lights. "I saw pretty things and I wanted to break them. I saw pretty people and wanted them under my loafer and begging. I wanted tears, and surrender." His lips thin, and the shadows darken. "You can't imagine how much it frightened me."

I start in surprise, and he smiles faintly at my reaction, but there's no humor in it.

"I thought I was evil," he confesses. "Only villains want to hurt people. I spent years burying it, fearing to look too closely at my desires. Which was foolish, of course—only in understanding comes acceptance. It took me a long time before I realized that not just any tears would do. Not any pain would ease the ache in my soul. They needed to be willingly offered. Given freely and gratefully."

Jasper rolls his shoulders back, and I realize he's uncomfortable. He directs that penetrating gaze on me again. "I'm sorry. I'm explaining this poorly. It's not something I've ever tried to put into words before."

Pulse shivering, I shake my head minutely. "You're explaining it perfectly."

Freely and gratefully. For the first time I wonder just how much pleasure a masochist must feel for their pain to become something they beg for.

On the board, I can suddenly see how clever his move is. If he pushes forward with his knight, I will be placed terribly to protect my major pieces. But most of my defensive moves still leave me at his mercy.

I move my pawn to C6, pre-emptively stopping his knight from advancing.

"Good girl," he murmurs, and I beam up at him at the praise.

Something kindles in his expression as he takes in my smile. I wonder if he'd be encouraging while he hurt me. What kind of comfort would come between the torments?

Feeling warm, I push my glasses up the bridge of my nose.

Jasper moves his other bishop to G5 to threaten my knight. "How did you meet your husband?"

My arousal sizzles out. "Ah. Henry was plumping out his extracurriculars for his Yale application, so we met at the nursing home my grandmother was moved to." Jasper's brows twitch at the mention of Yale, just slightly, and my smile turns caustic. Yes, nothing but the best for my dear husband. "Henry . . . he took an interest in me. I'm still not quite sure why. His parents were rather hard on him, and I think he liked playing the hero. His family was wealthy, you see, and terribly educated."

Jasper trains his eyes on the board, but the lines of him are carefully still. I know he's paying attention.

I lift my hand in a dismissive wave, though my throat thickens at the humiliating memories. "It's all very predictable, I'm afraid. He was kind to me, and so willing to 'teach' me to be a better person—in their eyes, of course. How I should dress, and talk, and eat so I could fit into his world. It didn't matter, though. His parents hated me."

It hurts to think of those early years. God, I was naive. Just a foolish little girl.

Maybe I'm making a mistake, telling Jasper all this.

I study his move. If he takes my knight, I can take his bishop. Is that an even exchange? Can I afford to give him this piece if he gives me one of his?

Into the lull I left, Jasper offers, "It took a long time for me to put a name to what I needed. What I was. *Sadist*. Dominant, too, but that was easier to wrap my head around—even a relief, in many ways. But then, once I finally felt I had it worked out, all I wanted was to experience it. To find the other side of my coin, if you like." The corner of his mouth lifts in a grimace. "The problem was, of course, that there are as many brands of masochist and submissive as there are sadist and dominant."

"There are?" I ask, curiosity bubbling past my unwelcome memories. "I thought— I suppose I thought you either are or you aren't."

Absentmindedly, Jasper runs his finger over his lower lip as he contemplates me, and I try to stop imagining what that lip would taste like. I wonder what flavor of sadist he is.

"Not quite. Some submissives want a full-time dominant, and others are only interested in giving up control during sex. Some want a combination of both. Some enjoy bondage, some degradation. Some like to be praised, and others like to be hunted."

His hand curls around the arm of his chair as he lowers it, and my heart trips over itself, speeding. I want to ask what it means when all of those things sound incredible . . . but I'm embarrassed about what the answer might be.

Flustered, I move my pawn to B5.

And am instantly embarrassed by how transparent a move it is. He'll be able to see through that with no trouble.

"Masochists are the same," he continues, watching me. "Some like particular types of pain—a sting, or thud, or burn, or slice, or a combination of those or many others. Some seek out subspace, others hate it. There are different extremes to which they may enjoy pain . . . No, it's not as simple as does or does not."

I feel his gaze on me again, and I pick up my tea to buy myself some thinking time. Maybe . . . some of that . . . would be okay.

Maybe.

Knight to B5. Jasper takes my pawn.

Okay, he's too strong in this position. I change the subject again.

"Henry craved his parents' approval as much as I craved his— but I also think I was the only person who had ever looked up to him, and he needed that as well. He proposed after five months despite their dislike of me, and I couldn't believe it. It felt so romantic to me, like a dream." I shake my head, annoyed that my past self was ever that stupid. "When we eloped, they disowned him. He hadn't planned on that. He thought they would forgive him anything. They didn't, and he didn't do so well after that."

We didn't do so well after that, either.

"You said he was in service," Jasper said, not quite a question.

I take a sip of my tea, then nod. "Yes, well. He didn't get into an Ivy like he'd planned, in the end. He didn't have the grades, and without his father's donations . . ." I shrug uncomfortably. "We sold his car to get started in a small apartment, and I worked in the local library while I studied. I did receive an academic scholarship, which helped a lot. It wasn't what he had planned for his life. It still felt like luxury to me, but it was a coffin for Henry. He resented . . . it."

I stop myself from saying "me" at the last moment, and Jasper catches my gaze like he heard it anyway.

With my pawn, I wipe Jasper's knight off the board with a tad too much aggression. "I think he decided to join the Army because he wanted so badly to play the hero again. That was always how he saw himself."

Jasper shakes his head, and I know what he must be thinking. It's no reason to join the military. Instead of replying to that, though, he takes my pawn with his bishop.

"Check," he says calmly, and I blink, redirecting my attention to the game.

His bishop is in line to take my king—the jerk. How did he manage that?

Ignoring the game, Jasper waits until he has my attention. "Soomin was both my wife and my submissive, but it was years before the cracks started to show. She wasn't a masochist, Eden, and I was starting to understand I needed that. I wanted more than her submission. I wanted her tears and her trust." He pauses and sighs. "But I wanted her to want that, mostly. And that wasn't who she was."

This isn't a session. It isn't work. He's meeting me halfway. Actually talking to me, the way I've wanted all of them to. Giving me his secrets.

I wonder if he'll tell me what's going on with the others. Why everyone is so tense.

I take my knight to D7, blocking his bishop and taking me out of check.

"Is that why you divorced?" I ask.

Jasper bends over the board, and I see the tension in him in the corded tendons of his lovely, careful hands. "In part. It . . . destroyed me . . . that Soomin felt she wasn't enough. I loved her, very dearly. I insisted she was all I needed, tried to make it true, but she didn't believe me." He adjusts the wrists of his sweater, his sharp misery coated in its inviting softness. "I'm not sure I believed myself by the end."

My teeth tug at my lip, chest aching for him. And, if I'm honest, for myself, too.

"The way you talk about it—the sadism, I mean—it sounds like a need. A . . . compulsion, maybe? Can you really just switch it off like that?" I ask, already knowing the answer.

He couldn't be with Soomin because she wasn't masochistic . . . if I want Jasper, it means I'll have to try. I mull over what he said before, about all the different possibilities. About how determined he's been to make me comfortable.

With Jasper . . . maybe I could try.

He looks at me then. His eyes are shadows and sadness. "No. I can't. That drive is part of me."

In one hand, Jasper collects his A1 castle and his king and moves them to D1 and C1, respectively. It tucks his king behind his pawns and brings his castle out from where it was trapped. My jaw drops open.

I stare up at him, outraged. "That's cheating!"

Despite his somber expression, the corner of his mouth lifts. "No. That's castling."

"You didn't explain that rule," I grit out in as even a tone as I can muster, fuming. This changes the whole board!

"Didn't I?" he says dismissively. "My mistake."

"Sadist."

Jasper inclines his head again. "As I was explaining."

I groan a little laugh and look at the board, my chin in my hands. I move my castle to D8, beside my king, with a pout.

Jasper's small smile softens, then he continues, "It's not enough to want to be right for someone. You can't carve away important parts of yourself to make your pieces fit. No matter how much you might want to."

There is so much pain in him as he says it, so much aching loneliness that I suck in a breath from the second-hand hurt.

He must have loved his wife deeply.

Jasper picks up his castle, and I can't help but stay his hand. He raises a stern brow, but for once . . . I don't feel like crumpling.

"I'm so sorry, Jasper. That must have hurt."

With his other hand, he captures mine and tugs it free. He squeezes it once, gently. "Yes. It did."

Jasper takes my knight with his castle at D7. "Tell me the rest."

I shift my gaze back to the board, finding it easier to talk while my hands are occupied, and take his castle with my knight, feeling like I'm falling into his plot. But even so, it doesn't even occur to me to hesitate now. "Henry was in the Army for a few years, and I had just finished my degree when he was dishonorably discharged —found criminally negligent in his basic duties."

Dead silence. Jasper sits back in his chair, and I can tell I've surprised him.

"It was sloppiness, really. I genuinely don't believe he would have done anything malicious, but he was always careless when things didn't interest or benefit him. Two men died because of his actions, and he was serving his time in a military prison when the strikes happened."

"You left him while he was in prison?" Sitting forward again smoothly, he moves his other castle to D1.

That was a hard time. I'd buried myself in work and tried to ignore the whispers of my coworkers. People took dishonorable discharges seriously.

They were a serious matter.

I smile ruefully. "I tried. Turns out, dishonorable discharges are expensive. His lawyers were expensive. Divorce is expensive. It took time. I was trying to get that sorted when everything happened."

His elbows on his knees, Jasper regards me with unnerving intensity. Needing to escape the attention, I shift my queen to E6 to put pressure on his queen. I think I've lost this game. Playing against Jasper, I'm not sure I had a chance to begin with.

"Do I remind you of him?" he asks seriously. "Is that why you've been avoiding me?"

His bishop takes my knight at D7 in a severe, clipped motion. He's right next to my king.

"Check."

I suck in a breath, but I'm not looking at the board. "No. No, Jasper, you don't. Not— Not really. It's just the wealth and I— I just feel like I'm saying the wrong thing all the time."

Rather than looking hurt or offended, as I feared, he seems to consider that. "Because you don't know the rules?"

I take my knight to D7, taking his bishop, for all the good it would do. This game is hopeless. I was lost before I began.

"Because I *hate* the rules." The words burst from me like a geyser.

Oh.

My hand flies to my mouth, mortified. "I'm sorr—"

"We've spoken already today about that word, Eden," Jasper says calmly. He moves his queen to B8, and I'm in check again. He examines my face. "The rules . . ."

I wrap my arms around my stomach, sitting back . . . but as I do, Jasper leans forward in his chair, chasing me.

"What is it you want from us, Eden?" he asks, so so gently.

I move to stand. "I need some water, I—"

"Come here."

My pulse thunders . . . but I can't escape the gravity of his gaze.

"Here?" I breathe, even as I step into him. Did I think he was darkness before? In the soft lights of the room, he shines like a star.

When I stand before him, he takes my damp palms in his, and dizziness swirls my brains. He doesn't say anything, but I sink to my knees. I couldn't say why, exactly. I'm sure there are thoughts floating somewhere in the mists of my mind. But curling up between his legs feels like breathing, like nature, like the home he tempted me with so sweetly when I first arrived.

My body softens, relaxing into the warm, reassuring strength of his thigh. Locks of my hair pool over his leg, tickling my collarbone, and Jasper takes a deep breath as I settle there, his eyes a galaxy.

From this close, I can see the flecks of silver at his temples. The delicate lines beside his eyes. He seems older today. Serious and tired and deeply thoughtful.

But I feel him tremble against me.

"Tell me what you want, Eden," he repeats.

My breath shivers out, and his eyes burn like banked coals. It's the way he looked at me that first day, when he and Beau kissed me and fingered me to climax.

I think of him promising family. His careful attention as I read. Every note he's left me. I think of how it might feel to curl up right here with a book, his hand in my hair, sharing passages and private moments. How thoroughly he's seduced me.

Maybe. Maybe I can hope for more.

And so, I grasp for the sun.

"Everything," I whisper. "I want it all."

Jasper's eyes sink shut, his lashes a dark veil over his thoughts.

But I feel him go someplace else. I watch him turn the whole world over in his mind—and whatever he sees there seems to pain him.

When he sighs, it's like a song. Sad, but desperately resigned.

"You deserve it all, Eden. You both—" He shakes his head, meeting my gaze. "You *all* do."

My eyes sting. Sting because I'm starting to believe it. I *do* deserve more.

I always have.

"I heard you in the music room with Lucien," he murmurs, and my cheeks flood with heat. Catching the look, his lips turn down. "My mother liked to hear my father play—she designed the intercom system so his music could play through each room of the house. Lucien must have accidentally forgot to turn it off."

He *heard* that?

"You sounded . . . happy." Jasper's voice is feather soft. "Were you?" When he captures my gaze, he doesn't let it go. "Was he?"

I think it might be impossible to lie to him, at his feet like this.

"It was one of the happiest days of my life," I whisper, and his eyes shine liquid bright. Wetting my lips, I add, "I think Lucky . . . I think he was happy too. I mean, how do you tell? He smiled a lot. But he always smiles a lot." Just thinking of it makes my lips lift. "But he wanted to spend time with me today too. That's a good sign, isn't it?"

When I look at Jasper again, all cracks and minutiae of emotion have vanished from his face. He's a perfect mask—solemn and pretty and impossible to read. Then it breaks, his eyes press closed and he looks tired again. No, more than that—he looks exhausted, sucked of life and energy.

"Are you okay?" I whisper.

It unnerves me more to see him like this, I think. I want him stern and cold and pretty again. This tiredness of his, it goes to the bone. I understand it. Too well.

I watch his throat work, then his reply sighs from his lips.

"Sometimes."

And I understand that too.

His hand strokes over my hair like the breeze of a breath, and I feel the tingles all the way down my spine.

Then his fingers curl, and he draws away.

I watch it happen. In so many tiny little ways, I watch him pull back.

And with a portentous, glacial crash, every hope and romantic breath in my body shatters.

"Eden," he says, so heavily, and I turn my face away.

In my name, in that one word, I hear the apology. The brutal empathy. The guillotine over my dreamy imaginings.

The tingles in my spine become ice daggers. Dread reaches up through black waters and pools in my stomach.

This wasn't a seduction. It was a rejection.

"I can't be anything to you. Not anything more than a friend." His words are careful, stilted. So painfully, gratingly unnatural. "But I *will* be a friend—I promise you that."

My lids sink shut, as my throat closes over. I duck my head, hardly noticing as my forehead comes to rest on his thigh.

I can't bear for him to see my face.

How did I not see this coming? How utterly I've just humiliated myself.

"Eden, I can't go through it again, do you understand? I can't fall for another person when we can't be what we need for one another." I hear him swallow, and his thigh quivers. "You will be happy with Lucien. With Beaumont, and Jaykob, and even Dominic. I meant it when I said you deserve happiness, Eden . . . it just won't be with me."

I feel the air change, lose its charge. Everything turns dull and flat.

"I've caused enough hurt," he whispers. "The kindest thing I can do for you is to leave you in peace."

How did I just spend the last hour questioning the lengths I would go to for us to be together and not realize he was explaining all the reasons why we couldn't?

I wasn't alone in an abyss with Jasper, after all.

I was just alone.

A fat, hot tear drops off my face and onto the fabric of his pants, and he falls utterly still.

How am I *still* such a foolish little girl?

I pull back from Jasper—too suddenly, but he'll have to forgive me that. It doesn't feel right, now, to be sitting here at his feet. Not when he doesn't want to keep me. Not when this thing between us is shockingly, embarrassingly one sided. Once again, I feel fooled into thinking I'd found a home.

Standing, I brush down my dress, and my eye catches the board.

His gaze touches me everywhere.

The pieces come into sharp focus, and I shake my head. "You've won, then."

When I look at him, finally, his eyes are humiliatingly compassionate. "You played exceedingly well. You have a mind for it."

I bite the inside of my lip. Hard. The tears well anyway.

Moving to the game, I knock over my king.

"But in the end, I always lose."

CHAPTER 23

EDEN

SURVIVAL TIP #3
Fight for yourself.
No-one else will.

I ready the dining table with a dull ache. In my muscles. In my gut. I don't know why it feels so wrong, really, like the planets are somehow out of alignment. I don't know why it hurts so much to lose something that never existed in the first place.

Maybe I'm just embarrassed.

Does your heart usually hurt this much when you're embarrassed?

Lucky brings in the rabbit and wild mushroom soup he made, and he's been darting looks at me ever since I made my way down from my room—where I fled in embarrassment after the abysmal ending to the games played between me and Jasper.

To me and Jasper.

"Eden, are you okay?" Lucky asks, an anxious frown creasing his forehead. "What happened with . . . him?"

Tanned arms wrap around my waist from behind, and my breath catches in surprise.

"Jasper didn't scare you off, did he?" Beau asks. Lips press to my temple, and he takes a deep inhale, breathing me in. "I didn't expect to see you down here tonight."

My insides sting hotly. Maybe Jasper did whip me, after all— and he didn't even need the flogger.

"No. It's— I'm fine." I try to pull out of his arms, uncomfortable in my own skin right in this moment, let alone against someone else's.

Beau only lets me pull back slightly, face dimming. He hesitates. "Eden, are we okay? The other day . . . we left things in a weird place."

"You mean before Dom nearly murdered me?" I attempt to joke, but he stays unusually serious, waiting.

Damn it. I don't want to talk about this now. I don't want to talk about him, or Jasper, or any of it.

"Should I fetch the potato?" I touch my hair, but there's nothing to fix; it's tied securely in its proper bun again. "You made a side, didn't you, Lucky?"

Lucky and Beau both fall quiet, looking at me.

I swallow, then nod. "I'll just go get that."

Beau pulls me back in, my back to his chest, his arms an unyielding vice. "Talk to me, darlin'. Did things not go well?"

I force a light laugh, and hate the way it sounds.

"Don't go charging after him with a knife or anything. I promise nothing happened." My throat is made of splinters. "Jasper was a perfect gentleman."

"That's when he hurts the most." Across from me, Lucky's face darkens, and the look is unnatural on him. The comedy mask turns to tragedy. Spring to dead, decaying autumn. "What did he say to you?"

"We just realized we aren't a good fit, that's all," I insist. I'm stretching the truth of "we" a bit far, but I think Jasper will forgive me for it.

He was very gracious, even while telling me I'm not enough for him.

Beau's hands run up my hips, and I try to let myself sink into his touch.

At my words, Lucky freezes. "You aren't a good fit for him? Or he isn't a good fit for you?" A strange look crosses his features. "Did he say . . . why?"

"Does it matter?" Beau says. "There are a lot of us. It's no surprise that it's not going to work out for everyone. As long as they're happy, then there's no problem."

Happy.

Right.

God, I need a distraction. Isn't it enough to have my past, my wants, and my soul flayed open, examined, and discarded? I have to rot away in front of everyone else too?

"I'm happy to see the two of you," I say rather than lying outright.

I draw Beau's arms around me more firmly, sure—fairly sure— that Beau, at least, has no interest in rejecting me. My hips nestle into his stirring interest, and Beau laughs low in my ear. The sound sluices over my stinging insides, drawing out the hurt like his very presence is enough to heal. I shiver as his hot breath tickles the sensitive skin below my ear.

"You have no idea how happy I am to see you," Beau purrs, then he snags my earlobe in his teeth and a furious roll of pleasure tumbles through me.

I squirm against him, and my gaze tangles with Lucky's. The frosty disbelief lingers, but curious heat begins to melt it. His sky-blue eyes flick to the man behind me, a questioning light to them. Beau's nod has his stubble catching the strands of my hair, sending quivers down my spine, and Lucky edges round the table. Taking Beau's lead, he takes my chin and tilts it up farther, helping his friend get better access.

Beau releases my ear, and his lips move to my neck, like a

whisper over my skin, and my eyelids droop. It's okay, isn't it? To bury my pain in someone else? It's okay if I want to use them as a cure for my loneliness and hurt pride? After all, they're using me too, right?

Would they want me without this deal? If they had to answer all the questions they want to hide? If they had to reveal themselves as nakedly as Jasper just did?

"I'm sorry if he hurt you," Lucky whispers to me. "I know how he can be."

There's something in that. Something that niggles at me, but my thoughts are starting to slip away under their hands. Their lips.

Lucky's thumb rubs across my mouth. Both of them move slowly, leisurely, not like they're trying to stir me up, but more like they're exploring, worshiping me with their hands and mouths.

It hurts.

It *helps*.

I kiss Lucky's thumb.

"You're so pretty like this," Lucky tells me on a sigh, resting his forehead against mine.

Everything in me grows soft and warm. In the next instant, Beau's tongue slides, slow and silken, over my sensitive flesh. I gasp, knees weakening, and Lucky ducks his head to brush my mouth with his, kissing the sound, rubbing his lips against mine. The competing sensations are too much—the wet heat against my neck and mouth, their bodies all over me. I remember the way they pinned me, sweaty and shirtless in the sitting room.

I whimper in pleasure.

Dom's clipped voice cuts through the snuggly, slick fog. "Is dinner ready?"

No. I don't want dinner.

I want kisses for dinner.

Lucky presses one more brief peck to my lips, then pulls back. I attempt to frown at him, but he just winks, twinkly eyed and flushed, and leaves for the kitchen.

Beau makes a frustrated sound against my neck—and I swear he mutters, "Like clockwork."

Whatever that means.

He nips me lightly before straightening, though his arms stay wrapped around me.

I clear my throat. "Yes, sir. Lucky's just finishing with the potatoes."

My pulse quickens at the electric flash in Dom's eyes. Oh. I called him "sir" again. It's slipping out as naturally as breathing now.

And he *likes* it.

The, ah, pressure in his jeans tells me so. *Not* that I'm looking. It isn't my fault it's just . . . there. Demanding attention.

Pretty damn worthy of it too.

Realizing my attention has drifted—and not at all subtly—I snap my eyes back to his face. He's studying me in that intent way of his.

"Not such a prude then after all," he mocks.

Does that really need to be the first thing he's said to me since beating up on Jayk? Even then, he wasn't really talking *to* me.

Embarrassment rocks me, and it follows a little too closely on the heels of today's earlier humiliation. He doesn't seem to be looking for a response, but the words slip out of me anyway.

"I really hate that word. Why is it that when women embrace their sexuality they're demonized as sluts, but when they don't, they're condemned as prudes and called frigid? There's no winning."

Flinging the door open, Jaykob stalks through and plants himself in a chair without a word. The door hits the wall with a *clang*, making me jump. He doesn't look at anyone as he pulls out his knife again, not even at me.

The lack of acknowledgement stings after we spent the whole day together yesterday—especially after Jasper—but I force myself to push the feeling down. I know Jayk had fun working with me.

Okay, "fun" might be a stretch. But he tolerated me yesterday. And that was nice.

"The angel or the monster, no?" Jasper strolls into the dining room with a disdainful look at the still-swinging door, controlling it with a neat catch and closing it with pointed, deliberate care. Which Jaykob ignores.

There's not a hint of our earlier conversation on his face . . . except that tiredness. That seems like it's there to stay. His dark gaze slides over me, coolly appraising, and he nods at Beau before moving to fix himself a drink.

"I— Yes. Exactly," I stutter. My pulse trips over itself, but I try not to seem too affected by him.

It would help if he lost that damnable cream sweater though. It emphasizes his shoulders, the Stygian darkness of his hair.

It's too inviting for how closed off he is.

The scrape of Dom's chair as he sits draws my attention. He gives me an impatient look. "I'm not demonizing anyone. I don't like hypocrites. If you enjoy something, say so. You feel something, feel it. People who put a stranglehold on their lives because they're too afraid to actually do what they want are pathetic. And frustrating to be around."

"Now ain't that the funniest thing, *partner*—I agree with you completely," Beau says in a sugar-sweet tone, and Dom gives him a sharp glare.

Beau squeezes my upper arms, then tugs at my hand until we're seated next to each other. Dom is on my other side at the head of the table. I mull over Dom's words, cut by how aptly, how neatly, they slap a label on me. As though being polite and doing as I'm told is somehow a failing, when they've made it clear that I'm living here at their mercy. Irritation pricks me.

One day I'm going to tell him to fuck off, and I'm not going to be able to stop myself.

And it might be soon, because my patience for just about everything is wearing thin right now.

I'm about to respond—politely, I think—when Jaykob snorts. The sound startles me. The last two times we were all together, he hardly engaged with the others at all.

"You don't know what you're talking about." Jayk rakes his eyes over Dom, the sneer in his voice clear. "Not everyone is lucky enough to just 'do what they want.' Only people with connected daddies get that luxury. Some of us actually have to make some tough choices and hold our tongues when rich assholes tell us to jump."

I close my mouth and duck my head to hide a smile. I forgot, for a moment, that the chip on his shoulder is at least as big as mine.

Dom's whole body turns hard and threatening. "This you holding your tongue?" he asks. "'Cause it needs work."

Staring darkly at Dom, Jaykob's lip curls like he's about to let loose.

Lucky enters with a fragrant platter of fresh roasted potato chips, then slows, tensing. After glancing around the room with new caution, he chooses a seat a watchful distance from Dom and far from Jayk. Calm and seeming bored by the altercation, Jasper brushes past Lucky with his drink—close enough that Lucky has to freeze so he can slide past—and the platter tumbles out of Lucky's hands. It clatters across the table, spraying crispy potatoes and cutting Jayk off mid-snarl.

"Cock-sucking, son of a—" Lucky sucks his lower lip into his mouth, reaching for the overturned platter as Jasper settles into the chair beside him.

Surprised, I sit up and help him right the pieces back onto the board, looking at his pink cheeks curiously. That wasn't like him; he's usually so graceful. When everything's righted, he slumps back in his seat, shifting it back slightly and not looking at anyone.

Jasper helps himself to a chip, unfazed, that cool, careful mask firmly back in place. Lucky's eyes drift to him, a crease between his brows.

Frowning, I look between them all, noting the tense, unhappy faces.

"Is it always like this?" I ask Beau in an undertone.

His gaze follows mine, and he shakes his head once. Needing to soothe my anxious tension, I help myself to an extra chunk of cheese.

"If you've got something to say, Ranger, spit it out." Dom is intent on Jaykob, and he looms at the head of the table, a dark, menacing presence looking down on his subjects.

Jayk rolls his eyes, not looking at him. It's the Jaykob I met that first day, full of bitter anger, and my heart tugs for him.

"No *sir*, not me," he mocks. "I only eat, shit, and think on command."

Jasper sighs and then looks up to study Jaykob seriously. It's a relief not to have that look leveled at me.

"I know it didn't come across well the first time, but I do apologize, Jaykob, for my assumptions the other day. I know better than that. Know *you* better than that, in fact, and should have held my judgment until I had all the details. You deserve better from me, and I can only promise I will not be so hasty in future."

Jayk stiffens, going from battle-ready offense to tense-shouldered defense.

"Is that what this is about?" Some of the menace seeps from Dom, the posturing. He seems earnest when he says, "Fuck. I meant to talk to you too, you know. You're a good soldier, Jayk. I shouldn't have gone after you like that. I trust you in our team without question."

Dom is only apologizing to Jayk *now*?

Like a muscle-bound wind-up doll, Jayk gets more and more rigid with each word. The sneer settles in like it's marked in the grooves of his face. He pushes to his feet, grabbing a bowl before Dom even finishes speaking.

"Know what? Food tastes better in the servant's quarters anyway." He stops in front of me, looking down with a smirk. But even that seems off, discomfited. "You feel like crawling through the dirt again tonight, princess, I'll fuck your ass so hard your crown comes right off."

"*Jaykob*," Jasper snaps.

Beau's hand tightens around mine under the table.

I ignore them both, searching Jaykob's rough face for the man who stood against the world for me yesterday.

"Oh, Jayk," I breathe.

Sharp teeth have clamped around my churning insides, shredding them as they twist. The wounds can sit beside the slices I've already received today.

His smirk drops at my whisper and a muscle ticks in his jaw as he pushes into my face. "I don't need your *pity*."

He slams a hand on the table beside me, and he might as well have my heart in his fist, squishing it to a pulp. A storm of fury, he makes for the door.

He's halfway there when Dom says, "Stop."

When Jayk ignores him, Dom stands and that spine-tingling sense of his power, his competence, washes over me again. "*Stop*, Ranger. That's an order."

But Dom's not looking at Jayk, he's looking down at a small, buzzing device.

Beau curses. "Where?"

Dom shakes his head. "We need a visual. Jasper?"

Jasper nods and stands as well. "We'd best go to the study."

They both look at Jayk's back where he still stands beside the door. He doesn't turn around but, after a long moment, his head drops back and his chest heaves.

"I'll meet you there."

"Fine."

I watch Jayk leave, wondering if he would accept a hug later, then roll my eyes at myself. Almost definitely not. I suppress a sigh.

I wonder if he'd give me one for my sake, if not for his.

Dom looks at Beau pointedly, then at me, then back to Beau.

Without another glance my way, he leaves the room. Beau presses his head into his hand, rubbing his forehead and avoiding my gaze.

My mouth twists. I wonder if Jayk's bitterness is catching.

"What's happening?" I ask, though I dread the non-answer I know is coming.

Jasper regards me through his pretty mask—impenetrable, except for those exhausted rings around his eyes. "It's nothing that need worry you. We'll make sure of that. You should get some rest, Eden. It's been a long day for you."

Hot embers start to smoke inside me.

"Don't patronize me, Jasper," I reply sharply. "And don't flatter yourself. Today meant nothing."

And, God, I wish it were the truth. I want it to be true.

I deserve better than all of this.

Jasper hesitates, scanning my face, and sadness sinks into his tired eyes. He inclines his head and leaves, the door closing with brutal softness behind him.

Bastard, bastard, *bastard*!

His truth-telling only extends to the past then, I suppose.

Is this my new normal? To be lied to and ignored every time something serious happens? Maybe *I'm* the wind-up doll, not Jayk. I do my one trick on command and then I'm to be put back in my box until they want me again. Despite my promises to myself that I can handle it . . . well, I'm starting to think that was the worst lie of them all.

Once he leaves, I look between Beau and Lucky, who linger like awkward teenagers. I know what they're going to say, and the vindictive Valkyrie starting to grow inside of me wants them to do it. To lie to my face. To palm me off with another platitude. These two who, out of all of them, promised friendship and trust.

Maybe it's another *scuffle*. It's a snarky thought, but really, whatever it is, surely I can help? Do they truly think I'm so entirely incompetent?

When both of them hesitate, neither looking at me, I snap. "*Well*?"

Lucky rubs both hands over his face. The look he levels at the door settles into something ice cold. As cold as Jasper's wintery goodbye. Beau is staring down at his bowl, and he flinches, just slightly, at my tone.

I push up from my seat roughly, throwing down my napkin. I start gathering plates.

Lucky's cold expression cracks. "God, Eden, don't do that."

The bowls clack loudly against one another as I stack them.

Beau's breath comes out in a low, pained gust. "Go meet them, Lucky. I've got this."

"But—" He looks at me like he aches. Not a playful, hangdog expression, but full of real pain.

It doesn't seem to make his mouth work, though.

Beau stands, then says gently, "Go on, now."

Lucky reaches for me, then seems to think better of it. "I'm sorry. I'm so sorry, Eden."

I duck my head down, blinking, trying to work out how many more bowls I can carry. They're hard to see for some reason.

The door snicks closed.

"Put them down, pet. You don't need to clean up after us."

That does it. That one word is like a raw flame and my veins are oil. I'm lit up from the inside out.

I slam the bowls onto the table, and they bounce, spilling and skidding across the table. One shatters at my feet but I pay it no mind, except to enjoy the reckless sound.

"No, I don't, because I am not a *pet*, Beau," I yell. I *yell* and I want to keep yelling. "I'm *Eden*, and I deserve better than this, damn you."

My rage is free and wild. It's as if, when I filled my lungs to shout, I finally breathed in properly for the first time. With abandon. Like my worries and irritations have been suppressing my lungs, and every time I bit my tongue, I was cutting off my oxygen.

But, at the end of the day, oxygen is fire fuel, and it's licking through my whole body now. Is it possible to burn alive from frustration? God, I *do* deserve better than this. I'm a survivor. I've fought my own battles for years. At some point this has to stop—I can't be a pawn forever. Surely, I'm a knight. I've earned that much.

I just . . . can't keep losing every match against them. They're not playing fair, and it hurts too much.

Beau just nods, those hazel eyes of his steady and soft. It reminds me of the day I met him. How easily he soothed me. How all my fear just melted like hot butter under that accent and those woodland eyes.

Maybe I gave in to that feeling too quickly.

"I am Eden. A *person*, not a doll, not your *pet*. And I am. Pissed. Off." My pulse races, thundering at my throat like a chariot charge.

Beau's lips quirk at that, just a fraction, and I see red. I lift a bowl, ready to throw it across the room. I don't want to hit him, I'm sure of that. Pretty sure, anyway. But I'm just so *mad*.

His eyes widen, and he makes a grab for my wrists, putting gentle pressure on the one holding the bowl until I drop it with a hiss. "Hey there now, easy. I'm not laughing at you, pe— *Eden*, I promise."

"*Promise?*" I try to shove him back, but, well, he's strong, and my rage doesn't lend me super strength. The muscles in his arms barely flex as he holds back my weight, so I make my voice like a lash. "Why should I believe anything you say? Why should I believe anything any of you say when you won't ever tell me the truth?"

"Look at me," Beau says softly, despite his firm grip.

I'm worried about getting snared in those eyes again. The woods are dangerous things, after all.

But maybe *he* should be afraid. I've strayed off the pretty path now . . . and fires and forests don't mix.

"I'm not nothing, I can help. I can contribute more than just sex," I tell his chest. "I'm not nothing."

My voice breaks on the last, and I bite my tongue to stop my anger from fountaining into tears. I tremble from the effort, caught in that awful, awful place between anger and misery.

"Eden, look at me *now*," Beau orders, and I do find my head lifting despite myself, uncertainty washing through my flames. Dousing them.

I eye him warily, swallowing and trying to hold on to some of that heat, but when he seizes my gaze, he holds it with resolute firmness.

"I *see you*, Eden. Of course you're not a pet." His grip softens on my wrists, and he lowers them until they rest against his chest. Slowly, eyes trapping mine like ivy, he threads his fingers through mine. He continues in a low voice, "We might not have spent much time together, but I already know you're clever—you kept yourself out of danger for years, then set up a home for yourself and taught yourself to survive."

His thumb runs over our hands, and I decide not to tug them away.

Just for a moment.

"You're resourceful, I know that too. You lived off the land with no one to help you. And the very fact that you're still alive tells me you're stubborn. A real fighter."

He takes a measured breath and then drops a sweet kiss to our hands, never untying me from his gaze.

"I've seen your kindness, too. With me, with Lucky. You were afraid of us when we first met, and you still tried to get us to run to save our lives. And you're so damn brave. You stood up to Dom when he went after Jayk with his hunting knife, and you with only your bare, tiny fists. I *see you*, Eden, and you're the furthest thing from nothing I've ever met."

My lips part. After a moment, I suck in a breath, getting a full, delicious inhale of Beau. More fool me, I think he does mean it.

252 E n s n a r e d

"You hearing me?" he presses.

I nod.

"Ye—" My voice comes out raw, and I clear my throat. "Yes, Beau."

Beau groans, deep in his throat. "Two of my favorite words on your lips, darlin'."

I work up a small smile, thinking hard.

Beau drops a light kiss to my lips. Then another. Then one more, this one lingering long enough to leave me breathless.

He pulls back reluctantly. "I have to go, but we'll talk later. We can talk all night tomorrow if you want."

Tomorrow. Beau's "day."

Beau is tense and anxious, and I can't help but want to ease his worry.

"If that's what you're into," I joke, weakly, and he grins crookedly.

"You going to head up to bed now?"

Hesitating for only a moment, I say, "I'll go upstairs."

Relief touches his smile. Giving me one last kiss, he leaves me alone, just like the others.

A small while later, my eyes drift to the carnage at the table. To my lovely, terrible rage. Then, quiet as the mouse they believe I am, I creep out of the dining room and up the stairs.

Enough is enough. I need answers. I need the full truth if I'm going to stay. For my own sake, I can't accept anything less.

Beau doesn't see me as well as he thinks.

CHAPTER 24

DOMINIC

SURVIVAL TIP #146
People are your biggest weakness.
None more than yourself.

This is the last damn thing we need. Multiple screens take up two walls of the surveillance room—it took us months to adapt the room from Jasper's study. The server power and capacity needed to store a week's worth of footage from thirty-seven cameras is no joke. Fortunately for us, between Jaykob's previous work as a mechanic, the military tech that was sitting around for the taking, and our extensive Ranger comms and equipment training, we managed to rig it up.

In the large, center screen, four men, armed to their pits, creep through the forest. The camera tracks their movement steadily until they move out of range. They have the same rangy, tanned look of the men we tangled with the other day. That in itself wouldn't be enough, but . . .

"Play it again."

Jasper taps a few buttons, and the men creep forward again.

"There." The figures pause. "Right hand. Tattoo. The others had the same mark, like a coiled snake."

Grim understanding lines my men's faces and something inside me settles, just a fraction. This isn't the place for the petty squabbles we've been descending into lately. This shit is a problem. A big one. And they'll face it like soldiers.

Beau is taking longer than I'd like, but I trust him to deal with the girl. Despite his crush, he'll follow orders. He's smarter than me. He's always been smarter than me.

He won't make the same mistake I did.

"How did we miss this?" Lucky asks seriously, studying the screen. "We have cameras all through these woods. They're still meant to be five days south, right? How are they now a day and a half *north* of us? Could they be leftovers from the ones we scattered when Eden was with us?"

"I didn't miss this," Jasper replies with a hint of snap to his tone. "They didn't come from the south. That encampment is still there—I've been watching the cameras around them the most. None of the motion cameras were set off until now. I don't know how they could make it around the woods near us without being caught by our sensors. Not unless they knew where they were."

It's only knowing him as well as I do that I can see the worry in the tightness of his jaw. The slight defensiveness. He's been distracted these last few days. We all have.

And there's only one reason why.

Lucky turns to regard Jasper, with surprising evenness for him, maybe even a hint of chill. He doesn't even blush. "I didn't say you missed anything. I'm just wondering how they did it. Are we going to suddenly have more guys crawling up our ass?"

Jasper's eyes narrow, but I speak up before he can cut into Lucky. This is not the fucking time. Soldiers. We're meant to be soldiers.

"He's right," I say seriously, funneling my irritation into the problem, the solution. One of us needs to keep our head. "Pull up the motion cameras—we have two more in the north region. Then pull up four of the closest static cameras on screens four to seven."

Thin lipped, Jasper nods once and bends over the keyboard. The screens around us flicker to life. The two other motion cameras peer into silent greenery. Leaves flicker in the light breeze, but that's not enough to set off the sensors.

Of the four static cameras, only one screen shows an image.

The cameras need a decent amount of maintenance—about half our trips are just to keep them functioning and free of wildlife —so it's not that unusual for one to go down every now and then.

But not three.

At least they're set up to record remotely, so we should still have the data up until the point they broke down. Or were cut off.

Jaykob grunts a curse and tension bunches Jasper's shoulders. "They were up this morning. I only paused long enough for one game of chess. *One*. But I was still catching up on footage from the night before."

Frustration ticks over me, but I force it down, reminding myself that he wasn't trained for this. He's only one man and we have over thirty cameras in operation. There's no way he can monitor them all twenty-four seven—his focus was on the main threat to the south, and even keeping up with that seems to have run him down to exhaustion. Damn it, I wish he'd spoken up sooner.

"Go back three days," I order.

A moment later, all screens show an image. It takes some fiddling, but we manage to pinpoint when the cameras cut out. First the northernmost, then the other two, each one progressively closer to Bristlebrook. There are no shots of any of the men, the cameras simply cut out, but in the footage from the second camera, just before it shuts off, there are four tall shadows cast against the small patch of grass.

These men are coming from the north. Not the south. Four

men, connected with the group that had chased Eden. Connected with the men Beau and I buried two days later.

But how do they know about our cameras?

"Pull up the southern cameras."

Beau enters the room without knocking and no one flinches. There's no way anyone can get in this room without the code—getting past the wall panel in the bookcase is tricky enough. I raise a brow, and he gives me a small nod, though the cool distance in his eyes has something stinging my gut. Our argument the other day still isn't sitting right with me.

But he's asking too much.

I cut my eyes back to the center screen as it changes to a view of a small stream. At the rightmost side of the frame, just in view, is the edge of a large camp. Two men are visible, facing away from the stream and into the woods, talking and laughing raucously. I can make out the snake tattoo on the rightmost man's hand where he's turned toward the camera. There's no sound, but I would lay money that there are more of them in that camp.

"I've been monitoring this group since we last spoke. They haven't moved. They seem to spend most of their time in their camp, but every now and then they duck out like this," Jasper says.

"Could they be leaving the camp without this camera catching them?" Beau asks, peering at the screen with a slight frown.

"They could," Jasper admits. "However, the cameras on five and seven would likely catch them if they were to move toward Bristlebrook. And one of the cameras on two, four, or six would likely catch them if they were to move north. There has been no sign of any activity on any of these cameras. It's impossible to know for sure, of course, but we placed them carefully. Any other route would be incredibly difficult for them to traverse."

"And none of the southern cameras are down?" Lucky asks worriedly.

Jasper doesn't reply, but the screens flicker as he runs through all the southern cameras. All show varying images of dense, dark woods.

We watch the cameras for a moment as I think. How did they know where the cameras were? They're concealed. Not easy to stumble on.

And how are they heading in a direct line for Bristlebrook?

"Bullshit," Jayk growls. "*Maybe* they got themselves equipment good enough to sense our gear. Maybe. But they're not fucking Ringwraiths. No way they don't show on any one of the cameras before they cut the feed. They knew where they were. And they knew the tech well enough to stop it tripping our sensors."

Lucky examines Jayk with a sudden half-grin. "Was that a Tolkien reference?"

Jayk scowls. "I had a childhood too, you know."

"Did you identify with the Uruk-hai?" Lucky asks seriously.

Ignoring them, Beau edges toward the screens. "So they knew where the cameras were but, what? Except for one?"

He grimaces dubiously.

Jayk flips Lucky off and then shrugs. "The live one is C30—we only installed that one last fall. Could be working off old intel."

"But who even knew about the cameras except us?" Beau questions. "Our old group knew we were installing them before they left, but they didn't see where we put them. Only we knew their locations."

Jasper turns his chair, and he studies me, chin on his fingers. I fight to keep every muscle from locking up. I know what he's thinking. I'm thinking it too.

I shake my head once. "That's not it."

"Heather and Thomas knew," Jasper says, silk over steel.

Her name is like an iron fire poker—one glowing amber, fresh from the coals. It sears through my gut. If I could, I'd wipe her name from their mouths, their minds. Fuck them for thinking of her. Fucking them for thinking *that* of her.

Heather was a lot of things, but she wouldn't have sold me out.

My lip curls. "She. Wouldn't. Do. This."

Beau pushes off from the wall, watching me. He sets his feet in a fighting stance, like he doesn't even realize it.

I taught him that stance. Fucker.

His eyes run over my face. "Maybe we should consider—"

My temper flares, and I have to unwrap my hands from their fists so I don't end up slugging him. My father taught me better than that. No punching subordinates. Especially no punching friends.

But I can't stop the words from swinging out of my mouth. "We don't need to consider shit. None of you liked her, fine, but that doesn't make her the enemy. She was a cop, for fuck's sake. She saved my life. She's not going to turn her back on all that because you bullied her on the goddamned playground."

"You and I have very different memories of how that went down," Jasper snipes.

Like he wasn't the worst of them all.

Fierce, gorgeous, brave, submissive Heather.

There doesn't seem to be enough air in the room.

Or maybe it's just that thinking of her always makes me feel like I'm drowning.

I pinch the bridge of my nose, hard, fighting for control. "None of that matters. We have four to the north, closing in. We have upwards of twenty to the south. While the south is stationary, we need to take care of the northern threat. Now. I don't want them anywhere near Bristlebrook."

Making the call eases some of the tightness in my chest. It clears my thoughts. Now isn't the time to be hurting over my ex or fighting with the guys. We have a job to do.

A home to protect.

"Beau, you're with me. We leave at oh-four-hundred tomorrow. I want them cleared out by the following day."

To my surprise, Beau hesitates, and my teeth click together. "What?"

"It's my night with Eden tomorrow."

The whole room catches its breath.

That drowning sensation starts creeping into my chest again, like my lungs can't get enough air. I could spit a dozen things right now, but for some reason my usual rage doesn't come to save me.

Why is he pulling this now? We have bigger things to worry about.

"I need you with me." My voice is low but thankfully even enough.

I always need him with me.

Beau looks uncomfortable, one hand rubbing his chest. He glances at Jayk, at Lucky. Jaykob just smirks, starts trimming his nails with his pocketknife. That fucking knife.

Lucky clears his throat, offering, "I can go."

But my eyes are trained on my friend. Steady, dependable Beau. He'd really choose a night with some girl over watching my back? Didn't he learn from my mistakes? Doesn't he know the girl will only break his heart?

Sometimes I'm not sure what was worse—losing Heather, or losing Beau's trust.

A pair of frightened, defiant gray-blue eyes wink into my mind. For some reason, they won't stay out of there. The fear in them stirs me. The bravery . . .

It doesn't matter.

She *isn't* worth it.

She's not worth the distractions. The risks.

She's sure as hell not worth the cracks that are spiderwebbing across our friendship.

"There are four of them. There's a good chance we'll need a medic," I grit out, hating that a hint of panic laces my voice. "Reschedule your damn date."

Resentment, clear as day, flashes across his face. His square jaw is tight, set—but fuck him for that. I *do* need him.

Because he's a doctor, of course, and we don't know how that fight will go down.

And because Beau always falls too fast.

Why can't he see that I'm protecting him, keeping him away like this? He doesn't need to get hurt again.

After too long of a pause, Beau's hand drops from where he was rubbing his chest and his expression closes over. "Yes, sir. Oh-four-hundred."

Relief crashes through me, and I reinforce my knees.

"There are four of them. Will you need extra hands?" Jasper asks, sitting back and glancing at Lucky.

Jasper's face is blank and serene as a glacier, but I know to watch his right hand. Long fingers worry his wedding band, which he now wears on his other hand. Round and round.

I force a grim smile. "To handle four? Two is plenty." And it is. Not a one of those four will have an ounce of our training. "Jaykob is right, though. Something about this isn't right. I'd feel better knowing we have people here watching the house. It could—"

"Ah." The surprised exhale from Jasper stops me short. His dark gaze has snared on a much smaller screen, set up on his laptop. He turns it. "It appears we have company."

There's a touch of humor in the tilt of his mouth.

My eyes drop to the screen, and I freeze, rage licking at my insides. The girl has the nerve to—

"Did you leave the bookcase open?" I demand of Beau.

His chin drops, face hardening. "Of course not."

She worked it out. The hidden latch that would open the hidden door in the bookcase. She crept down the short corridor, lightly enough that we couldn't hear her, and is now standing outside the door, studying the keypad panel with a small frown.

We watch as she appears to give up on that and presses her ear to the door.

Jaykob, of all people, snorts in amusement.

Anger spikes, but I hold it in check. Let it burrow deep into my bones, leak into my marrow. She's trying to *spy* on us? We've given the spoiled brat everything—every single thing she could ask for—protected her against *everything*, and she does this? Useless, dangerous girl.

"Dom," Beau says warningly.

I shake my head once, stalking to the door. I yank it open and grab her by the arm, ignoring her breathless gasp, and draw her into the room.

"Get on your knees," I tell her coldly.

Eden's eyes widen until they almost eclipse her glasses. There's tension in the air, snapping through it like electric currents. The others are shifting, hesitating. When she doesn't move, I step forward and lower my voice.

"On. Your. Knees."

I expect her to look to the others, to turn those big, pretty eyes on them and beg for help. But her wary gaze stays on me, tracking my movements the way a gazelle side-eyes an approaching lion.

But there's nowhere for her to run.

Interestingly, beside her nervousness lurks a touch of her own anger that she doesn't bother to hide. It intrigues me—just a little —but I push that feeling away.

Swallowing, she lowers herself gracefully, like she's done it a thousand times. Like the movement is a memory, preserved in her flesh.

As she does, Jasper releases a long sigh, the way people do when sipping spectacular wine or watching a breath-catching sunrise.

Her breathing settles as she sits back on her heels, hands folded neatly in her lap. Mine settles too, until we're breathing in the same rhythm.

It's always been like this for me. The more control I take, the more controlled I feel. The more they submit, the more the awful, discordant tunes of the world begin to bleed into something pleasing. It doesn't stop the fury—it's buried too deep now—but it takes the edge off.

I walk around her, enjoying the way she tenses, how her head turns, just a tilt, trying to keep me in view.

"What were you hoping to achieve by breaking into our private rooms and sneaking outside our door?"

"Answers." Then she lifts her chin and adds, "Obviously."

Lucky sucks in a breath and, behind her, Jayk sticks his tongue in his cheek, seeming to hold back a smirk.

My eyes narrow on the girl. That tone . . . She should be gagged for that alone. Gently, I brush my fingers over her hair, down to her jaw. Her whole body goes motionless.

Crouching beside her, I study the side of her face. Then wrap my hand around her throat in warning, arching her head back slightly so she has to look at me out the corner of her eye.

"You spoiled brat. Must be hard sitting here in safety while we take risks to protect you."

Her pulse thunders under my fingertips and there's no helping how hard I'm getting. It would happen to anyone like me, holding her like this. Nothing to do with her, not really.

"I can help," she pants.

As if she'd know how.

I feel the urge to tighten my grip, watch the nervousness grow in her eyes. I want to swallow her fear.

If Beau and I head off tomorrow, we'll miss my night with her as well, I realize. Not that it matters. I have no intention of touching her—it'd only encourage Beau's fantasy, and I'd rather spend the time fixing our shit than setting us both up for failure again.

I've failed more than enough already since the strikes.

I release her.

Don't push me, I warn her with my eyes.

She should pay attention. It's the only warning she'll get.

"We're going tomorrow morning. There's a small problem we need to deal with. Beau and I will be back in two or three days," I tell her, the picture of calm control.

The others watch me closely. I wonder if they'd leap to her defense if I pushed her now.

Or if they'd help me hold her down.

My words catch Eden's attention though, and her head whips around to look at Beau. Surprise and no small amount of disappointment tightens her expressive features.

"Oh. But—" Her teeth tug at her bottom lip, a hint of color pinkening her cheeks.

As if his earlier distance with me was a mirage, Beau's smile for her is slow and warm. That peach-sweet, cowboy smile has been melting hearts since we were seventeen. Biting back my scowl, I move in front of the girl, between her and Beau so she can't see that damned stupid grin.

"Look, we have bigger priorities than licking your pussy. But if you stay on your knees and beg, one of the others might oblige— makes no difference who does it, right?" As soon as the crude, stupid words leave my mouth, I want to reel them back in.

Beau tenses again, and I just stop myself from grimacing.

This isn't how I do things. She's just a girl. A civilian. An ungrateful one, sure, but what else is new? I'm here to keep her safe and to get on with my life.

I don't need to resort to this kind of petty bullshit.

I don't know why she's getting under my skin like this. It must be Beau. She's causing problems between us and that's why she's pissing me the hell off.

Eden's nostrils flare delicately at my insult, her lips pulling in like she's biting back her words again. She did not like that. Not one bit. The tiniest twist of curiosity tugs at me. I wonder if I can make the little librarian snap at me properly.

I wonder if she ever feels rage like mine under all that politeness.

I rake my eyes over her, then shrug one shoulder dismissively. "Though it's only Beau you'll really be missing—I wouldn't have touched you either way."

"Oh, *fuck you*," she hisses.

There it is.

Lucky whistles.

"Dominic," Beau warns again.

"Beaumont," I mimic. My eyes are locked on Eden.

One hand flies to her mouth, like she's shocked herself. Her eyes flicker to Beau then, looking for help.

Mistake.

In moments, I have both her tiny wrists trapped in my grip, and I'm dragging her to her feet, careful not to strain her arms. Eden yelps, then struggles, lighting my blood with the desire to trap. To subdue. I grab her around the waist and haul her against me, her back to my chest, her weight nothing at all. Running on instinct, I pass her wrists to Beau.

When he doesn't take them, I look up.

His jaw flexes in indecision. No surprise. He's never liked the discipline aspect of topping.

It's why he needs me.

I raise a brow at him. "She was specifically told to stay out of it. Instead, she broke into our private rooms and tried to spy on us. You okay with that? What did she say to you before you came up here?"

From his wince, I'm guessing the brat wasn't too honest about her intentions.

Eden kicks my shin, and I grunt. In her ear, I snarl, "Try that again, subbie. I dare you."

"I agree with Dominic." Jasper links his fingers, leaning on one arm of his chair. "She can't disobey orders like this. It's not safe, particularly given the circumstances. She's earned her punishment." He hesitates, then adds with a hint of frost, "Within reason, of course."

I shrug. "I'm reasonable."

Lucky's lower lip is trapped between his teeth, and he's staring at Eden squirming in my grip. Poor librarian—even Lucky seems more intrigued than inclined to help her. Jaykob is the only one looking at me, more direct and assessing than usual. But, after a long moment, he settles back against the wall, his attention flicking back to her.

Giving in, Beau sighs. "Sorry, darlin', the mob has spoken."

At that, Eden starts squirming in earnest, and I'm grateful Beau takes her wrists so that I can hold the rest of her.

"Wait!" She throws her head back, and I get an arm behind her back, bending her over at the waist toward Beau. He takes a seat beside Jasper and, holding her wrists, yanks her into place over his lap.

"I don't want to be punished!" she squeals.

That actually startles a real snort of laughter out of me. "People usually don't."

She's barefoot and still wearing the little sundress—the short, flippy skirt annoyed me all through dinner. The sight of her bent over and waiting is like a promise. A prayer.

I stretch my neck, eagerness thrumming through my veins. "What's your safeword, little librarian?"

"My— My what?" she stutters, squirming over Beau's lap again to get away from me. Then she freezes, looking up at him. "You're *hard* right now?"

The outraged offense in her tone has me biting back another laugh.

Beau doesn't bother to hide his, but when she twists again, he lets out a strangled groan. "Is this a punishment for her or me?"

I share a small smile with him, glad for the warmth back in his face. Then my brain catches up to what she said, and I snap around to look at Jayk, at Lucky, at Jasper.

"You didn't cover safewords?"

Jaykob gives me a lazy smirk. "We got to non-verbals."

Jasper hums in displeasure.

"What?" Jaykob's smirk takes on an innocent curve that looks profoundly wrong on his rough features. "Her mouth was full."

I turn my attention on Lucky, whose shoulders cave. He clears his throat, looking so carefully anywhere but at Jasper that it's painfully clear who he's trying to avoid.

"We kept it light," he says evasively.

Jasper is staring at him with unnerving intensity, then shakes his head and adds, "Eden and I didn't engage in a scene."

I kneel beside her head and despite the awkward angle, she looks up to glare at me. Reluctantly, I have to admire the courage that takes.

And the sheer stupidity.

"A safeword, little librarian, is a word you can say to make everything stop if we go too far or if something is pushing you past what you're comfortable with, and not in a fun way. Any word you like, but it should be one that you can remember easily in the heat of the moment. Any preferences?"

Her full lips flatten. "A word that I say to stop everything just so I can be asked to leave? Isn't the point that I just shut up and do whatever you want?"

My amusement dies a hard, abrupt death. Something sick and queasy churns my stomach.

"You—" For the first time in as long as I can remember, I'm lost for words.

Her head lowers again, her shoulders curving in protectively. Seeming to make a decision, Beau hauls her up, so she's sitting on his lap and curled against his chest. He looks as stunned as I am.

"No, Eden," I say finally, uneasily. "There is never, ever a consequence for using a safeword. Anything between you and anyone here . . . it's an agreement. Between equal, consenting parties."

I shouldn't have to explain this. How can she have this so completely wrong? How did *I* get this so damn wrong? It goes beyond like or dislike. She has the right to feel safe here, for as long as she wants to stay.

At the word *equal*, she tucks her head into Beau's chest but not before I see her mouth twist. I glance at Jasper, who arches a brow—a clear "fix this" demand if I ever saw one.

"Eden," I try again, "you don't have to do anything here that you're not comfortable with. I'm . . . sorry . . . if that hasn't been clear."

She murmurs something that sounds like, "*Brbrk*."

I frown. "What?"

Eden sighs, then lifts her head. She hesitates but, after a moment, she clears her throat. She lifts her eyes up to mine hesitantly. "I want Bristlebrook to be my safeword."

"Bristlebrook," I repeat.

Did she hear anything I just said? Damn woman.

She gives a slow nod and some of her long, dark hair falls forward. "It's only fitting," she says thoughtfully. "It's the first place I've felt safe since I can remember."

Beau releases a long breath.

"It's not feeling *safe* here, or with any of you, that's the problem," she continues, looking at each of us. "I don't like being lied to. Or coddled. I can help. I want to help. I can't bear to be bundled up and put on a shelf like a dress-up doll when you're done playing with me. I think . . . I think I would rather live alone than live like that."

I stare at her, feeling like I've been punched in the gut. I'd be the first one to admit that I'm not the best with emotions. That's what I need Beau for. But it's been a long-ass time since I've felt put in my place.

Still. This shit with the hunters is dangerous. Life and death. I might not love having her underfoot with Beau making cow eyes at her, but I don't want her to run back off into the wilderness and find herself prey to those assholes either. The thought of her, bright and tiny and defiant, in their hands makes me want to kill something.

Maybe we can bring her out later. On small trips. Out with Lucky to go hunting, or with one of us to fix the cameras. As long as we can see there's minimal danger before we head out, she can't do too much damage.

But not now.

The others have stayed silent, waiting for me to take the lead on this. I don't need to see the grip Beau has on the girl to know that if I fuck this up and upset her more, the two of us will have a serious problem.

I look at Eden, still on one knee. I haven't knelt for anyone in my life, and I wonder if she appreciates the view. But, for the moment, even I can tell I should lay off the domineering. At least a little.

"Three of our cameras are down," I tell her, deciding on a half-truth. We can start fresh once this shit is dealt with and she's not in danger of running. "That's a lot, even for us. It leaves us with some major blind spots. We need to patch them up quickly."

Stubbornness firms her jaw, and I raise a hand.

"It's rough terrain, and we need to move fast; you'll only slow us down. That's not an insult, it's just a fact. You don't know the way, or the area, and three dead cameras is too dangerous to leave for long." Not a lie, exactly, just not the whole truth. "But next time . . . next time we'll have you come along, even show you how to do it yourself so you can help us going forward."

Her mouth clicks shut in surprise. I straighten, then hold out a hand. "Fair?"

Eden looks at my hand as though I might have answers written on my palm. "You'll let me come out with you and be useful, just like the others?"

"You can go hunting with Lucky, fix cameras with us, and we'll even show you how to protect yourself, if you want," I say agreeably.

Everyone should know how to protect themselves these days. That just makes sense. We'd only take her out when we were there to protect her anyway.

Eden stands up from Beau's lap, right in front of my hand.

Would the damn woman just shake it? I don't usually make concessions. Does she have to keep pushing her luck?

Blue-gray eyes sear me; I can see her sharp brain picking apart my words as though she's a human caught making a deal with the faerie king, trying to spot a trick. I manage to stop myself from shifting.

Just.

"And you'll tell me the truth? Bring me in on everything, the same as the others?"

I narrow my gaze on hers. "You're not a soldier."

"Technically you're not anymore, either," she reminds me blandly. "And neither is Jasper, and he's still included."

I cross my arms over my chest.

"Or maybe," Eden continues, "it's because I'm a woman, and you think that I—"

"For fuck's sake," I snap. "*Fine*. Fine. Going forward, we'll tell you everything—*if* you agree to follow our orders. I won't have you going off half-cocked thinking you know best and putting yourself in danger."

She blinks at that, and Beau smirks.

"Because *the others* would be upset," I grit out.

Beau gives me a dry look.

"And for the *record*," I say to both of them, "Jasper has been training with us for years, had the same security clearance as we did, and we still don't bring him out with us most of the time."

Eden studies me. Sharp. Intense. Then she nods slowly. "Okay."

"Okay?"

She thrusts out her hand. "Yes. It's a deal."

I put my hand into hers and shake.

With her small, warm palm in mine, I have the strangest feeling that I'm handing over far more than I bargained for.

Maybe she's the faerie queen after all.

CHAPTER 25

EDEN

SURVIVAL TIP #267
*If you're hunting big game,
make sure you don't get gored.*

The forest vibrates with life. Sun dapples the thick undergrowth as it twitches with scurrying animals. Birds trill to one another, darting from branch to branch. Spotting a particularly dry patch of leaves, I correct where I'm about to place my foot and silently thank Beau for thinking to bring me supple leather boots among the multitude of lingerie. They're soft and silent and offer me far more protection than my last pair of shoes. My poor foot has only just recovered from treading on that stone.

I shouldn't be out here at all, really. I know I shouldn't. But despite all the quite reasonable conversations I've had with myself this morning, I still find myself tracking Dom and Beau through the woods while they make their way to the broken cameras. Dom's main argument against me coming today was that I couldn't keep up. All I'm doing is proving them wrong.

Right?

It's too late to turn back now, anyway. It's been hours, after all. I may not be a gun-toting hard-ass with buns of steel, but I am a useful person. I'll track them to the cameras, surprise them with my apparently shocking ability to keep myself alive for a few hours in the forest, impress them with my stealth, and then help them to fix the cameras.

Or watch them fix them.

To be fair, I really can't help with repairing wildlife cameras.

I can't delude myself entirely . . . this will probably end very badly for me. Either one of them could snap me like a Kit Kat—and gobble me up just as fast too.

But after they get over being pissed, maybe they'll be impressed?

Maybe?

Oh, their stupid muscles and stupid smiles and stupid kisses are making me stupid. I'm going to be in so much trouble.

For the third time in as many minutes, I study the ground. The trees. It isn't easy. They've left far less trace than most game. Still, they're two large men, and no skill in the world can completely disguise the impressions of their boots. Small leaves have been crushed with a heel here, a slide of dirt there. Making a decision, I push on to follow a few bent twigs.

Maybe I shouldn't be testing them so much. It's only been two weeks, after all, and Dom did make some major concessions last night. I probably should have waited, followed the agreed pace.

But the truth is, they terrify me.

I'm scared to death that I'm going to wake up one morning and all of that independence I've worked so hard for, all of that self-worth, will just vanish in a cloud of mindless orgasms. That they'll tell me what I want to hear, and I'll start nodding along like I always do and just find myself the pampered princess they've been treating me as.

I need more than that.

I don't want to be defined by who I am to them—I did that with my husband and that was a disaster. I need to be an equal. Free. I need to be defined by who *I* want to be.

And I want to be like this. Free and wild and brave and settled in the forest. It's so good to be back out among the trees.

I've been following them since dawn, and the sun is high in the sky now. Past noon, certainly. Surely Lucky has found my note by now—I left it in the kitchen, and he never stays out of there for more than a few hours. Even after my little white lies to the three of them, that will clear things up. I hope they aren't too worried I'm gone.

And I *really* hope they don't come after me.

Abruptly, a rough, masculine voice snaps an order ahead of me. It's far enough through the thick brush that I can't make out what he said, but I know it's Dom. Satisfaction and pure nerves crash through my veins, and I take a deep breath to settle myself.

I should call out, I know. Let them know I'm here. But the hunt is almost . . . thrilling. I wonder just how close I can get before I'm discovered. Why I'm craving that look of shock on Dom's face, I have no idea, but I want it badly. I want that smug confidence *gone*.

Slowly, and as carefully as I can manage, I ease my way through the trees, slipping behind anything that will hide me as I move forward.

Keep low, stay steady, and watch your damn feet, Eden.

In a few minutes, I can hear them. They're not making much noise, but definitely more than me. A few minutes after that, I catch glimpses of them through the trees. They're wearing their Army uniforms, to my surprise, and I can only see them because they're moving so purposefully.

"This . . . it . . . fine . . ."

Grimacing, I pick up my pace just slightly, wanting to hear what they're saying. I manage to get closer, close enough that I can see the stubble on Dom's jaw when he turns his head. I lower my foot . . . only to feel the fragile indent of a twig against my boot. Catching my breath, I glance down and move it to a safer patch of dirt before putting my weight down.

My heart pounds giddily in my chest.

"Yeah, well, if you didn't want to talk then you shouldn't have dragged me out here," Beau snipes in a tone I've never heard from him before. His accent sounds softer too, for some reason.

I slip between two trees, following.

"Heather wouldn't have done this. You out of all of them have to know that. You know what she was like."

There's a silence, and I edge forward, wanting to hear more. Lucky wouldn't give me any details on Heather, but I've gathered enough to know that Dom was hung up on her and she left with some guy called Thomas, who used to be part of their team. I haven't been alone with Beau long enough to ask any questions, and Dom, well, there's no way I'm going to ask Dom about her.

But what has she done now? I thought she was out of the picture.

"*What*?" Dom prods.

"Just trying to figure how to answer that without getting my ass kicked."

I struggle to split my attention between my feet and the conversation, but they're not moving too fast, at least.

"Just say it."

Beau huffs. "Fine. Heather was a lot. Sure, she was brave as all hell—I'll give you that. But she also had a knack for hitting a guy below the belt that you either didn't see or didn't want to."

"She was tough," Dom snaps.

I blink. He sounds so defensive of her. Uneasiness sifts through my gut. It doesn't sound like these are old, dusty feelings at all.

"She was a dick, and I could never tell if it was intentional or not. There's a reason the other three hate her, Dom—they didn't just wake up one day and decide it. She was always different around you and Thomas. Softer. The rest of them . . ." Beau trails off.

I shouldn't be listening in like this. This is not the way I should be hearing about them.

But I still don't make a sound.

"It's not like the others are innocent. Lucky put a snake in her bed, for fuck's sake."

I bite down on my lip hard to stop a giggle. Lucky's never put a snake in *my* bed.

Well, not the fanged kind anyway.

Beau snorts. "It was a garter snake. Completely harmless. And you know he only did that because she kept saying that he was too soft to watch anyone's back. She told him flat out that he should stay back with the women and children while she and Thomas went out on raids."

Dom stops abruptly, and I only just catch myself before I step into view. My heart hammers, then twists a little as I think of Lucky. I've seen him in action, and he's as fierce and capable as any of them.

"She was joking. She had a mouth on her, but she was only joking," he says, though he sounds uncomfortable.

Beau makes a derisive sound. "Yeah, real funny. I laughed a lot when I saw him hurting after that one. I don't even know how she always found the exact softest spot to hit on a guy, but she was a real pro. I thought Jasper was going to murder her on the spot."

Dom blows out a long breath. "And you?" he asks in a low voice. "She do that with you too?"

"She—" Beau groans. "Look, she never wanted to push me too far because she knew we were tight. But as charming and fantastic in the sack as she was when it was both of us, it hit me like a brick to the face when she turned around and made it clear she wasn't interested in me. She wanted you, Dom, and Thomas, and as soon as you weren't around, she made the lines pretty damn clear."

The queasiness in my stomach worsens. *Fantastic in the sack.* Well, that's just . . . great. I bet she knows all kinds of fancy tricks.

Maybe it's for the best that my night with Beau was interrupted. Damn it, why didn't I spend more time making Jayk or Lucky show me how to be amazing? I was so caught up in just being with them I didn't even think about *how* I should be with them. I should have taken notes. It's unlike me not to have studied.

I'm starting to seriously regret coming out here, and not for the reasons I worried I would.

There's no *way* I can reveal myself now.

"Beau—"

Beau cuts Dom off. "And I don't know why you still keep defending her. She did the exact same thing to you. As soon as she made up her mind on who she wanted, she left you in the dust."

"It wasn't like that," Dom says quietly. "She's entitled to decide who she wants to be with. She never hid that she wanted Thomas as well."

"I'm surprised the two of you didn't just share her," Beau mutters, and the bitterness in his tone makes me wince.

After a moment, Dom says, "That was never going to happen."

There's an awkward silence as they continue walking for a stretch, and I have to push to keep up.

Beau finally sighs. "I don't think she would have done this, for what it's worth. If there was one thing she cared about, it was keeping our people safe. She made the civs feel safe. She managed that better than any of us—it's why half of them left with her. I agree that she wouldn't have sold us out."

Sold them out? I'm missing a key piece of information here, I'm sure of it. I should have known I wasn't getting the whole truth.

"Thank you," Dom says.

They fall into silence, and I follow them, wriggling apart every detail from their conversation.

"Should we check C18 as well?" Beau asks, and they both pause.

I stop, suspended mid-step, more startled than I should be when he breaks the silence.

"It's out of the way," Dom replies, but he seems to be considering.

"But if they're taking the canyon pass, that'll be the way they go. It's longer to Bristlebrook, but sure as shit easier than this route. There's a good chance they'll avoid these cliffs, right?"

I frown. Who is "they"?

"It's worth a look. I'm not having them sneak around us. If they do take the cliffs, they'll be here for hours, and they're not going to take them at night unless they're taking a run at the Darwin award. We can come back." Dom's voice turns grim. "They should pray we don't find them while they're hanging from their fingertips."

My stomach drops. Trip to repair some cameras, my ass. What the hell is going on?

They start to move again and, with a start, I realize they've changed directions and are heading right for me. Swallowing a squeak, I swing deeper into the brush, ducking under a low, heavy branch. In just moments, they pass me, close enough that I could reach out my fingers and brush their legs.

I'm debating whether I should ease out of my hiding place and start following again when Dom pauses.

"What is it?" Beau asks.

My breath strangles. Did I leave some trace? Should I just start running now?

"Rock in my shoe."

As he stops to shake it out, I let out all the air in my lungs. My hand is shaking where it's pressed against the bark.

I'm okay. I'm safe. I spent years out here perfecting staying undetected in the forest. *I'm good at this.*

The pep talk helps. When they start moving again, so do I. I try to stay close, wanting to hear them if they start talking again, wanting to hear about this "they" they seem to be tracking. But now, I really don't want to be caught. It's one thing to follow after them when they're making a harmless trip to fix some equipment —it's another entirely to follow them into a firefight after being "sold out." So I hang back, just a little, far enough that they're out of view but still in hearing distance.

As we continue, my momentary panic starts returning to anger.

They lied to me. *Again*. How many times am I going to fall for this? Dom's words from last night ring in my ears. "We'll tell you everything," he said. He *promised*.

Actually no, that wasn't quite it. "*Going forward*, we'll tell you everything." His exact words.

God. Damned. Sneaky. *Lying*. Son of a—

I burst into the next clearing, not realizing until too late that the slight rustles and crunches ahead of me have gone silent. I only have time to see the flash of a gray, metal muzzle, and then I'm being yanked sideways, and my ears are ringing so, so loudly.

Face down in the dirt, I choke on air. My body aches and stings, and I'm shaking so hard against the ground I wonder if it's possible for one person to cause an earthquake. There's heavy pressure on my back and a hand—maybe?—on the back of my head.

I'm too stunned to even try to wriggle away.

Then the pressure eases. I'm flipped over, and Dom crouches over me, glowering down with ferocious fury. Movement draws my eye, and I look over to see Beau, white to his lips, staring down at the pistol in his hand.

Grabbing the front of my jacket, Dom hauls me to my feet. His mouth is moving, and his golden eyes spark like flowing lava. Deaf and numb, I recognize with a detached kind of curiosity that he's probably yelling at me, but the whining, ringing sound in my ears drowns him out.

I was almost shot.

My teeth start chattering. I try to make them stop—the jolting is annoying—but they won't obey.

Beau almost shot me.

Dom seems to realize that I can't hear him or, at least, I'm not listening. I watch interestedly as his brows lower. Scowling, he wraps his long, warm arms around me and holds me tight against his hard chest. One hand grips the back of my hair, pressing my forehead to his chest. The rims of my glasses press into my skin.

Why didn't I realize I was so cold until he wrapped me up?

His spicy male scent curls inside me like smoke and slowly, so slowly, underneath the almost too-intense pressure of his arms, my uncontrollable shaking fades, then stills completely. Warmth starts seeping back into my limbs.

" . . . should be far enough away. It's hours yet before we'd see them on either route based on their pace so far."

The words fight with the ringing inside my head, but Dom's voice is much nicer than that piercing wail. Low and deep and rumbling, it shivers through my numbness.

"Is she okay?"

I nod against Dom's chest, and he stiffens, then yanks me back. "You can hear?"

"You hugged me." I stare up at him as his eyes narrow.

"I applied pressure. It can help with panic attacks."

"Uh-hu—"

Beau grasps my shoulder and spins me around to face him. "What in Satan's holy asshole are you doing here?"

If I thought Dom was mad before, it has nothing on Beau now. He's still pale under his tan, and there's a harsh tension around his eyes and mouth.

I open my mouth.

He fists a hand in his short hair. "I almost shot you. I could have *killed* you. In what idiotic corner of your brain did you think sneaking up on two trained, *armed* Rangers was a good idea?"

Frowning, I try to speak again.

"We told you to stay put. You agreed. You lyin' to us for fun now? You think we tell you to do things to make us giggle? It's not *safe* out here, Eden. Do you have any idea what—"

Enough. I cross my arms over my chest. "No. I *don't* have any idea what is happening out here. If you hadn't lied to me—again— then I wouldn't have followed you. Who exactly are you trying to track down? What's really going on, Beau? Because from what I hear, you're not exactly gearing up to fix up some cameras." I glare at him, then at Dom. Taking a deep breath, I force myself to calm. "You said you would be honest with me."

Dom cocks a brow. "What I *said* was—"

"'Going forward.'" My mouth twists. "Yes, I remembered *that* part earlier." I sigh, looking around at the underbrush. "I just wanted to help. I—I thought if I showed you that I could keep up, that I'm not a liability out here, then you'd see . . ."

"You *are* a liability out here."

The acerbic tone from Beau makes my insides curdle, but I raise my chin. This is partly my fault, but it's partly theirs too, and I'm exhausted with all the lies.

"Don't worry about it. I'll make my own way back."

"It will be dark soon," he says, as though it might have escaped my notice.

"It does that at night." His lips tighten at my tone, which I ignore, along with the quaver in my stomach at the sight. "Despite how well you *see me*, Beau, I should remind you that I've probably spent almost as many nights in these woods as you have, even with your fancy Ranger training. I can find my way back. I remember the landmarks. I'll be fine."

"No." The clipped word from Dom finally draws my attention from Beau.

I expect rage but, as if he truly is always Beau's opposite, Dom seems calm.

He assesses me, taking in my small pack, my boots, my jacket, my small trusty knife. "The hunters that were chasing you are part of a larger group that seems to be heading to Bristlebrook. Our northern cameras went down, that wasn't a lie, but we think they were taken out. We're heading up to intercept them. We haven't spotted any other hunters in proximity—the rest seem to be camped elsewhere, and we have them under surveillance—but it's possible there are others we haven't seen. Your little knife won't do much against them."

Hunters! I swallow. Hard. Something cold washes through my veins. Memories of running through the forest, feet bleeding, chased by their threats and shouts flash through my mind. I swallow again, trying to work some moisture into my mouth, but I'm breathing too rapidly again.

Then their earlier conversation clicks. They were worried Heather revealed where the cameras were. That's why they were talking about her.

"They're—" I breathe through my nose, thinking. "That's who you fought with. Just after I arrived. The two of you went back out and . . . The scuffle. That's how you got that bruise."

It's a paler color now, almost impossible to see. Dom nods.

"Okay." I pinch the bridge of my nose under my glasses. "Okay."

They're coming after me. I'd *thought* there were more hunters than they killed in the clearing. There's a whole camp now?

And they know where Bristlebrook is—it isn't safe there any longer.

"I need to . . . " Run. I need to run. "I'll go. I'll leave, and then they won't come to Bristlebrook. They'll leave you alone. I'll . . . I didn't mean for this to—" My tongue feels thick and clumsy in my mouth. "I never meant to put you in danger."

"And how will they know you've decided to do that? You planning on handing yourself over?" Dom asks dryly.

I blink at him. Why is he not more upset? Isn't he meant to overreact to everything?

"We have it under control. You panicking was the reason we decided not to overshare. Besides, there's a good chance this has nothing to do with you. You might have just been unlucky enough to be in their path to Bristlebrook." He stares down at me from under his brows. "This'll go a lot easier if we don't have to carry you with us. You calm?"

Lightheaded, I nod. What does he mean, they're not after me? But . . . if they're heading toward Bristlebrook . . . if that's their goal . . . then he's right. They probably weren't targeting me specifically. I was just the side quest.

Am I really that unlucky?

"Are you calm?" he repeats.

"Yes, sir."

I nod again, more sure this time. Beau tucks his pistol away, and I swear his fingers still tremble. He doesn't look at me.

"Good. I don't suppose you told anyone back home where you were going?"

I duck his eyes. "I left a note."

And lied through my teeth to all three of them, but I'm not mentioning that.

"Great. Fantastic." Dom's eyes roll to the sky for a moment, then he shakes his head once. "They better have enough good sense to stay put. We should duck in front of C17 so Jasper can get a visual."

After addressing the last to Beau, he points at me.

"You. You want to prove you can keep up? Then do it. We're not stopping till we find a sign of them or it gets too late. When we do, you will stay put, out of the way, and not make a sound. Clear?"

"Yes, sir."

Dom surveys me then, cataloging every inch of my expression. He grunts, then stalks through the brush, somehow managing to make very little sound.

I give Beau a questioning look, and he points his chin after Dom, indicating for me to follow. He still doesn't meet my eyes. Can he really not understand why I had to come out here? He could have told me the truth too.

Trying to ignore the stinging hurt in my chest, I follow after Dom.

CHAPTER 26

JAYKOB

SURVIVAL TIP #138
If they think the worst of you,
be worse than that.

I swing the door shut on the washing machine and place my tools back in their holsters. It takes longer than I'd like—all I want to do is turn it on and see if it works—but discarding tools just anywhere is how you lose them.

Working at my uncle's car yard growing up, I saw plenty of sloppy mechanics losing their tools, or treating them so rough they were no good to anyone, and it ain't like any of us had the cash to just go buy replacements. You take care of your tools, and they'll take care of you. It applies for a wrench or blowtorch as much as it did for my weapons after I enlisted with my brother.

I scowl against the ache in my chest—the one that sucker punches me every time I think about Ryan—and glare at the tumble washer. I've been working on it for two damn weeks and haven't been able to fix it. I'm actually regretting the whole month I was "too busy" to look at it. It was funny when his royal highness was the one spending hours cleaning my socks, but now that it's Eden . . .

Whatever, it doesn't matter to me if she scrubs her fingers raw. I'm just usually quicker at fixing this shit, and it's starting to piss me off.

The guys are on my ass about it too—every one of them grilled me about it this week. Funny how they all managed to ask about the washing machine and didn't give me one single word of apology. Except for Jasper, but since he spent the whole time lecturing me about "not retaliating" and finding "appropriate ways to manage my anger," I'm not counting it.

I dumped a bucket of engine grease down the back of his fancy shirt.

That seemed to manage my anger pretty good.

Screw them all, anyway. One day I'm beating up on big-eyed librarians, and the next I'm their fix-it guy again? They're lucky I didn't torch the stupid Playboy mansion from under them.

It's not like any of them offered to help, either.

She did, though.

Tools secured, I turn back and hold my breath, hovering over the switch. If this doesn't do it . . . I flick the switch to "ON" and wait for the telltale lighting up of the small screen.

Nothing.

"Useless goddamned *junk*!" Frustration spills over, and I kick the broken thing hard, denting the metal door. A dent that I'm also going to have to fix. "No good to *anyone*."

I yank my wrench out of my side pocket, not sure if I want to go back in or just start beating on it. "Stupid son of a—"

"Hey, I'm sure the machine's mama was a nice lady."

My head drops back. I clench my teeth together and count to ten in my head. *Don't bash his head in. It ain't worth the wrench.*

"You know, likes a tumble, always wet."

I up my counting to twenty. Shouldn't have left my pistol in my room.

"Plus, she could probably take a real big lo—"

"Get out." I yank the dented door open and get back down.

Lucky laughs, ignoring me as per fucking usual.

He crouches down beside me, blocking my light. "Is it working yet?"

I shove him back so he overbalances. The light clears up, and I grunt in satisfaction. I put away the wrench and reach for the screwdrivers; I need to take the panel back out.

"Guess that's a no, huh?"

The panel's sticking and it takes a yank to pull it out.

"Not in a talking mood? That's cool. We don't need to talk. People talk too much, is what I always say. Talk about nothing really, just go on and on and on . . . "

My grip on the screwdriver tightens, and I imagine it plunging into his neck. It's long enough—could probably get him right through the voice box.

"And on and on . . ."

"Don't you have somewhere better to be?"

"Not really. Drying shed's stocked. Eden's hanging out with Jasper today." He grimaces and looks at the ground. "She wanted to smooth things over with him, I guess."

Of course she's with Jasper.

What would *those* two have to argue about? Whether caviar tastes better with crackers, or just on the tiny little silver spoons they were born with?

My mood sours further as I stare at the coils of wires I've been looking at for weeks. *His highness* is exactly who a princess like her would get all wet over, with his fancy books and fancy hair and *degrees*. The kind of guy who said things like "existential" and "grandiloquent."

I catch sight of my greasy fingers and scowl. Pulling out of the machine, I slam the door shut again, not bothering to re-secure the panel. What's the point? The damn thing's broken beyond fixing. Better to just get it out of here.

Lucky stares at me from where he's still sprawled where I shoved him.

"Why don't you go run off and play with them?"

They'd probably love that. Most annoying shit on the planet but everyone just *loves* Lucky. Ryan was like that. Probably the only reason I haven't actually beaten his head in yet.

Lucky's mouth twists in a way I'm used to seeing in the mirror. "Nah, I'm good."

My scowl deepens as I stare at him. I don't do the touchy-feely shit.

"She told me she was spending the day with you," I tell him, not really sure why.

She'd come in all pretty and pink-cheeked from the morning frost. Some idiotic thing in my head thought she was coming back to work in here with me. But that really was stupid. That day was a one off. She was hiding from Dom and needed the big bad monster to protect her.

If she really wanted to hang out, she wouldn't come to me.

This morning, she dropped off some breakfast and said she was spending the day out in the sunshine with the circus rat. And that just made sense. She doesn't fit in this grubby, dark place. Matter of fact, I'm starting to think I don't much fit in this place either.

"She did?" Lucky sits up and wraps his arms around his knees, an odd expression on his face. "Guess she changed her mind."

"Yeah, well, at least you made the shortlist," I mutter, resentment clogging my throat.

Lucky blinks, and his brows shoot up. I bite my tongue with another scowl and turn around, packing away my tools again. My mouth is running on stupid today, apparently.

"Whatever. We can have just as much fun!" Lucky insists with mind-numbing brightness.

"Fuck off."

He jumps up so he's sitting on the workbench beside me. His

ass is on my favorite rag. "Come on, you've got to be sick of being in here all day. Come spar with me. I'm rusty."

I tug at the rag. "I'll kill you."

"You try to kill me, I try to kill you—what are friends for, anyway?"

He lifts one cheek off the rag and does some wide, pleading thing with his eyes. I yank the rag out from under him with a grunt. "We're not friends."

Lucky presses one hand to his chest. "Well, now you're just being mean."

"Move."

"No."

I glare at him. "Get. Out."

He examines his nails. "Nah."

"For fuck's sake," I explode. "We are not friends."

Shoving away from the work bench, I stare around the barn, not sure what to do next. The uncomfortable ache I've had in my chest the past few weeks turns hot. I'll raid the doc's supplies later.

It's probably heartburn.

I pull Ryan's old pocketknife out of my side pocket, then start flipping it between my fingers—but I've never been able to nail the tricks the way he used to do. "You think I don't know I'm just some guy in the same regiment that just happened to be around when it all went to shit?" I scoff. "I don't *care*. You're all slumber buddies who like to braid each other's hair or whatever, that's fine. Whatever gets you hard. But leave. Me. The. Fuck. Alone."

The outburst feels good. They always do. But underneath that is a sick, gnawing feeling in my gut. There've been a lot of different run-ins with the guys over the years. It's always been pretty clear I'm the ugly duck of the heroic little swan crew.

Heather was the first one who made me seriously think about leaving, but it didn't get much better after she left. The shit the other day, realizing just what kind of person they really think I am . . . that's got to be the end of it. I don't belong here—and they don't want me here. Not really.

And as for her . . . well, whatever. She's just the latest girl around. She'll choose one of them, and there ain't a speck of doubt in my mind that I'm not making that shortlist either.

I realize I'm towering over Lucky. Wide eyed, he stares at me. "For the record, I braid my own hair. Beau's the only one with any skill at all, and he pretty much always refuses to help me."

My fists lift of their own accord and it's fifty-fifty whether I'm going to strangle him or chuck him out on his ass.

Lucky grins, lifting his own hands defensively. "No, Jayk! Dom already took my lunch money this week!"

I grab him by his shirt and drag him off the bench.

"I'm sorry. I'm sorry!" he says, laughing. "Dude, chill, I love this shirt. I'll stop, I'll stop!"

Huffing out a breath, I glare down at him. His dimple winks at me and, rolling my eyes to the ceiling, I let him go.

His smile changes in a way that makes me uncomfortable, and I'm just about to throw him out again when he says, "Look, just for the record? I never thought of you as just some guy who happened to be there. And I get that I drive you nuts and you're a grouchy bastard, but I like having you around."

He eyes my head. "And I would totally braid your hair too if you grew it out." His gaze drops down my body, and he grimaces. "I'm not braiding it anywhere else, though. I don't care who you are, manscaping is important."

I shove him toward the door again. "I manscape, dickhead."

"You manscape your dick head? Wow, you should talk to Beau about that. Pretty sure you're not meant to have hair there."

I pick him up and put his squirming ass over my shoulder, intending to toss him out this time, when the barn door opens. In the next two seconds, I've dumped Lucky and grabbed for the MK 16 strapped under the workbench. It's only as my fingers wrap around the cold metal that I realize it's just Jasper.

Tension brackets his mouth and lines his shoulders, and an additional crease forms between his brows as he glances between me and Lucky, who somehow managed to land neatly on his feet.

Flippy freak.

Jasper's next look at me is nothing short of hostile, and I slap the rifle on the bench and bare my teeth. *Smiling*.

He's always telling me I need to work on my body language.

When he doesn't say anything, I cross my arms and wait. Jasper doesn't come here without a reason—and it's not because he's worried I'm feeling up his boyfriend.

"Eden isn't here." It's not a question, but his eyes scan the barn anyway like she might pop out of a shadow. They linger on the door at the back.

Yeah. Right. Like Miss Manners is coming anywhere near my bed before she's due.

"I thought she was spending today with you," Lucky mumbles.

Running his hands down the front of his shirt, he stops when he seems to realize what he's doing. He crosses his arms, then uncrosses them. As if giving up, he shoves his hands in his back pockets and leans against the battered truck.

Idiot.

Bored, I consider the truck. I'm going to have to move that thing into the clearing beside the barn so I can dismantle this washing machine again properly. If I decide it's worth the effort.

The lethal look on Jasper's face eases as he watches Lucky.

"She told me she was spending the day working with Jaykob," he murmurs, then his face sharpens again. A dark brow crooks as he addresses me, "May I assume that she told you she was spending the day with Lucien?"

That pulls me from my inspection of the truck.

Huh. So she's a sneak.

"Wait. Wait, what?" Lucky shoves off the car. "Are you saying she *lied*?"

"And here I thought I was the slow one," I mock.

Where the fuck would she have gone?

"That stupid little girl," Jasper hisses. "She's gone after Dominic and Beaumont."

He stalks out of the barn, and we both follow on his heels. Jasper's always been better at the leaps in logic. But damn. My heart rate picks up. Dom and Beau are going to take out four hunters. This isn't a hiking trip.

Hell, she probably didn't even manage to follow them. She could be lost. There are tons of treacherous trails in those woods, and wild animals, and other hunters. It gets cold out. It'll be night soon. Did she even think to bring a jacket?

I mean . . . it's nothing personal or anything. Obviously. But she's like a kitten. I don't want to see a kitten get hurt either. Might have grown up rough, but I'm not a complete asshole.

Not all the time, anyway.

"Why didn't you realize she was gone?" I snarl, feeling dizzy. "There're cameras all through here. Outside the barn, the kitchen, the cave—"

Jasper stops sharply inside the glass sliding doors and then pushes into the kitchen. "She was in here earlier."

Impatient, I shrug. "Yeah, she made me breakfast."

"She made you breakfast?" Lucky shoots me a disgruntled look.

There's a piece of paper on the counter. Snagging it, I read the short note.

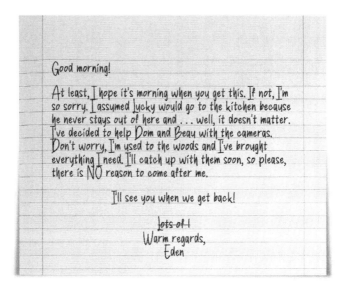

Good morning!

At least, I hope it's morning when you get this. If not, I'm so sorry. I assumed Lucky would go to the kitchen because he never stays out of here and ... well, it doesn't matter. I've decided to help Dom and Beau with the cameras. Don't worry, I'm used to the woods and I've brought everything I need. I'll catch up with them soon, so please, there is NO reason to come after me.

I'll see you when we get back!

~~lots of l~~
Warm regards,
Eden

Stomach dropping, I hand the note to Lucky, who skims it with a groan and passes it to Jasper. He glances at it, then crumples the paper between his fingers. Taking a deep breath through his nose, he smooths it back out and puts it in his pocket.

"It seems Dom was right. Eden is in dire need of discipline." Icy stalactites drip from his words.

I roll my eyes at him even as my own panic sets in. "She ain't a prisoner. She can leave whenever she wants."

Jasper's upper lip curls. "She's going to get herself *killed*."

He's so tense, I brace myself, wondering if he's dumb enough to take a swing at me. The shrink might be good at a lot of things, but brawling ain't one of them.

Lucky places a gentle hand on Jasper's chest. "She'll be okay, Jasper. She's smart—she'll have caught up with Beau and Dom. They'll keep her safe."

Jasper stills at Lucky's touch. His chin drops as he looks down at the hand on his chest. After a moment, he takes another breath and nods sharply. Then, wrapping his long fingers around Lucky's wrist, he removes his hand from his chest.

Without looking at the other man, he starts moving again.

"I'm pulling the cameras up."

Lucky's fingers curl into a fist, but his face stays expressionless as we follow Jasper upstairs. It only takes him minutes to flick through the cameras. We catch glimpses of her on C7 and then C14. Oblivious to the screens catching her movement, Eden walks confidently, a small smile on her face. She stops only briefly to examine the ground or the leaves.

Out in nature, with the trees and dappled light all around, she looks more than pretty. She's . . . she's one of those stupid words Jasper would use. A word like extraordinary. Sublime.

Breathtaking.

Damn it. Maybe it's not heartburn. Something is seriously wrong with me if I'm quoting I-only-drink-water-with-a-squeeze-of-lime himself.

"What were the stamps on those?" Lucky asks, then whistles low. "She's making good time."

Jasper flicks through a few more screens, and a flash of color on one makes him stop. A pink scrunchie is pinned to a tree.

Lucky leans in. "Which one is that?"

"C17."

Jasper pulls up the logs and rewinds through the video. When the time hits less than an hour, three figures appear. Beau and Dom loom over Eden, who is trapped between them, looking miserable. After a moment, she turns to the camera and mouths, "Sorry." She wrings her clasped hands.

Dom looks at the camera and shakes his head firmly. Grasping her by the back of the neck, he turns her and pushes her in Beau's direction. Beau grimaces, then walks her out of view. Dom gives us a final look, raising one hand in a clear "stop" motion.

"Pft," I mutter. "I'm going after them."

"Don't," Jasper tells me, sounding tired. "Just stay put. They have her. She's safe."

"Yeah. Right. Like they won't choose each other over her if it comes to it."

Worry scrapes at my insides. Anything could happen to her out there. Shit happens all the time—my brother is proof of that. Maybe she *should* be our prisoner. As soon as we get her back, I'm putting a collar on her and tying her to the damn wall.

Princesses shouldn't be let out of their towers . . . that's what monsters like us are for.

"Beau wouldn't let that happen." Lucky frowns.

"He wouldn't," Jasper agrees. "Neither of them would. We have our own job to do."

"Then maybe you should do it."

I work up a smirk at him, the one I know he hates, and let myself enjoy the flash of rage behind his eyes. In a lot of ways, he's just like her. Pretty, pampered. Something snarled and starless curls in my chest, beating alongside the panic. Someone like him couldn't protect someone like her. He'd never get how dangerous it could be for her, not really.

My sneer turns ugly. "First you didn't notice three cameras are down, and now Eden walks out. How did you miss that? You even know how to work these things? If she gets hurt, it's on you."

Jasper stiffens, lips pressed together. Beside him, Lucky sighs and gives me a disapproving look.

My smirk fades, and I glower back at Lucky. Whatever. Eden is out there, about to be in the middle of a firefight because of him. He should have been watching her. He should have made sure she was safe.

We all should have.

I should have.

Restless and uncomfortable, my eyes drift back to the camera where Eden dropped out of frame.

"They'll keep her safe," Lucky repeats.

I shrug. My tongue presses against the edges of my teeth until I taste blood. "Whatever. She dies, she dies."

Lucky shoves me then in a rare burst of temper. "Oh, shut the fuck up, Jayk. Don't say shit you don't mean."

I round on him, but Jasper stands and yanks Lucky behind him, giving me a warning look. My stomach clenches bitterly. Yeah, like I would take the stupid kid's head off for a shove.

Jasper spreads his hands. "Jaykob, I understand you must be feeling—"

I roll my eyes and flip Jasper off, heading for the door, sick of this. Sick of every-fucking-thing here.

If she's not back by tomorrow I'm going after her, whatever any of them say. I'll make sure she gets back to Bristlebrook and that every inch of her perfect little ass is safe—but then I'm done. These days, there's probably more than enough groups ready to take an asshole like me. Trained soldiers are in high demand, especially ones who know how to crawl in the mud.

All I know is I'm done being the cast-off. The embarrassment. The rude, uneducated lowlife who's going to fly off the handle. A risk to be managed. I'm tired of being feared and looked down on and knowing that, sooner or later, *she's* going to start looking at me like that too.

She's got enough Prince Charmings here.

Eden will get her fairy-tale ending—and I'll go play the villain somewhere else.

CHAPTER 27

EDEN

SURVIVAL TIP #1
Kill or be killed.

W e found their camp last night.

Or Beau did, anyway. He'd scouted ahead and came back forty minutes later saying they'd set up for the night. He and Dom then had a "strategy meeting"—I wasn't invited—and decided to rest for a few hours. Dom told me that they planned on surprising them in the early hours of the morning when they would be less on guard.

Dom told me because Beau still hasn't looked me in the eye once since the nearly-shooting-me incident yesterday, let alone spoken to me.

Now, the dark sky tells me it's hours before dawn, and Beau is bent over a small pan, preparing a quick breakfast over a low fire—the growth is too thick to worry about it being seen. One look at his stiff shoulders warns me against offering to help.

Rolling up my compact sleeping bag, I sigh. Dom's eyes settle on me again. He's been watching me almost as often as the trees, expression unreadable, and it's starting to make me nervous.

Glancing at him, I raise a tentative brow.

He looks over my pack, my boots, the canteen at my hip. "What else did you bring?"

I blink. "Um, well, I have a change of clothes, my compass, a small knife, a first-aid kit, matches, a lighter, water purifiers, rope, a flashlight, solar blanket, and rations." I think. I decide against mentioning exactly how much cheese I took from the fridge. We really need more goats. "Oh, and I have a small pot. And a book. That's it, I think."

"You managed to steal all of that without the others noticing?" Dom's voice is dry as dust.

I tuck my hair over my ear. "I was just . . . borrowing them."

"Uh-huh." He looks back out at the woods. "You know how to use this stuff."

It's not quite a question, and I stifle a sigh at the undertone of surprise. "Yes."

Dom nods. His thick black hair catches the dappled light through the trees. "You're different out here. Different to how I thought you'd be."

I glare, taking a seat beside him. "Useless, you mean."

The corner of his mouth kicks up, just a fraction. "Yep."

When I huff, he looks over at me again. "Don't give me that look. You put the help in helpless the last time I saw you out here."

"When you last saw me out here, I'd been running for days under threat of my life."

After a moment, Dom nods. In companionable silence, we watch Beau make breakfast.

I wrap my arms around my legs, and ask quietly, "Is he going to stay mad at me?"

Dom snorts, surprising me. He glances back at his friend, then down at me with a wry smile. "Beau's got no idea how to be mad—he was brought up too nice. He'll sulk until he gets over it."

"Sounds healthy." My heart sinks.

A warm, muscular arm shrugs beside me. "Or you could confront him about it. That works about half the time."

I grimace. "And the other half?"

"Makes it worse."

His golden eyes kindle with humor. I haven't seen that look in them before, like warm honey, and I have to look away as my cheeks flood with heat.

"Why aren't you more mad at me anyway?" I ask, flustered.

"I'm furious with you." Even without looking at him, his irritation is palpable. "There's just not much we can do about it now. I'll hand you over to Jasper for punishment when we get back. Then we can call it even."

My heart rate picks up. "Jasper said he wouldn't punish me without my consent."

Or at all.

I can't quite seem to put that into words though. Or why Jasper *not* punishing me sounds like the worse end of the deal.

"He won't," Dom agrees, then asks seriously, "But do you really think you don't deserve it?"

"I—"

"You put me and Beau—not to mention yourself—at risk with this stunt. And note or no note, I'm only about fifty percent sure the others will stay put. You lied to us."

"You lied to me first," I mutter. Dom glowers, and I raise my hands. "I know I made a mistake, but punishment is for children. I understand that I should have stayed at home, but if I'd had all the information—"

Dom is shaking his head. "That's the thing, Eden, you don't understand. Whether or not you had all the information isn't relevant, not when you're putting others at risk. You can afford to do that when you live by yourself, but not in a group. Not with us. I need to know that if I tell you to do something, you'll do it. I don't give out orders for the hell of it, and I also can't always spend the time to explain everything—at some point you're going to have to trust me. Trust that I know what I'm doing to keep all of us alive, and just do what I say."

I swallow. "I do trust that, Dom. That you'll keep us safe."

And I did. I haven't doubted that since he planted me beside him on that cliff face and laid waste to every one of the nightmares who chased me.

"If you did, you wouldn't have come out here." His voice is grim. "You think that if any one of the others had disobeyed orders like you did, that they wouldn't get punished?"

"You'd bend them over Jasper's lap too?" I ask tartly.

Dom's face hardens. "They would be so lucky. Trust me when I tell you that you're much better being punished as a submissive and a civilian than as one of my men." He sighs and rubs a hand over his jaw. "It's harsh because it needs to be. Your decisions can have serious consequences, Eden, and I need to know that you'll remember that lesson. Whatever you say, there's a difference between thinking you understand something and really *feeling* it in your skin."

Biting my lip, I think that through. Despite my serious lack of interest in "getting punished" there may be some teensy tiny point to what he's saying. Beau nearly shot me, after all. That would have haunted him for the rest of his life.

"It also works to clear the slate, work out resentment in a healthy way. Once your punishment is over, it's over. Lesson learned, no hard feelings."

I give up and stare at him then. "Just like that?"

His lips tilt up again. "Just like that."

This punishment sounds different to Jasper's . . . vocation. In a way, it's almost refreshing. No grudges. No guilt trips.

"Would you really call that a 'healthy way' though?" I ask, though I'm mostly teasing.

Dom rolls his eyes, then points his chin back at Beau. "You prefer that route? It's gentler, sure, but it might be Christmas before he forgives you."

Groaning, I bury my face in my hands. "You're not helping." I peek back up at him. "There has to be something else. He can't have been in relationships before and not be able to have a mature conversation when he's upset."

Dom turns back to the trees, the tilt to his mouth vanishing.

My eyes narrow. "Well? What did he do with the others?"

His lips press together in a grimace, and I try and fail not to notice how full and pretty they are. Not that much about Dom can really be called *pretty*.

"You know we shared," he says. Not a question. "If he was mad at our subbie, he'd come to me and we'd work out a suitable punishment. I'd facilitate the scene, set it up, and he'd use it to work out what he needed to get off his chest. But he's not good at initiating that kind of thing on his own. Too conflicted. All that Christian guilt."

I stare at him.

"Oh." As that sinks in, my shoulders slump, and I repeat more quietly, "*Oh.*"

Dom has made his position clear. He wouldn't touch me if I were the last woman on earth—and at this point, I might as well be.

So, no cathartic forgiveness scene for me. Unless . . .

"He wouldn't— Would he do that with Jaykob?" I ask tentatively.

"No." Tension bunches Dom's shoulders. "He wouldn't. He won't. You might have noticed, but Jayk doesn't play well with others."

"But maybe, it could be like that first night with Jasper, when he—"

Dom's brows slant down so hard, I cut myself off.

"That was a one-off," he says curtly.

My breath leaves me in a long, slow sigh. Fine. No working things out that way then.

Dom's eyes are on me, but I don't want him doing that read-my-face-with-his-golden-laser-eyes thing, so I drop my chin to my knees and keep watching Beau.

"I'm going to scout a bit. Back in ten," he says abruptly, pushing to his feet.

As he leaves, Beau looks over at him, then at me for just a moment before his gaze skips away. I'm debating whether or not to try the confronting-him method when I see what's in his hands.

"No, stop!" I yell, jumping to my feet. Beau looks at me sharply, but I'm on him in moments. "Drop it. Drop it right now."

"Eden, what—"

He doesn't drop the herb, so I slap his hand, hard. Beau releases it with a curse, but I've already pulled out my canteen.

"You don't have any cuts on your hand, do you? You didn't eat any of it, right?" I splash water over his fingers, grasping his wrist when he goes to move away.

"Stop. *Stop*, woman. It's Queen Anne's lace—wild carrot—it's harmless," Beau snipes, yanking his hand out of my grip.

My pulse pounds in my throat, and I scan his face. He doesn't seem ill. His pupils aren't dilated, no trembling.

My voice comes out much harsher than I mean it to. "It's *not* Queen Anne's lace." I bend down and pick up the stalks of the plant, avoiding touching the leaves. In a month or so, it will bud with tiny white flowers, but this one is bare. "*This* is water hemlock. See the purple splotching along the stem? Queen Anne's lace is entirely green and has tiny white hairs sprouting along the stem. This is hairless."

Beau hesitates, then reaches for the plant. I shove it deep in the pocket of my pants.

"No!" I exclaim. "Leave it be! Do you have any idea how poisonous water hemlock is? You really didn't eat any, did you?"

"No, I didn't eat—"

"You would have been dead within an hour!" My hands are shaking. "You shouldn't just grab any plant if you don't know what it is! You should know better than that."

Beau's jaw clenches and, for a second, I think he's going to yell back at me. But after a moment, he steps back and picks up the pan. He dumps the contents in the bushes. Still not looking at me, he stalks to the small brook and starts washing the pan. His back is like a wall.

I take a deep breath, willing myself to calm down. In a brief moment of clarity, I wonder if this is how he felt when he fired on me yesterday. The thought of what could have happened . . .

"Beau—"

"What happened to breakfast?" Dom asks from behind me, and I jump about a foot in the air.

He eyes me. "Remind me not to put you on watch duty."

I lift my chin. "We had to get rid of breakfast."

Dom frowns, but Beau stalks back. "Leave it, Dom. Let's get moving."

The large man looks between us, then shrugs cautiously. "Fine. Let's go."

I'M ON A TIME OUT, and I hate it with every fiber of my being. As soon as we started the approach to their camp, Dom and Beau nestled me under a large boulder well out of the way and told me to stay put until they came back for me. At least Dom had left me with sweet words of comfort: "If we're not back in an hour, we're not coming back. If that happens, head to Bristlebrook."

I could punch him.

Anxiety churns my stomach. It's only been ten minutes or so, but the minutes drip by like treacle. For once the scents of damp earth and fresh air do nothing to pacify me. I've been straining to hear something, anything, as though listening harder will actually bring the sounds closer.

I get to my feet, needing to move. They didn't seem too worried, and I vividly remember how easily they handled the hunters last time. They know what they're doing. And if I want them to give me and my skills the benefit of the doubt, the least I can do is offer them the same.

But, God, it's *different*.

What if something goes wrong? This isn't *like* last time. Last time the hunters were running blindly, confident they were chasing down one unarmed woman. This time, they're prepared. They're expecting trouble. They'll have someone on watch. It will be so much harder for them to be caught unawares.

I worry my lip between my teeth as I think about that. Why *would* they take out the cameras? So we lose visuals, sure, but *why*? So they can get more men through the woods unseen? Didn't Dom say that the rest of the men were elsewhere? Without the cameras here, how can we be sure there aren't more?

And if the hunters *were* taking out the cameras just to hide their own tracks, then why wouldn't they have just avoided them, since they clearly knew their location? They *had* to know that the dead cameras would be noticed.

It . . . doesn't make sense.

There's no reason to tip us off like that.

Which means . . .

Panic ricochets through me just as the first crack of gunfire shatters the silence.

It means this is a trap.

Without stopping to think, I bolt toward the sound. It's followed by a series of rapid blasts. I'm not sure what I can do, if there's anything I *can* do, but I can't sit by and listen and do nothing when they're walking into a nightmare.

Branches whip at my cheeks and arms, and I force down memories of my last flight through these woods. I'm not the hunted this time. I grip my knife.

Never again.

Why why *why* didn't I think this through last night? Or this morning? I'm the worst kind of idiot, fretting about Beau being mad at me and worrying about punishments when I should have been considering what lay ahead. The very real, actual danger they would be facing. *Stupid*. Dom is right—I'm not ready to face this kind of threat.

I slow as the sounds start getting louder. The gunshots are deafening, and I can hear shouting now. I think I catch Beau's voice amid the racket, but I can't be sure. Pressing a hand to my chest, I take a deep breath.

Think, Eden. I can't go rushing in there. I need to see what's happening. Looking around, I try to find inspiration. My eyes dance over the brush and green twice before settling on the tall, heavily branched trees. It makes me think of Lucky, whistling from the treetops as he fired down on the hunters.

Tucking my knife into my belt, I hurry around until I'm as close as I can get to the clearing without revealing myself. Carefully, quietly, I climb a large, overhanging tree. It takes more effort than I'd like—my upper body strength isn't what it should be—but I manage it. My ears ring and my pulse thrums a staccato beat in line with the gunfire. I'm desperate to hear Beau or Dom, but I can't tell voices apart in all the yelling.

Keeping low on a thick branch, I edge forward until my head just peeks from the leaves and I can see down in the clearing. When I do . . .

I press a hand to my mouth.

Carnage.

There are more than four men here. Three bodies are sprawled and splattered in the clearing, one over by the tree line. I try to avoid looking at the gory chunks torn from their sides, their heads, and just take in features, clothing.

Not Beau.

Not Dom.

My relief is short-lived though. Heart in my throat, I watch as men move behind the tree line, leaning out to fire shots and then curving back behind protective trunks. Gunfire flies in every direction, and it's hard to make anyone out in detail.

I notice, though, that one crack of noise sounds louder than the others. Closer. Turning my head slowly, I can just make out a man dressed all in dark brown lying flat along another branch, just a few trees over from mine. His branch protrudes far out over the clearing and he's much farther forward than me. He fires down into the trees, a killer in the canopy.

My bladder starts to quiver, and I press my forehead to the branch beneath me, breathing shallowly. *He hasn't seen me. I'm okay. Everything is* fine.

"Fuck! Beau, get that goddamn sniper!"

My head lifts at Dom's rough order, eyes scanning the clearing. I can't see him. I can't see either of them.

"Kind of busy right now," Beau shouts back with a grunt, as though the air has left his lungs.

Relief makes me dizzy. *Alive.* They're both alive.

Then what Dom said registers. The sniper has to be this man in the tree. The way he's lying on the branch, he must be almost impossible to see from below. But from up here . . .

Fear locks my muscles for a moment. It's crazy. I can't do this. I can't do anything about this. I'm a librarian, not some G.I. Jane. Sweat beads at my temples, under my arms.

I can't do nothing.

With more effort than I'd like to admit, I unclench my grip on my branch and ease back as slowly as I can. I do *not* want to draw attention to myself. When I'm sure I'm deep enough into the leaves that I won't be seen, I stand and, holding nearby branches as I go, make my way toward the adjoining tree.

The benefit of these woods is that the trees have grown densely, so it's not too hard to work my way from tree to tree until I think I reach the one the sniper is on. As I clamber quietly onto one of its nearby limbs, a bullet collides with the trunk behind me, smashing a deep gouge in the wood and sending splinters flying.

My hand wraps around my throat to catch myself before my scream escapes. I have to swallow it back three times before I'm confident it will settle.

I really hope Dom or Beau doesn't accidentally kill me while I'm trying to help them.

Frozen, I wait on the branch by the trunk, waiting to see if the bullet disturbed the shooter. When nothing shifts in front of me, I shakily get down on my hands and knees.

After a moment of hesitation, I pull my pocketknife from my belt. It will make climbing more difficult, but being armed makes me feel better.

Marginally.

The limb is thick and wide and it protrudes far over the clearing, so it takes a few moments of shuffling through the cloud of leaves before I catch sight of the sniper. When the boots come into view, I breathe a sigh of relief. Despite the thick branch, I was half-sure he'd have felt me moving along it and that I'd clear the leaves only to find myself facing the barrel of a gun.

I pause again about a foot from him, realizing I have no idea what to do next. Stab him? How quickly can he turn around and point that thing at me? I nervously realize we're about fifteen feet in the air.

I have to do *something*.

While I hesitate, the sniper tenses and fires off three more shots. Stomach bottoming out, I don't think. I throw myself forward and push his legs to the side, hard. He yells, twisting and trying to keep his hips on the branch, and his flailing pushes him more off balance.

But he keeps hold of the firearm.

The gun spooks me, and I shuffle up quickly and shove at his hips, wanting him to let go.

His lower half falls off the branch.

The man's eyes widen in fear, and he drops the weapon to clutch at the branch as he begins to slide off, only just catching himself from a complete fall. The gun drops to the ground, splitting apart, and a sob escapes me, but I quickly turn my attention to the dangling man. This close, I can see his eyes are brown, and his face is gaunt and dirty. He looks like someone who used to frequent my library. He's young —younger than me, definitely. He could be anyone.

"Help me," he gasps, scrambling at the tree limb for leverage. "Help."

He was shooting at Beau, at Dom, I remind myself, trembling. *He wants to kill them.*

My throat closes over. *God, he's still a person.*

I edge closer, not sure if I'm going to help pull him up or stab his fingers to make him fall. I don't recognize myself right now. The sounds of the firefight fade into the background.

"Please," he says, brown eyes soft and begging.

I reach for him with both hands—one to help, one to kill.

More quickly than I can register, he grasps my wrist. "Bitch," he snarls. "Sam'll have to miss out this time."

And he yanks me, hard. Unbalanced on my knees, I go flying, but at the last minute I twist and try to use the knife in my other hand to catch on something, anything, to stop my fall.

It does catch, puncturing deep into something thick and tough, and the jolt changes the angle of my fall. Momentum spins me and brings me in close to the tree again, and I hit the man's back with my front. The knife jerks down, sawing through whatever it's caught on. Something warm and wet sprays over my face, blinding me.

The man screams and releases my wrist, and he arches, throwing me back. My stomach drops out from under me as I realize I'm falling. I throw my arms out again in pure panic, blind, not sure which way is up. Something hits my right arm in a burst of shocking pain, then my shoulder, then I manage to catch onto something solid and rough, which slows me for just a moment before the momentum tears me away and raw scratches rip down my arms.

I hit the ground, and I remember to fall to the side and crumple as I land on something at once soft and hard. I read about that, the falling, that's what you're meant to do. Parachuters fall that way. It's how not to die. I'm pretty sure that's what I read. Or maybe that was what *not* to do.

Everything stops.

Am I dead?

I don't feel dead.

I'm thinking about parachuters so that has to be a positive sign.

In fact, after a moment of lying in shock, I feel very much alive and very much like I hurt *everywhere*. Very much like I can't pull enough air into my aching lungs. I can't open my eyes—something wet and sticky is coating my face. Sounds have gone quiet around me, and I wonder if that's real this time or if I've been deafened again. But there's no ringing in my ears.

It's just quiet.

I want to lie here and feel sorry for myself. To catalog each and every injury and assess how bad it might be before moving, but that would be stupid. Because *someone* has to have survived, and if it isn't my guys . . .

Shakily, I wipe at the blinding liquid over my eyes—I don't know where my glasses have gone—and then stare at my fingers. Thick, garish red coats them. Even a little blurred, I can see that much. Breathing through my nose, I force myself to wipe the rest away and then pull myself up.

The man is under me.

Scrambling back, I can't help the screech that leaves me then. My knife sticks out of his back, buried to the hilt, and his neck is bent at an unusual angle. My mind jars on the image. I only just stop the inane urge to shake him awake.

Injuries not conducive to life. Isn't that what they say?

Nausea rises, and I only just turn to the side in time to empty my stomach noisily. Bile, hot and acidic, scorches my mouth and burns my nose. But even when I squeeze my eyes shut, his body is imprinted in my mind.

When I'm finally done, I take deep, gulping breaths, and my gaze darts around the clearing, searching for any movement. Someone has to have heard that. The scream, if not the vomiting afterwards. I need a weapon, and I need to leave. Now.

I look around for anything else. I spot the gun that he dropped at the base of the tree but, reluctantly, I decide against it. It looks broken, and even if it wasn't, I have no idea how to use a gun. Even if I did, I doubt my vision is good enough to hit anything reliably without my glasses.

Crawling forward, I eye the knife, trying not to look at what's beneath it. I also try not to smell the urine and feces he secreted when his bowels released. Grasping the hilt, I grimace at the sticky feel to it. When I tug, it doesn't come easily, and my wince deepens.

"Come on, come on," I beg under my breath.

Bracing myself, I yank it hard, and I have only a brief moment of victory when it comes free, as a hand clamps over my mouth, and I'm wrenched away from behind.

CHAPTER 28

EDEN

SURVIVAL TIP #109
Break when you need to.
Preferably in the arms of a gorgeous man.

I scream. I try to bite the hand, twisting as hard as I can and kicking back to try and free myself. If I can stab him, if I can just get the knife around, then I can stop him. I've done it once now—what's one more life on my hands? I fight wildly, violently, but the grip doesn't loosen, doesn't do more than dislodge tears from my panicked eyes.

"Enough, fuck, darlin', stop fighting me. Easy now."

I fall still, heart hammering in my chest.

"That's it, you can drop the knife now. There's a good girl."

A shudder goes right through my body, down to my toes. The weapon drops from my numb fingers.

"That's good. If I let go of your mouth, can you promise me you won't scream? Stay nice and quiet for me."

Beau's slow, soothing words by my ear start to settle my rampaging heart. His breath is warm and light against my chilled face. I nod, and his grip over my mouth eases until he's cupping my chin, his thumb making tender tracks along my cheek.

"I found these. They're banged up, but they should still do the trick." Gently, so gently, he slides my glasses back on my face.

Needing to make sure he's okay, I turn to look at him. His mouth is a breath away and the air between us tangles. The warm brown in his green eyes seems to glow, and to my horror, I feel tears well up again.

"Beau, I—" I press my hands against his chest. Blood is sticky between my fingers.

"I know, sweetheart."

A pair of brown eyes in a too-young face flashes into my mind, pleading. I shy away from the memory, and the flashes that follow, each one more tactile, more visceral than the last. The feel of my knife puncturing through thick skin, the spray of hot, salty blood against my face, the foul stench on his limp body.

"Stay here with me, Eden," Beau orders. Then he makes a sound of frustration deep in his throat. "I need to signal Dom, okay? It'll be loud."

Burying my fingers in his shirt, I nod again. Breathing through my nose, I focus on Beau, scanning his body for injuries. There's a cut on his left arm that's bled a bit but seems to have stopped. A bruise is coming up on his right cheekbone. Blood and mud splatter his clothes, but the blood doesn't seem to be coming from him. He's less injured than I am.

Beau lets out a piercing whistle, followed by two shorter hoots, lower than the last. I don't flinch.

"Are they all dead?" I whisper as we wait.

"They better be, or I just called them all over to say hello," Beau says. Studying my face, he winces. "Sorry. They're all gone, darlin'. Dom's just done the final sweep, but I'm sure we got them all."

We. That includes me, I realize, that acidic, gnawing nausea building in my stomach. I got one too.

"Easy there," Beau murmurs, pulling me closer.

A whistle sounds to our right, and Beau calls out, "Here."

Dom appears through the brush, dark and fierce and bristling with a palpable energy. It's hard to tell with my vision out of focus, but I'm sure color runs high along his cheekbones. He looks both of us over, brows raising slightly at my bloodied hands. I bury them deeper into Beau's shirt, not wanting him to see how badly I fucked up this time.

And I did. It's not a mess, I didn't bungle it. I *fucked up*.

"We're clear. There's the brook back the way we came where we can clean up."

Clean. A laugh sticks in my throat. A Macbethian urge to scrub at my stained skin rises, but look how it turned out for her. Some things can't be wiped away.

"She okay?"

"She's alive," is all Beau says.

His hand wraps around the back of my neck, and he urges me forward. Something relaxes in me as he takes charge. Suddenly, I want to turn it all over to him. He can take responsibility for all of it, for all of me. Dom and Beau, the other men, they know what to do in these situations. With these kinds of feelings. I was so, so wrong to think I could do it myself.

"You dropped your knife."

When I turn, stomach dipping, Dom is ducking to pick up the pocketknife. *My* pocketknife.

"No."

My voice is barely audible, and he's scooped up the bloody, awful thing before I can stop him.

"Here."

I stumble back a step into Beau. "I don't want it."

I sound panicked, and after my vomiting fit, my throat is raw and sore. Dom stops and studies me, and I cringe away from that knowing stare.

He tucks the little knife behind his belt and lifts his hands.

Tears prick my eyes again, and I swallow twice, trying to keep it together. Beau's hand moves to the middle of my back, and he nudges me.

"Come on now, let's get cleaned up, have something to eat. You'll feel better with something on your stomach."

The way it's seething right now, I'm sure I'll bring up anything that I try to force down but I just nod and let him lead me through the forest. I feel golden eyes on my back and try not to let my shoulders hunch. This is exactly what they wanted to avoid. Me meddling in things I shouldn't be meddling in. Dom should be saying "I told you so" right now. The least I can do is actually listen to them, the way I should have done in the first place.

I never should have left Bristlebrook.

What's wrong with being pampered and coddled, really? If it makes them happy, and it means I'm not doing . . . *this* . . . isn't that better?

What's the point of having choices if I just keep making the wrong ones?

When we reach the water, Beau stops. I stare blankly at the scene. The sun beats down between the trees, sparkling over the clear water. It whispers and burbles around the stones and branches, running in a playful path through the greenery. The grass is soft and thick, almost mossy, and the loamy earth has a kind, welcoming give under my feet. My teary vision gives the scene a hazy glow, the details blurring into each other prettily.

It confuses me. I feel like a whole day must have passed, a century, but it's only been a few hours. It's not right. It should be night, all black and shadows, bare tree limbs catching and tearing at my clothes.

I must have stared too long, because Beau's hand wraps around my wrist, then his fingers skate down to twine with my bloody ones.

I look up at him, and his face is throat-closingly soft.

"Oh, darlin', I'm so sorry," he murmurs. Not taking his eyes off me, he raises his voice. "Dom . . . "

There's a beat of silence, then Dom says in a low voice, "I know. She needs it."

A crush of tiredness, of sadness, squeezes me. Needs *what?*

Beau strokes the pad of his thumb over my hand in slow, soothing motions. "Eden, sometimes we use kink as a way of processing things. To help get feelings out in the open."

He's so unusually grave that I force myself to pay attention to him. Why is he talking about kink? Why on earth would he be talking about it *now*?

"Eden, Dom and I . . . we want to help you. Will you let us do that?"

To process things? I try to keep up. My mind floats back to my talk with Dom before all of this mess, about how the two of them set a scene to work through Beau's issues, but the memory just makes my stomach sink further.

"Are you—" I have to swallow; my throat is so raw and dry. "Are you still mad at me?" I whisper.

Beau's expression breaks, and his eyes sink closed. I watch his Adam's apple bob as he swallows too. Finally, his eyes drift open, and he whispers back, "No, darlin', I'm not mad."

"Then, what . . . "

"Do you trust us?" he asks again. "To make you feel better? You can stop it at any time."

We're so close that our breaths mix, match, until we're breathing together. His eyes are the woods that kept me safe for years, steady streams and hidden nooks.

"I trust you with everything," I tell him.

Slowly, he nods. "Well, alright then." He squeezes my hand, and his next smile seems to bury all the sadness in his face. "Get yourself some water, Eden."

I don't need a drink. But, wanting nothing more than to get the blood off, I kneel by the water's edge. I submerge my hands, then rub at my face and rinse out my mouth. Taking a handful of the coarse sand, I scrub it into my skin, managing to get the worst of the blood off my neck and arms.

"Now, now, darlin', you're gonna need to get wetter than that."

I glance up just as Beau reaches over his back and pulls his shirt over his head in one motion. My tongue sticks to the roof of my mouth. Beau without his shirt is . . . a sight, and it must be a common one, because he has a delicious golden tan across his whole torso. There's a light dusting of dark gold-brown hair across his chest that narrows to a trail that beckons me to his waistline. I hesitate before blinking the water from my eyes.

Seeing him like this with pure clarity might be enough to stop my heart.

When my gaze finally makes its way back to his face, some of the cold blankness in me recedes at his twinkling eyes. The sudden mischief in them reminds me of Lucky. There's color rising in his face, too, like he's just gone for a run.

How is he so *normal* right now? He just took a life. *Lives* probably. Even knowing who they were . . . That boy was young. Twenty, tops. Did he really deserve to *die*?

Beau bites his lip as he watches me too, and sadness flashes across his face before his smile returns full force. He kicks off his shoes and unbuckles his belt, and I suck in a breath as I realize he's half hard already.

"What are you—" My voice sounds strangled.

"I don't know about you," Dom says from behind me, "but I don't bathe fully clothed . . . and you're filthy."

Dom is leaning against a tree, and I need to crane my head over my shoulder to look at him. He's still vibrating with that odd energy, like he's about to spring back into motion at any moment.

It's in the twitching of his fingers, his tense muscles, the restless way he keeps shifting.

That intense gaze fastens on me.

"Strip."

A shiver of warning runs down my spine. The way they're standing, one at my front, one behind, feels deliberate. I'm reminded of the way a wolf sends a runner to chase down prey into the jaws of his brother. A frisson of nervous energy tingles over my skin.

I wet my lips, eyes darting between them. "I— Uh. I'll clean up when we get home?"

Why did that come out like a question?

Beau's brows lift up, and I try my best not to notice, but he's, well, he's really hard now.

"That wasn't really a suggestion, sweet girl." Beau's crooked smile deepens, and he takes a deliberate step toward me. "You should do what he says, hmm?"

I scramble back. He's still smiling, but there's an unholy light to his eyes. Something pagan and dangerous. I realize abruptly that I may have underestimated my charming doctor. Dark and feral needs lurk under his good nature.

Beau steps forward again, and I stumble to my feet, not taking my eyes off him. The threat in him is illicit, delicious, and my breaths come faster.

"Remember your safeword, darlin'?"

Fear and excitement thrill through me, and my somber thoughts grow blessedly quiet. I wet my lips. "Why do you need to know my safeword?"

My pulse throbs in my neck, my core.

"Oh, I know your safeword," he confides, and the way his eyes slide over me is vile. Erotic. "Just making sure you do."

The back of my neck tingles in warning, and my nipples tighten into sensitive nubs even as I recognize he's giving me a choice. My still-red hands clench in the material of my pants.

I don't want choices right now.

Taking a deep breath, I stop backing away.

"Bristlebrook," I whisper.

The tension in Beau doubles. His gaze flicking up over my shoulder is the only warning I get.

"Good librarian," Dom croons, deep and threatening, right beside my ear.

I scream, twisting away as he plucks my glasses off my face, rendering the world instantly fuzzy. I'm not sure why I run, only that the adrenaline that had been dying in my body bursts back to life, my panic from the clearing returning in full force. I realize that Dom is naked—he must have stripped while I was occupied with Beau.

Beau steps forward to catch me and grabs me by my hair, yanking me against his body and pressing his mouth to mine in a hard, hot kiss. I gasp into it as liquid heat pounds through my body. His open belt buckle presses into me, and he shoves between us to unfasten my pants.

Dom growls behind me and adrenaline wars with drugging, luscious lust, jolting me back into awareness. I bite Beau's lip hard enough to taste blood and dart away when he rears back. Dom is right there, large and threatening, and I duck wide and bolt.

Never have I felt such a delicious mix of fear and excitement. The panic *is* different—my nervous heart skitters at the thought of them catching me and, at the same time, I desperately want them to. I want them to take me, claim me, fuck me against the soft earth. I want them to have me completely at their mercy.

There's a low laugh and a curse, then strong, heated arms wrap around me at speed, and I'm taken to the ground. Dom rolls, protecting my body with his as I go down, and I end up pinned beneath him. He yanks my pants down and off in one brutally efficient move, then he comes down on top of me. His naked erection pushes against me, and I shudder.

When I catch my breath, I push up to bolt, but his rough hand clamps around my throat, and he wrestles me until I'm seated atop him, my legs split over his thigh, my back to his chest. With his wide hand pressed against my thundering pulse, and another arm around my waist, he pins me to him. I can feel his thick, hot length against the seam of my ass.

Dom makes a vicious sound of satisfaction deep in his throat, and I writhe against him. Every movement, every breath, rubs us together, and pleasure rips through me.

"*Behave*," Dom orders, voice rough.

Nervousness and lust make me lightheaded. Every hard, muscled inch of his chest is pressed against my back, and he grinds his rigid cock into my backside shamelessly.

He wants me, I realize. Dom *wants* me.

Wickedly wet, I squirm, helpless in his hold. The hand around my throat tightens threateningly, and I can't hold back a breathless moan.

Breathing hard, Dom presses his lips against my ear. "Submit, little librarian. No matter where you run, we'll chase you down."

His other hand wraps around and rips my shirt down the front, tearing right through the soft fabric. My instincts tangle until I'm not sure whether I need to escape or beg for him not to stop. Shuddering, I struggle, trying to push away from him. The movement only grinds my ass against his dick, my clit against his rough thigh. He yanks me deeper into his hold, and I soak his leg on the shuddering backslide through my panties.

Dom groans. "Or fight if you want. It turns me on."

He yanks down my bra so my breasts spill over.

"Fuck. That's a sight," Beau says roughly.

Forcing my heavy eyes open, I see Beau towering over us. Moisture rushes to my core even as terrified goosebumps race over my skin. His zipper is lewdly parted, and his hand is wrapped around his cock as he strokes himself coarsely.

Dom cups one of my breasts, and his large hand spans most of the bared flesh. He grips it roughly, possessively, still grinding against my ass, then he takes my nipple and rolls it hard between his fingers.

Crying out, I arch my back, and his teeth bite down hard into the soft skin between my neck and shoulder, holding me in place as he does it again, and again, switching between my breasts until they're both sore and red and abused. Reaching up, I try to find purchase in his short hair, but can't, and my fingers press into his scalp desperately. He doesn't even flinch at my efforts, greedily touching me however he pleases.

Beau kneels and bends over us. Dom pauses his abuse and squeezes my breasts together—an offering to his friend. He releases his teeth from my neck and licks the small wound there like an animal, trailing his tongue up to my ear.

I tremble, and Beau drops his mouth to my breasts and sucks the offered nipples into his mouth, first one, then the other. It's scorching and wet and silky soft after Dom's rough treatment, and I feel it everywhere. Dom licks the shell of my ear, and I shudder again.

My pussy aches and throbs, but Beau hovers out of reach, touching only himself. I squirm, this time not to escape but to grind against Dom's leg, to try and press against Beau, anything to ease the vicious ache.

Dom's hand squeezes warningly at my throat. "Stay still. This isn't about you. You're ours to suck and fuck and play with however we want."

"Our pretty slut." Beau scrapes his teeth over my nipple, then turns his attention to the other one. "You're doing so well, darlin'. Keep fucking his thigh, just like that."

I moan, arching into Beau, not sure why their words turn me on so much, except that, abruptly, I'm completely freed. I don't need to worry about what to do, or what I've done. I'm only here for them. A vessel for their pleasure. The prize for their hunt.

Nothing bad can touch me here.

Dom buries his face in my hair, breathing hard. "That's it," he croons. "Such a good little murderess."

The words sink through my pliant body like a block of ice. My emotions scatter, and the raw pleasure-pain sensations rocking through my body only confuse me more. I jerk in Dom's grip, but he holds me fast by my throat. Beau grasps my hips, locking me in place against his friend.

"No," I whisper.

"*Yes*." Dom's hand around my throat lifts to my chin, and he turns my face roughly. He kisses my cheek, then my jaw with heart-breaking tenderness. "You did kill him, right? Pretty, bloodthirsty girl."

Beau's mouth starts trailing from my breast down my stomach. "It's okay, sweetheart. We have you. You're safe now. You taste like a wet dream, you know that?"

My skin feels oversensitive, and the wet drag of his tongue is almost too much. Tears sting my eyes, and I try to blink through the fog of lust and pleasure.

I want to melt into Beau. Run from Dom. I want them both to fuck me.

I want them to leave this alone.

"Wait. I—"

Dom chuckles in my ear as Beau nips at my hipbone. Frustration spikes, right beside a sharp flare of desire. I'm caught, but I don't want to play anymore. Right? This isn't the mindless fucking I wanted. Why won't they just let me forget? Why can't they let this be easy?

Fearful brown eyes flicker through my mind.

"*No!*" I kick out, but Beau catches my legs easily, splitting them wide, and pinning them back over Dom's thighs. I catch Beau's hair in my fingers, and yank hard enough that he groans.

"Pull it again, gorgeous. It'll only make me come harder," he pants, smiling at me.

"You still remember that safeword, killer?" Dom taunts,

rubbing his thumb along the column of my throat. With his other hand, he brings his fingers between my thighs and dips underneath my soaked panties, playing lazily with the wetness there. I'm startlingly close to a brutal, terrifying brink. Dom kisses my cheek again, and this time I feel the cruelty in the tenderness, the absolute mockery.

The burning lust flares into something hotter, angrier.

"*Fuck* your safeword," I snap, then try to push away from them for real, fed up with this game, this teasing.

This *hurts*.

Beau licks my lower stomach, right above the line of my panties, still holding my legs back over Dom. "I'm gonna pass on that one, darlin'. You're looking like a much better option, all wide open and wet for me."

I hiss in rage, even as my stomach quivers.

His head drops lower, and Dom spreads my lips under the clinging cotton so that Beau's mouth brushes right over my clit through the fabric. Then he *sucks*. Twisting violently as pleasure decimates me, I manage to tear one of my legs free and kick out, clipping Beau on the shoulder. I throw my head back at the same time, and Dom's grip loosens around my neck as he shoves me aside to avoid the headbutt.

I roll away, and the three of us stare at one another, crouching in the grass, breathing hard.

Beau rubs his shoulder. His eyes are still filled with dark promise. "Nice hit."

"That how you took him down, killer? You kick him off that tree?" Dom smirks. "Or did you just use your little knife?"

"Oh, this little knife?" Beau says. He pulls my stained pocketknife from Dom's discarded belt and tosses the stained, guilty thing at my feet.

I recoil, staring at it. My heart takes on an unsteady rhythm. *"Help me."* The memory of his voice lacerates my thoughts. It eviscerates my arousal.

"Fuck you," I snarl, except instead of spitting venom, my voice breaks. There's still blood on the blade.

"Hmm," Dom says, watching me, and I tear my eyes away from the knife to watch him back.

The smirk is gone now, for some reason, and I can't read his expression.

"You wearing all that blood as a trophy, pet?" Beau asks softly. "Or are you ready to wash it all away?"

I clench my bloody fingers and glare at him, at both of them. My vision is blurred and my breaths are starting to hitch. Using my forearm, I swipe at my eyes, not wanting to cry in front of them. Somehow that makes me feel more exposed than the breasts spilling from my bra.

Dom starts circling me again, and I tense. "What do you think, Beau? She might taste better nice and clean."

Beau nods, moving around me. "Maybe you're right. She looks like she needs to cool off."

My head whips around as I try to keep them both in view. "This isn't funny. I don't want to play this game. I just . . . I just want to go home."

My heart *aches*. Abruptly I feel more alone than I have in years. I bite the inside of my lip against the hot, thick pressure in my throat.

"Home," Beau muses. His voice becomes gentle. "Where's home, darlin'?"

I open my mouth, then shut it, off kilter. Dom steps closer behind me, always moving. I'm not sure why, but I can't make the word leave my lips. *Bristlebrook.* One word and I know they'll take me home. They'll stop.

I shake my head once.

Dom scoops me up from behind with surprising tenderness and takes me over to the water. I turn my face away.

"I don't want to," I mutter thickly.

"Too bad," he says, but he's not teasing anymore, or nasty. He sounds almost . . . kind.

He lowers me into the water until my feet brush the coarse sand. The crisp water laps at the mangled bra beneath my breasts. Without a word, he reaches around and unhooks it then tosses it to the side. His hands linger on my back, tracking small circles up and down my spine. When he reaches my panties, he eases them down my legs until I step out of them.

I'm completely bare, now, and I shiver. The chill of the water takes me over, seeping in deep.

Killer.

"Why did you kill him?" Dom asks in a low voice.

I pull back from the question and find my back pressed up against a wall of warm, naked muscle. Beau. I don't understand why they're pushing me like this. I'm stinging with shame and anger and a new, sour kind of self-loathing.

Turning around, I look up at Beau, wanting to believe he'll make this torture stop, wanting him to take control and make it all go away again.

Please.

"Ah, darlin'." He cups my cheek. "You're breaking my heart."

Dom's hands flatten over my back, and his thumbs start moving more firmly, washing the cool water over my sweaty skin. He's close enough that his heat warms me.

"You did it because you liked it, right?" Dom muses in a low voice. "Because you wanted to see him hurt. Did you want to watch him die, Eden?"

I shake my head numbly, and a tear slips down my face. Beau wipes it away with his thumb. He wets his hand again and grasps my chin, then starts wiping and rubbing at my face in smooth, deliberate motions.

"Then you did it because you wanted to be the hero?" Beau asks. "You wanted to prove to everyone that you could do it?"

Every accusation is a bullet, and those awful feelings dig deeper.

Help me, please.

"*No*! Will you just l-leave it alone? It's done now." I *hate* the way my voice trembles. I try to work up a glare, but I'm empty of rage.

I might throw up again.

Help.

"It is done," Beau agrees, though he sounds pained. "Done for him. Forever."

"Stop it!"

"Why?" he demands.

"Because I didn't want to kill him!" I yell, and my voice breaks on the shout.

I'm sorry, I'm sorry, I'm sorry, I beg the boy in my head.

The tears spill over like acid, as though all of the painful knots in my chest have liquified into some bitter fluid I need to eject from my body.

My knees buckle, but Dom catches me from behind, lifting me from the water. Beau wraps his arms around my waist, and my arms and legs twine around him like that's their natural place. I sob into the crook of his neck, and one sob turns into dozens of heaving, ugly hiccups.

"I know," Beau whispers. "I know, Eden. We've got you."

His cheek nestles against the top of my head, and another set of hands starts washing down my back with the rough sand, then moves to the nape of my neck and down my arms. The scrapes of the coarse granules in direct contrast to the soft, rhythmic caresses.

"I didn't want to," I choke out between sobs. "I didn't want to do it. I don't want to hurt anyone."

Beau lets me shatter, and Dom tends me, and after a while my tears start to slow until I'm raw and hollowed out. Beau lets me down, my body as limp as a marionette. He turns me until I face Dom, then starts unbraiding my hair. Pressure I hadn't realized I was feeling eases, and his fingers running through the strands make me shiver.

Dom tilts my chin up. "Front now," he murmurs.

I sniff and look up at him between my lashes, embarrassed by how blatantly I'm breaking down in front of him. He seems to have no such worries; he scoops up more sand and picks up my arms, rubbing them down and rinsing them off at the same unhurried pace, apparently unfazed by my tears. Between Beau's hands in my hair, and Dom's on my body, the last tension bleeds out of me, and I let myself drift, safe and secure between them again.

I can't remember the last time I've ever felt so . . . cared for.

Or how little I felt like I deserved it.

After a while I start to notice the droplets clinging to Dom's chest, the stubbled line of his jaw . . . the bloodied gash along his arm. Lips tightening, I reach up to touch it gently, rubbing some of the blood beneath it away.

"That's a present from that sniper, you know," Dom tells me, not taking his eyes from where he's sluicing water over my neck.

My fingers pause.

"I was caught between the trees. A few more shots, and he might have had me."

I study his face but see no sign he's lying to make me feel better.

He meets my eyes. "You very well might have saved my life, doing what you did."

Dom's words burrow beneath the numbness. Shaking my head, I keep wiping at the blood on his arm. His arm. Just a slight change of angle and it could have been his chest.

"He didn't need to die," I whisper, finally. "I could have stopped him without . . . doing that."

He turns my chin so I can't look away from him. "Why didn't you?"

"What?"

"If you could have just stopped him, why didn't you?" he repeats.

"I—" I try to pull my chin away, but he has a good grip. Beau's hands are soft in my hair. "He attacked me, he . . . he tried to throw me off the tree."

Dom nods. "So you stabbed him."

I flinch. "I just tried to stop myself from falling. I didn't mean to. He— I—"

"So he threw you off the tree and you tried to catch yourself and you both ended up falling. Seems to me like he made his own bed."

"Stop. You're making it sound like—"

"Like you were defending yourself," he interrupts. "Like you were defending us. You saved your own life, and mine, and the only reason he's dead is because he tried to hurt us."

I swallow, hard. Another memory flickers. Not of brown eyes, but an ugly snarl. *"Bitch,"* he'd called me, right before he threw me to my death.

Beau tugs my head back until I'm looking at him, almost upside down. "Dom and me, we killed eight between us out there. You hatin' on us as much as you're hatin' on yourself right now?"

"Of course not," I say impatiently. *It's not the same thing.*

As if he can see the thought on my face, his eyes flare. "It sure *is* the same thing. You don't get to be down on yourself for doing what you had to unless you're going to put the same blame on us."

I open my mouth to argue, but the words don't come. My brow tangles. What else *could* I have done? I could have stayed where they left me, or stayed in my tree, but then what would have happened? That sniper had them pinned. Would I rather Dom or Beau be killed? My gut lurches at the thought.

I decided weeks ago that I didn't blame them for shooting the men hunting me. They kept me safe.

I kept them safe too.

Another wave of water washes over me and this time, it washes away more than the filth on my skin. The acid in my gut seems to ease away with their words, their care. It's like my doctor just punctured my flesh and let the poison out, right before it could fester, and Dom bandaged me back up.

A sweet, heavy pressure rolls into my chest. Gratitude, and maybe something else. Something I'm not quite ready for just yet, but wonderful and hopeful all the same.

Leaning forward, I press my lips against Dom's wound.

CHAPTER 29

EDEN

SURVIVAL TIP #293
*Cleanliness is good for the soul,
but being dirty might just be your natural state.
Embrace it.*

A breath sighs out of Dom, like relief or maybe satisfaction, and it pebbles my damp skin. He cups my cheek and presses a kiss to the top of my head. It confuses me a little. Dom is stern, imposing, bossy. I didn't know he could be so tender. Maybe Beau brings it out in him.

Or maybe I'm starting to.

"I'm sorry I didn't do what you told me to," I murmur against his skin. Which is partly true. It's also partly a lie, I realize. I may regret the life on my hands, but they're right—I can't regret keeping them safe. With a settling sense of clarity, I know that I would do the same a dozen or more times if I had to.

Despite the chilly water, Dom is still hot to the touch, and I keep my forehead pressed to his bicep. For the warmth, of course. I shiver, though not from the cold, and Beau shifts closer as well, until I'm fitted snugly between them. Awareness floods me of how close we are, how naked. Just a tangle of limbs and heated skin pressing against each other in the river.

Dom hums. "And after we had such a specific chat about that, too."

His tone is dry again, so I know he's not too mad. I lift my head.

"I just realized it was a trap," I explain in a rush. "They could have stayed hidden and not touched the cameras, so there was probably more of them, and you were going to walk into the middle of it, and I just *couldn't* let you—"

Beau lets out a snort behind me and bends to nip at my earlobe. "'Course it was a trap, you little idiot. It's always a trap."

Dom rolls his eyes, but a smile lurks in his mouth. "Cute of you to worry, though."

Glaring, I pinch his nipple. He lets out a sound suspiciously close to a yelp and bats me away, then snags my wrists again in one of his. Beau chokes on a laugh but makes no move to help. His fingers trace around my hip, then skate down my inner thigh.

Golden gaze narrow, Dom ducks his head until his lips brush against mine. "You're becoming more of a brat by the second."

With every word, his lips tantalize me, a barely there caress. My tongue darts out to tease at his lips, though I almost faint at my own daring. It is *Dom* after all. But he's flirting, I'm sure he is, and he just went to all that trouble to pull me out of my own head. He wouldn't do that if he were indifferent. That goes above being nice, surely. I feel skittish about making assumptions after Jasper's rejection, but . . . I felt his hands on me before. His body under me. There was no mistaking his interest then.

Or now, for that matter. I arch closer to him, and Dom's eyes simmer with amusement.

I worried, for a moment, that between the heavy conversation and the frigid water that his interest might have . . . deflated. But it's still there. All big and heavy and . . . interested.

Dom snags my bottom lip between his teeth with warning

pressure, gaze locked on mine. Then he sucks it into his mouth, tongue swiping at the small hurt. I sigh, lids drooping.

Beau laughs softly and kisses the back of my neck. "Hmm, so it's like that, is it?"

Closing the last half-inch between us, he presses his length against my ass and lower back. I wriggle back brazenly. The angle makes Dom's dick brush against my stomach, and I tremble. *Two* dicks. What do I even do with two?

However it works, I'm ready to try.

My arousal from earlier still burns through me, but it's no longer soured by bitterness and shame. A bit of sadness, maybe, but there's also gratitude, and trust. I want these men, these kind, selfless, brave men who protected me and gave me a home for the first time in my life. These men can use me in any way they want.

And I'm going to enjoy the hell out of it.

"I think we still deserve our prize, don't you, Beau?"

Beau yanks my hips against his cock and rolls them back with a low groan, then he does it again and again, using my ass like a toy to fuck against. "You've been bad today, darlin'. You want to show us what a good girl you can be?"

I whimper, my pussy growing slick again in a way that has nothing to do with the water. I want to clutch at Dom so I can brace against Beau's carnal assault behind me, but he still has my wrists, holding them against his chest, and it leaves me off balance. I have to scramble to brace against each selfish, ravenous stroke so I don't collapse. It doesn't seem to bother Beau; he just holds my hips where he wants them and makes himself feel good.

Another vicious thrust and my breathing turns ragged.

Dom slaps my cheek lightly to get my attention, and I gasp. "He asked you a question, little librarian."

The flush has returned to Dom's cheeks, and he drinks in my expression, devours it, until I'm sure he's seen everything I've ever thought or felt about him, about them.

"Yes," I gasp out. "I—I can be good. I'll be good, sir. Please, I want— I need—"

Dom's lips slant over mine, and he claims my mouth, invading with his hot, silky tongue. His kiss is aggressive, but not rough like Jaykob's was. Dom is deliberate. This is an exploration, a strategic takeover, and his tongue works against mine with a determined skill, demanding a response. I turn soft, malleable, ready to give myself over to whatever they want to do to me. Pleasure simmers through me.

Beau slips his hand around my waist and, without warning, begins to play with my clit, circling and rubbing it as he keeps fucking against me. I'm already on the edge. Pressure builds too quickly, and I want to tear my mouth away so I can whine and beg, or take in some air, but neither of them let me move. They just take and take and take.

I sob into Dom's mouth and crack my eyes open to find him watching me, heavy lidded and hungry. He sucks on my tongue.

Unable to hold back even if I wanted to, I come so hard around Beau's fingers, my vision winks out. Dom yanks his mouth away as I cry out, my voice raw and strangled with pleasure.

Dazed, I blink a dozen times, sucking in air and shaking.

Beau runs a possessive hand down my spine and squeezes my ass. "Very pretty."

Dom releases my wrists, and I catch myself against his chest, enjoying the firm skin under my fingers. My breath is still coming in quick pants, but I take advantage of my freedom and skim my hands over his chest and arms, down the ridges of his abs.

When I reach the length of him bobbing out of the water, I hesitate. I glance up at him between my lashes to find him watching me with some bemusement, like even he's not quite sure why he's letting me get away with touching him like this.

"Don't go getting shy on us now," Beau says in my ear.

He takes my hand in his and wraps it around Dom's thick dick. My breath hitches.

"Nice and firm, darlin', just watch your nails."

Dom's cock is warm and swollen through the length, the wide tip flared and ruddy and begging for attention. Beau moves my hand in a steady rhythm and the water begins to churn around us. I'm surprised it isn't steaming. He feels so good, silky and hard all at once, and every twitch under my palm makes me want to pant. I give myself over to Beau's murmured instructions, loosening my grip now, tightening here.

I lose myself to their rhythms, how they press me between them, the way they use me to push one another's buttons—to push mine. This is their specialty after all, looking after each other as much as they look after their sub. It's their tandem understanding, their friendship, their ability to share desire and these vulnerable, perfect moments together. I see it now, so clearly.

Dom widens his stance as I look up at him nervously, wondering how he's taking my bold touches. It wasn't like I'd asked. He cocks his head at my attention, raising his brow in question. Then he just crosses his arms across his chest and glances away, like he's vaguely bored. Like he's accepting his due as our king and commander.

Beau moves my hand down, urging me to fondle his balls, to rub the sensitive patch of skin below his sac until Dom's indifference begins to falter. We return my hand to his cock, and the scorching throb in my fist and the dark flush of color over his cheekbones betrays his lust. I shiver back into Beau, pressing my thighs together against the ache.

I want to service him properly. I want to make our commander shake.

With a whimper, I stroke him again, this time not guided completely by Beau, and rub my thumb over the swollen tip. Beau's teeth catch my earlobe and tighten in warning, and I snuggle against him, enjoying the sting a little too much.

Dom's gaze cuts back to consider me and, this time, amusement lurks in the golden depths again. "Do you want to please me, pet?"

This time, the name doesn't grate.

Deciding honesty is something a good girl would strive for, I nod. "Yes, sir."

Lips twitching, he says, "Good." Dom brushes his lips against mine. "You should see the way he comes apart when he gets a nice, warm mouth around him. He's a beast."

My eyes widen at the crass, careless words.

His eyes flick to Beau. "We should take her to the bank. I want to see you take her mouth, and if we do it here, she'll drown before she gets you off."

"Great plan." Beau picks me up and tosses me over his shoulder with a cheerful bounce.

I squirm on instinct, and Beau's wide hand claps against my ass painfully. "Stay still for me now."

His fingers linger as he walks me to the bank, sliding between my thighs to tease at the wetness between my legs, then spread it between the cheeks of my ass. I want to jerk away from the invasive, delicious touch, but I really do want to show them I can obey. Despite running off earlier, I did take it seriously when Dom told me he needed to trust me.

So I stay as still as I can, trembling as Beau's fingers explore through my folds, grazing against my tender clit and then teasing against the tight, puckered rosebud until my breaths are coming in sharp pants. I try not to tense, though he must feel me quiver every time he rubs me there.

These slow touches are no less shocking than Jayk's sudden invasion, but also deeply intimate, like Beau has decided he has every right to my body and will use whatever parts of me he wants. Breathlessly, I wonder whether he's planning on fucking me there.

Is that even something I want?

Despite my embarrassment—or maybe because of it—I'm soaking and restless again by the time we reach the edge of the water. Beau's thorough touches have left me slick and ready everywhere between my thighs and ass cheeks.

His slippery fingers press against my tight hole again, past the clinging inner ring, and I arch into the touch, whimpering. Beau groans and bites my hip, hard enough to leave a mark, and pulls out with a small tug. He sets me down but holds me to his side.

I'm grateful for the support—I'm sure my knees would buckle under me if he left me to my own devices. Burying my face into the side of his chest, I press a few small, shaky kisses against his skin, and he strokes my shoulder soothingly.

My feet touch something soft, and I realize Dom has unrolled his pallet over the grass.

"Kneel."

The command does something intangible but wholly visceral to me, and I'm kneeling before I've even registered what Dom said.

"Very nice." Beau runs his hand over my head, like I am the pet they'd called me. "That's perfect, sweet girl."

"Hands and knees," Dom commands. "I want you bent over."

I'm shocked by the rush of desire that accompanies his words. I bend over, on display for them both. Dom is behind me now, and he has to see the moisture glistening between my folds.

"Spread your legs wide, darlin', and arch your back." Beau kneels down beside me and presses down on the center of my back until I'm arched obscenely. My breasts are thrust forward and my legs are spread wide, ass in the air.

My breath catches. I'm so exposed like this. There's no hiding anything and, even though my skin buzzes with expectation, a bout of self-consciousness hits me.

Beau cups one of my breasts and squeezes. "Fuck. Do you have any idea how beautiful you are?"

He plucks at my abused nipple, and I squeak, though I force myself to stay still like they told me. His words filter in and the nervousness fades almost as quickly as it came. Beau's thumb soothes over the sting.

Dom releases a deep sound of satisfaction. "So you *can* listen."

He kneels behind me and runs a possessive hand down my back.

His voice turns dark. "Which means you've just been choosing not to."

His hand claps hard against my left ass cheek, and electricity jolts from his hand directly to my clit. "Count them for me, pet. You get fifteen for not following orders today. If you lose count or squirm away, we start again."

The sting is chased by a hot ache and my pussy clenches around nothing.

Fifteen? I can do fifteen, right? That's not many. It's just five, three times. I can do that. He's not even hitting me as hard as Jayk did—though Jayk was inside me at the time, so it's a little different.

Dom's hand comes down again, harder and with a sharp sting, right over the first ache. "Am I going deaf, Beau? Did you hear counting? 'Cause I'm sure our subbie is not stupid enough to ignore me while I have my hand on her ass."

"No, sir, I did not hear a single peep myself. Could be the gunshots messed with our hearing?" Beau tweaks my other nipple, hard, and I yelp.

"I—" I start, but Dom speaks over the top of me.

"Or maybe something happened to her tongue in all the mess. Why don't you make sure her mouth is in working order, doc?"

"Seems like the responsible thing to do," Beau agrees.

I look up as Beau moves in front of me, fisting his hand in my hair. The beautiful, hard length of him juts from his body. His other hand wraps around my chin, and he presses against my cheeks until my mouth pops open. I expect him to shove in, but he cranes my head back further until I'm looking him in his pretty green and gold eyes through my clear lenses.

"You need me to stop, you hit my legs, okay?"

"Okay," I say, though the word is garbled through my pinched cheeks.

Beau inches his cock between my lips, teasing me with it. I

swipe at the head with my tongue, enjoying the warm, slightly tangy taste of his pre-cum. He backs out and, with the way he's holding my mouth open, I can't follow him. I can only wait for him to gift me with another taste. I whine in frustration, and Beau lets out a husky laugh.

"You want more, pretty girl? You want to swallow my dick?"

He's feeding it to me before I can answer, the glossiness from the first pass easing his slide past my lips. Greedily, I tighten around him, sucking him in and running my tongue around the underside until he backs away again so I can focus on the fat, flared head. With his fist in my hair, I can't move at all, so I just accept what he gives me.

Beau rocks back and forth in slow, lazy movements, taking my tongue where he wants it and murmuring encouragement. The musky scent of him makes me dizzy, like I'm supping on ambrosia or some kind of decadent alcohol that makes me liquid and light and needy. My skin tingles, and my nipples feel painfully tight, my pussy wet and hollow and clenching around nothing.

I want to be touched. *Now*. I *need* to be.

Beau pushes in deep with a rumbling groan, and I look up at him pleadingly.

His tongue teases his lower lip, and his expression becomes pained. "Fuck me. Those eyes of yours, darlin'. I like it when you beg me."

I run my tongue along the root of him, flattening it along the underside of his length, and his head drops back.

He pulls back and then pushes in again with a short, chastising thrust. "You like having my cock in your mouth? I'm going to spill inside you, darlin', and you can have every drop. I'll smear it all over your tongue so you can taste me all the way home."

I moan then, growing wetter. As I do, a hand crashes down hard on my other ass cheek, and the unexpected pain sends me rocking forward. I choke on Beau's dick, and he clutches me tight against him, letting the contractions in my throat work over its tip.

Tears leak from my eyes and, desperately, I suck in air through my nose, whimpering as Dom's calloused hand soothes over the sting. Then, as if to mock the moment of tenderness, he rakes his nails over my ass, adding a new scorch of pain over the easing prickle.

Beau pulls back, yanking my head off him. Saliva clings to my mouth, and I only just stop my hands flying up to wipe it away. I gasp for air.

"Hmm. I still don't hear—"

"One!" I cry out, and my voice is hoarse, maybe from shouting, or crying out, or maybe just from strangling on Beau's dick. "One!"

"One *what*?" Dom's voice is unbearably patient and the warning in it makes me quake.

"One . . . spanking?"

Dom's hand comes down on my tender flesh again. "Try again. We're still at one."

Panic shimmers beside desperate need, and I don't know if I want to shy away from the blinding pleasure-pain he's delivering or melt into it.

"One, ah, one . . . um." *Shit, shit.* I tense, readying for another blow.

Beau runs his thumb along the sensitive column of my throat and whispers, "Bit of respect might do you some good here, darlin'."

I blink, dazed. "One, *sir*! Sir. Thank you, sir."

"Spoilsport," Dom mutters. His fingers track so lightly against my hot, stinging skin that goosebumps race down my spine. "The 'thank you' is nice, though."

I heave a sigh of relief. "Yes, sir. I'm so—"

I'm cut off with a squeak as the next spank comes out of nowhere, lower this time, right above the seam between my thigh and ass.

"Two, sir. Th-thank you, sir," I stammer out.

Breathing through the bright, radiating sting, I wait for the ache to settle in and bring that delectable flush of heat. Before it does, he strikes twice more in quick succession against the middle, meaty flesh of each cheek.

"Ow!" I yelp and tears leap to my eyes, even though I don't feel like crying again, not really. Dom's hand pushes down on the small of my back until I arch again, keeping my wet folds presented to him. I feel them part and want nothing more than for him to bury himself inside me.

The sharp pain is blurring at the edges, mixing with the older hurts, layers of stinging and aching and delicious heat that licks across my skin. It's lighting me up, making me airy and breathless, and I curve into the callouses on his hand, wanting him to scrape me with them again. "Three, sir, thank you. Four, sir. Thank y—"

Beau's erection shoves between my lips, catching me by surprise. I instinctively press my tongue against him to push him out, but he ignores me, rocking in more deeply and holding me in place by my hair. His warm, masculine taste fills my mouth, and I relax around him, sucking on him to drag out more of that wonderful flavor.

Two dicks. I have to remember there are two. They're both so distracting, I keep losing myself to one, then being surprised when the other claims back my attention.

"Don't you *dare*."

Beau drags himself out of my mouth and then slams back in, rough but not so deep that I gag.

"Forget."

He thrusts in and out again. He swells against my tongue as he claims me.

"About."

His shaft stretches my lips. My mouth waters, and I can't spare the air to swallow, so my saliva soaks him on his backslide, making us sloppy and wet and messy.

"Me."

Burying himself deep, he grinds against my mouth, and my nose tickles against the small, coarse hairs at his base. He's at my throat now, and he works himself against me. Tears do spill over now, but I'm flying high on his taste and smell and the raw, coarse way he's using me for his pleasure.

Forget about Beau? I'd sooner forget to breathe.

Just as I'm about to gag, he pulls free, and Dom's hand slaps down again, hard. I gulp down air around a sob. Beau tilts my chin to study my face, but my mind is frantic.

Oh shit, what number am I up to?

Dom's hand lifts, readying for the next smack that will take me back to one.

"*Five*! Thank you, thank you, sir. It's five." My breath hitches tearily. *Ten more to go*, I think, heart tangling somewhere between sinking and soaring. I look up at Beau through my tearstained lashes. "Thank you, Beau."

Beau runs the backs of his fingers over the damp tracks on my cheeks, then lingers against my abused, saliva-slick lips, dipping in to caress the silky inside. "You dangerous thing."

I jump as Dom's fingers dip between my legs at the same time. The full fury of my lust centers on my throbbing clit, so close to where he's teasing me. Beau removes his hand and brings his cock back to my lips, and I whimper, caught between slipping into the feeling of Dom in my pussy and wanting to please Beau.

Making a decision, I lean forward to lick at Beau eagerly, then tongue his slit, stealing the bead of moisture welling there. Beau lets out a string of curses, and I'm rewarded by Dom thrusting two fingers inside me. I clamp down on him instantly, clutching at the filling pressure, and he pushes them in and out. The wet suck is loud, obscene, but I couldn't care. I redouble my messy efforts on Beau's cock, moaning shakily around it, and Dom leans down over me to circle my clit with his other hand.

"Is this what you want, pet? Say the word and there's no more punishment, I'll make this pretty pink cunt come for me again, and Beau will spill all over your tongue. We'll even cuddle before we head home."

What?

Beau backs up as I pause, watching me consider. I twist to look over my shoulder so I can read Dom's expression—something sounded off in his tone—but he smacks me again, and I snap back around.

"Six, sir, thank you," I say absently, and Beau snorts.

"Brat," he says affectionately.

A smile touches my lips, but my brow scrunches in confusion. Dom crooks his fingers and rubs tauntingly against a spot inside me that makes my vision haze. My mouth drops open on a long, moaning exhale.

No, pay attention, I order myself dizzily.

"W-why would you do that?" I force myself to ask, and I ignore the husky, needy sound of my voice.

Dom is silent for a moment, then he finally says, "No need for you to be punished if you don't deserve it, right?"

I blink a few times and hold myself still, so I don't fuck against his hand like I really want to. My thoughts are drunken, floating, but something similar to hurt trickles through.

He's testing me. He's testing me *now*?

He'll follow through, I know, and deliver me the orgasm he promised . . . but he won't fuck me, and he won't ever do this again. Dom made it clear that he needs to do things a certain way.

He's seeing if I can handle it.

Anger spits through my giddy lust. "I am taking my punishment, *sir*. If you have a problem delivering it, then maybe I should find someone else to finish it. Jasper, maybe? You said you'd hand me over to him, right?"

He wasn't there to hear how Jasper rejected me, but I've seen enough to know sharing with anyone but Beau bothers him.

Dom's hand tenses on my backside. "You want your punishment?"

I do turn to glare at him then. "I didn't use my safeword."

"No, you didn't."

My glare softens, just a touch, as I take him in. He's so tense, the muscles on his stomach are quivering, his face is flushed and strained and his eyes golden fire, and his deprived cock is dark and stiff and glossy with his need.

I'm growing softer, wetter in response. I've been so caught up with how good they're making me feel, I hadn't fully registered how much they were getting off on having me like this, spread out for them to enjoy.

I lick my lips and deepen the arch of my back. Dom's eyes drop to where his fingers are still buried deep in my—God, what had he called it?—my pretty pink cunt.

Even thinking the filthy word makes me shudder.

"I earned my punishment, sir. Please give it to me," I murmur. "Let me show you I can be good."

I glance back at Beau so he knows I include him in that. Beau's pupils are dilated, and his chest works with short, sharp breaths. He meets my eyes with a look of pure, carnal promise.

"All right, pet, no more warming up. No more counting. Brace yourself." Dom pulls his fingers from my pussy, and I sigh at the loss. Then he adds, "You get two more for being a sassy brat. Don't threaten me with Jasper again."

That makes me grin, but I do as he says and steady my stance.

Beau grips my chin. "I'm going to fuck your mouth now, darlin', and I'm not gonna stop till you've taken every last drop." He taps my jaw. "And don't go biting me, even when it hurts."

I release a shaky breath. "Yes, Beau."

Beau strokes my cheek, then lines himself back up at my mouth, which I open obediently. Watching me, he makes a sound somewhere between a grunt and a groan. He fills me slowly, completely, and I take in every expressive twitch and grimace on his face. When he's completely seated, he nods to Dom—and then things speed up.

Beau starts moving rough and fast just as Dom starts raining blow after blow in quick succession, and it's all I can do to hold on and let it all happen. The spanks hurt—some stinging and sharp, others solid and aching, and Dom's hands move around my ass as if to make sure there will be no inch of unbranded skin left to sit on.

Beau's length rubs between my sensitive lips, and he reaches down to cup his own balls where they slap against my chin. The taste of him floods me, fills me, mixing with the salty tears that start streaming down my cheeks, both from the impact on my ass and the way Beau taps the back of my throat with each vicious thrust.

Rather than making him hesitate, the sight seems to drag the selfish cruelty back out of my sweet doctor. He holds my wet, desperate gaze and groans as his thrusts grow harder, sloppier, more frantic, and a lost, drugged expression takes over his face.

Dom growls behind me. "Ten." *Slap.* "Eleven, twelve." *Slap, slap.*

The last one almost makes me grit my teeth against the brutal sting, but I hold it back at the last second, sobbing around Beau instead.

"Fuck," Beau moans, watching the glistening join of his dick and my lips. "Fuck, fuck, fuck."

The pain from Dom's hand is starting to transform to pure heat, sinking into my bones, my veins. It's like lava, light and scorching hot. My clit throbs in time with each blow, my core clenching and leaking moisture. I'm craving each spank as much as I dread it.

"Fifteen," Dom snaps, and the strain in his voice makes me whimper.

The blow is precariously close to my cunt, and I cry out, arching deeper in offering. *Please, please, please.*

Beau's fingers in my hair tighten, and he grips his base with his other hand. He stops thrusting and pulls back so only the fat head of him remains in my mouth. "Stick out your tongue."

I stick it out as far as it can go, making sure it's flat along the sensitive rim like Lucky showed me the other night. Taking the second of reprieve, I catch as much air as I can, and my panting blows cool air over his heated flesh. I can taste him leaking onto my tongue.

Beau's face is tight with furious lust, and he starts to work his length with brutal strokes.

"You take it all," he demands.

I can't talk, can't move, so I just agree with my eyes, wanting to show how much I want this, how much it turns me on. I want him to brand me with his taste. I want to smell him for days. I want him to flood my mouth and drink him down like nectar.

It only takes five rough strokes before he stiffens, shudders, and spurts over my tongue. Holding me tight, he rubs himself over the full length of my tongue, against my lips, spilling his seed helplessly everywhere he can smear it. It's like a marking, like he's claiming me, and a euphoric, dizzy sense of satisfaction makes me moan.

Unable to help myself, I close my lips around him and suck him in, savoring the flavor, loving that he's owning me like this. I drink down every drop, licking him clean, licking my own lips, until he softens in my mouth.

Finally, with a sweet sigh, his hand loosens in my locks, and he slips from between my lips.

"Perfect, sweet girl." He ducks down and presses a quick, hard kiss against my mouth. "You're absolutely perfect."

I'm trembling now, on a high of lust and happiness and pure feminine satisfaction.

"Two more." Dom's voice is hoarse, like he's as affected as I am.

My breath hitches, and I brace myself. Moisture is running down my thighs, and I'm so empty I want to cry. I'm so close to the edge now, I think one brush against my clit will send me shooting off like a bottle rocket.

Dom's hand comes down, harder than any before it, and I yelp. It doesn't quite hurt anymore, though. It melts instantly into heat, and I shiver, my cry turning into a needy moan.

"More, *please*, sir. Please give me more," I beg.

"Shit," Dom curses, then clears his throat, though it barely disperses the gravel. "Yes, pet, you get one more."

His knee pushes at the inside of mine, nudging it wider, and he presses a hand between my shoulder blades until my face is pressed against the pallet. I get ready for the smack but, instead, his fingers run up my inner thighs, smearing the wetness there.

"You have a greedy cunt, pet." He moves up until he reaches my pussy, circling my opening with his index finger. "I can see you clutching for something to fill you up."

He spreads my folds and grunts, and even the cool air is too much against my sensitive flesh. "So swollen and pink. That needy clit is just begging for attention."

I let out a long, low whine, lost to words, to sense. I want to shift, just to see if I can push his hand to where I need it. It wouldn't take much. It would probably make me come.

But I don't. Because this part is for Dom, not for me.

I bite my lip against a sob. Beau runs what I'm sure is meant to be a soothing hand down my spine, but it only stokes me higher.

Dom hesitates. "You really are a good girl, aren't you?" he asks, voice a little softer. "You've been very patient for us."

I shiver, waiting, hoping.

"One more," he promises.

The blow comes, but not against my ass. He strikes me right against my clit, and the sharp sting is all it takes. The light and heat that had been building in my body bursts behind my eyes, and I come on a long wail, pleasure exploding in my core and all the way down my spine.

CHAPTER 30

EDEN

SURVIVAL TIP #72
Enjoy your victories.
Your next loss will come soon enough.

I'm a shivering, sobbing mess when I come to, and Beau has curled me up so I'm nestled limply against his chest as we lie together on the pallet. The chafe of his chest hair against me makes me shiver happily, and I don't want to move.

I think my mind just melted.

Except . . . I look over my shoulder and see that Dom is sitting back on his heels, watching me with a hot, satisfied look on his face, like it wasn't me who just came hard enough to see stars. The restlessness has bled out of him, and he's lost the twitchy, electrified pulse that felt so lusciously threatening before.

His thick cock is dark and swollen, desperately leaking precum against his stomach, yet he seems . . . content.

I lick my lips, and Dom's brow kicks up. "I think you're done."

I frown, pressing my cheek against Beau's chest. His heartbeat is still unsteady, and he rests his chin on the top of my head.

"I don't want to be done," I reply, and I can't even find the grace to be embarrassed by how petulant I sound. Dom's brow hikes further in warning, and I rush to add, "Sir. Please. I . . . I want to make you feel good too."

Dom hesitates, and Beau tilts my head up, dropping sweet kisses against my lips, my chin, my cheeks. He rubs his nose against mine, and I hum in happiness.

Beau glances over at his friend. "I think she can do one more. You could use it."

"And I said she's had enough. We're done for the day, Beau." His jaw flexes. "Don't push it."

Sleepy, and not liking the snap to Dom's tone, I roll a little and reach out for him. He stares at my palm like I presented him with something unexpected. Something special.

His face softens, and he takes my hand.

My heart softens too, at the shine in his eyes.

Picking something up from the grass, Dom moves in so he's behind me, then tugs my head back. I expect a kiss, but instead, he cradles my gaze in his, and slowly, so slowly, he slides my glasses back on. I hold my breath—I don't think I could find air if I wanted to.

Dom's large hands whisper over my cheekbones, and he watches me with such focus, moves with such studious care as he tucks my glasses gently behind my ears, that my heart takes a hard, aching hit.

When his hands fall away, I remember to breathe, and I let my head rest back in the nook of his neck. My legs are still twined with Beau's. The three of us are pressed as close as we can be without them being inside me. A drowsy calm falls over me, and I snuggle against them, deciding not to question the sweetness.

But Dom doesn't seem inclined to let me sleep. In a serious voice, he asks, "Are you okay, Eden? That was a lot."

Beau's hand trails idly over my thigh as I frown. I don't know if he's referring to the fight, or the man I killed, or all the scarily intense sort-of sex, but whatever he means, I don't really care—I'm stuck on one word.

He's calling me Eden again, and I don't think I like it.

I think I want him to go back to calling me "good girl" . . . or even "pet." It doesn't sound like such a loaded word while we're all naked like this.

Stretching like a cat between them, I rub the back of my head into his neck. "Mm-hmm, I'm good, sir. Perfect. I'm perfectly perfect."

"Perfectly perfect, huh?" he asks, sounding wry.

"Mm-hmm."

His fingers track down my side, almost hesitantly. "Well, okay, then."

I sink into the touch. I could probably slip under this feeling and drown here, and I wouldn't even struggle.

Beau kisses my shoulder lazily. "Our pet looks good on you," he says to Dom.

At the endearment, I melt, but a small amount of tension steals into Dom's embrace.

"Hmm," is all he says.

I nestle in closer, sleepy and dazed. I don't want him tense. I want him limp and sated and thrilled with me. I try not to read into his lack of reaction. It is Dom, after all.

"You should see what the three of us can manage in a bed, darlin'. We'll have to find one next time."

Dom's hand falters from its stroking motion on my back. Then it drops, and he squeezes my hip.

I sigh into the touch, my brain puddled between my ears. I don't want to—can't—overthink this. Dom and Beau have me wrapped up like their favorite present. It *is* perfect. The three of us like this, clean of secrets, is one of the most perfect things there is.

I want it to stay like this.

And there it is. In this moment, it all feels so clear. Almost easy.

It's like they washed away the last of my doubts with river water and liquid orgasms.

"I want to break the deal," I say, calm and sure. "I don't want any more conditions attached to me staying at Bristlebrook. I'll stay because I deserve to be there. Because I contribute as much as anyone, and it has nothing to do with sex." I don't even stumble over that word anymore. What a wonder two weeks can work. "No more lies. No more hiding things. Not 'going forward.' From now on, I'm there because I want to be, and because you want me to be, and for no other reason."

For a long, long moment there is only the sound of their breathing and the babble of the water along the stones. Beau and Dom are both tense and still beside me.

Then Beau eases up on his elbow, turning so he looks down at me. "You . . . want to end this?" he asks. "End . . . us?"

They really are terrible listeners.

I reach up and run my finger along his jaw, enjoying the scrape of his stubble. "Not even a little bit."

He relaxes, his breath rushing out. "Thank God, darlin'. I was really worried I was going to have to arrange a kidnapping for a second there."

I smile, but Dom sits up behind me, pulling me up with him. There's a knot between his dark brows.

"What about the others? What does this mean for them?" There's a hint of steel in his voice. "You're choosing Beau?"

"*Us*," Beau clarifies, and Dom glares at him.

"No!" I push down a flair of panic, shaking my head. "No, I'm not choosing anyone. I care about all of you. I'm attracted . . . I mean, Lucky is so beautiful, and free, and I just *laugh*, you know? Every time I'm with him. And he really listens to me, for hours and hours he listens." I smile, warmed through just thinking about him. "And Jayk, well, he pretends to be so brash. He even believes it, I think. But he's patient—we took apart the washing machine together, even though I'm sure it took twice as long to have me there. He's so smart, and he doesn't give himself half as much credit as he deserves. And Jasper—"

Well. I don't need to talk about Jasper.

Feeling their eyes on me, I shake my head. "And then there's you . . . " Shyness slips over me like a shadow, and I look up at Beau from under my lashes, then dart a glance at Dom.

The green and brown in Beau's eyes dance together. "What, no compliments for us?"

I lift a hand to hide my smile, feeling my cheeks color like a sunrise. "I—I like you too."

"You like me?" Beau teases. "Like, *like* like me, or?"

Huffing a laugh, I meet his eyes. I take a fortifying breath. "You make me feel safe, and I've not felt that often. A few weeks ago, I didn't think anyone *could* ever make me feel that way. I've been fighting my fear my whole life. Since coming to Bristlebrook, I've felt safe, and it's given me the chance to think, really think, about what I want for myself for the first time ever. And I'm trusting you to listen to that."

Beau's teasing smile fades, and he's staring at me now with the same intensity he had when we were in the river, while they dragged my pain and confusion out of me. Slowly, not breaking eye contact, he nods.

I nod back, relieved. Resolved. "Jasper told me that some people, some . . . submissives . . . like to be dominated all the time, others not, that everyone negotiates their own boundaries."

When I glance at Dom, he finally looks at me, serious and introspective. "He's right. You want to renegotiate?"

"I do, yes."

"Good."

I blink. "Good?"

Dom sighs. "Eden, there's a reason I don't take on soft spoken submissives. There's just too much risk of getting it wrong. I'm not always great at picking up on signals. I need to trust that they'll speak up if anything isn't working for them. If they're uncomfortable or unhappy." He meets my eyes. "Renegotiation is always on the table."

My mouth drops open as I think that through. "Just like that?" I ask in a soft voice.

At the reference to yesterday's conversation, Dom's lips quirk. "Just like that." He directs a tense-jawed look at Beau. "Your dominants should have explained this all to you."

"*We*," Beau replies, his tone dripping with poisoned honey, "haven't had a chance to sit down and have a proper conversation about all this. Keep gettin' dragged away."

Dom rolls his eyes.

Before they can keep bickering, I lift a hand to get their attention. "I don't want to be a full-time submissive," I say firmly. "I hate having rules about my life dictated to me. I want to be able to speak my mind without worrying about the consequences. I want authority over my time and my choices. *Always.*"

Dom considers me, golden eyed and dangerous. "And your body? Do you want full authority over that?"

My mouth goes dry, and it's a struggle not to look away. "Not . . . always."

His mouth curves up on one side, just a little, as I try not to fidget.

Beau rubs his chest, then glances at Dom. "We never wanted a full-time submissive. Not really. This arrangement was never meant to be all about kink. It was meant to be the start of something. A relationship."

I purse my lips primly. "And do you always start your relationships by lying? Or were you being experimental?"

Dom snorts, and Beau laughs uncomfortably, then bites his lip. They're still red from kissing me senseless. He edges in close to me and shoots me a sinful look under his lashes. "That was all Dom's idea," he confides. "*I* voted for honesty."

"Seriously?" Dom mutters dryly. "Unbelievable."

The heated way Beau's looking at me makes me shiver. It takes me longer than I'm proud of for my brain to start functioning again, but I finally manage to work up a frown.

And I really hope it looks at least somewhat disapproving and not just desperately aroused.

"Don't blame him—you should have been honest regardless. You're responsible for your own decisions. You're an independent adult." My gaze slips down to his bare, deliciously firm chest. An X-rated, beautiful, well-developed, *well-endowed* . . . I catch his smirk and snap my eyes away, cheeks flushing. "You— You're just as much at fault."

Dom snickers, and I twist to give him a stern look. "And don't *you* laugh, you lied to me too. All of you did. It's incredibly patronizing."

His smile fades. "I was trying to keep you safe."

I stifle a sigh. "Yes, well, as darling and"—I wave an exasperated hand—"*macho* as the impulse is, I'm not some fragile ornament, or something for you to *keep*. I know you mean well, but the lying has to stop. You need to trust me to be sensible." My voice turns tart. "You do understand that I don't actually *enjoy* putting myself in danger? Given all the information, I do usually choose to keep myself far away from it."

Beau's cheeks color, but Dom sighs. "We talked about this. Sometimes I—"

"Don't have time to explain, yes, I heard. But you did then. You usually do. You chose not to." I hold his gaze, even as his eyes narrow. "I'm not a soldier, Dom. You might need to try a different approach because I don't enjoy being treated like one."

There must be something wrong with me that his stern look kicks my heartrate up again.

"Cut me off again and we'll make it another fifteen," Dom replies, and my breath catches. I don't think I can take another fifteen right now though. My butt is bruised as it is. Then he gives me a contemplative look. "I'll try, Eden. You might need to remind me. My track record at working with civilians is . . . not the best."

"I will," I say sweetly, and Dom swats my hip.

"Good," he replies.

My heart is racing.

It's rather exciting, speaking your mind.

I laugh, feeling light. Surprisingly so, after the last few hours. "So that's it then. The deal is over!"

At my laughter, Beau's face kindles, and he gives me that slow, melting smile again. "I guess it is." He runs a finger up my arm, then along my collarbone. "So how exactly am I going to win alone time with you now? You're going to have all of us fighting for your attention."

Despite my best intentions, my mind slips to the sparring session I happened to briefly glance at the other day. They were sweaty, and wrestling, and pressed up against one another . . .

"Hmm." I pretend to consider that as his finger trails back down the curve of my breast. Breathlessly, I murmur, "I guess you'll have to convince me that you're worth my time."

His pretty hazel eyes widen in surprise, and he shoots me a cheeky grin. "Now I wonder how I'll do that."

"You're both getting ahead of yourselves," Dom cuts in, and I look back at him. His eyes linger on Beau's hand on my chest before they lift to meet mine. "The set days were in place to keep things fair. Even. It's not easy to share, Eden."

I purse my lips, studying him. "Yes," I say slowly, "I understand that it's easier for you all when I don't get a say. But it's not working for me."

Dom rolls his eyes with a short, hard sigh. "That's not what I meant."

"Then what did you mean?" I ask testily. I'm not about to let him ruin my glow, no matter how distracting he is, all damp and dark and gorgeous in the sunshine.

"I think he means, darlin'," Beau says, "that Dom and I have tried it a few times. Negotiating jealousy, issues, keeping everything in balance . . . it was a lot with three people involved, on all sides. You're talking about six."

Beside me, Dom tenses.

"Five," I correct quietly, wrapping an arm around myself as I think of the awful chess match.

Dom's shoulders unbunch. "Yes, five."

I look up at him, confused. "You know about Jasper?"

"Sorry, Eden, I forgot you and Jasper didn't work out for a minute," Beau says quickly, glancing between us and giving Dom a quelling look. "Five, then. Five people are a lot to keep happy."

Dom mutters under his breath, and I sting over how easily Beau says it, like it was a thing of no consequence.

I suppose it isn't, really. I suppose Jasper and I were never really a possibility.

Seeming to sense my mood shift, Dom looks at me. I feel him regard me for a long moment, and I avoid his gaze like it's my last mission on earth.

I clear my throat. "I know it won't be easy, okay? But we're all adults. If we have any problems, we'll just have to talk it through. And I will do my best to keep it fair."

"Just like that, huh?" Dom says.

I lift my chin and look at him through my glasses. "Yes. *Just like that.*"

His eyes take on a secret shine, and Beau nods. "She's right. We need to try this the right way. The hard way."

Beau's words make me bright, like fairy lights are being strung up between my ribs, and I lean up to kiss him again. "Thank you."

The forests in his eyes dance, alive with possibility. Beau cups my jaw and pulls me in for a low, thorough kiss. "I hope you know you're mine now, darlin'. Be prepared for everything that comes along with that."

His. Theirs. And I also get to be mine now, too.

Beau presses another light kiss to my lips. "Eden, I don't always say the right thing. But I promise I'll work on it. I think you're fierce, and intelligent, and resourceful as anything—I was yours the minute you told us to run and save ourselves." He rests his forehead against mine. "Take good care of me, sweetheart."

My lips curve up, and those lights in me turn star bright. "I promise."

After a long, sweet moment, I look at Dom, who's watching me like I'm a puzzle, an impossibly knotted string. He's sitting so close, but just out of reach.

"I won't hurt them, Dom," I promise softly. I can see it in him, that protectiveness of them. I feel it too.

"Don't make promises you can't keep, pet," he replies, just as softly.

Then he shakes his head, and the moment breaks. "It's done, then. But without the deal, the consequences are all on you if this goes south."

That seems fair, at least. "Yes, sir."

He stands up, and I can't help the way my eyes trail over his naked body. When he starts tugging on his pants, I hide my sigh of disappointment.

"Do you have a canteen?" Dom asks. "You should have some water."

"Mm-hmm. In my bag."

Dom tugs at the straps and opens the flap, pulling it forward to check the contents when an avalanche of . . . supplies . . . falls out. He picks up one of the condoms, then looks at me with a raised brow.

Beau splutters a laugh. "*Ten*? Darlin', you were coming out here against our orders." He rubs a hand over his jaw. "I like your ambition, but were you really thinking we'd use all of these?"

My cheeks heat. Rather than respond to that, I dare to start pressing small kisses across his chest, licking at the gentle glistening of sweat on his skin.

"Water." Beau hands me the canteen, and I drink without complaint. I drain it, surprised at how thirsty I am.

"Come on," Dom says. "We should get moving."

My arms twine around Beau's neck, and I snuggle in. I don't want to leave this place just yet. The circle of Beau's arms is a wonderful, glorious sanctuary.

Beau groans . . . and I hate that the sound is resigned. "He's right. We won't get back until well after nightfall as it is."

I shake my head and kiss his neck. "Mm-mm. Comfy here."

A warning slap against my ass startles me into lifting my head.

"Ow." I frown, glaring up at Beau.

Dom snorts in amusement, and I glare at him too.

He smiles back languidly, some of the stiffness in his muscles relaxing as he looks down at me. "Move that ass, or I'll bruise it, gorgeous."

I huff, but a smile bubbles at my lips. "I think you already did that."

Beau kisses my forehead, and Dom's slow smile deepens. "*One*."

I drop my legs and get up quickly enough that my head spins, and Dom laughs. Beau begins collecting his clothes, and I grudgingly do the same with a sigh.

As Dom slings on his pack, he looks over at me thoughtfully. "How are you feeling about the rest of it, Eden? The shooter?"

Another unwelcome thought. How do I *feel* about it? Sick. Sad. *Sorry*. But . . .

"I do understand why I had to do it," I say finally, and the words don't feel like a lie. I swallow. "I would do it again."

Please don't let me have to do that again.

Dom nods. "You should talk to Jasper." At my expression, he lifts a brow, then shakes his head. "We might have helped with your initial panic, Eden, but kink isn't a substitute for therapy. This kind of thing leaves a mark. You should talk to him."

"And I promise he's better at dealing with trauma than he is at relationship advice," Beau adds wryly, and I snort softly.

The thought of opening up to Jasper again makes my stomach

churn in a different way. I remember curling up at his feet and staring up at the gorgeous veil of his eyelashes. The way the world just fell away.

For me, anyway.

I couldn't have made more of a fool of myself.

"I'll think about it," I promise, when both of them keep staring at me. Dom opens his mouth like he's about to argue, but Beau shoots him another quelling look. I smile softly at him. "I'm okay. For now, I'm okay. He—they all—wanted to hurt us. He would have killed me, or taken me back to Sam, and I—"

I cut off as Beau turns stiff as a board. "What?" I look at him. "What did I do?"

Dom and Beau exchange a look loaded with meaning, and alarm skitters down my spine.

Hard golden eyes impale me. "That name, Eden. Where did you hear that name?"

"What name?" I stammer. "Sam? That's their leader. He's the one who almost caught me."

His eyes press closed.

"He wasn't in the clearing that first day," Beau says, dull shock ringing through his tone. "We didn't see him in the woods later. We couldn't have known. But, shit . . . We didn't even question her when we took her home. Dom . . ."

Beau yanks his shirt on, shaking his head.

"You're sure?" Dom asks me urgently. "You're *sure* that was the name?"

"Y-yes." I glance between them. I feel a sudden draft. Looking at my mangled bra and ripped shirt, I abandon them and reach for my bag. I pull out my spare set of clothes and get dressed as quickly as I can. "What am I missing?"

"This is important, Eden. What did he look like?" Dom asks, then kneels to re-pack my bag for me with swift experience.

I run a hand over my tangled hair, trying to catch up with this abrupt shift in tone. "I— Well, he was a little older. Maybe early fifties? Short beard. Salt and pepper hair. I— I don't know what else. Medium build, but he was strong? I remember he was strong."

"*Fuck*," Beau curses as he yanks his pack up, and an ice-cold weight lands in my stomach.

Beau doesn't swear. Not like that.

When Dom hands me my pack, my hands are trembling with foreboding.

I glance around the clearing. All evidence of our messy, perfect tryst is gone. Dom and Beau's faces are wiped of emotion too. They're back to pure soldier mode now. If the aching weakness in my muscles wasn't screaming at me, I could almost think it hadn't happened.

"Please," I ask, and Dom pauses. "Why does that name matter? What does it mean?"

Dom looks down at me, and my knees turn to water at what's in his eyes. I know it's bad then. It's really bad.

For the first time since we met, Dom is *afraid*.

"It means this trap wasn't meant for us." Dom looks away and slings his rifle over his shoulder. "It means Bristlebrook is under attack."

CHAPTER 31

JASPER

SURVIVAL TIP #199
*When you discover your fatal weakness,
either protect it at all costs . . .
or destroy it.*

D amn it!"
I hit the desk in frustration, then push back in my chair, scowling at the screens. Scrubbing a hand over my eyes, I sigh. There's a twinge in my back that tells me I'm not as young as I used to be—I'll be paying for sitting up in this chair all night and most of the day. My stomach is tight with hunger but I'm reluctant to stop long enough to get myself some food. I caved and had breakfast, but lunch had been due hours ago.

Why would that group just sit there? It doesn't make sense. The spot is exposed, and the closest source of water is a fifteen-minute trek away. But there are men camped there—they slip into frame often enough that I'm sure of that.

Ever since Eden arrived and alerted us to the hunter issue, something has been off. My instincts have been screaming at me for days. We're missing something critical. *I* am missing something critical, and I don't want to fail again. Jaykob may have been crude, but he had a point: I've missed too much already.

Perhaps there is a flavor of self-flagellation to my tired vigil, where the sadist in me relishes even my own penance. But a few uncomfortable nights aren't enough to make up for missing the cameras, or for Eden running off.

And that's not even to mention my greater failures.

With another heavy sigh, I push myself back over to the desk and rewind one of the videos that has been bothering me. The picture is clear, from yesterday afternoon just before dusk, from a camera just half an hour from Bristlebrook. The trees are sparser here, and there's a wide view of the forest. A woodpecker with a small yellow patch of feathers above its beak swoops in and perches on a nearby branch. My brow creases.

"Shit, Jasper. Did you even go to bed last night?"

A thousand needles prickle at the nape of my neck, then down my spine to the backs of my legs. Cursing myself inwardly, I glance down at the small screen on the desk which shows the hall and wide-open door. Yet another thing I missed.

I don't turn, keeping my eyes locked on the tiny woodpecker. Looking at Lucien is always a mistake—one I avoid whenever possible. I don't need to look, however, to know my seeming indifference slices into him. His hurt is a tangible, sour taste at the back of my tongue. He's been stiff and uncomfortable around me—almost cold—ever since our conversation in the kitchen, and I can't blame him for it.

"I'm working, Lucien," I remind him politely, and rewind the video again, trying to focus on the little bird.

"Oh, sure, but I thought . . . Look, I just think you—"

Lucien huffs, and there's a strangled, frustrated whine to it that teases at the dark mood I'm in. No matter what constraints I put on myself, hearing charming, chattery Lucien become tongue-tied around me is one of my most secret delights. One that makes my dick stir and thicken instantly, every time.

Unable to resist it now, I turn my chair so I can see him. His cheeks are flushed the exact shade of pink that always makes me want to bite them, and he's carrying a tray of food, looking like the star of one of my favorite maid and master fantasies.

I wonder if he knows how irresistible he is like this, servicing me so sweetly. Lucien's desire to please is so natural to him, so wound up in his perfect, innate goodness, I doubt it occurs to him to do it for any other reason than to be kind.

And therein lies the full sting of my Lucien problem. How can I be distant and unfeeling toward someone so deserving? How much longer can I resist delivering him the pain and control and *love* he craves, when I so badly crave the deliverance also?

But how can I say yes, when the last tattered shreds of my honor hang on my resistance?

"I made you dinner," he finishes in a rush, avoiding my eyes. "You, um, you should take a break."

The painful tempest inside of me decides to batter at my heart, like it might knock it right out of my chest. "You made me dinner," I repeat softly.

The pink in his cheeks spreads to his ears, and he glances at me. Our gazes tangle, and whatever he sees in mine makes him suck in a shivery breath.

Casually, I cross my legs, hiding my now-insistent interest. His parted lips are a sin unto themselves.

"I made it for Jaykob too," he mutters defensively. "It's no big deal."

Tearing my gaze away is more difficult than I'd like, but I take in the meal he made me. Healthy, the way I like it, simple poached pheasant, a side of grilled vegetables, and . . .

"Kimchi," I breathe.

I lean forward, taking the tray from him. Stunned, I take a bite and need to stifle a groan. The fermented Korean staple is sour, spicy, and tangy, and it brings with it a rush of homesickness so strong I'm almost dizzy with it. It's ridiculous, in a way, because I *am* home. But it's nostalgia of a different kind—for a time, and certain moments, and people I haven't seen in far, far too long.

I taste it slowly, rolling the flavors and feelings over my tongue before I swallow. To my surprise, tears prick the back of my eyes.

"Is it okay?" Lucien asks, shifting, after the silence stretches longer than manners call for. "I've never made it before, but Eden found the recipe in one of the pantry cupboards and we made it together. We— I mean, she thought you might like it."

My breath leaves me heavily, caught on the chest-twisting picture of Eden and Lucien working together in the kitchen to make something so sweet and personal just to make me happy. Just because I might like it.

Eden's brilliant, sharp eyes caress my mind. Her sumptuous hair. Her quick wit and kind concern.

The glorious effortlessness of her submission.

I set the tray onto the desk, needing some distance from their heartless, thoughtful gift.

Damn her. And damn him. I am not a selfless man—they shouldn't torment me like this.

They should take one another and run far, far away.

Reaching out, I catch Lucien's wrist, pulling him over to me. He follows easily, that awkward tension in him falling away as soon as I take charge, as it always does. Lucien stands over me, but through that one touch, he's at my mercy.

The power of it, the heady awareness that I can do anything I want to him, seeps into me. He would let me. He would let me take him to his knees and fuck his pretty mouth until I came down his throat and he would say nothing but *thank you*. I could pull him into my lap and just *hold* him, for hours, and he would stay there happily.

Or he would have, before Eden.

Now, I'm not so sure. He indulged my foolish, selfish, impulsive request not to fuck her, and I am both mortified and darkly satisfied that he did. But his patience with me has to be wearing thin, and as much as the psychologist in me tells me it's for the best, that I should continue backing away, the man in me wants to claim him now. I want to claim them both, to demand their affection and tangle the three of us into such a knot that none of us could ever be unsnarled. I want to undo my hard work, unswear my vows, and abandon my resolution to leave them unbroken.

But that truly *would* be foolish, not to mention selfish beyond all belief.

His skin is warm under my chilled fingers, and I stroke the vulnerable flesh at his wrist. The pulse there kisses my fingers with swift little presses.

"Thank you both, Lucien."

I watch his throat bob. Unable to help myself, I link our fingers together and squeeze gently. After a moment, he squeezes back, a dazed expression crossing his face. He leans against the desk, as though needing the support.

"I used to make kimchi with my parents," I venture in a mild voice, though I know I'm inviting him in when I should be pushing him out. "It was my mother's recipe, and it was important to her that we all contributed. She said it was like holding our culture in our hands. She left a lot behind when she came here, but she'd joke that some things were sacred. It didn't matter if we were having bibimbap or caviar, we'd almost always have kimchi as well —and it had to be kimchi that we made ourselves, by hand, together."

Lucien's mouth curves on one side, just a little, teasing me with a dimple. That chill he's been keeping between us melts like sugar on my tongue. "I don't know how I feel about caviar and kimchi."

"You don't know what you're missing, I promise you."

I look back at the screens, but I don't see them now—just memories of my mother grinning up at my father, her hands deep in a messy bowl of cabbage the color of a burnished sunrise. My father sweating every time he took a bite, because my mother also liked her kimchi to be as hot as the sun, and he had never had a head for heat.

Lucien has never been afraid of a little heat, though.

"You don't talk about them much." There's more than a hint of a question in his voice.

"Don't I?" I say, though I know it's true. Then I add more quietly, "I think about them often."

Lucien presses our palms together more fully, and my stomach does a low, hard flip.

"I miss mine too."

Hesitantly, he strokes a thumb over my hand where we're joined, and I know I should pull away now. This is getting too close.

But I don't. Not just yet.

Surely I'm breaking no vows by just holding his hand. I've come far closer to breaking them in the past. A little hand holding is nothing.

"Why haven't you made her recipe since we've been here?" he asks.

Because I have no family to make it with.

Strange, I never made it with Soomin, either. She had always had her own recipe, and she preferred to make it herself.

"It takes a long time to make," I say instead. "And I wasn't sure anyone else would have a taste for it."

"It wasn't that hard," Lucien disagrees. "And Eden likes it. She loves Korean food."

I blink, unsure why that surprises me. "She does?"

He looks far too amused. "You know, you really should just talk to her one day without all the fancy interrogation tactics. The two of you have a lot in common. She's also raided your mom's old collection of K-dramas. Or maybe it's yours."

I know Eden and I have a lot in common. Books, and philosophy, and tea . . . and Lucien. Precious Lucien. Precious Eden. They will be beautiful together, I know. Pure, precious, and *happy*.

"My mother loved them, and I couldn't bear to throw them away." I smile, then give him an arch look. "They're far too sappy for my taste."

"Uh-huh," Lucien says, and his dimples are definitely toying with me now. The sight of them makes my chest throb—and my erection go absolutely nowhere. There's just enough sass in his voice to warrant a little lesson in manners.

If he were mine.

He must see something of what I'm thinking in my face because a tremor runs through him, and he glances away. "Anyway, the kimchi's not too bad. Bit of ketchup and it'd be totally edible."

Pardon? I'm pulled out of my thoughts. Even for Lucien, that's . . .

Settling back in my chair, I release his hand and catch his wrist again. I yank him forward so he's off balance and press down in warning. "You put ketchup anywhere close to my mother's recipe, and I will empty a bag of rice on the kitchen floor and make you pick up every last grain with a pair of tweezers between your teeth."

Lucien's mouth drops open, and he seems caught somewhere between laughter and horror. "Your creativity is a little frightening sometimes, you know that?"

I know that I want to press him into the wall and choke his laughter with my tongue.

He was your patient, I remind myself. He was for years. You have far too much influence over him. It would be unethical.

But images of the last time my weakness overcame me are quick to spring to mind. The day his stupidity reached new heights —literally—and he somehow convinced Beau to race up that cliff-side. Without gear, without a plan to get down.

Without his brain, apparently.

I made him repay every minute of the unbearable hours he'd terrified me. I tortured him until tears tracked down that cheeky, bratty face and his dimples tucked themselves away in apology.

Until he was unbearably hard, throbbing, and mindless with the need to come. Until he apologized, and begged me so sweetly, and my raging fear slaked itself in his torment. The grateful little whimper he gave when I finally allowed him release has gotten me off more nights than I can count. The way he snuggled into my side as I tended him afterwards . . .

"What are you thinking about?" he asks in a low, husky voice.

I glance up to find his eyes stuck on my lap, those parted lips sucking in air and taunting me with the pink slickness just inside. Of course, from the angle he's now standing at there's no hiding the erection pushing at my slacks. *Damn it.*

"Eden," I lie smoothly, and hate myself when he flinches.

"Right."

I watch his throat bob as he swallows, feeling filthy. A prince of muck and shame. He deserves better than this, better than me. If only he didn't believe he was in love with me. If only he recognized this for what it was and let me go, then I wouldn't need to keep pushing him away.

"You didn't fuck Eden," I blurt, and his tense, hurt expression swings back to me in disbelief.

Immediately, I want to bite my tongue off. I *need* to push him away. To unclamp my grasping fingers from his heart. To finally snip the last threads of hope that tie him to me. I need to free him, the way he deserves to be freed. I should mind my own business.

But I'm tired, and rumpled, and sore.

And terribly deficient.

Unlike Eden, Lucien doesn't stammer. He blinks once, then looks at me from under lowered brows.

"Not with my cock," he admits. Then his voice lowers, becomes hushed. "I fucked her with my mouth. I fucked her until she came on my tongue."

He says it like a confession, like he's whispering to a priest of some forbidden communion. His eyes are on my face, and I wonder what he hopes to see. Jealousy? Anger? I have no right to either, though both suck at me like diseases preying on a weak constitution.

"How did she taste?" The insidious question slips out of me, but the need of knowing is an instant obsession. I've imagined it, many times. Every time she crossed and recrossed her legs while she read in the firelight, when she had the audacity to sass me about the library, when she knelt at my feet like she was born to it. I've imagined her taste, her smell, the sounds she would make.

How pretty her lashes would look tangled with tears.

Lucien's blue eyes darken, and I can see the lust and more than a hint of vindictive satisfaction lurking behind them.

"She tasted like she wanted me."

Releasing his wrist, I catch his shirt and tug, so he's forced to bend down further over me. "Tell me how wet she was." Stroking down his cheek with my other hand, I ask, "Did she soak that beard of yours?"

Lucien shivers, but he traps my eyes. "Over and over."

I was right—my sweet soldier is taunting me.

"She wrapped her legs around my ears and grinded on my tongue. She begged me for more. She begged for my cock."

Jealousy clutches at me. It's not fair, not fair at all given my decision—but I'm furious that he had her and I did not. That she had *him*, when I would let my soul expire to do the same. My hand drops to the seam of his jeans where he strains against the thick denim. I rub him roughly through the fabric, and he gasps in shock, bucking into my hand.

"But you didn't give it to her," I croon.

I squeeze his length, just this side of painful. Lucien moans, then grits his teeth against the sound, clearly trying to control himself. Blue eyes flash defiantly at me. "Her mouth was incredible, she let me use it twice."

Of course she did. Lucien has a beautiful cock; she *should* worship it.

But only when *I* say she can.

My grip tightens, and he whimpers, tensing, but I see the submission sliding over him. The fight leaves his body, and he pumps into my punishing touch. Adrenaline thrums through me, pressure building in my balls. My heart stutters and twists.

What am I *doing*?

I release Lucien as quickly as I grabbed him, ignoring the way my chest throbs, avoiding the devastation and humiliation crossing his face. I'm shaky, unsettled. Damn it, I know better than this. I decided *against* this. What happened to my control?

Kimchi and dimples. A toxic combination.

Forcing myself to relax—or at least seem to—I look up at the screens again, realizing with irritation that I've somehow skipped the camera ahead to present time, losing my place on yesterday's feed.

"Really, Jasper?" Lucien's voice trembles with hurt. "What the hell are you doing with me? Will you make up your damn mind? Can't you see that I want you?"

Shame has sharp teeth, it seems, and it minces my insides as I bring up yesterday's feed from that camera on another screen.

"Damn it, *look at me*. I deserve an explanation. What is it? First I thought you wanted Eden, but then you broke things off with her, and I thought maybe . . . But then, with Jayk, you pushed me away again, and I just—" Lucky lets out a hard, frustrated breath. "What *is* it? Is it that I'm a man? Because I hate to break it to you but there's no way you're indifferent to me. I—"

My fingers halt on the keys, and I can't help but turn to stare at him, flummoxed.

"What does you being a man have to do with anything?"

"I—" His mouth opens, then clicks shut as he frowns at me. "Doesn't it?"

I quirk a brow at him, utterly at a loss to this turn in the conversation. "Was it me jerking off that gorgeous cock of yours that made you think I wasn't interested in men? Or me oiling you up and having you parade around as my most exquisite furniture?"

That was a particularly weak day for me. "Or was it the way I bent you over to see how you would take that hook up that pretty ass of yours?" I shake my head, disbelieving. "No. I wouldn't change a thing about you, Lucien."

Color floods his cheeks again, but his pulse is hammering, and he has the look of a sub pushed almost to his limits. That look wrecks me, floods me with the need to protect him. The pain is only fun when I can make it better.

"Then *why*?" He thrusts his hand into his hair and grips it. "Jasper, what is the damn problem?"

"Why can't you just leave it be?" I hiss. I rub my forehead, trying to fight against the urge to pull him into my arms.

"Why?" He laughs, and there's a hysterical edge to it. "God damn it, Jasper, can't you see that I'm in love with you? I'd give you anything, *everything* you ask for. You want me too. I know you do. You have to."

"And what about Eden? You want her, don't you?" I snap, pushing out of the chair.

"So? I want you both. We could all have each other. I'm sure, if you apologize, she'll—"

The single tear that slid off her cheek as I rejected her still scalds my skin.

I shake my head once, cutting him off. "Just be with Eden, Lucien. She's lovely—she'll make you happy."

"No, Jasper." His voice drops low. "It's not *enough*."

I grit my teeth, hating the ring of truth I hear in that statement.

"You're attracted to her," I say mildly, turning back to him when I've managed to gain control of my expression again. My heart gnashes against the cage I press it into.

"She's not a dominant, and neither am I. We can't be that for each other." Lucien glares at me. "Not without you. We both need more."

Panic makes my head light. "You're a switch, Lucien. I've seen you do it."

"Dominating isn't the same. It doesn't *fill* me," he says, unrelenting. "And I don't think I can do it with her. Maybe it's just been too long, or maybe I just realized I prefer being the submissive, I don't know, but I couldn't."

No.

A mismatch in kink, especially one as fundamental as this, is devastating. It's the reason my marriage failed. It's the reason I gave Eden for turning her down—one that wasn't the whole truth, but still a valid one. I sensed no deep desire for pain from her.

If Lucien can't switch . . . if he doesn't want to dominate . . .

His eyes find mine again, brimming with pain and confusion. "I *couldn't*, Jasper. She's gorgeous and funny and smart and she tastes like a dream. With her, I can finally breathe again in a way I never could before, not even with you. She could be my best friend, I could love her completely, easily, but that edge . . . that thing, that takes me somewhere else, that thing that calms me, and makes me feel safe, and broken . . . it just wasn't there without you. I couldn't help it. I didn't want to, but I just kept thinking how much I wanted you there with us, taking both of us for yourself. I want her. I might even need her in a way you can never give me, but I need you too. I need you to take control. I need to see her make you come. She should be there next to me, both of us kneeling for you, and—"

"Just shut *up*, Lucien," I snap, cutting off that drugging, impossible picture. Because it is far, far too easy to see. My Eden, crawling on her knees to me. Rewarding her with Lucien's cock. Both of them, *mine*, to pet and hold and shatter as I like. "It will never happen."

There's a long, terrible silence.

"Why? Just answer that, Jasper. I deserve to know why."

The pain in his voice paralyzes me, and I loathe myself for putting it there.

Why? The why would lay me naked before him. It would flay the flesh from my bones and leave me no place to hide. It might kill me to tell him why.

But I've tried everything else.

He's right.

It's time for Lucien to know it all.

CHAPTER 32

JASPER

SURVIVAL TIP #32
*Your fight will give out at some point.
Prepare for the consequences.*

I breathe in through my nose, calling on every meditative technique I ever learned to pull myself back into some shaky semblance of control. Two, three more breaths later and I'm able to stare at the screens, at that bird flying in and settling on that tree branch.

Why. Where to begin?

"My wife—" I start, then try again. "My relationship with Soomin . . . it was so straightforward, at first. She was a darling. Sweet, intelligent, and a wonderful, trained submissive. You met her. You know."

Lucien leans against the desk, watching without speaking, and I'm grateful. This is a difficult thing to articulate. It's hard to talk about her; harder still to talk about her with *him*.

"It only took me a year to realize Soomin and I weren't well matched. Her masochistic tendencies were very light, and I hungered for more."

I can't look at him for this. Not because he won't understand, but because I know he will, and too well. My eyes drop to my ring, and I absently realize I've been spinning it. I take another deep breath and force myself to still my hands.

"For seven beautiful years, it was worth it. Or, at least, I was able to convince myself it was." I swallow, and then lower my voice. "And if I sometimes trembled with the need for more, to push her in other ways, darker ways, I learned to suppress it. I quashed that part of myself viciously, not even allowing myself the fantasy of it —because even in fantasy it felt wrong when I was vividly aware that she wanted no part of that particular facet of my soul."

Lucien shifts, but when I glance at him, he just nods at me to continue without meeting my eyes. A small frown mars his forehead.

"Over time, the signs of strain began to show, both in her because she was sharp enough to notice how much I held myself back, and in me, for the holding back. And I loathed myself for the weakness. For the misplaced guilt I saw building in her eyes. But we went to the club, we experimented. We loved one another, so we made it work. We made it work right up until . . ." My voice catches, nervousness closing my airways. I gather myself and continue, "Right up until I met someone. A young soldier who changed everything."

Lucien has gone so still, I'm not sure he's breathing. His golden hair is half twisted in a bun on his head and half cascading over his shoulders. The harsh fluorescent lights shouldn't be flattering, but I'm not sure it's possible for him to look less than devastating to me.

"Young, gorgeous Lucien," I say tenderly, and his chest hitches, though I don't hear a sound. He's turned his face from me, and I wish he wouldn't. I want to read every thought that crosses his expressive face. "Who wouldn't have been in awe, meeting Lucien? A soldier who had moved through the ranks at near record speed. A young man who, while a confident bisexual, was also a conflicted, submissive-leaning switch with heavy masochistic tendencies. It was like seeing a notice for my own demise. He was to be under *my* care as a high-priority patient—and I was madly, urgently attracted to him."

Fresh from my promotion, I was feeling good. I'd debriefed Beaumont, Dominic, and most other members of the platoon by that stage, and we'd gotten on well enough. I'd wanted to brush up on my notes before meeting with Jaykob after reading about the incident with his brother, and thought Lucien would be a straight-forward assessment.

Right up until I saw the shameless interest that lit up his eyes, and all the shadows and needs and fears that hid behind them. I saw those dimples begging for my tongue.

Straightforward, my lily-white ass.

Now, those dimples are nowhere in sight. That boy might have matured into an incredible man, but right now, he's still the picture of vulnerability.

I force myself to go on. "This *boy* was a cruel joke on me—both on my marriage, and on my profession. It was beyond absurd. Me, a thirty-five-year-old happily married man, an experienced psychologist, lusting after a twenty-one-year-old *patient*. It was . . . a cosmic unkindness beyond my imagination."

Leaning against the wall, I sigh. "So of course, I locked that down too, into the same place I pushed my sadistic self. I could indulge neither. Perhaps those fantasies could play with one another there, but I was determined never to peek into that box of shame." Hardening my tone, I add, "You must understand, Lucien. I loved my wife, genuinely, and she deserved the loyalty I promised. And you—you defenseless, flawless thing—deserved a therapist you could trust, who would help you without guile or agenda. For all our sakes, the box could never be opened."

But, curse him, Lucien was a flirt, and curious, and he tested all my limits. Through his sessions we talked about his work, of course, and also his sexuality. His fears and worries about being seen as a submissive. His own calling, for pain and tears and pleases and thank-yous that so perfectly, desperately matched my own. His recitations of fantasies and desires that had me sitting swollen and dripping pre-cum in my chair as I took dutiful notes. His curious, hungry, and entirely inappropriate questions about me.

Present-day Lucien looks at me, finally, intensely, but for once, I can't read him.

"The lines started to blur. Soomin and I became more involved with events on base. You started showing up everywhere, at barbecues and charity auctions and, worst of all, you began frequenting the club. I shouldn't have been surprised—there weren't a plethora around . . . and I was intimately aware of your needs."

I glare at him, unable to help myself, remembering that furious, helpless panic I'd felt on seeing him there. Lucien's lips tighten, but he doesn't look away from my wrath.

"I started taking Soomin to the private rooms for our sessions there, not sure who I was trying to protect. Perhaps both of you. Perhaps only myself." I swallow, some of my glare softening. "I knew seeing you like *that*, shattered and tearstained, might be something too big to fit in my box."

It would have been. It *is*. Every time, despite the soul-souring shame, I have to admit in the most shadowy recesses of my heart, that he is perfect. This gorgeous, likable man whose masochism rides him as deeply as my sadism does me. Whose mischievous spirit is so enduring and bright, he's impossible not to love.

So while his cries are delicious, and his pleasure addictive, what keeps me up at night is that moment. The one where he gives himself over to me completely, where he looks up with perfect trust and heartbreaking faith. It's the moment where I know I've satisfied something deep inside him, and the relentless craving inside me has also eased. It's better than any orgasm I've ever had.

And *fuck*, I want that again. But I won't have it. Not ever.

This has gone on long enough.

"Soomin noticed, of course. She wasn't stupid. And over the

next three years, I devoted myself to convincing her that I would never take advantage of my patient, that I loved her, that I didn't need to feed the darkness inside me."

Old hurt spills over, and I can't keep it from my voice. "I meant it, Lucien. I truly did. Even if she wasn't my best friend, even if I didn't love her, the imbalance of power between you and me was—*is*—far too great to ever be palatable. In the end, though, she didn't believe me. She left. She left, and I was alone with the promises that I swore never to break."

And here it is. The hard part. And I will explain it to him, though I know him well enough to know he won't accept it. It's why I've held my tongue until now.

Every step closer to him hurts, but I take them, until we're a breath apart. Always close but that space never closed. It takes several moments before he meets my eyes, still with that unreadable, intense expression.

"Those promises are still promises, Lucien, even though it's been five years and an apocalypse since our divorce. Because you are still too young, you are still my patient, and I still have an ethical responsibility toward you. I've been a mentor and a guide to you, and you have confused those feelings with a crush. It would be wrong to take advantage of those feelings."

Lucien's face darkens like a gloaming sky, but I cut him off.

"It's not psychobabble, Lucien. It's called transference and it is a very real phenomenon." I cup his chin, unable to help it. "I *promised* my wife you wouldn't be mine. I made promises to myself when I took on this profession not to cross certain lines."

I stroke along his jaw, knowing it might be the last time I allow myself to do so. He's tense and furious, his eyes wet with the worst kind of tears. Hot, filthy shame makes my throat tight too.

"Since we've been living here, I've slipped more times than I'm proud of. Somehow the box pries itself open, and I relive a new brand of failure as a husband, psychologist, and dominant. You have to understand. It's *terrible*, Lucien. The things I've done to you—I am the villain I always feared myself to be."

"*Done* to me?" Lucien asks, and there's a dangerous, bladed edge to his question. His eyes flash. "Are you finished?"

Unsettled by his tone, I frown, searching his face. I'm not sure I've ever seen him look quite like this.

I nod, and he nods back, like we're agreeing.

"Good."

Lucien shoves me back, hard. "Who the fuck do you think you are?"

He grabs my shirt and yanks me close, and I brace myself against him, stumbling. He turns us and shoves me against the wall. His strength surprises me, though I know it shouldn't. He's just never turned it on me before. I finally recognize the raw, unfiltered fury for what it is.

My heart twists until it snaps, severing itself from all vital blood flow. It has to be why my chest hurts so much.

"I am not some tender-hearted schoolgirl who's never had her skirts flipped before," he snarls in my face.

Every inch of him is pressed against me, as if in protest of the space I always kept between us. Irritated that he's missed the point, I open my mouth, but he slaps a hand over it.

"No. You had your say, now you listen, you stupid, old, patronizing *fuck*." I narrow my eyes on him over his palm, not at all sure about this flip in our roles. "I've lived through war. I've had my heart broken. I've been fucked in every hole I have. I've dated, and killed, and loved, and lost. I've survived an apocalypse. How *dare* you stand here and tell me I don't know my own mind?"

He takes his hand from my mouth and smears his thumb over my lips, the way I've done more times than I should have.

"Do you have any idea how condescending you sound? You think we're the first people who have ever fallen in love that shouldn't have?" Lucien grinds his dick against me, rubbing against mine through our pants, and I can't help my grunt. "And

I'm sorry, but your wife is gone, and there's no ethics board here to rake you over the coals. How can you say this is a lie? Do you even really believe that? No matter who you are to me, who you've ever been, *this* is real. These feelings exist whether you want them to or not. They always have."

Enough. I move to push him off me and find that I can't. It's galling to admit, but he is stronger than I am. My heart pounds unsteadily. His eyes narrow on me, so close to mine. I can taste him from here.

My lips purse as I scramble for my usual cool. "Yes, Lucien, I do believe that my duty to you is real. Ethics don't stop existing just because no one is around to enforce them. I didn't stay away from you because I didn't want to lose my job. I stayed away because it's wrong. You don't fully understand your unconscious drivers, what is pushing you toward me. And my own lust is simply a case of countertransference, responding to your infatuation. You were so young when we met, it—"

Lucien growls, and I'm a touch intrigued by this wild, angry side to him. I want to wrap a chain around his neck and force an O-ring in his mouth and hear him growl just like that around my dick.

But that would be counterproductive to this conversation.

I swallow, needing to get myself back under control. It's utterly shredded. Having Lucien pressed against me like this is the purest torment. I've never allowed myself the pleasure and would never have allowed him to take it. But he *is* taking it.

It's not my sin if he takes it from me, surely.

"I'm twenty-eight years old," he says against my lips. "I'm a grown-ass man, Jasper."

I meet his eyes, forcing steadiness I don't feel. "And I'm forty-two. It's no small difference, *Lucien*."

"Eden's only twenty-seven, she's even younger than me."

My chest squeezes at the petulance in his voice. "Eden is not, and has never been, my patient. And I wasn't too thrilled about her age either. But it's a moot point—there is nothing between Eden and myself."

Lucien licks the seam of my lips, and I shudder, then glare at him for his daring.

"Liar," he says. He rocks his hips against me again with a helpless groan. "I've seen you staring at her tight ass. You love her big eyes and pretty tits. You love that she's curious and nervous and yours to do whatever you want with. You love that she's young."

He stares at my lips, and I'm shocked again when he reaches down and cups my cock through my slacks, running his hand jealously over the length. Impatient, he pulls down my zipper and pushes his hand inside until he finds bare flesh, like a child grasping greedily for every scrap of candy he can find while his parents aren't looking.

My breath hisses out. There are objections, somewhere. I should stop this. But his hand squeezing my dick is strangling my brain cells.

"But this isn't just for her. It's mine, too. You said yourself you want me. Fuck your transference, Jasper. Life's too short."

He strokes me roughly, punishingly, and as he does, the pressure keeping me to the wall lessens. In seconds, I have him flipped so he's back where he should be. Under me. His hand is still down my pants, and I wrap my hand around his throat. I barely stop my eyes from rolling back, and I can't stop myself fucking his fist.

"I should whip you raw for grabbing me like that," I hiss.

He gives me another long, firm stroke, and my pre-cum coats his hand. "I would have to be your submissive for you to punish me," he taunts.

That hit lands. Hard. I've lost control of this conversation, this argument. Myself. I tangle my hand in his hair and wrench his head back.

Then I press our mouths together for the very first time.

It's a relief, a break in a storm, a burst in a dam. I'm not gentle. I take his mouth with my tongue, punish it with my teeth. Lucien kisses me back desperately, hungrily, sucking on me. His fury melts under the onslaught, and his hand stroking my dick gentles just enough to become dizzying. His beard bristles against my chin.

My orgasm builds swiftly, and I groan into his mouth. It's been more than five years since anyone else has touched me like this. Maybe I've never been touched quite like this.

Lucien pushes me back again and it surprises me enough that I stumble. He drops to his knees and takes me into his scorching, soaking wet mouth before I can stop him.

Wrong. *Wrong.* This is all wrong. I shouldn't let this happen.

I look down, gripping his hair, ready to tear him off me, when he looks up. Those blue eyes drown me. My dick is wet where it meets his lips, and his mouth is like a furnace. Instead of ripping him away, I fuck into him like a punishment, staring at him as he takes me. He rubs his tongue against me expertly, ravenously. Greedy, greedy boy.

How dare he feel this good?

How dare he wreck and ruin every promise I ever made?

His throat closes around the tip of my dick as he swallows, and that ends me. My balls tighten, and, pressing deep into him, I unload every filthy fantasy and broken promise right into that perfect mouth. I come hard, and guiltily, and finish panting in shame.

I press a hand over my eyes, as if that can block out the sight of my betrayal as I come down. My thundering heart starts to slow, and my thoughts begin to filter through again. I stumble back, pulling out from between Lucien's lips and grab at my rumpled slacks, turning and tugging them back up.

What have I done?

"Jasper?"

I just barely repress a flinch at Lucien's tentative voice. I should go to him now, be a good dom. I should soothe him, somehow, and say . . . say what? He got what he wanted. What he *thought* he wanted. I was the one in control here. I have the power. I was the one who should have stopped this.

I can't look at him. I can't stand—I think he might have sucked my knees and my backbone out of my cock. Sitting heavily in my chair, I stare up at the screens, wanting to cry for the first time since I realized my wife was dead.

"Jasper, I know that got a little . . . out of hand, but we should talk. This is— It's a good thing."

That silly bird with the yellow feathers above its beak flies into the screen again and lands on the branch.

Talk? For once in my life, I don't think I have anything to say. I've finally done the unforgivable. Years of brushing close to it, toying with disaster. Years of resistance, and I still failed him.

I watch the bird hop on the branch, absently wondering again why it bothers me. Then I blink, lean forward. That bird isn't on yesterday's reel. It's showing on the camera for today, for now. The exact same bird, with the exact same feathers . . .

A different kind of dread soaks my bones.

"It's looped."

"What—"

"Not now, Lucien. Look at this."

I rewind the feed from yesterday to the time I had before and set the feed from today back a few seconds. The images are mirrored on the adjacent screens. When I think I have the times about right, I hit play. The exact same bird swoops in at the same angle, headed for the same tree, and perches in the same place. Same time. Same image. My stomach falls, but I also feel a breathless rush of relief.

This is it. *This* is what I've been missing.

"It's looped," Lucien says, repeating me. "Jasper, this means—"

"That we have no visuals. These cameras are useless."

He pulls at his topknot of blond hair, the one I mussed beyond repair when I fucked his face, and his eyes shift as he thinks. "How could they do that?"

I shake my head, some of my soul-clenching nausea receding as I focus on the problem. Not much, but some. "If they have twenty-four hours of footage, and someone with a bit of know-how, and they knew where the cameras were, it wouldn't be too hard to set it up on an automatic loop like this. We've been hacked."

"Jasper, if we can't see them, they could be anywhere. They wouldn't even have to avoid the direct trails," Lucien says, growing serious and tense as the implications hit. "There could have been dozens of them waiting for Beau and Dom. Jayk's right. Eden could be in danger. The guys could be. We have to—"

"Except that the hunters don't want them—at least not as a priority," I interrupt, everything sliding into place in one neat, terrifying picture. "It was a lure, to break up our forces, leave us vulnerable. Eden might be a draw, but they couldn't have known she would go after them. What they really want is—"

"Bristlebrook," Lucien breathes, paling. "They're coming here, while the others are gone."

If they know about the cameras, they know about this base. Electricity, water, animals, gardens, weapons—Bristlebrook is a motherlode.

I glance at the screen of the camera closest to us, right outside the house. One of the few I'm sure couldn't have been affected.

It's just now dark, and the shadows are lengthening across the clearing. Dread fills me.

"And the best time to attack would be"—on screen, a lick of fire creeps up the side of Jaykob's barn—"right now."

CHAPTER 33

EDEN

SURVIVAL TIP #5
The people you love dearest will most likely die,
and it will hit you like a bullet to the chest.
Brace for impact.

The acrid smell of burning wood is the first thing that tells me we're too late. The raging amber light filtering through the leaves and the blistering sound of gunshots confirm it. Shouts and cries of pain ricochet off the trees, making it impossible to pinpoint where they're coming from.

We kept to a steady jog for hours, not slowing or stopping once despite the savage aches and pains from our earlier run-in. But while Beau hovered around me the entire way, Dom pushed us to *move*, radiating a tight, edgy determination that told me with frightening clarity how worried he was. That, more than anything, kept me on my feet.

But our furious flight wasn't enough. We realized too late.

They're already here.

Dom ducked away a few minutes ago to get a better look, and I take the opportunity to suck in a few labored breaths while Beau stands watch. There are lines of tension around his eyes and bracketing his mouth.

Dom pops out of the trees like a phantom, and I only barely strangle my scream.

"Lucky and Jasper are pinned behind Jayk's truck. The barn's an inferno at this point, and they're too close."

"Any eyes on Jaykob?"

Dom jerks his chin in a negative, and my breath hitches. *Jayk.*

Beau's hand finds mine and squeezes, but he keeps his eyes on Dom, who only spares me a tense glance.

"What about the shed? Can we get to the weapons?"

"It's right in the line of fire. No chance," Dom replies. He checks his gun. "I'll take the rear from the trees—you get to Bristlebrook. Cover the tree line and keep them off our guys' asses."

Beau shakes his head. "I'll take the rear. I can do more good on the ground if the others need a medic."

Dom hesitates, then nods, jaw tight. "Fine. Keep your comms open."

Reading between the lines, I'm guessing the rear is going to be more dangerous. I bite my lip against saying something silly—like begging them to stay safe.

Smoke is creeping through the forest now and it burns my nose. I can't see the blaze from where we are, but it has to be big to cause this much thick, filthy air. An inferno, Dom said.

My stomach sickens.

I try to zero in on the shouting, desperate for any reassurance that my guys are safe, but I can't make out individual voices no matter how hard I strain. Jasper and Lucky are pinned? What does that even mean? Are they hurt? And where is Jayk?

"What can I do?" I whisper. My hands are shaking, and I press them against my thighs so they don't notice.

"Stay put, Eden," Dom tells me in a low voice. "I need you to stay out of the way—*really* stay out of the way this time. We can't be worried about you right now. Go to the cave with the animals.

It's hidden. No one should find you there. If we don't come for you in half a day, don't wait any longer. Leave at night and move fast."

Bile rises in my throat. "But you—you'll come back for me. You'll be fine, all of you. We got here. We're *here* now. Everything's going to be okay."

Beau tugs me to him and presses his mouth to mine in a fierce kiss. "Be safe, pet."

Tears fill my eyes and the adrenaline of the last few hours catches up to me. But that's not what they need right now. They need to be thinking about the others, about getting them out. I force myself to breathe and swallow down the thick lump in my throat. It's coated in ash.

"You too, Beau," I whisper, touching my fingers to his cheek, slightly coarse from his stubble.

I sear his face in my mind. I want to go back to the three of us tangled in the moss and that brief moment when everything was okay.

His cheek lifts under my fingertips in a half-smile, then he pulls back and leaves. My heart hammers as I watch him go. I turn to Dom. I'm about to speak—though I'm not sure what to say—when he takes my hand. He buries it inside his.

"Come with me," he says gruffly. "I'll get you as close as I can."

He holds his rifle in front of him, releasing me when I follow him without question. The urgent speed from earlier has vanished. Dom scans the trees as we move steadily, ducking from one to the next as cover. We stay back from the exposed line of trees closest to the clearing.

As we move farther from the fire, I notice there's a creeping hush over this part of the forest; the shouts and bangs and snaps of bursting, burning wood seem out of reach. Around us is a thick, deadly quiet. Smoke mars the way and the flickering light transforms everything into a smoggy, nightmarish haze.

Still, as we move closer to the tree line, I catch glimpses

between the leaves and need to stifle my sobs. The barn looks like something from a hellscape—an angry orange blaze with a blackening skeleton underneath. Flashes of gunfire light up the darkness like fireworks.

Jayk.

"He wasn't in there, right? He got out, didn't he?" I can't stop my shaky, panicked questions.

Dom doesn't stop moving, but his lips tense. "I don't know."

I bite my lip, nodding. Nodding too much. I'm about thirty seconds from a panic attack.

I think of Jayk's guitar and his messy bed and the photo of the woman in the dress and the boy with the missing tooth. I think of how he kissed me and his smirk and the look in his eyes when I asked to work in his barn beside him. Mostly, I just pray he wasn't in there when that barn went up, even though I know he barely leaves it. My palms feel sticky and the thickness in the air makes my breaths rough and sore.

Abruptly, there's a flash of movement in front of us and before I've even flinched back, Dom has lunged forward with the even, deadly speed of a viper. The man lurking in the bushes is disarmed and disabled in seconds, lying at his feet.

"I—"

Dom lifts his hand in a silencing gesture, and I bite my tongue hard enough to draw blood. After a moment, he nods and grabs my wrist, tugging me closer to the tree line.

"Did you kill him?" I mumble, shocked at how quickly that happened.

"Yes."

I swallow hard, then follow him through the darkness, stepping around the body. From here, we're about a hundred yards from the action. There are men everywhere, firing toward the barn. There are men all through the trees too. It's hard to see through the smoke. It's chaos. Pure chaos.

My heart lurches at the sight. Shifting, I see they're not firing on the barn, but toward Jayk's truck, which is parked beside it. In a frenzied, disorganized group, they're slowly converging on the vehicle. Jasper and Lucky are pinned behind it, Dom said, and now I know what that looks like.

"Fuck. They're too close." Dom grunts, then looks down at me, clearly distracted. "I have to go. You can make it from here."

I know I can. The cave is only fifteen yards away, and away from the action, but I hesitate, eyes dragging back to the awful scene.

Dom nudges me. "*Go*, Eden."

I should. I'll only be in the way, and this is far too much for me. This is far more than one man in a tree. I'm really, truly just about to leave when Jasper roars.

"Lucien, *no!*"

I spin back around to see a slender figure push from behind Jayk's truck. The smoke clears enough for me to see his golden hair catch the light. He fires wide, running sideways into the open field, and throws something toward the cluster of men who are far too close. A few men drop under Lucky's bullet spray, but he's so *exposed*.

I lurch forward and hardly notice as an arm wraps around me and yanks me back. Clutching at my throat, I try to track the wild mix of bangs and shouts. My eyes dart everywhere, trying to work out what's happening.

Then Lucky jerks once, twice. I can *see* the heavy impact on his body pushing him back.

My heart lurches. "*No.*"

Lucky drops, and the clearing lights up seconds before a huge, roaring explosion decimates the area where the group of men were standing. The arms around me tighten as Dom throws us behind a tree, and I squeal as shrapnel ricochets into the trees, peppering them with small, sharp thuds.

Grenade, I realize when my brain and heart restart. He threw a grenade. Lucky threw a grenade right before he—

The images of his puppet-like jerks, his crash to the ground, play on repeat in my mind. Tears squeeze between my eyes as if trying to dislodge the horrendous reel.

"No. No, no, no, no."

Something shakes me. "Stop, Eden."

I recognize Dom's growl, but there's a rawness to it. I can hear the devastation in his voice. That does it. A sob escapes.

He shakes me again. "Stop. We don't have time for this. I need to get to the house if I have any chance of keeping the others safe. You need to be safe. Tears later, you have to pull it together now."

The *others* safe. Because Lucky . . .

I can't help the low groan of pain, and I push my forehead into Dom's chest. His stern orders ground me, a little, but this is too much.

His hand finds my chin, and he pulls my face up to his. "Enough. Go, little librarian. I can't keep you all safe at once."

The beautiful amber light in his eyes captures me. I can see the barely restrained urgency in him, but also the worry. He has to go. That starts to sink in. I draw in a steadying breath. He has to go, and I'm standing here panicking. I'm not a soldier. I can't compartmentalize and keep my fears locked down so easily. I can't just let him . . .

When he looks back toward the barn with barely concealed frustration, I can't help it. I step into him and rise up on my tiptoes so I can press a light, nervous kiss to his mouth. Dom goes entirely still, and watches me as I drop back down on my heels. For the first time in hours, I have his complete attention.

"Be careful, please," I choke out as red stains my cheeks. "And save them."

Dom's golden gaze rakes over my face, and he gives me one slow nod. Then he turns, jogging through the shadows like he was born to them, slipping into the house.

Sick, terrified, I turn toward the cave, knowing there's nothing more I can do here. I can't do anything for any of them. I don't have training or even a weapon. I'm not like Lucky, keeping a convenient stash of—

My breath rushes out of me.

Lucky's hidey hole.

I stop, flooded with a focused sense of calm. No, I can't go back to the farm and the safety of that hidden cave. Maybe I *can* help.

I'm truly shaking now, but I push off in the other direction, not looking at the carnage behind me, and *run*.

CHAPTER 34

JAYKOB

SURVIVAL TIP #151
Don't be a hero.

God damn it, *no*!

My chest seizes as Lucky hits the ground, already limp. *Idiot*. Brave, stupid *idiot*.

Pressing around the corner of the shed, I wring out a few rounds toward the tree line where some fuckers have started getting bold. It won't take long for them to work out that if we had more frags, we'd be using them. Lucky is sprawled a few feet from the truck where he and Jasper had been trapped, the burning barn illuminating his figure in shadows.

Not moving.

Fuck.

I grit down against the rush of sick, icy horror. Memories of Ryan, of getting the news, threaten to rise up, but there's no way I have time for this shit. Pulling on the tricks the head-doctor taught me—because no way will I admit it, but they do work—I force myself to take in my surroundings, to catalog the shitty visuals of my present. At the same time, I press against the peeling, slick flesh of the burn wound running up my side, letting the pain anchor me. Okay, not exactly what the posh prince recommended, but it works.

This is bad. I just made it out of the barn before the exits became unusable, only to get trapped behind the drying shed. Thanks to Lucky, we're now free of the cluster over the far side that was closing in, but there are still too many in the trees trapping me here, and I'm running out of rounds.

If I could just get *into* the shed, I'd have a lot more fire power to work with, but trying now would only buy myself a quick plot in an early grave.

Jasper might be able to get out from behind that truck now, but the way he's edging around it makes me think he's gunning for Lucky over safety.

What's left of him, anyway.

I grit my teeth, and peer round the corner of the shed toward the trees, wondering if I can make a run toward Bristlebrook. A bullet whistles beside my head, and I jerk back.

Yeah, that's a no.

Heat from the barn sends sweat trickling down my spine. I weigh up whether to go to Jasper, but he's even more exposed than I am. Not to mention that running through the clearing without cover, even ten yards, would probably be enough for them to put my lights out.

I check my magazine, grunting when my exposed burn tugs as I move. Less than a dozen rounds. When I look up, Jasper crouches and creeps out into the clearing toward Lucky's body. Two bullets fly from the trees—one goes wide but the other slashes the air right beside his neck. Jasper doesn't flinch, doesn't make any move to get out of the way, just keeps moving toward Lucky. Firelight flickers over the determined set of his jaw.

"Hey, asshole!" I shout at him. "Get back behind the truck."

There's no point. The kid's probably gone anyway. You don't take two bullets to the chest and make it without heavy-duty and quick medical intervention. Jasper's just going to get himself killed as well, and I . . . don't want that.

Jasper ignores me as neatly as he did the bullet. *Damn* it. This is *not* protocol. Panic fires through me. I lean out and fire toward the trees where the shots came from, shouting wildly at the stupid, untrained shrink.

"This is *goddamned.*"

Faces pull back and weapons gleam from the shadows.

"*Stupid.*"

The shots shift away from firing on Jasper and start piercing the flimsy shed around me. I grunt and duck lower. This is a bad angle for me, but if I move around the shed, I won't be able to cover Jasper for shit.

"*Hero.*"

I fire back twice and look back at Jasper, who's pulling Lucky behind the truck.

"*Bullshit.*"

Hollering in wild relief, I lean out to fire again and I ring on empty. "Fuck."

I toss down my now useless MK 16 and tug my Beretta out of my belt. It *maybe* has the range to reach the far tree line.

Maybe.

Unless something changes fast, we're toast.

CHAPTER 35

BEAU

SURVIVAL TIP #224
*If you can protect your family,
you've done the best anyone could hope for in this life.*

A hunter leans out from behind his tree and pops off two more shots at Jasper, and I'm grateful. It makes it easy for that silent, deadly calm to take over, letting me shed the healer and become the killer I need to be right now.

Wrapping my hand over his mouth, I punch my knife between his ribs, angling precisely so I puncture his heart. He's the third in the last fifteen minutes.

I felt for Eden, when she took that life—I understand her pain better than most. I'm not like Dom, who can focus on a job and not flinch at the fallout. I've had a lot of different blood stain my hands, but the blood from delivering death never washes out the same way as blood from surgery.

I was born to save lives, though—and while sometimes that means picking up a scalpel, other times it means the knife.

I lower the man to the ground, dismantle his gun and toss his ammo. It's no use to me, not half so good as my own weapon and not easy to carry with the rest of my gear, but I'm not about to let some other opportunist pick it up either.

Hearing movement close by, I grimace and move quickly behind a large boulder, watching as three men jog through the trees. Trying to get a better angle, I'm guessing. I hesitate for a moment, then let them pass. Three in close quarters is too risky; they'd have too much chance to alert others. I need to pick them off—it's the only plan we have right now—and if I'm caught . . .

Well, if I'm caught, I'm not going to have much to worry about anymore, I suppose.

I heard Jasper call out for Lucien earlier, and the blast that followed, but I haven't had a chance to get a visual. I can only hope it was our damage.

Allowing myself a moment, I edge forward and look out at the massacre. From this angle, I see Lucky lying between the truck and the burning barn. Burning embers rain down on the ground around him, and the fire lights him up well enough that I can see the dark stain flooding his chest. My breath stalls.

He needs medical attention.

Now.

But, almost as bad, Jasper seems to have abandoned the truck —and his God-given common sense—and is out in the open, moving toward him. If I hadn't just killed the hunter standing here, he would have had a short, clear shot to Jasper's skull.

With sharp relief, I see Jayk's head as he peeks around the shed. He shouts at Jasper, but I can't make out the words. Bullets fly toward him.

Shit. This is bad. Some mighty kind of bad.

The shots are coming from these trees though, if I can just take the hunters out maybe they'll have a chance to make it back to Bristlebrook and Dom.

"Hey, you're not—"

Heart thundering, I whip around and tackle the man to the ground before he can move from confusion to deadly force. He's a big bastard, but I'm not exactly light either, and he gasps as the breath is knocked from him. I force my hand over his mouth, and he punches my ribs as we grapple in the dirt. Grunting, I try to get my knife up, but the move unbalances me, and he flips me on my back.

Rather than going for the kill though, he pushes up. "Where are they all?" he snaps. "Where are all the women? Families?"

He punches my ribs again, and I groan.

"Sam said—"

My blade finds his throat in the next instance, buried to the hilt. His hands come up to meet it, his eyes wide in shock, and I twist before yanking it out. Blood spurts down, coating me, and I shove him to the side so his weight doesn't pin me.

Families? Women? It's been a long time since we had any here, but when we kicked Sam out . . . well, that was a different story. I wonder if he lied to them so he could get his revenge or if he genuinely doesn't know everyone else cleared out years ago.

Wiping my face with my forearm, tasting thick copper on my lips, I push back up. I move toward the sounds of gunfire. The why doesn't matter now. There's no time.

Please, God, don't let any of them do anything too stupid. Let me save them.

I don't know if the brief prayer means much, but I figure it can't really hurt either. My mama used to send up little prayers like that on the daily. "Never hurts to show your respect," she used to say. "You never know who's listening."

We're going to need someone listening to our prayers today.

I approach the shooters carefully—there's at least four here, and who knows how many others nearby. This probably won't end well for me. I wish Jasper and Jayk were in kits the way Dom and I are. If they were, I could let them know what I have planned on our comms and this plan would have a much higher likelihood of success. But they're not stupid. If I create a big enough diversion, they'll take the opportunity to run. They'd better.

With a sting of regret, I think of Eden and how pretty she was as she lay nestled between me and Dom by the waterside.

I'm so sorry, darlin'.

Don't see why I can't pray to her too. Being with her is about as close to a religious experience as I've had in years.

Taking out my radio, I open the speaker and give my final words to Dom. My best friend. My partner.

I owe him that much.

I turn it off before he can respond and tuck it away, swallowing hard.

Then I tighten my grip on the knife, unholster my pistol, and move in.

CHAPTER 36

DOMINIC

I train my rifle on the trees and pick off two assholes who are rounding the far side of the shed to get to Jayk. They go down silently, with a spray of blood that snares the burning light.

Thick smoke from the treated wood hazes my view—not the worst visibility we've fought in, but not ideal. The barn is starting to groan now. It won't be long before it goes down, and Jasper and Lucky and that damn truck are too close to it for comfort. It must be hotter than Satan's ballsack already.

I briefly worry about drones spotting the heat signature, just to top off this shitshow, but shrug off the thought quickly. We haven't seen any in years and there's not much we can do about it now in any case. Fortunate or dead seem about our only outcomes in this whole hot mess.

I consider my position. My vantage from the upper-story window in the music room is good, and my rifle can handle the distance no problem, but it doesn't give me visibility through trees, and the hunters are hidden in the shadows. I'll be hard pressed to pick them off unless they expose themselves.

Soon enough they'll get bold, I'm sure, but if they charge out in numbers, then my guys are fucked. No way I can take out more than half a dozen in the time they'll take to get to them.

And that's not counting damage the barn will do.

I eye the hole gauged in the middle of the clearing, the bodies splashed around it, and have to admire Lucky's balls, even as my throat tightens. Disobedient little shit had kept a frag in the house after all, despite my safety lectures, and I'm glad as fuck he did. Right now, I'm dreaming of a dozen more just like it. He gave Jasper and Jayk a chance with that move. A slim one, but a chance anyway.

My chest aches. For the first time, I'm not sure how we can make it out of this one.

A creak in a floorboard behind me has me spinning with a curse. I'd thought it'd take them longer to decide to come around and use the house. Reluctantly, I draw away from covering the guys and creep to the door, pulling out my pistol.

Another creak sounds in the hall, and I tense, getting ready.

"Dom?"

Yanking myself back, I press the grip of the Beretta to my forehead and pray for strength. "*Eden?*"

Opening the door, I move to grab her and then have to stop. She's . . . loaded up. She has a bazooka slung heavily over one shoulder—the fucking military grade rocket launcher she and Lucky stole from my room—and a duffel bag hanging off the other. She's panting, red cheeked and wide eyed.

"What the hell did you do?" Reholstering my pistol, I pull her inside and take the bazooka. It's not light, and I don't know if I'm pissed or impressed. "Eden, I appreciate the thought but this thing is useless without—"

"These. I know, Lucky showed me." She unslings the bag and

unzips it quickly. "I couldn't carry that fancy box thing so I just grabbed a duffel."

Nearly a dozen rounds spill out, and I flinch at the careless way they're packed. My heart is thundering in my chest, and I decide now isn't the time to yell at her about weapon safety. There are high explosive rounds, anti-tank rounds, illumination, smoke, area defense munitions . . .

"Eden," I breathe, kneeling beside her.

She looks up at me nervously. "I'm sorry, I know you said to go to the cave, but I was thinking about . . . anyway I remembered about all the weapons, and I thought, if I could just get them to you then—"

I yank her to me, cutting her off with my tongue and kissing her thoroughly. When I pull back, she stares at me, breathless and dazed and looking like every fantasy I never realized I had. A rumpled, repressed librarian with more courage than I ever gave her credit for.

Then I hear shouting though the window—Jayk?—and a spray of gunfire, and I come back to earth.

"You did good, pet. Real good. Is there more?"

Blinking a few times, she sucks in a breath and then nods. "Yes, loads more. I just couldn't carry them all."

Relief and desperation spikes. "Okay, listen to me carefully. I need you to bring me some things."

I quickly describe the weapons I need while loading the bazooka. I have no idea what Lucky has stashed—I thought we used most of what we grabbed from the base—but the damn guy was a magpie.

Is a magpie, damn it.

I lift the loaded weapon to my shoulder, and Eden gets to her feet.

"Eden?" I say as she turns to go. When her eyes lift to mine, as big and intelligent as the first time I saw her, I murmur, "Thank you."

She gives me one slow, shy smile before she darts off, and I watch her go with a mix of pride and worry. That girl may have just saved our asses for the second time in less than twenty-four hours.

Forcing myself to refocus, I turn back to the fray. This changes everything. I have the firepower to smoke these assholes, trees notwithstanding—I just need Beau to get out of my way.

I pull out my radio, but just as I do, it flicks on, and Beau starts talking into the line before I can get a word in.

"Okay, buddy, this might be it, and I don't have time to argue with you, so for once you're just going to have to listen. You're the best friend I ever had, the best friend I ever could have had. I know the last while has been rough between us, and I'm sorry about that. I never should have let anyone get between us, and I ain't proud I let my jealousy get the better of me. I just . . . I want you to be happy, Dom. You deserve it all."

My throat closes over, and my head starts to spin. It never happens during combat, not ever, but pure horror starts to cloud my senses. I try to speak over him, but he has the line open, not letting me get a word in.

"You take care of our girl, okay? 'Cause that's what she is, even if your stubborn ass wants to take its sweet time admitting that."

"You cut this shit, Beau. Cut it right now," I snap into the radio, but he can't hear me. There's no point. I know what this is, and he's making this one sided. "I can take care of this, idiot, just get your ass gone. Open the damn line."

"I think I can take these guys out, Dom. Or most of 'em anyway. Jasper and Jayk, they'll have a bit of time—not a lot, mind, but a bit. Now Lucky's cleared out the other side, they should have a straight shot to you. Cover them."

Beau swallows, and it slices through me.

"Take care of yourself, too, Dom. I love you."

The radio cuts out, and I immediately try to open the line so I can yell at him, stop him, *something*, but he's disabled comms like I knew he was going to.

"Fuck!" I shout, shaking.

This is some kind of sick cosmic joke. I have all the firepower I could want, but I can't use it without guaranteeing his death.

With unsteady movements, I take my rifle and press it to my damp eye, desperately searching through the scope. Sure enough, within minutes I make out a scuffle just beyond the tree line. Shots are fired, metal gleams and surprises, furious shouts follow, though they're too far for me to make out words.

My finger hovers over the trigger, but I can't see clearly. It's too dark and there's too much smoke. There's no way of knowing if I'd be shooting Beau or one of the fuckers who were trying to steal my family from me. Despair constricts my lungs.

I lift my head and see the moment Jayk makes the decision to bolt, taking advantage of the reprieve, as he should. He pushes off the shed and runs over to the truck. Someone shoots at him from the far side of the woods, close to where Eden should be, and I swing my rifle round. Visibility is easier on this side, and I pick the too-bold hunter off with a single headshot.

Looking back, I see Jaykob slide in next to Jasper and Lucky like he's just stolen second base. The spark of relief is momentary. A man backs out of the woods where the commotion is, firing into the trees—at *Beau*—and I shoot him in the back with ruthless efficiency.

Come on, Beau, get out of there.

Jasper and Jayk seem to be arguing as Jasper pulls Lucky's limp body over his shoulders.

All of you, move your asses, I urge silently.

Jayk grabs Jasper's rifle and nods at him, and I brace. They're going to do it. They're going to—

Something bursts from the trees and takes off at a furious run. The figure is coated in blood and limping, but I'd recognize him anywhere. My heart stutters, and I fire behind him wildly, hoping to deter anyone from sticking their head out, trying to give him every spare second he can get. Jayk spots him too and turns around to join my flurry of shots, covering Beau—and covering Jasper, too, as he starts staggering toward the house with Lucky hanging heavy over his shoulders.

Bullets fly past Beau, and he begins to weave. Deciding Jayk has this for the moment, I grab the bazooka and settle it over my shoulder, lining up my sights.

Men have started to pull out of the trees from several directions, clearly deciding they have our men on the run. Beau clears the truck and keeps going, and Jayk runs backwards with him, firing in every direction. I grimace for a moment, deciding where to aim, when the barn groans.

My grimace turns into a dark, predatory grin.

Perfect.

I line up my shot and wait a few seconds, knowing timing is going to count here. I don't want to take out our guys by accident. But when the hunters start pressing close to the barn, I fire.

It only takes moments. The fragile barn bursts open like a microwaved peach, spraying burning projectiles across the entire clearing, decimating the tree line in all directions and blasting out half the windows of Bristlebrook. I throw myself down as a plank of wood hurtles through my window and shatters the glass across the music room.

I push myself back up and grab my rifle, breathing hard. Sweat drips down my temples. The entire clearing is annihilated, a true apocalyptic wasteland, complete with fire and bodies and limbs. I spot someone pulling themselves to their feet and blast them down. Nothing else so much as twitches.

I scan the scene but can't see my guys anywhere. That's a good thing, given the extermination I'm looking at, but I hesitate, pulse pounding. I should stay put, keep covering from up here in case anyone is stupid enough to decide that this isn't enough—in case there's anyone left to make that decision—but that was a big blast, and I have no idea if Beau and the others were clear or not. And then there's Lucky . . .

I grab a few grenades and my rifle and run downstairs, seeing the sitting room overturned and covered in sparkles of glass. Lucky is sprawled behind two overturned couches, Jasper crouching over him.

"Where's Beau, Jasper? And Jaykob?"

Jasper doesn't even glance up, but I can see the raw terror in every move he makes. He rips open Lucky's shirt, and blood makes it stick slickly in several places. I go still at what's revealed.

Lucky's whole chest is slippery and red, and Jasper's hands hover over it, shaking.

"Wake up, Lucien," he commands, and the snap to his voice is pure panic. "*Now.*"

He begins tearing at his own clothes, then presses the scraps against the pulsing holes, looking lost. Looking at the location of the wounds, and the blue-tinged cast to Lucky's lips, I'm guessing he has a collapsed lung and that wound is sucking in air dangerously.

Without Beau, without an emergency crike, I doubt he'll make it. Damn it, where *is* he?

Cursing, I look around and spot the med kit Beau left out here while he was flirting with Eden. And I can't believe it, but his crush might actually save the day here.

I yank it out and pull out the sterile dressing we were taught to use for this situation. There's one here with a valve, but that's beyond my expertise. It's been years since I did my first responder training. I clean the wound quickly with Beau's wipes, dry it, and then place the dressing over the chest wound, securing it on three sides.

I'm leaning down, trying to decide if his breathing sounds steadier, when I hear a low growl.

"You are dead fucking weight. I should leave you on the damn grass. Should leave all your stupid asses. Gonna get me killed like an asshole. Dicks. None of you are worth this shit."

Jayk stumbles in through the now-open space where the glass sliding door used to be, one of Beau's arms over his shoulder. My heart actually flutters in dizzying relief as I rush over to help.

They're all here, I reassure myself, and it's like feeling floods back into my numb body. *All here.*

Though as I glance back at Lucky, the relief fades quickly. Those wounds are far from nothing. Not to mention, there's no guarantee the danger is over yet. I scan the clearing again, but nothing moves except flames dancing over dead grass.

"Like anyone's coming close again after that," Jayk scoffs, and I just grunt, not ready to trust it.

Pulling Beau's other arm around my shoulder, I move with Jayk to get him beside Lucky and Jasper. He's covered in blood, but I can't see where it's coming from. There doesn't appear to be a head wound. His left leg looks the worst, with a deep cut in his thigh that's leaking blood.

"I'm going to kill you for that stunt," I bite out under my breath.

Beau laughs, though it sounds pained. "Well, I wouldn't want a good speech to go to waste."

When he catches sight of Lucky, he sobers. "We need to get him to the med bay. Now."

Jasper and I lift Lucky gently. We're moving, fast and efficient, toward the med bay when Jayk asks a question that has more violent force than any bomb I've set off today.

"Where the hell is Eden?"

Chapter 37

Lucky

SURVIVAL TIP #178
Kisses are better than oxygen.
No, Beau, it's a good tip, don't take my—

My first thought is that death is more uncomfortable than I hoped for. I mean, after the wars and the apocalypse and all, I kind of hoped that I'd catch some kind of break in the afterlife. Some cushy ether or a nice fluffy kingdom in the clouds. Heck, I'd take reincarnation. Bring me back as a tiger or something—I've got no problem picking my teeth with a poacher's tibia.

I try to shift and realize I do have some form of body. I can move. It's just that moving sucks and sends bolts of pain everywhere.

Really, it's not fair that it hurts this much. If I have to hurt for my sins, I'd really have loved for it to be in some kind of sexy dungeon scenario. I bet Lucifer is the daddy of all sadists. I could get down with that.

"Lucien."

Noise starts to filter in, and I'm pretty sure I heard my name.

Or maybe they said "Lucifer." I might be getting the dungeon after all.

Each breath is agony, sending spasms through my body, but between those spasms, I feel something else. Someone is gently stroking my face, right along my hairline. I'm no expert, but I don't think Luci would be this sweet to me. Eden's the only one who has touched me this tenderly in a long time. The soft touches are almost worth the spasms.

"I'm going to kill you for putting me through this, you selfish boy," someone says, and the low voice triggers warm shivers through me. Even with my foggy brain, I recognize that voice, though I've never heard that rough, choked tone from him.

I'm alive then, that's good. Jasper may not be the prince of darkness, exactly, but he's close enough. The rough sheet around my bare waist registers, and the warmth of Jasper's hand in mine. He's close enough that I can smell him, but his usual parchment and ink scent is clouded by smoke and sweat.

Memories of the barn and the hunters, the frag and the truck, come back to me sluggishly. Ah, shit. What happened? If Jasper's sitting next to me then it worked, and we got free. No idea how the fuck that happened, or how I made it out of that one. I didn't run out into the open expecting to live, that was for sure.

My lids are heavy and gritty. It takes a few attempts before they crack open. The room is dimly lit—no lights are on, but candles flicker around the room. Generator's crapped out, then. I recognize the med bay, but how the hell did we make it here? Last I knew, we were well and truly fucked.

As they always do, my eyes drift back to Jasper. There's no urgency in his body language, though I can vaguely hear an argument from behind the door. He's close beside me in the bed, his head pressed against the mattress beside mine. His eyes are shut and soot dusts his face, hair, and eyelashes. My heart tangles when I realize he's been crying.

I didn't know he could do that.

The slow, sweet touches along my hairline continue. He's never touched me like this before. Not even during aftercare, that I can remember.

My throat burns with thirst, but I ignore it. Every breath stabs and spasms, but I ignore that too. I just watch him. The pain makes sense now. It always hurts around Jasper.

I'm okay with it. I would take a lot worse than this to have him here. He's safe. Whether it's because of what I did or by some other miracle, Jasper got free and isn't dead behind a truck right now. Life is good.

"—where she is. We need to look for her."

The door slams open abruptly enough to make me startle, which in turn sets off a thousand-lash punishment through every inch of my body. I groan, and Jasper's head lifts sharply to stare down at me.

"Is he awake?" Beau asks, ignoring whatever Jayk was snarling at him about.

I work up a smile for Jasper, wondering how awkward this is going to be. He didn't seem happy after our liaison in his study, and—

In the next instant, Jasper has my face cupped between his hands, and his mouth crashes down on mine. His tongue prises between my lips, tangling with mine in desperate urgency. I sigh into the kiss as he holds my face close, and I taste a sting of salt. I realize more tears have escaped him, and I try to gentle the storm, easing back until I'm pressing soft, comforting kisses against his lips.

"It's okay," I whisper between kisses. "I'm okay."

Actually, I can't hold myself up. I'd say I feel weak as a kitten but I'm pretty sure a kitten could kick my ass right now. Still, even weak and dizzy and with every movement an agony, I wouldn't stop this for anything.

Jasper's kissing me like I matter.

He finally pulls back, sucking in a deep breath, and settles me back into the bed. He gives me a dark look as he pulls out an embroidered handkerchief from his slacks and cleans his damp cheeks with zero shame. The look promises punishment, but I'm starting to float.

I abruptly remember we have company and lift my eyes to Beau and Jayk, who are both staring at us in shock. Jasper and I have never been that *overt* in front of anyone before. And barely in private either. I can't keep my lips from splitting into a wide grin.

Beau's lips twitch in response, and Jayk just scowls.

"How do you feel?" Beau asks, moving forward. He pulls his stethoscope up from around his neck and presses the chilly metal against my chest. Jasper watches him with concern.

"Horny," I respond, then cough when my raw throat protests.

Jasper stands quickly and pours me a cup of water as Beau gives me a dry look.

"You have no idea how lucky you really are. An inch either way and either of those bullets would have ended you in seconds. As it was, I wasn't sure you'd make it."

I'm not really sure how to respond to that, so I just say, "I knew you'd take care of me, doc."

Jasper makes a sound suspiciously like a growl as he hands me my water, and I shoot him an innocent look.

Beau removes the stethoscope from my chest and studies me. "So how are you rea—"

"He's fine," Jayk snaps impatiently, seeming to break out of his momentary surprise. "He's talking. We're all thrilled you're alive yada yada, and Beau can keep patching you up all night, but for now just tell us where your fucking stash is."

I frown, confused. "My—"

"Your stash, your hidey hole, whatever you call it where the weapons are. We've been searching for it for a day and a half."

"Are we still under attack? Why are you all here when—"

"For fuck's sake," Jayk bursts out, and that interrupting thing is getting really annoying.

Still, he looks more agitated than I've ever seen him. He steps toward me aggressively, and Jasper steps in front of him, cutting him off. Jasper may be tall, but Jayk has him well and truly out-muscled. And yet Jasper looks as cold and calm as he ever has. I'm going to get hard despite how shitty I feel if he keeps defending me like this.

Beau grimaces. "Jayk, I said I'd ask him. Step out if you can't control yourself."

Some of that floating sensation starts to fade as I take in the tension in the room. I meet Beau's eyes, knowing he'll give it to me straight.

He nods at me. "The hunters have scattered. Eden brought Dom an arsenal from your stash, and he blew the bulk of them to pieces while we got to safety. There's no sign that they're coming back to the house—wouldn't be much point now anyway, since it's shot to hell, and they've realized there are no women here like they thought."

Jayk hisses in impatience, but Beau doesn't react, keeping his gaze steady on mine. This is all sounding like good news so I know there has to be more.

"In the middle of this, Eden went back to get more weapons."

My stomach sinks, only now reading the fear and worry in Beau's face.

His voice turns husky. "That was over eighteen hours ago. We haven't seen her since. Dom's out looking, but . . . we don't know where to start, and there are tracks everywhere."

I shake my head, not understanding. She was meant to be safe. Out of all of them, they were meant to keep her safe.

"You're not—" Trembles crash over me. "You can't be saying that—"

"Eden's missing," Jayk bursts out, and I recognize the agitation for what it is. Fear. "And we think they took her."

CHAPTER 38

EDEN

SURVIVAL TIP #340
That sound behind you?
Oh, yeah, you're fucked.
Eighteen hours earlier

The duffel over my shoulder is even heavier than the damn bazooka, but I managed to get most of what Dom asked for. As I make my way back out of Lucky's secret cave, I realize the sky is darkening now, banishing even the filtered light through the trees. I wish I hadn't dumped my pack with Dom. My flashlight would be useful about now.

I'm not usually skittish in the forest, even at night, but there's something about knowing there are men who are willing to murder me and everyone I care about that really changes the tone. The shadows seem to shift unexpectedly and every tiny crack and rustle makes me flinch. But I adjust the duffel and keep moving, swallowing down my nervousness.

I just need to get back to Dom.

I've hardly been moving for five minutes when a prickle lifts the hairs at the back of my neck. Glancing around casually, I don't see anything, but that doesn't mean much. My eyesight is shocking at the best of times, and between the sinking light and the hazy woods, I'm pathetically vulnerable.

I pick up the pace, hoping I'm imagining things, when a sharp crackle sounds to my right. That was too loud, and too close.

Nope. No, thank you.

I move to my right and stumble on a log I didn't see. I bite my lip and step over it, looking around again. Damn it, why is everything so dark? After a tense moment, I start moving again, and as I do, a low, taunting laugh follows me.

Fear ices my veins, and I give up, jumping into a jog. My muscles protest, telling me we've done too much over the last few days, but there's no way I'm slowing down.

I'm not alone.

I know I shouldn't, but I can never help myself. I look over my shoulder, sure that there's someone right behind me. But there's . . . nothing.

The relief is only slight, and I whip my head back around in time to see a wide, stocky chest. I slam into the man, and his arms come around me with none of the kind firmness of my brutes.

These arms *are* familiar though.

Slick horror makes me slacken, though I can't back up. I escaped before—I don't think I'm lucky enough to do it again. I look up, knowing who I'm going to see.

"Well, hello, sweetheart," Sam croons. "I think it's about time you came with me."

AUTHOR'S NOTE

Okay, okay, but that was only an itsy bitsy teeny tiny cliffhanger. Just think how mad you would have been if I'd left you hanging on Lucky! I'm only a teensy bit of a sadist.

Guys, thank you so much for reading. It was such a big, huge, scary, fun, amazing, emotional thing to publish this book, and it makes me so teary happy to think of people enjoying these characters that I really do have an unhealthy obsession with at this point.

If you did enjoy the book, I would be grateful beyond words if you'd consider leaving a review. They're honestly an author's lifeblood and one of the few ways we can really push to get our work seen, so they mean everything.

CONTINUE THE SERIES

Break your heart on Entangled, available now

Entwined is out July 16th - pre-order the epic conclusion here

CAN'T WAIT?

Are you desperate to know what exactly went down on the day the world died? When everything went up in smoke and our favorite characters' lives were changed forever? Do you want to see Jayk get his pride shredded? Beau realize he'll never see his family again? Jasper and Lucky desperately trying not to collapse into one another? Dom fighting for his men, the civilians, for *survival*?

Of course you do. You're a total masochist. It's okay, this is a safe space.

Head to my website (https://rebeccaquinnauthor.com) to sign up to my newsletter and you'll receive each episode of Day Death as they're created. Released as often as I can get to them and remain sane, we'll experience that deathful day from the perspective of each of our main characters.

I mean, who doesn't want to see six hearts shatter forever . . .

ACKNOWLEDGMENTS

Oh boy, I'm too much of a sap to write these things. Already crying. Let me just pour another glass of red (that will definitely help, Becky, you *genius*).

Okay! I'm good, let's do this. I'm going to go more or less in chronological order here, so first up, my sister, Nicky. Years ago, she read the first, crappiest draft of half of this book. She bounced ideas, gushed, did all the things. She breathed life and enthusiasm into this book, and it wouldn't exist without her.

I'll thank my fiancé now, because his was and is a continued effort. No, he still hasn't read it. I think he's scared. Honestly, I don't think I could shock him more than I already have over our thirteen years together but here we are. Thank you for being a cheerleader, always. For listening to me gush and babble nonsensically at you about book things and book people and characters and ideas that I'm sure you have very little interest in. You make a good show of pretending, and I adore you for it. Thanks for always waving that foam finger.

I'd thank my baby, but let's be real, this book is here in spite of you, you adorable little time suck.

Brianna Bancroft, you deserve a podium, a trophy, and all the love. You were my first ever proper critique partner, and when I say this book wouldn't be here without you, it's not even the slightest exaggeration. Exchanging chapters with you was the only thing that kept my procrastinating, imposter syndroming ass in line. Your encouragement and support and squeeing kept me writing in a way that nothing ever has before and I am so, so grateful. You're an amazing friend, author, and human.

To AK Blythe, alpha-ing with you is much newer but no less fun. You always manage to catch me with love right when the doubts are kicking in and you're one of the few people I've met who has a mind as filthy as mine. Never stop writing, I can't wait for you to release!

To every single person who beta read for me, edited for me, worked on my cover, promoted me on socials, or contributed to all the thousand different things that go into making a novel, THANK YOU! The Bookstagram and Booktok communities are so incredibly lovely, and I've been overwhelmed with all the support you've given me. I appreciate each and every one of you. So much.

To my wives, WH Lockwood, LH Blake, Letizia Firmani, and Letizia Lorini. (Okay, big tears now). I could write a whole book as a love letter just to the four of you. The support, advice, giggles, and talent that you guys have and are willing to share is just staggering. It's hard to find people who share your big passion, and this is a hard job. The courage all of you have in pursuing that passion is nothing short of inspiring, and your willingness and selflessness in sharing your time, experience, and skills is absolutely humbling. You are all perfect examples of how, as writers and as women, we're stronger together, lifting one another up, and helping wherever we can, and you inspire and push me to be better every day. I can't love you enough for it.

Doesn't hurt that your books are all genius level, gold star crack cocaine, and every single reader should track you down on Goodreads and devour your back catalogs. DO IT!

Okay, last one. Lety, the other wives are just going to have to forgive me for this, but you really do need a special, additional mention. Plaque. Statue. Crown. When you found me, I was wondering aimlessly through Facebook, looking for beta readers, only half sure I would ever publish anything, taking my sweet ass time as usual to make a decision.

Then I met you.

And by God. What a whirlwind.

I swear I don't even know how it happened. One moment I was there, the next I had the most constructive novel critique I've ever been given, was being talked into pub dates, and socials strategy. I was overflowing with laughter, and glowing with someone who felt as passionate about my book as I did, and helpful information, and ideas, and you're FORMATTING my BOOK, and holy crap, now I'm publishing. And it's because of you, it really is. You did it. You're the most determined, impassioned, talented, skilled, kind person I've ever met. You shared so selflessly, supported so fiercely, that you should practically be considered co-author at this point. You deserve every bit of success you've had and every bit that will come, and there is so, so much more in store for you. In thanks, I give you Dom.

Whew, okay. This is too long but whatever, brevity isn't my thing. Gushing is, so this was always going to be a massive scroll. Sorry not sorry.

About the Author

After spending her career publishing other writers' wonderful words, Rebecca Quinn decided to unleash her own. Turns out, she's a little debauched. Rebecca loves writing inclusive, character-driven reverse harem romance with heart, humor, and kinky heat —or romance with bromance, as she calls it.

Rebecca lives in a coastal town south of Sydney, Australia. She spends her days cuddling her young son and her fiancé, getting far too invested in her DnD campaigns, drinking too much wine, playing board games, and—of course—reading as many novels as she can get her grabby little hands on.

If you want to keep up to date with the next books in the series, bonus content, new series, filthy memes, and ridiculous chats, come get Quinnky with me on my socials, or sign up to my newsletter via my website.

Printed in Great Britain
by Amazon